MW01092338

FORBIDDEN LOVES

Paris Between the Wars

FORBIDDEN LOVES, Paris Between the Wars
Second Edition

All Rights Reserved © 2008 by Patricia Daly-Lipe
Previous edition copyrighted in 2004

No part of this book may be reproduced or transmitted in any form or by any means, electronic or mechanical, including photocopying, recording, or by information storage and retrieval system except by a reviewer who may quote brief passages in a review to be printed in a magazine or newspaper without written permission from the publisher and the author.

This book is a work of fiction based on true happenings. Some names, characters, places and incidents are either products of the author's imagination or are used fictitiously. Any resemblance to actual events or locales or persona, living or dead, is entirely coincidental

J Published in 2008 by:
JADA Press
Atlanta, GA
JADA www.JadaPress.com

ISBN: 978-0-9800629-3-9
      0-9800629-3-4

LCCN: 2008922125

Printed in the United States of America

I dedicate this book to the memory of
Katharine Elisabeth Johnson Highleyman

Other Books by Patricia Daly-Lipe

LaJolla, A Celebration of Its Past

Myth, Magic & Metaphor,
A Journey into the Heart of Creativity

Messages from Nature,
Short Stories and Vignettes

AWARDS

AWARDS RECEIVED FOR THE FIRST EDITION

OF *FORBIDDEN LOVES*

Trophy, JADA AWARD WINNING NOVEL

1st Runner-Up Fiction, 2006

Best Books Award, USABookNews.com

REVIEWS

"Better to have loved and lost than never to have loved at all – well, yes and no. Read 'Forbidden Loves' view of this age old dilemma."
   Rita Mae Brown, author of eleven novels, poet and two-time Emmy nominee

History With a Twist. I adore fiction and I adore Paris, but this fascinating story kept me glued to my seat. The characters and situation, always more compelling when based on true life, were beautifully drawn. What a wonderful window into a time that we know about but have not witnessed! And how brave of Ms. Lipe to share these intimate details. She draws us in and keeps us reading until the final page.
   Erica Miner, Author *Travels with my Lovers* and *Murder in the Pit*

"I greatly enjoyed this excellent recreation, almost a recollection, of the seeming distant but really so recent past that still shapes our present world. This is an amazing evocation of the Paris of a time when it truly was the cultural and intellectual heart of the west. Famous personages are-were a part of everyday life in a concentrated mix of cross-fertilization that would be difficult to imagine happening today. All of this in the context of an improbable, but ultimately plausible love story. Read this story and be transported back to a magic, vanished time. You will find this one of those books that quickly captivates and may not allow you to put it down. I would highly recommend this book to lovers of Literature, History, France, and of course Romance."
   Felix E. Westwood, Vietnam Veteran, Woodbine, Md.

"Congratulations! This is superb work. I appreciate the quality, the substance, and the style. Very well done."
Dr. M.P. Cosman, Esq., (died March 2006) author, attorney and President of Medical Equity, Inc. One of her 14 published books was nominated for the Pulitzer Prize and the National Book Award and was a Book of the Month Club Dividend Selection.

"A very pleasant surprise. On the surface, Forbidden Loves is a romantic 'coming of age' novel about love, loss, and redemption. It throws in a surprising ending to boot. But it's not 'just' a love story. As the novel works out its story line, it brings to life a society and a culture that would otherwise be hauntingly unfamiliar to today's readers."
   "Daly-Lipe spices up her story with side trips to such diverse areas as the history of aviation, the American exile community in Paris, modern art, Hannibal, and the Catholic church. The diverse characters include Charles Lindbergh, James Joyce, and Gertrude Stein--and each of them belongs in the story."

"I don't want to give away the plot of Forbidden Loves. It takes many unexpected twists before it arrives at the ultimate twist at its end. The story is worth reading without anticipating anything but surprises. This is not the type of book I normally read, nevertheless, I enjoyed it enormously."
Robert Goodman,,founder and past president of PWSD, (originally San Diego Publishers Alliance), Board member of PMA, The Independent Publishers Marketing Association, CA.

A Letter from the Ambassade de France aux Etats-Unis
Dated Washington, April 20, 2005

Thank you so much for your... wonderful book on Paris between the wars. I really appreciated it and your endeavor to search for the places and the facts of your mother's life in Paris and make a great book of it is admirable and impressive. I wish your book a great success.

Sincerely, Jean-David Levitte

From England: *I have just finished (Forbidden Loves) and I must say... it is beautifully written.*

(It is) structured...well and within that structure expresses emotions so poignantly. The descriptions of places, moods, atmosphere and people make one feel a part of the story.

(Patricia's) ability to put on paper straightforward piece is interesting as it is very well thought out and carries itself in a very serious fashion and therefore the reader does not want to put the book down.

(Patricia Daly-Lipe) obviously did a lot of research and (her) ability to let that research flow from (her) fingers as if (she) had been there (herself) is great. I liked the quotes at the beginning of the chapters as they added live thoughts of others, which gives a sort of authenticity to that period. Very much the Bloomsberry set. Poetry was almost the essence of their being. I wondered if it had anything to do with that uncertain period between the wars.

Again, well done.
Putzi; Oak House, Surrey, England (the house used in the movie 'Finding Neverland')

Tapestry of social norms, history, and culture: Based on facts, this book, a historical fiction, is filled with the author's ardent research and life experiences in Paris. One feels the life of Paris come alive. Once I began to read the novel, I couldn't put it down. It is a story that draws you into it like a magnet.

Carol Cook, communications specialist

All ten of us in the book club enjoyed this trip to Paris between the wars. We could see the freedom lost to our grandmother's friend shackled by Catholicism while the artists and aviation buffs relished their time in history. Fabulous read.

A book club winner, April 14, 2007, Letitia O'Conor

ACKNOWLEDGEMENTS

"All written history (is) a compound of past and present," state Barzun and Graff in their book, *The Modern Researcher*. They explain that the instrument which the historian uses to look at the past is his or her own mind. The obvious bias in this historical fiction is my prejudice toward the little I remember or knew about my mother's life in Paris between the wars. I was benefited from letters written by mother, her beau, my grandparents, as well as letters preserved by my grandmother and written by my great-uncle, The Right Reverend Monsignor William A. Hemmick, from the front lines, WWI.

To discover the so-called pulse of the period, I read original works, listened to the music, studied (and enjoyed) the art, traveled to Paris and Provence, and tried to interview anyone who might still be alive and remember the period. For the latter, I am grateful to have known the late Mrs. Francis LeBaron (Regina) Smoot of Washington, D.C. An accomplished artist, she had studied art in England and Europe during the thirties and kindly read pertinent parts of my manuscript and confirmed their authenticity.

Thanks also to my late Tante Tiffie, Mrs. (Raymond Harper) Shenstone of Princeton, New Jersey. In a recently discovered document, we found a copy of a letter she had written on board the *S.S. Manhattan*, leaving Bordeaux and the war, dated September 25, 1939. Beautifully written, we have incorporated some of its contents to give a true flavor of France at the onset of WWII.

The French poetry is my own translation. The dialogue of James Joyce, Hemingway, Gertrude Stein, Coco Chanel, Virginia Woolf, Sylvia Beach, and Ambassador Herrick is taken from either their written work or newspaper accounts and should be considered authentic. Although the story line is fiction, the time, places, events and activities are well researched and can be authenticated.

Thank you to Harry Houghton, docent, San Diego Aerospace Museum and Dan Clemons, Lindbergh and Eddie Rickenbacker Collector, San Diego, for information pertaining to Lindbergh and

Spirit of St. Louis, some of which they said had never been published before.

Thanks Bill Gine for taking me for a ride in his 1910 Model T and Herb Cook of Johnsonville, Tennessee, for showing me how his 1926 Model T was driven.

Steele Lipe who not only took me for a ride in a biplane, but traveled with me to France, lived through years of research, and was sympathetic to my desire to see this book published. Without his encouragement and support, this book would probably never have been completed.

"Be patient with all that is unsolved in your heart and try to love the questions themselves ... Do not seek the answers, which cannot be given you because you would not be able to live them. And the point is, to live everything. Live the questions, now. Perhaps you will then gradually, without noticing it, live along some distant day into the answer."

Rainer Maria Rilke

Chapter One

There is nothing stable in the world; uproar's your only music.

John Keats
Paris, 1928

"The War confirmed that the Western world is culturally bankrupt," claimed the gentleman sitting at the far end of the long rectangular table the restaurant had set up in the back of the dining area. "Certainly, Western civilization as we knew it before 1914 is lost forever."

The room was warm and stuffy. Smoke was puffed into the air from cigarettes by both men and women. I was certainly not one to take on this habit even though many physicians argue for the cigarette's pathophysiological innocence and psychological benefit. Nevertheless, despite the cigarette's supposed attributes, the mood was grim.

"Was it the War that destroyed the romance we knew before or was all that an illusion?" I had to lean across the table to see who was speaking. It came from a lady with the look of stoic dignity. "Did that catastrophe then destroy illusion and put truth back in its place?" Silence prevailed as everyone around the table seemed to be contemplating her somewhat caustic comment. After taking a sip of wine, she continued. "Yes indeed, which was truth and which illusion?" The lady's name was Virginia Woolf, an elegant woman in her mid forties, her voice very clipped and so refinedly British, it was a bit difficult to understand. Again, her question appeared to be rhetorical since she continued, this time without a pause. "For my belief is that if we live another century or so; if we have the habit of freedom and the courage to write exactly what we think, then perhaps our relation, not to each other, but to the world of reality will … "

A dark haired, fair skinned lady with piercing blue eyes on her right finished the sentence with embellishment, "allow us to grow and know the truth." Clearly, this was not a timid group. The evening meal had been taken away and only liquid refreshments remained on the table. This was the time for talk.

The theme for this evening's discussion was the aftermath of the Great War. I was honored to be included in such a prestigious group of writers despite being not only too young to have shared their experiences, but having been, until recently, living on the other side of the Atlantic where vestiges of war were unknown. However, I did have one relative who had crossed the ocean and had courageously participated. Before we left Washington for France, my mother gave me a copy of a letter my Uncle William had written from the trenches. I had placed the envelope with the missive in my pocket before leaving our apartment in anticipation of possibly sharing it with this eminent group.

Soft sounds of sotto voce chattering surrounded the table until another lady clicked her glass so the rest of us would listen. During the war, she had driven an ambulance. "I saw it on their faces," she said somberly, "the wounded and the dying. They had sacrificed their lives for an ideal." Heads nodded. "And why? Did they hate the Germans that much? No, for the French, it was '*La Gloire*' that was France. For the Americans, it was 'for democracy'. And for me, nursing and driving the wounded was 'the right thing to do'. But that was in the beginning. Soon, it became my life. For years I knew little sleep, few baths, constant exhaustion, bombs, gas, filth, dirt and blood. I stopped questioning. I think that my emotions overtook my intellect. Maybe I became less civilized but maybe, just maybe, I am more civilized now." I discovered later that she was an American who had spent most of her adult life in France. No wonder she had such an objective perception of the war.

Sitting adjacent to the American was a middle aged lady dressed in black. She appeared to be in continuous mourning for what she had experienced. Her words confirmed what I suspected. "When you have been through a war like the last one, you come to believe in the supernatural. I saw boys lying on their stretchers just before they died. I listened as they talked to their sweethearts back home.

It was just as if they could see them standing next to their cots. Yes, anything is possible when you have experienced that war."

Timidly, I took out the document my mother had given me. It seemed appropriate to the present atmosphere. I asked if I might read what my uncle had written. Miss Woolf nodded her head.

"Thank you. My mother told me that my Uncle William, her brother, was under gun fire almost constantly as he administered to the sick and dying on the American and French fronts during the Great War. He is a priest. Mother gave me a copy of a letter he sent home. It is dated April 29, 1918. Uncle William was with the American troops under Foch."

I paused, taking a deep breath. The room was silent, faces around the table staring at me blindly, their expressions belying inner thoughts. Unfolding the paper, I cleared my throat and gathering courage, began to read. "It seems as if hell itself were let loose; the roar of the battle is so terrific. I am scrawling this in a cave right near our front lines. Several officers share it with me and we sleep on straw and live the lives of moles … Never in all my life have I seen such days of horror. We are constantly under shell fire day and night … The strain is something terrible. At midnight the food wagons come by and we get a hot stew and coffee as most of the men's work is done by night and we sleep during the day when we can. Then at dusk I crawl out and bury the dead in a deserted garden by a ruined house. There are no coffins even, but just a big trench and there the poor mangled bodies of our men are laid, and I hurriedly read the funeral service over them and sprinkle them with Holy water. I seem to be sort of numb with horror and the tragedy of it, but manage to get through it somehow. The battle is raging all about of us and it sounds like the crack of doom. God knows what the outcome will be. Our men are splendid, courageous and enduring and are putting up a splendid fight and I am glad to have a chance to be with them and help them … The ruin and desolation all about are beyond words as a perfect hail storm of shells is falling. The tragic prevails, of course, as they bring the dead and wounded by stretchers … I was also quartered in the same town on the second line, where Lt. Col. Griffiths was killed, and whom I buried."

For several minutes, no one spoke. Carefully, I folded the document and returned it to my pocket.

Finally, Sylvia Beach, whom I had not noticed before, broke the silence. First thanking me, Miss Beach proceeded to tell how she had delivered pajamas to Serbian troops traveling between Paris and Belgrade. "I too observed the death and dying your uncle described." In Paris, she witnessed the death of ninety-one worshipers when the Church of Saint-Gervais received a direct hit from *Grosse Berthe*. Everyone present knew about Big Bertha, the largest gun ever made. It was named after the daughter of Krupps, the German armament manufacturing family. Again there was silence. Some took sips of wine. Some took a drag on their cigarette while others took to methodically stirring their coffee, as if the solution could be found in a cup.

A young student-writer at the other end of the table finally broke the silence with a brash statement: "The WORD. We need to concentrate on the word," he cried out. I heard a giggle and rejoiced in the change in atmosphere. "We writers have an obligation to humanity," he continued. "This obligation can be defined by the written word." Smiles returned to the somber faces. "After all," he upheld, basking in his new celebrity, "doesn't language define human experience? Think about it. Its power to shape and remake the world could be said to invoke even the power of God." Looking around for approval and receiving enough for confidence, he finished with a flourish. Raising his wine glass, he announced, "I am speaking about the written word. Use it, engage in it and let it take over."

"Hear, hear!" they teased the young enthusiast, but toasted him nevertheless.

A gentleman named William Carlos Williams had just joined the group. His mood was not so gay. Somberly, using the literary reference, he brought the gathering back to the prior discussion. "It is difficult to get the news from poems. Yet men die miserably every day for lack of what is found there."

An older man, whose solemn yet earnest voice rose two octaves as he spoke, the words coming slowly but distinctly, declared, "We cannot allow another desecration to take place. Do you all realize that nearly nine million soldiers were killed between 1914 and

1918? That's an average of 5,600 each day. I feel the Germans are plotting. Yes, plotting, despite the fact that they were required to surrender their military fleet. I know the Treaty of Versailles forbade them from manufacturing military aircraft or tanks. But we would be naïve to think that there will be no more battles, no more wars. Look at old Field Marshal von Hindenburg; he won't last another two years. The German Republic will fall and, God forbid, I feel something tyrannical will take its place."

"Old man, you are wrong. We have seen the war to end all wars. It will never happen again. I remember this war vividly. I was there. I saw trees as round as a man's thigh literally cut down by the stream of lead," gasped another octogenarian.

"He is describing the effects of a machine gun," a British lady seated to my right explained. "The machine gun could fire five hundred bullets a minute."

"We must work hard, write, let the Word take over," piped in the same enthusiastic young writer at the other end.

"Enough! Words are like sweets. Too many of them make you sick." This came from Cecil Lewis who, I was told, had been a pilot in the war. Too bad Michael hadn't stayed.

"Right. We can't go back to pre-1914, but we can learn our lesson and move on." Several agreed, several disagreed, but one thing was clear, at least to me. This conversation was helpful both to understand the past and to learn of options for the future.

Most members of the group were foreigners; only one appeared to be French. I wondered what the French gentleman was thinking. Turning back to my British neighbor, I whispered, "After their land has been desecrated, their young men slaughtered, their homes, farms and countryside reduced to rubble, I wonder how they feel listening to us, Brits and Americans?"

"Young lady," said a middle-aged British gentleman sitting directly across from us, "you may not know it, but it is a matter of record that in 1917 there was a mutiny among French and British soldiers. They had walked out of the battle. The Germans, however, did nothing. Perhaps they too were worn out."

"I remember the end of the summer in 1914 when the Germans were coming down to take Paris," interjected the octogenarian. "It was the Battle of the Marne. A horrible day for both sides and that included the British forces who were helping the French. Thousand were killed. The French and British army came close to defeat and was only saved by the use of Paris taxis who rushed 6,000 reserve troops to the front lines. The German commander, General Helmuth von Moltke, proved to be indecisive during the invasion and his failure to give clear orders resulted in field commanders ordering a retreat. What is truly frightening, my young American friend, is what the general said about war."

I felt as if I were living in the midst of the battle itself. These men had experienced such horrors in their lifetime.

Without waiting for a request, the old man explained that the German General had said that in his opinion, perpetual peace was a dream."

"A dream?" We couldn't believe such a statement.

"A dream indeed and not a beautiful dream either. He said that war was 'an integral part of God's ordering of the universe'."

Now we were truly shocked.

"Yes, the General believed that the courage and fidelity to duty and a readiness to sacrifice that troops exhibit in war are the noblest virtues man can have. Therefore, he felt war was indispensable. Without war, the world would become 'swamped in materialism'. I am quoting what he said."

I was receiving more education than any school or university could have taught me. How privileged we had been in the United States.

The sole Frenchman overheard what we were discussing and switched seats to come next to me to explain the facts. "Libby, if I may call you by your first name (I nodded), what I overheard you discussing earlier was a conspiracy. It was Caillaux, the banker and our ex-premier, who plotted with the Germans and caused the mutinies in the French army. What you were talking about, I think, was the breakdown of one of our offenses against German trenches north of the Aisne River. You see, Caillaux had instigated a movement called 'defeatism' and it worked, especially in Russia, because after years of fighting, the morale was very low. We desperately needed the American soldiers and are forever grateful of their help."

I was humbled and grateful that my nation had come to the assistance of the French. I had not known the war nor did I have friends killed or maimed.

"Almost nine million men lost their lives and almost twenty million were wounded, Libby. Don't forget that the soldiers killed were mostly young and able, the strongest, most spirited, and most promising members of the human family."

"Yes, and don't forget the millions of private citizens who perished from starvation and violence," added Sylvia Beach who had moved over to our side of the table.

"Libby," the Frenchman continued, "you must go to the *Arc de Triomphe* and pay your respects to the burial spot of the Unknown Soldier. He was buried there in 1919 to symbolize all the Frenchmen who lost their lives in assuring their country military triumph in the Great War."

I wished my husband had stayed to hear these facts about the war. But Michael had left. An aviator not a writer, at least he could have discussed the aspect of the fast development of aviation which resulted from the war with the pilot Cecil Lewis. A kindred spirit, I gathered, since both men chose to live dangerously. "Safety last," Mr. Lewis had said.

Glancing to the other side of the *café*, I searched for the table where Philippe and his Mother had been eating when we first arrived. It was empty.

"War or fighting is like a dance because it is all going forward and back, and that forward and back movement, that is the reason that revolutions and Utopias are discouraging they are up and down and not forward and back." That came from Gertrude Stein who was at the far end. I was surprised how quiet she had been up until then. She continued, recounting a time toward the end of the war when she and Alice were in Nimes helping to care for both French and American soldiers. "The Armistice had just been declared and I remember a remark a wounded French soldier made when I told him, 'Well here is peace.' The soldier replied, 'At least for twenty years.' War is a dance going forward and back."

"What do you think, Libby?" asked Francis, a young man whom I had met at Natalie Barney's soirée. He and I were the youngest members of this exclusive circle.

"Excuse me? I mean, what are you asking?" I was still thinking about 'the dance'.

"Do you think our generation is culturally deprived? Just because we didn't go through the war, does that mean we can't sympathize?"

I considered the question in light of the horrific realities we had heard earlier. "Francis, you use of the word 'deprived' but I may have a different understanding of the word. My father has a fine library. Some of his books are in Greek; some Latin. I never learned Greek. The only Latin I know I learned in Catechism classes. Perhaps I wasn't exposed to the classics because I am a woman. But maybe if I had an opportunity to read the great thinkers of the past, I would be better equipped to put in perspective some of the life changing events these people have been discussing." I looked over at Miss Stein and wondered if she had studied the classics. She was always wearing loose clothes reminiscent of Greek tunics and had sandals on her feet like the philosopher Socrates probably wore.

While Francis, the Frenchman and I were talking, several serious female writers at the table were moving onto a different topic. We stopped speaking to listen.

"The artist," Miss Stein was saying, "is not someone apart from the rest of the world." She was describing the artist as being more sensitive, more receptive to the wave of the future, someone who would ultimately inundate the rest of the public. "No one is ahead of his time; it is only that the particular variety of creating his time is the one that his contemporaries who also are creating their own time refuse to accept. And they refuse to accept it for a very good reason and that is that they do not have to accept it for any reason."

I shook my head. This was impossible for me to understand.

"That brings us to another point, doesn't it?" piped in an energetic feminine writer.

"That's Djuna Barnes," whispered the Frenchman as he stood up ready to leave at any moment. Clearly, this was not a discussion he wanted to follow. The debate that ensued related to women's rights, equality and woman's uniqueness.

"Just now, women are being enfranchised. But among the younger people, there is complacency."

"The battle has been won," a younger woman reasoned, "so why is there a need for public action?" The older lady seated next to the speaker wrung her hands.

"Literary effort is the same as love. It is inseparable from the occasion that provides its impetus," Djuna Barnes continued, ignoring the young authoress. "Listen to my friend Natalie Barney. She says you can't separate art from life. Now, can you? What's more, I believe that art belongs to women." Miss Barnes was not about to give in. To me, her extreme feminism was annoying.

"You know what they say about the English language? While it has profundity; it lacks any sense of depth. *La langue francaise se parle, l'italienne se chante, et l'anglais se crache.*" This was the Frenchman's attempt to alleviate the tension and turn the conversation around. Although a few laughed, the serious feminist debate continued. He shrugged his shoulders and, as he was about to leave, murmured, "*La Belle Epoque est définitivement terminée.*"

It was getting late and I was getting tired. Besides, I was starting to feel guilty about being out so long while Michael was at home alone. It was time to leave. I was also too exhausted to follow the logic of the discussion any longer. I hadn't slept well in the past few days. Excusing myself, I found my hosts, Miss Stein and Miss Woolf and thanked them for including me. Graciously, they asked if I needed an escort. Assuring them that as we lived very close by, I would be quite safe, in actuality, I was glad to have the short stroll home to be by myself.

It was a cool spring evening. The air was fresh and I could smell the blossoms and the dampness of the dewy grass, and feel the dry bark scaling off the trees though I could barely distinguish their forms in the pale street lamplight. Crickets chirped defying the silence of the night. The sound was comforting and familiar. The Seine continued her voyage downstream, her small rivulets lapping at the stone embellishments which held the *Île St. Louis* together.

This island in the Seine, a jewel in the heart of Paris, was now my home. Although we had been here only two months, Washington seemed like a lifetime away and I was not unhappy about that. I loved the island and I loved Paris, but tonight I was tired and a bit confused.

When we arrived at the restaurant, Philippe and his mother were there having a quiet dinner at a table near the window. I was sorry not to be able to spend time with them, but we had been invited to participate in a writers' dinner party and regretfully had to pay swift compliments and move on to the group in the back room. Something about those two, seemed so familiar, so comfortable. Now as I walked home, it was not the fascinating conversations of the writers' table that filled my mind; it was the consideration of a feeling I had, a feeling toward Philippe. This was a new emotion and I was not at all sure it was appropriate.

With these thoughts and feelings running rampant in my mind, I reached the *portiere* of our building. Madame Metz, our dear, most observant concierge was leaning against the great door. "*Bonsoir, Madame Whitacker.*"

"*Bonsoir, Madame Metz.*"

"*Madame, votre mari est déjà chez vous.* Your husband is already home."

This seemed like a perfect opening on her part for me to give an explanation of my coming home alone. To satisfy her insatiable appetite for news which could be too easily translated into gossip, I explained that we, my husband and I, had been with friends at *Le Rendezvous des Mariniers*, a hotel-restaurant further up on the *Quai d'Anjou*, not far from our apartment. However, Michael had been bored by the conversations. He understood aeroplanes, not books, and had only escorted me to the dinner because he had been invited for my sake. I understood his leaving early and felt perfectly safe walking home unattended, though probably not the most appropriate thing to do.

"*Oui, Madame, je sais, I know,*" our caretaker replied before I had completed my account. She attempted a smile but was somewhat despondent.

Despite her demeanor, I smiled back ready to pass through the entry and up the stairs. But it was the way Madame Metz shrugged her shoulders and looked at me with probing eyes that made me hesitate. Just before closing the doors, she whispered, "*Mais il n'est pas seul*. But he is not alone." Then, having delivered the message she originally intended, *la concierge* caused the heavy wooden *porte cochère* to bang shut, dropped the wrought iron latch into place, and disappeared into her dark apartment on the ground floor.

I let her words pass over me as I ascended the stairs to our apartment on the second floor. Aware of the late hour, I quietly turned the key, gently pushed open the door and entered.

It was silent and dark inside with only flickering strands of light coming from candles in the hallway. I removed my coat and as my eyes adjusted to the dimness, tiptoed from the foyer to peek into the salon. The room was dark except for a glow from the fireplace. My eyes followed the sound of the crackling flames and then I saw him. My husband was standing in front of the fire, his back to me, his body silhouetted against the orange blaze. Silent and still, not sure of what I was truly seeing, perhaps not wanting to give in to the sight, I allowed my eyes more time to focus. Michael was naked. His tight buttocks and his tall slim torso teased my sensibilities. Although he was my husband, I had never seen his body like this before. How handsome. Would he take me now? I had waited so long. I was ready. I had completely forgotten *Madame la concierge's* message.

Then, about to move closer, I saw it. Michael was not alone. It had been difficult to adapt to the dark in front of the firelight, but slowly I became aware that there was a hand around Michael's thigh. Long, thick fingers were stroking Michael's skin. A man's hand. *He's with a man! A man is on his knees in front of Michael. Oh, how could this be? Michael, you're a degenerate, you're …* But none of these words reached my mouth. Stunned, I fell back against the wall and slowly slid to the floor. With my arms pressed across my chest, my head dropped and my body shook uncontrollably. When I finally looked up, Michael was standing over me. This time he was wearing trousers.

23

"Stay away from me." Tears streamed down my cheeks. Michael leaned over to help me up. He was murmuring something I could not understand. This was like a dream . . . a nightmare. "Leave me alone; don't touch me!" Warily, I sat on my haunches, braced myself against the wall and slowly drew myself up. "I must leave," I whispered clinging to the stair rail for support.

"No, no," pleaded Michael, "I, please, I, I can explain" as he came toward me.

"No, don't. Don't!" I put my hand out to keep him away. Michael stepped back, his face betraying his anxiety and, I hoped, guilt. Blindly, I made my way to the kitchen. The telephone was hanging on the wall next to the sink. In the dark, I groped for the receiver. When the operator came on the line, I gave Pamela's number.

"Pleeease," he begged, standing at the doorway.

"Pamela. This is Libby."

"Hello, Libby dear. I assume you are calling about the writers' party. Did you enjoy yourself, dear?"

"I, Pamela, I can, can't talk about that right now." I was having trouble getting the words out.

"Libby, are you all right?"

"I, I, I need to see you, Pamela," I said, tears falling uncontrollably. "May I come to your home? Please excuse … I mean …. I need, I need to stay for the night." I realized that this was bold, but what could I do? I had to get out of the apartment. I could barely breathe; trying to choke down the sobs at least long enough to speak with my friend, my new friend, the only person I could turn to at this moment.

"Of course," replied Pamela. "I will send Frederick over right away. Libby, what is wrong? Are you … "

"Yes, no, I mean, oh I don't know what I mean." At that point, I was shaking so badly that I could hardly hold the phone. All I knew was that I had to get away from Michael ….quickly.

"Can you be ready in half an hour?"

"Oh, yes, yes, thank you," I gasped replacing the receiver. Michael was watching me from the doorway.

"How could you? You brute. I hate you," I said, shocking myself. I had never used those words before. He made a step forward. "Stay away from me." I swung out as if trying to slap him, but he was quick to duck. Then fearing he might retaliate and strike me back, I ran blindly down the hall to my bedroom and locked the door. Turning around, I faced the room. This was a room we had shared. Heaving with silent screams, I fell on my bed and sobbed.

By the time Frederick arrived, I had packed a small suitcase. Without speaking to Michael, whom I scarcely saw standing near the glowing embers remaining in the hearth, I left.

Chapter Two

*"Though we travel the world over to find the beautiful,
we must carry it with us or we find it not."*
Ralph Waldo Emerson

It was a social whirlwind that blew me into my new life. The winter season was my time to be *presented* to Washington society. The year was 1925.

I not only survived the debutante parties in Washington, but flourished in the fun of being on my own, away from family supervision. Furthermore, I was encouraged, even by Mademoiselle, my old governess who still supervised my activities, to do so. The dinners were a bit tedious, but afterwards we had dances and I loved the music. *Every mornin', every evenin' ain't we got fun? Not much money, oh but honey' ain't we got fun? There's nothing surer; the rich get rich and the poor get poorer.*

This was considered the credo of the roaring 20s and we were on the right side of society, flaunting our wealth and not in the least embarrassed about it. All the sadness I had seen in France just the summer before when I had accompanied my parents to Paris, seemed so far away and, for a short time, I cleared my mind of those memories. I was having fun. *Yes, we have no bananas* made sense. We were literally *Puttin' on the Ritz*. The music transported me to another world.

Although I danced with several young men, I was often sitting alone. When a handsome fellow named Michael Whitacker saw me by myself, he would come over and ask to put his name on my card as if he had to fight for a place in line. When we danced, the music and the atmosphere carried me beyond fear and timidity as we glided across the floor keeping time to the rhythm. Unfortunately, usually toward the end of the evening, the orchestra began playing the fast new, hot jazz. I preferred sitting those out. Michael respected my point of view.

There is nothing graceful about that kind of music and to be honest, it offended me. I saw girls doing things I really did not think were decent, things like the *shimmy*. They allowed the boys to hold them in a way that made me blush. Some even permitted the boys to kiss them in public. My parents called those girls *flappers*. In a way, I was almost jealous. They looked so happy. What I envied was their ability to be completely carefree, easygoing, almost indulgent in their immodesty. Definitely not brave enough to allow even the slightest impropriety, I would never have dared having a *sweetie* or even discussing such things with my girl friends.

Although I had attended plays performed at the foot of the Washington Monument, I was never allowed to go to a nickelodeon. Shakespeare had taught me little about romance or flirtation, so I couldn't put a name to the feelings I had when a boy held me a little too tightly. My body enjoyed what better judgment forbade. I was troubled by this conflict, emotions seizing what thoughts banned, and I had no one to talk to about it. Mademoiselle always supervised when my friends came over and I surely could not share these feelings with her.

Nevertheless, I survived the entire debutante season intact. I met the *proper* young people, which was precisely what my mother and father wanted for me, and, in the end, they were rewarded with the result I believe they anticipated. Michael Whitacker, the most eligible bachelor of all the brilliant, slick-haired young men, proposed to me. My parents were thrilled. I was in shock.

Like my father, Michael had attended Georgetown University. Unlike my father, he never completed his studies. "Those Jesuits are tough, brilliant, good teachers, but strict," he said. Like many young men of unlimited means, he was filled with wanderlust and decided to leave the University and travel. He went backpacking in the mountains of Peru and rafting down the Amazon River in Brazil. He seemed to crave excitement and challenge, always looking for adventures demanding stamina, strength of character, and danger. Apparently, he believed overcoming fear was the key to being strong. His latest quest for adventure was learning to fly. "With an aeroplane," Michael propounded "I can combine all my passions." Passions? I would never have used that cherished word to describe a sport activity. "Besides," he continued, ignoring my look of astonishment, "didn't aeroplanes prove their worth during the Great War?" I admitted that I was not well informed about the 'War to end all wars' even though I had recently traveled to Europe with my parents. It just didn't seem like a good idea to recount my experience last summer so I simply said, "I heard a few horror stories."

When my parents included me in their annual trip abroad, Mr. Myron T. Herrick was the United States Ambassador to France. Soon after our arrival, my parents were invited to an intimate cocktail reception at the Embassy. To my surprise, I was included. No wonder my mother had a new Chanel dress tailored for me the first week we were in Paris.

When we were together, my mother and I spoke French, but not in front of Father who barely understood the language. At the embassy, I was delighted to be introduced as the young lady with a perfect accent and fluent in both languages. Mr. Herrick shook my hand and then decided to test me. I passed with flying colors and was presented to an attractive older French couple who graciously helped me understand the appreciation the French had for American soldiers. "They came and risked their lives to help us defeat the Germans." Acknowledging my age, they were careful not to be too graphic. I could sense, however, just looking at the furrows in their faces and the way they clenched their hands, they had been subjected to such nightmarish things as I could not begin to understand.

Meanwhile, Mr. Herrick was describing an event that had made a lasting impression on him. His audience was in rapt silence, so we walked over to listen.

"A great harvest moon was rising over the city near *Notre Dame*. It seemed to rest on the corner of the façade of the Cathedral. The French flag was blowing steadily across the face of the moon. In the fleeting moments while this spectacle lasted, people knelt on the quay in prayer."

"An extremely powerful image," my father said. He paused, and then asked, "Why were the people praying?"

"I was wondering myself," the Ambassador replied. "There is an ancient prophecy that says the fate of France will finally be settled upon the fields where Attila's horde was halted and driven back and where many battles in defense of France have been won. It was explained to me that the people were pointing to the French flag outlined across the moon because it was the *sign in heaven*. It meant the victory of French arms. The prophecy of old, they believed, had come true and France would once again be saved on those chalky fields."

I could feel chills run down my spine and, looking at others in the room, I was not the only one to react that way. As Mr. Herrick walked away to welcome new guests, the gentle old Frenchman I had been conversing with whispered, "Who would live, my child, if the future were revealed to him? When a single anticipated misfortune would give us so much uneasiness? When the foreknowledge of one certain calamity would be enough to embitter every day that precedes it? I think," he continued wistfully, "it is better not to pry, even into the things which surround us. Heaven, which has given us the power to foresee our necessities, has also given us those very necessities to set limits to exercise that power." His words were confusing, but the way he spoke belied pain and anguish.

His wife put her arm around the dear man. A tear fell down her cheek. "Libby, my child, I don't think you know. We lost our son in the war. He would have been your age when he died."

These people had been through such misery. Listening to their stories brought to mind the images of war I had seen while walking the streets of Paris. Sights like the remnants of buildings, once private homes, now reduced to pieces and parts. Or the holes from bullets wedged into cement walls that lined the boulevards.

I began to recognize that my life in Washington was almost too perfect. We had never run from bombs flying through the air or listened to breaking glass as bullets riddled holes in windows just above our heads. No one in our family had been lost or injured in battle. Exposure to these calamities and their influence on people's lives made me realize how much I needed to learn about life.

But all this was too much to share with Michael. While my thoughts had lingered on last year's experiences, he was expounding upon the merits of air travel.

"Yes, perhaps the only good thing to come out of the war was aviation. Just think about it. Before the war, the highest speed achieved by an aeroplane was about 60 miles per hour." *That seems pretty fast to me*, I thought. "But, amazingly, by the end of the war, planes could fly at speeds surpassing 130 miles per hour. And that's only in the space of four years." He was so engrossed in his subject, I don't think he cared whether I was impressed or not. Despite my lackluster interest in his obsession, I loved watching him get excited, his hand squeezing mine tightly as he made a point.

"If there is a silver lining to the conflict, it will be found across the Atlantic in France," he added with a flourish. But I didn't understand and wasn't afraid to admit it.

"France was devastated by the war, Libby. Her only chance of recovery from her economic slump, in my opinion, will come from building aeroplanes. Her government is becoming heavily involved with aviation and I have learned that they are giving financial priority to testing and developing aeroplanes." Clearly fervent, Michael took hold of both my hands and, looking straight into my eyes, proclaimed, "Libby, that's why I want to live in Paris."

At this, he let me go with one hand and swung me around with the other. The world traveler had decided to have his next adventure as well as make his fortune in France and I was dizzy. In fact, he could have said nothing more enticing to me even without the twirl. I envied Michael. The idea of living in Paris sounded wonderful to me. Wistfully, I thought how easy it would be to leave the restricted routine my parents imposed. The French lifestyle would suit me perfectly. Perhaps it was naïve, but that's what I thought.

Many nights after coming home from the dances, I'd curl up with Mr. Ted, my stuffed bear, and fantasize about being held in the embrace of a handsome young man, his arms around my waist and his mouth coming close to mine. Before the kiss, I would wake up embarrassed by my own thoughts.

Although the young man in my dream was too vague to identify, by the next evening or afternoon party, I would be excited to see Michael again. Sometimes instead of dancing, we held hands and I listened to him talk about flying. When he escorted me home after a party, he would kiss me on the forehead before letting me in the door.

At that time in my life, being kissed on the forehead was romantic. But Michael never said he loved me. This should have been a clue.

I understood his love of aeroplanes and I understood his wanting to go to Paris, but when he told me he wanted to speak to my father about our future, I didn't understand.

"You want to marry me?" I asked incredulously. Although the parties lasted the entire winter, our time together had been relatively brief.

Despite what I was feeling or thinking, especially since I never dared to express any private thoughts to my parents, the proposal was accepted by my father. Immediately, my mother changed like a chameleon. The once strict, domineering and distanced mother, who gave me instructions but never hugs, suddenly turned into a loving and caring parent, making me into her treasured pet. Caring or not, it was back to the Chanel standard.

The summer before, no sooner had we arrived in Paris than my mother arranged for a car and driver. While father took care of business concerns, mother and I were driven to *29 rue de Faubourg St. Honoré*, the salon of Gabrielle 'Coco' Chanel.

"My dear child," mother explained patiently, "Mademoiselle Chanel is all the rage among the Parisian *couturiers*." I had never heard of her. When we entered the small dress shop, I was introduced to a petite lady in her mid-forties. She was not fair like us, but gallically dark with well defined features. I thought her face severe, but not mean. She was skinny and talked with a cigarette dangling from her lips. Her hands were forever busy adjusting, pulling and pinning material on customers as they stood patiently. It was clear that when it came to her trade, Mlle Chanel was a very serious woman, but she could be droll and witty as well. After Mother told me about the dressmaker's past, I realized why Mlle Chanel needed to be both sharp and amusing.

Gabrielle Chanel was born out of wedlock. At the age of twelve, she was placed in an orphanage. It was from the nuns that she learned how to sew.

"How did she come by the name 'Coco'?" I projected interest as I took these first steps toward developing a new rapport with my mother.

"Happy to oblige," she told me. "After leaving the orphanage, Coco received her nickname at a *café* where, as a young woman, she responded to a challenge. Standing up before all the customers, she sang about a girl who had lost her dog. The dog's name was Coco."

I laughed, my admiration mounting for the lady, amazed how definitive Mlle Coco could be about her opinions. She pontificated without stopping, continuously adjusting, fastening, sewing and clipping her client's dress.

"Fashion is not simply a matter of clothes," she pronounced while pinning up a hemline. "Fashion is in the air, born upon the wind. One intuits it. It is in the sky and on the road." Mother and I were spellbound. Going to her salon was equivalent to attending a literary soirée, a social event and a dress performance all at the same time. I was overwhelmed and delighted. My mother, on the other hand, simply approved the work Coco designed. "Any lady who prides herself as being part of fashionable society is a regular patron of Chanel" was my mother's proclamation.

"What counts," said Mlle Chanel, referring to the material, the buttons, even the thread, "is that all the elements be beautiful." We returned many times, often for less than five minutes, simply to have a fitting.

Now here we were in Washington living this fashion statement all over again. This time, however, it was not for a reception, but for my wedding. I was to have the perfect wardrobe, the perfect hair style, the perfect manicure. I was driven to Elizabeth Arden's Beauty Salon, the Red Door on Connecticut Avenue, then off to dress salons, seamstresses and boutiques. Michael and I had to attend the obligatory 'pre-Canna' conferences with our parish priest. I have no recollection what was said.

One afternoon, my father took me to the State Department where we went through the formalities of my obtaining a new passport. Libby is not my real name. When I filled out the form and wrote my baptismal name, Elisabeth, it seemed like an omen. My Christian name is spelled the French way with an 's'. If it was destiny that I should live in France, I had every reason to feel positive about what I was doing. But an inner voice kept chastising me. I couldn't understand and chose not to listen.

Meanwhile, family friends were giving parties in my honor. The parties were more for my parents than for me. Weeks went by. I was in a daze. When I went to bed at night, I cuddled with Mr. Ted. As a young child, Mademoiselle gave me hugs when I needed them, but it was her job. I desperately wanted the warmth of another human being who really cared about me. For the moment, I only had my teddy bear and the poor fellow was getting more than his share of kisses.

The big day finally arrived. The gown of white satin which my mother had chosen was quite long and slightly draped to one side with a square yoke of antique rose point lace reaching to the waistline. A long court train fell from my shoulders and a tulle veil, which was held close to my head in a cap of orange blossoms, fell over the train. The satin sleeves covered my arms tightly and stretched to a point at my index finger with tiny white buttons running underside from my wrist up to my elbow.

When I was all laced, buttoned and tied up, my father came into the room. He took a good long look at me. Although he said nothing, he couldn't conceal a big grin. My aunt handed me a bouquet of white orchids and lilies of the valley to carry in one hand, while my father took my other hand and gave it a squeeze before placing my arm through his. Slowly, because the gown was not designed for easy maneuverability, he walked me down the stairs to the foyer. At the foot of the stairs, we paused and I had a chance to look at my reflection in the hall mirror. The gown was stunning. The bouquet was beautiful. I was the picture of what a bride should be except for my complexion. It was almost as white as my gown. Hopefully no one else would notice. If only the feeling matched the picture of beauty and composure, but what I felt inside did not match. This was a performance, a charade, like the ones I used to play with my little girlfriends. I glanced at my father. This man, whom I had put on a pedestal, was proud of me. I flushed with new-found confidence. It was just enough to keep me going.

We turned to the right and slowly passed through the dark mahogany double doorway into the drawing room. Someone began playing Mendelssohn. Our baby grand piano had been moved to the back near the entrance to the dining room. While I was upstairs being dressed, the house had been decorated with spring flowers, yellow and orchid in the drawing room, with yellow forsythia and jonquils in the dining room. Chairs were set up in rows from the piano to the front facing the window. Now, as we walked slowly down the side aisle created beside the chairs, all I could see was a blur of faces, all staring at me. The music changed and with the invigorated tempo, we walked between the guests to the front window where there were huge garlands and vases laden with flowers.

I didn't notice Michael until my hand was placed in his. My friend, Mary Louise, whom I had chosen as my maid of honor, took the bouquet from my other hand. Until then, I had been completely unaware of her or the best man's presence. The perspiration was profusely working its way around my body as I gritted my teeth and grimly subjected myself to the ritual. We faced the priest. All I could see of him was a black silhouette against the brilliance of the afternoon sun which came flooding through the front windows behind the altar. I don't remember any of the words, but I must have repeated the proper lines because all of a sudden, the priest said, "And now you may kiss the bride." My first kiss! Michael's touch was soft, tentative and quick. The piano began playing again. Michael was pulling me away from the priest and walking me through the assemblage of guests. From the corner of my eye, I could see people blowing kisses and hear them calling out congratulations. We walked down the aisle into the dining room. The chairs had been removed, leaving only the dining table in the middle of the room. China plates and silver trays laden with finger food surrounded the centerpiece, a huge five layered white cake with a tiny bouquet of pink and blue flowers adorning the top.

The guests came swarming around us and between nibbles of watercress sandwiches and sips of champagne, congratulated Michael. People I barely knew hugged me and wished me luck and happiness. I would need more than luck, but said nothing. Someone had placed a plate of food in my hand, but I couldn't eat a bite.

Suddenly, my mother appeared at my side. She wore a gown of beige georgette crepe draped to one side and a large straw hat of a darker shade of brown. "It is time for you to cut the cake," she coaxed. At last, the final ritual. Michael's hand guided mine as we cut the first slice from our wedding cake. His hand was cold.

And then it was over. My friends escorted me back upstairs. It took two of them to get the wedding dress off. We were so worried about tearing the lovely lace. My traveling dress, again chosen by mother, was tan and brown crepe. To match, I put on a small brown hat, brown shoes and a black coat trimmed with brown caracul. As a final touch, the double strand of pearls my father had given me was placed around my neck. In the little dressing table mirror, I saw something sparkle and looked down. It was the sun refracting light off the ring so recently placed on my finger. Oh, how beautiful it was! I rubbed my other hand over the smooth surface of the blue sapphire and the rough points of the baby miners' cut diamonds encircling it on the platinum band.

Each of my girl friends insisted on holding my hand to stare at the ring. They could take my hand and admire it, but I wasn't about to take it off. The ring and the kiss, what was next? I couldn't help but shiver. The girls must have sensed my angst for soon they left me alone so I could compose myself. I needed to calm down. I also needed the time to say goodbye to my little room with all its mementos of childhood, including Mr. Ted. Wiping away a tear, I gave my bear a final hug, took a deep breath and descended to the foyer where Michael was waiting.

My parents and their guests waved and shouted as we walked down the front steps. Mademoiselle was there too, waving and crying before she turned and went back inside the house. Arm in arm, Michael and I walked down the first set of steps. I stopped for a moment at the landing, turned around and took one last look at the only real home I had ever known. I loved that house.

Michael pulled my arm. Slowly we descended the second set of steps, passed through the gate, crossed the sidewalk and were ushered into the limousine parked on Massachusetts Avenue. Hans drove us to the station to catch the late afternoon train to New York. From the solemn look on his face, his eyes gazing solidly into mine,

I think this man who had known me since I was a small child, was the only one who understood how I was feeling at that moment.

Michael and I didn't say much to each other on the train. We exchanged trite comments like: "Did you enjoy the wedding?" *Wasn't this the biggest day in my life?* Wasn't I supposed to feel elated? Instead, my stomach was upside down. It sounds silly, but what I really wished I was doing was not sitting in this train with Michael, but rather lying in bed clutching Mr. Ted. I wasn't like the other girls, giggly and fawning over boys, and yet I was one of the first among my girlfriends to get married. "Yes," he had replied, "Very nice. Thank you." *Why is he thanking me? Aren't we supposed to get beyond this level of conversation? Why isn't there someone here to help me understand?* I was ready to cry, but smiled weakly instead. Michael did take my hand in his and, for a brief moment, held it tightly. I couldn't tell if he cared or if he needed reassurance. We were both ill at ease. I comforted myself with the thought that perhaps all newlyweds felt this way in the beginning.

Once in New York, Michael made all the arrangements. We had to secure transportation to the ship. Although we weren't scheduled to sail until the next morning, all booked passengers were allowed to spend the first night on board the beautiful *SS Berengaria*. It seemed safer than going to a hotel and then having to get a cab to the ship in time for an early morning departure. I thought it would be romantic to spend our first night together listening to the quiet lap of the surf, looking at the stars and then settling down to the calm of our cabin with its porthole and view of the city lights.

Unfortunately, the luxury was wasted on both of us. That first night we drank quite a bit of wine. I don't remember what we said to each other or what we did, but I do remember we slept in separate bunks. The next morning, no sooner had we left the port of New York and watched the skyline fade from view than the sea became extremely rough. The ocean was covered with white caps as far as I could see and the swells mounted as we began our voyage across the Atlantic.

"It isn't dangerous, is it Michael?" I asked as we stood at the rail waving goodbye to America.

"Certainly not," he replied stoically. "Not if the Captain has chosen to continue."

Rolling seas, small chops, rain, gloom … three hours of undulating and rough movement, and I was the first. Holding back as long as I could, I finally abandoned ladylike demeanor and vomited over the side of the ship. My relief was short lived.

"Who would separate waves from sea and say, 'These are waves but this is the sea.' Yet thoughts of waves forget thoughts of sea."

Never before had I felt like this. Perhaps it wasn't only the movement of the ship that had made me so sick. My nerves were frayed. I had eaten little and drank more than ever before. At home, we only sipped a small glass of wine with dinner. But I wasn't alone in my distress. As the voyage progressed, the situation on the ship worsened and many passengers came outside hoping the fresh sea air would relieve their nausea. Days later, the seas calmed, but by then Michael and I were in no mood to enjoy the voyage. The severe bouts of *mal de mer* left us physically drained.

There was really nothing the stewards could do to make our voyage enjoyable, although they tried by bringing us chamomile tea, dry bread, Dramamine pills, and encouragement. After a quick stop near the cliffs of Dover, we crossed the Channel and arrived at our destination, the French coast. With shaky legs, we disembarked.

From Le Harvre, still queasy, we took a train to Paris.

Initially, we stayed with Michael's mother whose apartment was in the fourth *arrondissement*. Often she spent the spring and summer months in Paris, leaving Michael's father alone with his business in West Virginia. She had also opted to stay in Paris and had not attended our wedding. Opinionated and a social snob, always attempting to be better than she was, his mother was difficult and hard to please. It wasn't long before we found a charming little apartment. Both of us were grateful that our stay was brief. Besides, with his mother sleeping in the next room, romance was still on hold. It remained that way even after we moved to the *Île St. Louis*. Now I knew why.

Innocence is not bliss. It is a driving force that can send some of us headlong into situations we don't take time to consider.

Chapter Three

Where there is marriage without love, there will be love without marriage.

Benjamin Franklin

Paris, 1928

What I had just witnessed with Michael and another man was shocking. As I waited for Pamela's chauffeur, Frederick, to pick me up, my mind was a whirlwind of memories, concerns and apprehensions. *If I'd been truthful with myself, I knew something was strange about Michael from the beginning. But in the short time since our wedding in Washington, the trip across the Atlantic, and settling into our apartment, what I knew instinctively was blocked as my rational mind took over. Blocked that is, until I met Philippe.*

Images of my parents, of my Washington friends, and my new friends in Paris came to mind. I couldn't tell them. And what about Philippe? Did he know about Michael? Perhaps, on the other hand, he did know and that is why he seemed to be flirting with me. But then what about his mother? What would she think, especially since she had just been introduced to us as a couple at the restaurant? Could she, with the discerning eye of a caring mother, see her son's interest in me? *Where is my mind going?* My focus went back to what I had just witnessed. *I saw those hands, those big, hairy hands.*

Frederick had come straight to the apartment to fetch my bags. "We will be there straight away. Don't you worry about a thing, Mrs. Whitacker." As he opened the rear door of the limousine, surely he could see how distraught I looked.

Gingerly, I stepped inside the limousine still shaking, but I tried to control my speech. Once settled in the plush back seat with a warm wool blanket Frederick had placed over my knees, I mustered a murmur of thanks. He smiled knowingly and was about to close the door when I asked, "Frederick, could you please do me a favor? Could you, would you, please call me Miss Libby, not Mrs. Whitacker?"

"Of course, madam; I mean, Miss Libby. I will do whatever you wish."

The drive to Pamela's across town passed in silence. I reclined in the comfortable leather back seat thinking about the day I met Pamela. It was the very same day I was introduced to Philippe, the day my life would change forever.

April, 1927

We had only been in Paris a short time when Michael and I were invited to a reception by Philippe de Beau, an amateur pilot Michael had met at Le Bourget Airstrip. The party was to honor and christen Count de Beau's new aeroplane. Unusual in itself, for us, it was even more unusual and exciting since this was the first party we had been invited to since arriving in Paris. For the drive to the aerodrome, Michael borrowed a 1925 Alpha Romeo called a Tipo-6C-1500. Bright red with two bucket seats, a windshield that turned down flat and wire wheels, it was a snappy little sports car. I didn't ask where he found it or who was lending it to us.

"This car is the prototype of the famous Alpha Romeo P2 Grand Prix car," Michael explained. I had no idea what he was talking about, but it was great fun setting out to the country in such style. The seats were deep and covered with pillowy hair cushions, upholstered in long-grain leather. A walnut-paneled tonneau cowl was rolled up behind.

The cool, refreshing wind tried to tease the scarf from my neck, but my hair, now bobbed short in the modern style was secure under a yellow cloche crammed well over my forehead. This was secured with one of mother's precious jeweled hairpins. She had given it to me in a moment of rare affection. Michael was also fashionably attired with his foulard flapping in the breeze as we drove out of the city of Paris and into the country. City streets became poplar lined lanes and the fumes of Paris were replaced by fragrances of early spring. Flowers were in full bloom and the green grasses swayed in a light breeze. Shadows cast by stately old trees with alternating patterns of light, dark, light, dark were almost hypnotic. The wind created the only conversation as the comfy car rolled through the scenic countryside.

All too soon, we arrived at the big field that was Le Bourget Airstrip. Windsocks indicated the wind direction flew from each corner of the field. Michael explained that all planes land into the wind and the flag designation helped pilots determine their landing pattern. More fluttering flags representing different countries: Switzerland, Belgium, The Netherlands, Italy, Jugo-Slavia, Bulgaria, Czechoslovakia, Estonia, Latvia, Lithuania, Poland, Spain and Portugal adorned the facades of various aeronautical clubs whose small lightweight aeroplanes lined up in rows at the other side of the field. Michael drove toward an area where a group of smartly dressed people had gathered. I could see heads turn as he pulled the dashing little Alpha next to a low slung Cadillac Phaeton. Unlike our little sports car, this automobile had a rumble seat in the rear, classic chrome bumpers, and twin mounted head lamps jutting out below the winged hood ornament. "Why would anyone want such a monster car?" I asked recognizing only size and opulence.

"Some people prefer those heavy giants with their powerful V8 engines," he replied crisply.

"To me, they are simply big, noisy, and flashy."

Michael maneuvered the little roadster carefully avoiding the protruding running boards of the *pleasure mobile*.

"Why are you parking here, Michael?"

"So I can keep this car blocked from the dust that is blowing across the field." Thus the big Cadillac would serve another purpose, securing us from the dirt.

As I slid out of my seat, my high heels sank onto the soft soil. Suddenly I realized how difficult it was going to be to walk. Perhaps I had not dressed appropriately after all. To make maneuvering even worse, the wind had picked up, determined to whisk off my hat. Michael was eager to go ahead and mingle and was less than gracious about having to wait for me to hobble across the dirt field.

Approaching the gathering, we were greeted with a loud din punctuated by an occasional high-pitched twitter. It sounded as if everyone was talking at once whether anyone else was listening or not. Michael was visibly thrilled to be around people who loved the sport of flight, but I was excited just to be out and about socially. Apparently, the big news was that the Brevoort and Lafayette Hotel Group in New York was offering a $25,000 prize for the first pilot to cross the Atlantic Ocean nonstop. The conversation was in French and I had no problem understanding what was being said. The hope, of course, was that a French pilot would win the coveted prize. There was some misgiving that an American group was coming up with the funds, but the French sought the prospect of enhancing their aeronautical industry. Winning would be most helpful.

Michael could not understand what was being said, nor was he tuned into the tension that existed between the French and Americans. I was torn, sympathizing with the French, recognizing their need for recognition after the horrors they had been subjected to during the war. However, I was an American. Besides, since I was invited to this gathering only because I was Michael's wife, I decided to voice my opinion.

"Perhaps this will be a way to bridge the gap between the French and the Americans?" I suggested in French.

"*Au contraire*," retorted a tall mustached gentleman in the group. "We've had quite enough of these wild and reckless New World people."

Michael, not understanding, murmured something about flying across the ocean. The mustached gentleman turned bright scarlet. "Oh, I am so terribly sorry. I did not realize you were Americans," he said in pleasant *cocktail* English. "Your wife has such a perfect accent and I, well, I only …" *Poor Michael. He was going to have to become used to this sort of thing.* Graciously excusing ourselves from that group, we went to find our host.

It was not difficult to locate Philippe de Beau. He was leaning against the fuselage of his new toy, one arm patting it like a soft puppy, the other hand gesticulating as he spoke. Though not terribly tall, maybe five feet nine, he gave the impression of being a big man. He was also, I thought, quite handsome. His hair was dark brown and slicked back from his wide intelligent-looking forehead. His eyes were brown with flecks of gold and they sparkled when he smiled. The pipe between his teeth added to his jaunty air. Several people stood around him, smiling, eager to hear whatever he was saying.

"Do you remember the small planes at the beginning of the war? The pilot's job was to spy on the enemy's positions and report back to a courier soldier who would then jump on his horse or motorcycle and report to the officer in charge. Can you believe the pilots from the opposing sides would pass each other in the air and wave? It was the chivalrous thing to do. 'Hello there, having a nice spy?'" Philippe laughed heartily and the group laughed with him.

I was captivated, not so much by the conversation, but by the man. I didn't realize my feelings showered my face.

"What are you grinning about?" Michael whispered.

Embarrassed, I began to whisper back a translation of Philippe's antidotes to distract Michael.

"Of course they eventually smartened up and armed the planes with grenades; that is, after trying handguns. The planes also had machine guns, but first they had to find ways to shoot *through* the propellers so they didn't shoot the propeller off," Philippe explained with a giggle. "But with the grenades, they had little darts to toss off, aiming at the other spy planes. Then, there were bigger aerial darts we called *flechettes*. The Germans call them *fiegerpfeile*. The planes would fly over the opposing troops only long enough to toss out some of these *flechettes* and, should anyone get hit, well, I wouldn't want to describe the gory picture."

"The French are ..." I began, but Michael cut me off demanding that I pay attention and translate later.

"These aerial darts were clumsy but most effective. They were dropped in clusters and reached a velocity of 200 meters per second," Philippe added, then paused to take a puff from his pipe.

"How much did these *flechettes* weigh?" asked a thin, serious looking gentleman with horn-rimmed glasses and a white broad brimmed hat.

"They weighed about twenty grams (about 2/3 of an ounce Michael told me when I translated this) and were approximately twenty-five mm long (about one inch, I think he said) with a caliber of 5.67 mm."

"That's about 1/4 of an inch," Michael whispered. He didn't want to interrupt Philippe, but he was making it difficult for me to listen and continue the translation.

"They had a sharp pointed nose on the striking end and a fin on the tail. Both sides used thousands of them. You can still find them all over the countryside where the battles were fought."

"We found some in Germany when I went there with my parents," I added to my interpreting to Michael. "They were on the ground near the spot where we picnicked."

"Did the pilots use these aerial darts to kill the other pilots, too?" asked a masculine looking woman with an absurd little red hat perched atop her straight short brown hair.

"What did she ask?" Michael wanted to know. I translated. Clearly, my husband was fascinated with the discussion. I was fascinated with our host.

"No," continued Philippe, replying to the last question. "These darts are only effective at high speeds. If you put one in an air gun, it could kill. However, you would need to create a force strong enough to initiate a high velocity and a proper projectile to reach a moving target. Much too difficult, especially since the pilot had to fly the plane as well. Nevertheless, your thinking is right on target with the military intelligence." This brought a huge grin to the red-hatted lady's face. "Soon after the invention of the *flechettes*, the planes were equipped with mounted guns. This time the pilot could line himself up with the opponent spy plane and shoot. Unfortunately, the first plane equipped that way fell to its demise. The gun shot off one of its propellers. Ha! Ha!"

The group tittered.

"Oh, there you are, *mon ami*," Philippe called out to Michael, disentangling himself from his audience. He gave Michael the perfunctory *baiser* on both cheeks. I was left behind with no introduction.

Michael could not wait to add his knowledge. "I hate to disagree with you, my dear friend," my husband, the serious student of history, began. "But this was not the first attempt. It was Roland Giros, the Frenchman, who had devised the first mounted gun."

"*Ah, oui*," he said making a sweeping gesture with his hand. "Leave it to the French to make such a stupid mistake."

Such a gentleman, I thought.

"You misunderstand me, my friend. Monsieur Giros mounted the gun but put metal deflectors on the propeller. He was successful on six missions."

"*Ah, bon.*"

At that point, I wished Michael would stop, but I knew that he was persistent when making a point.

"Yes, well on the seventh mission, he wasn't so lucky. The deflector gave way and he shot himself down. Unfortunately, he was behind enemy lines."

"So you see how it is with the French?" Philippe added cheerfully, not the least perturbed by Michael's intrusion into his discussion.

"But do consider that after 1910, most development and racing of early high-speed aircraft has been concentrated in France," Michael continued, not understanding his host's simple good manners.

Philippe, however, had by now clearly lost interest in the conversation. He stared directly at me for a second before he said, "Michael, I assume this is your lovely wife you have finally brought for me to meet." I could feel my face turning red. Michael never looked at me with eyes like that. Philippe was not only looking at me, he was looking through me, as if probing my very soul.

"*Enchantée, Monsieur de Beau*," I mumbled hoping to (yet fearful that I might) receive the traditional kiss on both cheeks. But he did not kiss me. Much worse. He put his hands on both of my shoulders and held me in place as though I would try to escape his gaze. In French he whispered, "Madame, you are absolutely beautiful." There was silence as he continued to stare. I completely forgot my husband standing beside me. Michael, on the other hand, was utterly unaware of any impropriety. I was sure of that since he had already turned away to seek other flying buddies. Fortunately for me, because my face must have been crimson and I felt hot all over, another friend arrived and the chatter recommenced.

Michael and I mingled amongst the guests. From time to time I caught Philippe glancing my way. Each time, my face tingled with school girl embarrassment.

Waiters carrying trays with glasses of wine and hors d'oeuvres scurried around the guests. Ardent conversations continued. The theme was universal.

"Do you really think it is possible that a man will be able to fly across the Atlantic? So many have already died making the attempt."

"What about lasting that long with no *toilette*?" This came from a coquettish young lady brandishing a long cigarette holder.

"Don't be ridiculous, my dear," replied an athletic looking man sporting the latest chic, rakish white hat with a black band. "We are discussing something quite serious here."

While I was listening to this banter, Michael had wandered off to join a group of men standing to the side of one of the hangars. They were having a serious conversation of their own. It was apparent that he was well acquainted with this clique and appeared much more at ease with them than he had been with the chitchat of the mixed group. Watching his behavior again made me wonder what the future would hold for us. Was he really going to make a career out of aviation? Would I be left alone most of the time? Or would I be included in his adventures? Looking around Le Bourget aerodrome, I examined again the dozens of small, private company banners and flags and the many small, sporty planes. Obviously, the private sector was very involved in flying. Perhaps Michael was right. There might be a great future in aviation.

Suddenly, out of the blue, a feminine voice broke my reverie. "How do you do? My name is Pamela," she said, her English clip and precise.

The lady who had suddenly come up behind me was certainly more suitably dressed for the dusty field than I. Wearing jodhpurs and slim brown riding boots, she was tall and elegant and had the unmistakable look of an English equestrienne. Under her brown brimmed Tyrolean hat with its jaunty green feather, her deep blue eyes impressed me with their sharp, penetrating gaze. I did not intend to be rude and hoped she would consider my hesitancy a mark of formality.

"Err, oh, how do you do, Pamela? I'm Libby."

"Short for Elizabeth. Yes, I know. Your husband has told me all about you."

Suddenly I was on the defensive. *Michael knows this woman?* She appeared a bit older than I but was certainly an attractive lady, athletic looking and slender.

"We met at the Morgan Bank," she replied answering my naked look of surprise. "My husband is Director of the bank. Michael came in wishing to set up an account."

I had to smile. So this is not a romantic liaison after all.

"I happened to be there, in my husband's office that is, arranging for a dinner party. You know, telephone service can be so erratic these days. I think your husband assumed I was Victor's personal secretary. Now he doesn't recognize me in my hunting attire."

"But you look too clean to have been riding," I blurted out before realizing how gauche that must have sounded.

"I haven't been riding. I am more comfortable in pants and this is the only acceptable way I can wear them."

I was a bit confused.

"I consider myself a modern woman. Victor and I try to behave as equals. This is one of the ways I express myself. He has no problem with my behavior. I rather think he enjoys it. Moreover, I love to shock people. I detest common behavior. Don't you?"

I didn't know how to reply.

"Oh dear, now I think I have rather shocked you."

"Yes, no, I mean, I admire your courage," I stammered. Pamela appeared pleased with my observation and I began to relax in her company. Deciding to be daring in my own way, I elected to state my opinions on a subject I had never before discussed with anyone.

"I believe in the equality of the sexes, too." Now where had that come from? This conversation was opening up thoughts that I must have locked up in my mind for years. "However," I brazenly continued, "in the United States, women only won national suffrage a few years ago, in 1920." Remembering the many conversations about politics that I had with my father, never my mother, I reasoned that I was more of a modern woman than I had given myself credit for. Boldly, I continued. "Don't get me started. I have a passion for politics, but my family does not feel it is appropriate for ladies to talk about such things."

"My family is more liberal. Maybe that is the difference between the British and the Americans?" Pamela giggled.

Her easy manner made me feel more relaxed. Still, I was amazed at her outspokenness. At the same time, I was enjoying the freedom of conversation we were having.

Pamela continued. "Isn't this grand? Being at Le Bourget, I mean. We are taking part in the making of history. Don't you agree? Everyone is talking about transatlantic flight. Can you imagine being able to fly to your home to America? The trip would take hours instead of days. Why, great ocean liners could become figments of history."

I shuddered, remembering only too clearly my honeymoon experience on one of those big ocean liners. Yes, flying across the Atlantic would be nice, but I wondered if that could ever become a reality.

"They have to make the planes a bit larger," she added nodding at the collection of small planes lined up on the side of the field. "These flimsy machines don't look terribly safe, do they? And, of course being so small, there wouldn't be the amusements and the camaraderie you experience on the big ships. I do so love their grand dinners." It was an odd comment from one so slender. She didn't look as if she could finish even the first course.

"I don't suppose you would be able to eat at all or even get up and walk around, would you?" I asked, glancing at our host's little plane parked not far from where we stood.

"Can you imagine reading a book on a plane? It would be difficult with all the bouncing and bumping, wouldn't it?" We both stared at the little plane in thought. "Imagine crossing the whole Atlantic Ocean with absolutely nothing to do, sitting for hours and hours. I, for one, simply could not do it," She declared emphatically.

I had to laugh. A true Brit, this lady had brought the whole amazing feat down to the bare bones. And honestly, I could not see this vivacious woman sitting still that long either.

"Well, well, I see you two are getting along nicely."

I swirled around and was face to face with Philippe. Immediately, I blushed. Most assuredly, Pamela noticed.

"Please allow me to show you two lovely ladies my new Puss Moth monoplane."

Although little, it appeared quite impressive until we were next to it. Up close, my doubts about the joy of flying increased. The two cockpits looked small, tight and uncomfortable. On the other hand, with the beautiful wings spreading out, I could conjure up the feeling a bird must have of soaring, gliding. The wind, the sensation of being closer to the sun, warm caressing rays wrapping around my shoulders. Philippe took me by the hand. Something made me realize he had been talking and I hadn't heard a word.

"… called a barnstormer. But while a friend is helping me work on this Puss Moth monoplane, I still really love my original biplane." He took us over to another plane. Tapping the lower wing fondly, he told us, "She flew in the Great War." Pamela and I marveled at the sight of this quaint little plane.

"I did have to make some necessary modifications," he continued with pride. "For one, I have installed a second cockpit."

He looked unabashedly at me. I could not meet his eyes afraid that I might blush again, so I continued to look at the cockpits. It *would* be worth the discomfort of being cramped in such a tight place, flying with the wind in your hair, up into and through the clouds, dancing with the gods.

"There is a nice long exhaust stack to warm your hands on along the starboard side of the fuselage," he stated as if he thought I was thinking about the cold. Of course, I had no idea what an exhaust stack was, but warm hands sounded good. The plane's off-white metallic paint glistened in the late afternoon sun.

Philippe's enthusiasm was transporting me to a place I would never be. Looking at the complexity of his aeroplanes, I was sure that for me to fly was out of the question, although I was glad to share his hopes and dreams. I was honored and I think Pamela was also that he was taking the time out from his other guests to speak with us.

The afternoon drifted into evening. Already, it was starting to grow cool. I hadn't thought to bring a coat, especially with an open-air car ride back to Paris. Pamela came to the rescue.

"Let's all go to the *Château Madrid*," she suggested. "We can take several people in our Duesenberg. Surely Michael can find someone to accompany him in the Alpha." As the word spread among the remaining guests, everyone thought it a splendid idea. I had never been to the famed *Château Madrid*, but heard it was a restaurant favored by artists, mainly because it was supposed to be reasonably priced. It was reputedly *"irrefutably sumptuous in its cuisine"* according to Pamela.

Laughing and chattering, everyone headed for the motor cars. Michael was only too happy to follow in the little Alpha and had no trouble soliciting a fellow to accompany him.

I found myself seated in the back of Pamela's ritzy Duesenberg between two robust Frenchmen who smelled of cigars and cologne and talked and laughed nonstop. I was warming up both physically and emotionally. The mood was contagious. I laughed and even contributed once or twice to the gay conversation telling them some of the legends of old that I had heard, especially concerning the island where I lived.

"Parisians are mostly themselves in restaurants," the man on my left was saying. "Like the waiter who suddenly one day out of the blue, confessed '*the problem of being*' while serving me a croquet-monsieur." We all laughed heartily even though I didn't understand. I was having so much fun that I never questioned being without my husband, with people I barely knew.

"A *croquet-monsieur?*" I finally asked after the chuckles had stopped. I had heard of a *croque-mort*, meaning undertaker, but an undertaker has nothing to do with food.

"Oh, yes, it is marvs, as you English would say," replied the Frenchman to my right looking at Pamela. "It is the most Parisian of sandwiches. It was first served back in the good old days of 1910 in a *café* on the *Boulevard des Capucines*."

"But what does it mean?" I persisted.

Looking back at me, he explained. "Literally translated, it means a hearty bite of monsieur." Now he was laughing too hard to continue.

Because the ride had been so entertaining, before I knew it, we had arrived. One of the traveling companions took my hand helping me descend from the car. I was grateful not only to keep from falling but the crowds in front of the *Château Madrid* Restaurant was huge and could have easily consumed me.

We had to shove our way in. I was in the middle of our group getting jostled and tapped. Once I felt someone pinch me from behind, but when I turned around, I could only see a blur of faces also pushing their way in. Was it Michael? Or perhaps Philippe? I hoped it was Philippe. Such a thought. I surprised myself. Truly, this evening had developed into more than I had expected.

Once inside, I became acutely aware of the noise. Corks popped, glasses clinked, and people laughed and called to each other across the room. Smoke filled the air. There was decadence in the *devil-may-care* atmosphere. It reminded me how little enjoyment I had experienced since my wedding.

Once accustomed to the noise, I could make out the tinkling of a piano in the background. Pamela grabbed me by the hand and waltzed me through the crowd to a table in the rear. "We're going to have fun this evening." Pamela smiled at me.

This was the real Paris, and I was finally part of it. I could feel myself becoming someone I had never known before and it was thrilling.

"Dance with me, *chêrie?*"

It was Philippe. I rose and followed him in a trance to a crowded spot where couples were already dancing.

"You need a drink. You're not relaxed yet."

A glass materialized. Standing with Philippe beside the dance floor, I obediently sipped the smooth red wine. My body warmed and my inhibitions began relaxing. A smile literally exploded across my face.

That's more like it!" Taking the glass and placing it on a nearby table, he spun me around in a Charleston. *"C'est très excitant, n'est-ce pas?"* he laughed.

My feet felt as if they never touched the floor as I bounced and swirled in time to the lively rag. I never danced to these tunes during my debut, but here I was and it was fun. Time and space dissolved. I was flying around and around, up and down. A little more wine and the room, the lights, the rhythm spun me round and round. When I finally sat back down next to Pamela, I was tipsy, not just from the wine but from sheer bliss.

By now the table was covered with food. We began with the first course consisting of two platters. We had a choice of *boeuf à la mode*, or *fillets de sole bonne femme* accompanied by *caneton aux navets, champignons farcis* and other vegetables cooked as only the French can. Then the waiters cleared away the plates and brought new dishes for the *salade* followed by cheeses. One way or another, the guests were able to continue the flow of conversation and eat at the same time because, in what seemed like mere minutes, the platters were bare. A different wine accompanied each course. The finale consisted of an assortment of tarts and *crème caramel* accompanied by coffee and a bottle of *Sainte Estèphe*.

Only when I had finished and was a little too full, did I realize that I had not seen Michael since leaving the aerodrome. Nor had I missed him.

1928

At this point in my reverie, Frederick stopped the car. We had arrived at Pamela and Victor's house. Once inside, both Pamela and her husband gave me a hug and escorted me to the library. A fire glowed at one end of the small room. It was near the warmth the Statlers placed me, in the midst of the soft, downy cushions of a loveseat. Victor stood to one side. Pamela took the chair next to me.

"Brandy?" Victor asked.

"Yes, do," insisted Pamela. "It will help you relax. Victor, pour me some too." Without a pause, Pamela, never taking her eyes off me, continued, "Libby, what has happened?"

I took a sip of the brandy. I had never tasted this drink before but it was sweet and soft. I could feel the tingle of the thick liquid as it passed down my throat. Not accustomed to strong liquor, I enjoyed the warmth that followed my second sip and relaxed a bit. Less inhibited, my emotions began to flow as I slowly poured out the whole story ending with, "I should not have been so presumptuous as to think I could burden you with my problems."

"But of course you may," both protested in unison.

"We are friends," said Victor, looking warily at his wife.

"Now, Libby dear," Pamela began as she sat next to me and put her arm around me. I didn't realize I was sobbing. "My dear girl, you have had enough for one evening. The guest room is ready for you." I made a feeble attempt to protest, but Pamela was insistent. "You are tired, your nerves are frayed, and there is nothing to be done at this hour of the night." She took my arm and guided me to the guestroom where the bed had been turned down.

Chapter Four

Do you know that conversation is one of the greatest pleasures in life? But it wants leisure.

William Somerset Maugham,
The Trembling of a Leaf (1921)

P amela saw to it that I was comfortable and had everything I might need before going to her own room. Later, she told me what she and Victor had discussed up in their bedroom.. I think she was not only telling me what they said to each other, but she was showing me how a loving couple can share their concerns. This is what I remember Pamela said about that night.

"Libby, when I came up to our room, Victor was already there. He was pacing the floor. Knowing his actions reflected concern for your welfare, I suggested that we call Philippe. He felt it was a bit premature.

"I walked up and snuggled against his tall handsome frame and when he wrapped his arms around me, I suggested what you, dear Libby, needed was a warm, kind, gentle man. Someone to hold you, soothe you like he does for me. He kissed my forehead and gave me one of those tender looks. I love him so much and it is that kind of love that I wish, we wish, you could know too. But he was right to be worried about the implications of calling Philippe. Remember, Libby dear, you are a married woman.

"While we were having this discussion, Victor and I were still holding each other. Libby, it is as if he and I can read the other's thoughts. After a few minutes, he let me go and began to pace the room again. I went to the bath and began to undress, sure he would come up with a solution. While I was combing my hair, he called me back into the bedroom. Now Libby, I must be honest, and this may be difficult to hear, but what he asked was if I thought that you and Michael, if you two had, if I thought you two had ever …"

I blushed and slowly shook my head.

"No?"

At this point, Pamela, who had also turned a little red, confided, "Libby, I have to admit that although you never told me this outright, I guessed that it was so. Please forgive my indiscretion. I told Victor that I didn't think you had. He chided me saying, 'But how do you know? Not your astrology, is it?' That wasn't nice. Libby, I take my studies seriously and he shouldn't tease me."

I didn't tell Pamela, but I could sympathize with Victor on this point. I remember when she had asked me out to lunch and confided in me her interest in astrology. It was the day after Lindbergh's memorable flight.

May, 1927

I had awakened that next morning quite late having come home after midnight from the party at the *Café Madrid* celebrating Lindbergh's arrival. A glimpse at the clock told me that it was almost eleven. The room was full of light. Michael's bed was empty. After slipping into my robe, I walked past the dressing table and saw a piece of notepaper propped against the mirror.

> *Have gone to the Club for a luncheon in honour of Lindy, our new American hero.*
>
> *Love, M.*
>
> *PS: Hope I didn't disturb you.*

I was about to put the coffee pot on the stove when there was a knock at the door.

"Madame. Madame Whitacker?"

It was the unmistakable voice of Mme Metz.

"Coming," I called, as I rushed to the door and pulled it open.

Mme Metz smiled a wide grin and held out a small bundle of papers.

"A letter arrived for Madame," she said. "And Monsieur asked me to deliver the American paper." Her disdain for the newspaper was unmistakable from the tone of her voice.

I paid a compliment about her scarf, thanked her profusely and, noting that other tenants did not receive such service, handed her a sizable tip. I knew that an insulted concierge could make life miserable.

The letter was from my parents. Actually, it was from Father. Mother was not much of a letter writer. I suddenly missed my father. He was very formal and respectable, rarely displaying emotion. He worshiped the ground his wife walked on although, in public, he didn't even hold her hand.

This letter expressed the hope that I was happy and enjoying my new life. Atlantic storms had brought an unusual amount of rain to the city and Mother was afraid she had lost the roses to flooding in the garden. Father wrote about the latest political gossip, not excluding his own prejudices. The letter also contained a brief discussion about finances. His daughter was to be careful when budgeting for household needs. He had set up a fund from which Michael could draw for any domestic necessities. Probably as a result of my mother's prodding, he asked if I had taken on a housemaid or was I going to attempt house cleaning and cooking myself?

Then, as if it were an afterthought, he added that Uncle Christian had dropped by saying he hoped that I would pay a visit to his ex-wife's daughter, Natalie. Apparently, she had a salon in Paris. A letter of introduction was included.

I was not clear about the circumstances surrounding Uncle Christian's marriage. His ex-wife, Alice Pike Barney, was an artist. No, she was more than an artist. She was a wealthy and eccentric lady who defied all the social norms. As an artist, a writer, a playwright and theater director, she used her wealth for the benefit of the arts and the artistic community instead of philanthropy. Although my mother would never admit as much, I read in the paper and hear enough conversation to know Washington society was shocked. That a lady of her stature and wealth would choose to be a painter, much less a director of plays was, in their minds, proof that she "did not know *her place*". She and my uncle had resided down the street from us in Washington. Alice called her home Studio House. She had a stage for her theater productions on the first floor and an extensive art studio in the back of the building for her pastel portraits, many of which were of Washington socialites. It was a unique house by Washington standards. One day, Washington society would come to thank this talented, albeit bohemian, lady for converting the nation's capital from a cultural swamp to a capital of the arts. Of this, I was sure.

Since his marriage had not lasted, I was surprised that Uncle Christian should still wish that I meet Alice's daughter, a daughter from the first marriage and quite close to my Uncle Christian's own age.

As father's letter concluded, he and my mother sent their best to Michael and to their dear Elisabeth. The postscript added that Mademoiselle had sent her best wishes. She was residing in New York City and I should send her a note. "Do not forget Mademoiselle gave you the best years of her life," was my father's final admonition.

My life in Washington seemed so distant that it was difficult to relate to the contents of the letter. It dawned on me that I didn't even regret being so far away from the city that had been home all my life until now. Putting the letter aside, I took up the bulky *Herald* and headed back to the kitchen for the day's first cup of coffee. This was going to be a lazy day. How Michael had the energy to get up so early was beyond me. Lindbergh's flight excited me too, but at this moment, I was happy just to relax and read about it in the newspaper.

A little before dawn, May 20, 1927, Charles A. Lindbergh, armed with six ham sandwiches, a gallon of water and no caffeine or stimulants of any kind took off from Roosevelt Field, Long Island, New York, at 7:52 am. It was raining. The runway was muddy. The plane was extremely heavy. The article stated that by itself, the plane weighed 2,300 pounds. However, with 450 gallons of fuel equal to 2,750 pounds, the weight exceeded the load of any other monoplane load ever recorded.

Just thinking about so much weight leaving the ground was more than I could comprehend. Just as I never could understand how the great ocean liners stayed afloat despite Michael trying to explain it to me. As I continued reading the article, it became obvious that I was not alone in questioning the feasibility of flight. There were many factors against Lindbergh including a slight tail wind, which would, I believe, force him down, not up. However, he had his supporters, including mechanics and others who believed he could do it. Together they pushed on the wing struts and soon Lindbergh and the *Spirit* were on their way. According to the article, *the propeller, which had to be set from the outside, was put in a cruise position, a setting that gave greater efficiency for cruising, but less at low speeds such as taking off. As if these challenging factors were not enough, the plane missed hitting a power line on take off by a mere twenty feet.*

How tenuous life is. Right from the outset there was such a fine line between success and disaster, a mere twenty feet. Life lived to the fullest was life lived on the edge, wasn't it? Perhaps this was the attraction of flying for Michael. As for me, for the time being I was content to enjoy Lindbergh's flight vicariously.

According to *The Herald*, it was surmised that for over one thousand miles, Lindbergh had to fly inside the fog because the airplane was too heavy to climb to a higher elevation. At times, it was reported, he had resorted to using his flashlight to monitor the buildup of ice growing on his fragile airframe. With no front windshield, he had to look out the sides, or rely on a periscope he had mounted to the left of the instrument panel. He also had an ordinary magnetic compass mounted from the ceiling at eye level to confirm his calculations. Since the compass faced away from him, he had hung a mirror in front of it so he could read the directions. To his right, on the outside, was the earth inductor compass, an instrument which I had to ask Michael to explain. The paper's explanation was that the earth inductor allowed the pilot to turn at an exact heading.

"The initial heading New York to Paris is 065 degrees. The actual compass heading of the airplane depends on the wind. Lindbergh flew low whenever possible to detect any drift or deviation from his heading by observing the wind streaks on the waves." Sometimes Lindbergh must have had to skim just above the ocean surface. I could imagine the rough swells lashing up trying to draw him in. Later, he was quoted as saying that the drone of his engine became "a lethal lullaby, lulling [me] into a nearly endless sleep." What a frightening thought and what a vivid picture. When I had hung over the side of the *honeymoon* liner looking at rough seas, aside from feeling sick, I remember being mesmerized by the swells. I could almost visualize mystical sea monsters, their scaly arms and paws reaching for the hull attempting to pull the vessel into the bowels of the ocean.

According to the newspaper account, before beginning the actual flight, Lindbergh had analyzed every possible detail which he check-listed in a little notebook, along with point-by-point calculations. Clearly, this meticulous concern was necessary when he was putting his life on the line.

I was completely absorbed in the newspaper report when another knock at the door brought me back. A glance at the clock suggested that I should be mortified to be found still in my dressing gown. The knock was repeated. I sighed and then resigned myself to being interrupted during my quiet time. Assuming it was the concierge again, I got up, tossed my hair, pulled my waist tie to be sure my robe was properly cinched and went to open the door.

"Bonjour, ma chérie!" Pamela drawled in her throaty French as she swooped inside, threw her arms around me for a moment, stepped back, and then held me at arms length. "Well, and what do we have here? A true lady of leisure? Just look outside. See the sunlight. It is a beautiful day and I am taking you to lunch."

The prospect of another adventure was too good to pass up. Besides, I couldn't resist my new friend's enthusiasm. While I changed, Pamela sat on a stool at the kitchen counter and picked up the paper I had been reading.

"Certainly puts a new meaning to this island you are living on, doesn't it, Libby dear?" Pamela called out, referring to the name of Lindbergh's plane.

Concentrating on what to wear and hurrying at the same time, I barely heard the question, but Pamela didn't seem to need a reply for after a few moments, she continued.

"Well, my goodness, Libby, look at what Booth Tarkington has to say."

I ducked into the kitchen to see what she was reading. It was the society page of *The Herald*, a part of the paper I hadn't yet reached.

"The headline reads: *Increased Freedom Is Only Hope for Happy Marriage Holds Tarkington*. He says," she continued, glancing up to see that I was close by, *"that modern marriage is the cause of increased unhappiness in the human race. Sort of equates it with war as a necessary institution. Says it is unnatural for two humans to be shackled together. The rules for marriage, he feels, need to be changed. He suggests 'the best brains of the race should be devoted to making it as little dangerous as possible to the affected individuals."* I nodded absentmindedly and returned to finish dressing.

"Libby, dear, can you hear me?" Not waiting for a reply, she persisted, trying to draw me into conversation. "I love his stories, don't you? Have you read *Penrod?*"

Emerging from the bedroom with my new Chanel navy cotton skirt and a white linen, full-collared blouse, I did respond. "Oh yes, Tarkington is one of my father's favorites too."

Pamela wasn't sure I had heard the quote. I had and I found it disturbing, but talking to Pamela about it then didn't seem appropriate. Perhaps once I got to know her better. Although she was a happily married lady, I sensed she might some day help me understand my marriage. After all, she had been with me when Michael not only did not show up at the restaurant, but was inebriated, drinking in front of the fireplace when she escorted me home. This time, however, I wasn't ready to be honest with her, much less with myself.

"You look lovely, my dear. You might want to bring a cardigan. Don't forget your gloves. Oh, sorry, I sound like a mother hen."

The limo was waiting out front. Frederick sat with his back against a large tree and a smile on his face, happily watching the activities on the Seine. Barges and small boats passed by in the daily comings and goings of Parisians and tourists. By midday, it was mostly tourists. Birds were busy nesting in the tree limbs. Their chattering added to the pleasant sounds of the island. Down the ramp in front of my building, horses were being bathed by their owners, splashed with cool, soothing water after a morning of heavy labor pulling a milk wagon.

Pamela had told me that Frederick was German, but didn't miss his homeland at all. She made comments about the recent war in which his country had suffered, but such an ignominious defeat did not upset him. "We had enlisted his services in England before the war and he has become part of our household." Pamela lowered her voice, "If the truth be known, it is probably our cockney cook who assures Frederick's loyalty." We giggled as we approached the car.

"Hello, Frederick?"

"Oh, so-so-sorry, Madam," he stuttered, probably embarrassed to have been caught daydreaming.

"We won't be going terribly far," Pamela informed him as he opened the right rear door of the gleaming black Duesenberg. "Please take us to the *Café de Paris*."

Evidently, Pamela came to the *Café de Paris* often because although the inside was packed, the maitre d' led us to a table overlooking the *Champs Elysées* and the passing parade of pedestrians. Chatter filled the air. "There is nothing inhibited about the French, is there?" I couldn't agree more. "They like to talk and their language lends itself so well. It is melodious, song-like. It carries itself rhythmically from line to line, don't you think?" I smiled and listened as Pamela continued. "The language is inherently philosophical. I guess you know that already since you are so fluent, but I have come to appreciate the nuances only after years of listening and learning. I guess we Brits don't have a terribly good ear for languages, or maybe most of us are simply too conceited about our own language." Without taking a breath, Pamela asked, "Have you had the *salade niçoise*, Libby?" I nodded. "I try to eat lightly at midday despite the local habit of large three course meals. Being British, I try to make a habit of using my afternoons constructively and not wasting them on a nap."

Since I had been such a late riser that morning, I felt guilty for having wasted time. *Le Printemps* in Paris! What could be better? As poet e e cummings says, the world is "mud-luscious" and "puddle wonderful".

It was a bit stormy when Michael and I first arrived in Paris, but the rains were short and sweet. Today, Paris was fragrant with flowers of every hue and with new bright-green leaves on the trees. On the *Champs Elysées*, pedestrians passed back and forth along the wide sidewalks while on the street, cars mingled with horse drawn carts and carriages. Pamela went ahead and ordered for both of us although I did manage to sneak in a request for a *cafe noir* before the meal.

"Quite American," she chided with a giggle.

I winced at the reminder that at this late hour I was just beginning my day.

"I was sure your husband would be at the luncheon for Lindbergh," continued Pamela.

Lindbergh had just won the coveted prize and brought glory to the United States and Michael and I had been part of the thousands the night before to pack Le Bourget Airstrip to greet our hero.

Pamela was talking and I had to shake myself to return to the conversation. With another sip of the strong coffee, I returned to the moment.

"What a great and brave man your Lindbergh is by the way. We are all most impressed and actually delighted that it was an American who would make the first transatlantic flight. You know, as sad as I am about the disappearance and probable death of Nungessor and Coli, I have to tell you, their departure did have an amusing side to it."

The French were devastated. What could have been amusing? "What do you mean, amusing?" I asked.

"Amusing? Yes. Well, the French do have a way of doing things. Can you believe their aeroplane, *The White Bird*, was stocked with caviar, bananas and gallons of coffee? I understand Lindy would have left with nothing if someone had not stashed sandwiches in the cockpit."

"I know he was fastidious about weight, but I never thought he would do without food," I replied. "How did you find out about the sandwiches?"

"Oh my dear, I always read *The Herald* before leaving the house. Wonderful paper your *New York Herald*. I am so glad they have a *Paris Edition*. But then, after all, Paris is where *it* is happening."

Another coffee was brought and I sipped slowly enjoying its rich aroma.

"When is your birthday?" I was rather shocked that Pamela would ask.

"My birthday? August 13. I was born in Canada at my grandparents' house, *Idalia*."

"May I ask what year?" she persisted.

"1906. May I ask why you want to know? I don't have any English friends so perhaps this is proper form?"

"Oh, please don't be annoyed, my dear Libby. I should have explained."

"Explained what?"

"You are a practicing Catholic, are you not?"

"Yes, I am. My uncle is a priest."

"Your Uncle William?"

"Why, yes, but, how did you know?"

"Your Uncle William is quite well known. He is a Monsignor, not merely a priest. We knew him because he spent several years here," she said, making a seeping gesture to include all of Paris, "before he left for Rome."

I told Pamela what little I did know about my uncle. "In Rome, the *Principessa Doria* offered my uncle an apartment on the third floor of her *Palazzo Doria*. Overlooking the Piazza Venezia and the Forum, the apartment has its own chapel."

"Libby, your uncle is not only a priest, he is the only American Canon of St. Peter's Basilica. Normally, a *Monseigneur* in his position would live behind the walls of the Vatican, but your Uncle William chooses to have his own apartment, his own servants and more or less, his own lifestyle from what I have been told."

"I don't really know too much about my uncle although I did meet him once in Washington when I was fourteen. He was being honored as a hero-priest."

"What did he do to deserve that title?"

"He served in the front lines as a soldier-priest during the Great War and was called the Patriot Priest of Picardy. Initially, my mother told me, he had joined the *Croix Rouge* in Paris and was a great help particularly because of his command of the French language." Pamela listened attentively. "I remember my mother reading to me from a newspaper article something about his cheery smile and kindly words to the boys in khaki. It was so graphic, I remember the lines. *Father Hemmick was like a welcome sunbeam in the semi-darkness of the dugouts and in the mud and water-soaked trenches and the shell holes of no man's land.* He was a true hero, Pamela. An American making such sacrifices for the French. God was looking out for him, I am sure. Mother told me that he was under gun fire almost constantly as he administered to the sick and dying on both the American and French fronts. She let me have the cable dispatch that was sent in 1918 when he was with the American troops under Foch. When we go back to the apartment, I will fetch it."

"Libby, I would be most interested. Just meeting him, you would have no idea he had been through such traumas."

"I am amazed. You actually knew my family? This is wonderful, to be so far away from home and to meet someone who, in a sense, already knows me."

The *salade* was served and, to my relief, the waiter was not at all miffed that we ordered so little.

"Quite cosmopolitan, the *Café de Paris*. That is why it is always so crowded. Most customers are from abroad. Believe me, we Brits and you Americans are good for the economy, and the French know it."

"My father is always lecturing me about being careful with money. I've watched many of my compatriots and they don't appear to have any qualms about splurging."

"Different economy, my dear. The dollar goes a long way in France these days." Pamela pointed out that *The Herald* was the newspaper of choice for all nationalities living in Paris. "I always enjoy reading about your politics," she said with a chuckle. "I don't mean to be irreverent, but my dear, to think that Mr. Scopes should be convicted for teaching evolution; well, really. And the speeches made by your Mr. Bryan; you would think we were living in the last century not the twentieth!"

I was taught the Darwinian theory of evolution in school and agreed with Pamela. We chatted, enjoyed our lunch, and then I told her about my Uncle Christian's request.

"Your Uncle Christian? Is he William's brother?"

"Yes, my Mother was one of eight. Seven boys and one girl. Only Uncle William and Uncle Christian and an uncle in Buffalo whom I have never met are still living. Uncle Christian enclosed a letter of introduction to Natalie Barney." I began to explain Uncle Christian's connection to the Barney family, but Pamela interrupted.

"I do remember that wedding. They were married in a joint civil ceremony with Alice's daughter, Laura, and Hippolyte Dreyfus. Then, because your Uncle was Catholic and Alice was a widow, their marriage had to be sanctified. I recall this took place at the Church of Saint Joseph, Avenue Hoche."

"Sanctified? You mean the marriage had to be blessed by a priest so that it would be accepted in the Catholic Church?"

"Exactly. But you as a Catholic should know this better than I. So to continue the story, at least as much as I can recall, their marriage made the headlines in almost every major paper. I'm afraid some, or to be honest, most reports were not complimentary. They wrote: *Widow, 61, Gives Away $3,000,000 To Wed Boy*. To prove that theirs was a love match, Alice placed her money in trust for her daughters saying she would live on the interest alone."

"How old was my Uncle?"

"Twenty-six, my dear. You were only six at the time, but I am surprised your family hasn't spoken about it."

"No, at least not that aspect of the story. I know my mother is extremely loyal to her brothers and my father never interferes in her family affairs. So I guess it was considered inappropriate for me to be told anything that might be considered negative."

"Well, I must say, from what I know, it was amazing the marriage lasted as long as it did. Nine years, I think."

"Learning all this now, well, I don't know what to do. Should I go ahead and present my letter to Natalie Barney?"

"Go of course. I know Natalie quite well. She has a marvelous salon; calls it the *'Academie des Femmes'*. Always groups of interesting artists and writers there. I should be happy to take you."

Before we left the *Cafe*, I had to ask, "By the way, did you have a special reason to ask my birthday?"

"Oh, yes, I am sorry. I forgot all about it when we began talking about your uncles. Let me begin by saying that I respect your religion and I do not want you to think I am some kind of heretic – which of course to a Catholic, I am, as an Anglican. However, I do like to help people. As a hobby, I have learned astrology."

I was intrigued. I knew what the word meant but I had never known anyone who was involved with it. "Please tell me … tell me … well, I don't even know what to ask."

We both laughed.

"If you tell me what time you were born, I can work on your chart. That will give me information about you. I am not a psychic or a fortune teller, but I can classify your character traits and perhaps advise you about what to avoid, or what you need to learn."

"I don't know what time I was born. And I am afraid I can't ask my mother. She would never accept astrology. Besides, I would find it difficult to make such a request and never without a proper explanation. Can you work out a chart without the time?"

"Of course. It will not be as complete. No matter. With your permission, I will begin right away."

As we left the restaurant, I noticed that we were practically the last customers. Time had passed quickly. Frederick was waiting outside, his cap shading his face. Again, he looked immersed in thought as he leaned against the side of the vehicle. Pamela had to prod him as before.

"Oh, terribly sorry, I, uh, I …"

"Don't worry. I don't blame you for enjoying the sights." Frederick was visibly flushed. "The young ladies of Paris are lovely and should be appreciated," Pamela counseled.

"You always know what is on my mind, Madam. Don't know how you do it, but you always know."

Pamela laughed and whispered to me as we climbed in the back of the limousine, "I did his chart you see."

1928

Pamela sighed. "I remember our lunch," she said looking to the ceiling with a smirk. She chuckled and then decided to continue her rendering of the evening when she and Victor were more or less trying to decide my fate.

"Libby, I so enjoyed our conversation that day and hope I did not offend you about reading your chart."

I shook my head.

"Well, to get back to the other evening, Victor did apologize about belittling my astrological studies saying he simply believed we had to deal with the facts. Then he gave me that special look as he came to me and put his arms around my waist. He held me tightly." Pamela was looking inward, reliving that moment. I watched her silently.

"I could feel … " She smiled at the recollection. Then looking at me, she whispered, "Compassion for you turned into passion for me." A grin slid across her face. I gritted my teeth as I realized what Pamela was confiding but I said nothing. She was sharing something so personal, so intimate and yet she was also educating me. I was but a student, a novice, still wet behind the ears. My feelings were genuine, but unexpressed. I thought I had come close, but as yet never experienced the love and passion this couple shared. Although shy and embarrassed, I was grateful to Pamela. Now I had something real to dream about and I knew, some day it might come true.

Pamela, seeing that I was accepting her tale, in her clipped British bluntness continued without apology. "When our fervor exhausted itself and I lay on the bed feeling a warm glow, Victor rolled over and slowly sat up, dangled his feet off the edge of the bed ready to get up and pace again. I could tell he was already in another world absorbed in thoughts unrelated to our passion.

"Out of the blue, he asked, 'Isn't Libby a Catholic?' Libby, his mind was focused on your situation and he had come upon a possible solution. What about the Church? Suddenly we both stared at each other and in unison shouted, 'Have the marriage annulled.' I threw my arms around the dear man and pushed him back down on the bed. Then we hugged and kissed like young lovers, happy for you and secure with each other."

I smiled, understanding more than I probably should have.

Chapter Five

And there is a Catskill eagle in some souls that can alike dive down into the blackest gorges, and soar out of them again and become invisible in the sunny spaces.

Herman Melville, Moby Dick

May 21, 1927

After Philippe's party at Le Bourget for the christening of his new plane, I read all I could about the coveted $25,000 prize offered by the Brevoort and Lafayette Hotel Group in New York. For the week prior to Lindbergh's arrival, *The Herald* had reported that two French pilots, Nungessor and Coli, had attempted an East to West crossing but were still missing and presumed dead. It was rumored their plane had not perished in the great Atlantic, but had crashed in the rugged mountains of Maine, which meant they had actually made it across. So far no trace of them had been found. Also four Americans had died attempting to fly across the vast expanse of ocean spanning three thousand six hundred and ten miles. From what I had read in *The Herald* and what Michael had told me, I was beginning to feel personally acquainted with every nautical mile.

Now, the contest winner was about to make himself known. A twenty-five year old American, Charles Augustus Lindbergh, was reported to have made the flight single handedly. Earlier this morning, he was sighted above Ireland and was now approaching Paris. We knew. This would be a day to remember: May 21, 1927.

I shelved my own news about our illustrious neighbor, Mr. James Joyce, whose book I had just purchased on the *Rive Gauche*, as I was ushered with Michael into the back seat of a big black Daimler parked, its engine running, in front of our building. Inside, an unsophisticated looking young woman smiled agreeably.

"All right," she addressed the man sitting to the right of the driver. The older gentleman nodded to his chauffeur. The car turned and crossed the bridge to the right bank. As soon as we left the island, we were in the midst of a traffic jam the likes of which I had never seen before. Those who were not in motor cars were out on the streets looking up. Arms extended, hands pointing, everyone wanted to be the first to see the tiny aircraft as it passed overhead.

Michael was involved in a serious conversation with the gentleman in the front seat, Mr. Brennan. He apparently was also a Washingtonian. Although he was currently stationed for his work in London, Mr. Brennan had come to Paris to spend some time with his daughter, Gina, the young lady sitting next to Michael. How Michael had met these Americans, I could not guess, content simply to settle comfortably next to the window in the plush back seat. The car was so long I could stretch my legs out in front of me and not touch the divider.

Listening to Michael speak about the flight, I couldn't resist a smile. He was so earnest and so well informed on this subject. This part of his personality made me proud.

"Lindbergh's plane is a new design of the M-1," he was telling Mr. Brennan.

Turning to me, Mr. Brennan explained, "'M' for monoplane, and '1' meaning the first in a series." Then addressing Michael, "Did you know that this design came from Claude Ryan's redesign of a French monoplane he had seen in a journal?"

I was thrilled to think that the French had, even in a small way, participated in this historic flight.

Michael, not terribly sensitive to the plight of the French, ignored Mr. Brennan's observation and continued his commentary. "This new design does away with the swooping rudder of the French Spad type."

"Weren't most of the planes flown in the Great War, biplanes?" It appeared that Mr. Brennan was not without some knowledge of the subject.

"Yes, that's right, but actually, aviation experts agree that the one small plane, which exceeded the rest, was not a biplane but a monoplane. It was the German Fokker designed by Anthony Herman Gerard Fokker."

"But wasn't he Dutch? And didn't he help the Germans?" Mr. Brennan continued to display his fund of aircraft history or maybe just the history of warfare.

"Yes, he was educated in the Netherlands, but his first factories were in Germany. However, after the war, he went to the United States and established factories there," replied Michael, happy to excel Mr. Brennan in his repertoire of facts. I continued to marvel at the husband I hardly knew, but I was also afraid he might offend this nice gentleman who had been willing to drive total strangers to the aeroport. It was so comfortable to relax in his luxurious car. The seats were not only soft, but still gave off that new-leather odor I loved.

"Tell me more about Lindbergh's plane," Gina asked, anxious to get back to the event of the moment. I noticed that she had not taken her eyes off Michael since we entered the car. Her question was asked with such a student-like seriousness, I wondered if she was learning to fly. Although the numbers were small, women were taking to the sky. I didn't think I could ever attempt such a thing, but it would interesting to know a woman who did have the nerve to do it.

"The San Diego based Ryan Flying Company had contracted William H. Bowlus, an aeronautical craftsman, to build the M-1," Michael continued. "Lindbergh heard about the plane's success and, determined to compete in this lucrative trans-Atlantic venture, took a train from Missouri to California. Can you believe, it was only three months after he arrived in San Diego that this venture began?"

I let my mind wander as I watched the sky turn from blue to grey with pink streaks from the setting sun. Somewhere out in that darkening sky there was an American pilot in a tiny aeroplane, perhaps lost, trying to find Paris before it was dark. With half an ear, I listened to Michael.

"The small factory type office was little more than a shed in a field. Its owner, Franklin Mahoney, and engineer, D. A. Hall, agreed to work with Mr. Lindbergh and build a plane to his specifications. From what I understand, it was a godsend for the struggling little company. They'd been left with six monoplanes and no buyers after T. Claude Ryan sold the company to Franklin Mahoney. Ironically, when Lindbergh's initial telegram arrived from St. Louis, Mahoney and his associates thought it was a prank."

"So what made them reply?" asked Gina continuing her quest for details.

If I had asked that question, Michael probably would have ignored me.

"You know what I heard? When Frank Mahoney saw Lindbergh's telegram, he laughed and called it a ruse and threw it into the trash."

"No!" we chorused.

"Yes! But his secretary disagreed with his actions. She pulled the crumpled paper out of the trash bin, reread it and advised her boss to reconsider."

"Aren't women wonderful?" I burst out laughing. Michael wasn't amused and continued past my comment. Gina gave a slight smile.

"Maybe it was fate. After all, they had nothing to lose. So they decided to answer the request." Michael had brought a satchel with him and pulled from it a stack of papers. "According to *The Herald*, J. Eddy, Secretary of the Ryan Flying Company, said that the next day, the St. Louis Company was asking for a promise of delivery. Here's the quote: 'This was no prank - thank God. We were sort of numb. It was such a blessing we felt like celebrating, but didn't know why.' "

"But I thought you said the secretary was a woman."

"Different secretary. That was Miss Georgia Coddingham, Mahoney's personal secretary."

"So it was she who really saved the company," I said smugly, feeling almost as if I myself had been part of the story.

There was an awkward silence.

"Perhaps Mr. Lindbergh has already arrived," I said, instinctively looking up, but the sky was void of any object except a few small pink clouds. As we moved slowly in traffic, Michael was eager to continue his tale.

"As soon as he arrived in San Diego, Lindbergh wanted to begin. Once the construction was started, he and Hall took a walk to the San Diego library. Using a world globe, they measured and calculated a theoretical range of four thousand miles needed for the new airplane."

"Starting from scratch?"

"Yes, measured with a piece of string. Lindbergh knew others were preparing to cross the Atlantic. If he wanted to win that coveted prize, he had to hurry.

"The work began on the twenty-eighth day of February. Since time was of the essence, the factory manager used wing ribs he had on hand from the first M-1. But the fuselage had to be a new design."

"Am I correct that no previous airframe structure had ever been built to handle the weight Lindbergh had in mind?" ventured Mr. Brennan.

"Indeed, Mr. Brennan," Michael replied. "With the fuel needed for the distance, the plane would weigh over 5,700 pounds."

"How much does the plane weigh without fuel?"

"About 2,400 pounds."

Now the traffic was at a standstill. Looking out the side window, it seemed that everyone who had a car was on the road heading for the airport, while the rest of Paris stood on the sidewalks scanning the sky. A revolving electric sign had been put up at the top of the Selfridge building with letters six feet high flashing the latest Lindbergh news. Stores were closing and anyone who had an American flag was waving it. Even little children ran around clutching tiny batons brandished with the stars and stripes. For once, I was proud to be an American in Paris.

Meanwhile, Michael continued to enlighten his captive audience. "The plane was given a metal superstructure and a wooden wing which was mounted slightly above the fuselage. The wing is moderately thick, with wood spars and ribs covered with cloth. I saw a similar plane at *Le Bourget*. The leading edge of the plane is formed out of mahogany plywood and is braced to the fuselage by streamlined steel tube struts."

"And the fuselage?"

"The tubing and the tail surface are both made of steel. The motor can be quickly removed in case of an emergency."

"The motor can be removed?" Gina and I laughed as our question came out in chorus.

"Yes. The motor comes out easily by removing four bolts. The power plant, the engine, can be replaced in thirty minutes if it needs repair."

I looked at Gina and whispered, "How could he get out and change the motor while up in the air over the ocean?" Fortunately, Michael didn't hear me.

There were a few moments of silence. This was not a subject either Gina or I had learned in school. We had studied poetry, history, grammar, but never aviation and motor technology. These were facts I could barely comprehend; but they were also facts that were changing my world overnight. "Maybe we will fly to the moon some day like that futuristic writer, Jules Verne, wrote in his first novel." Fiction was quickly becoming fact. I don't think anyone heard me.

It was Gina's turn to speak. "He certainly needed all the help he could get if he were going to endure a more than thirty hour non-stop flight. Anything could happen in the air, couldn't it? I mean, he could and he probably did experience turbulence and ice storms and heavy rains and who knows what else?"

"That's right." Michael stuffed his papers back into the satchel.

"This may sound stupid," I ventured timidly, "but how did he know where he was going? I mean, there is nothing to look at crossing the ocean, except waves, and I guess the sky above when you can see it, if it isn't cloudy."

"That's an exceedingly intelligent question, my dear," Mr. Brennan answered kindly, immediately endearing him to me.

"The Pioneer Instrument Co. of Brooklyn, New York built his earth inductor, which also supplied the magnetic compass. Simplicity and independence of operation were what Lindbergh believed in." Michael had actually acknowledged my question, but his response showed that I was in over my head now, so I decided to keep silent. There was so much to learn. I wondered if Michael would have the patience to teach me about compasses and earth inductors and all the other aspects of this mysterious new vocabulary.

"Imagine making this trip alone?" Gina craned her neck out the window as the car continued to inch its way. It was now growing dark.

"Quite right," her father nodded. "This is a first. On long flights, it is normally the custom for another person to accompany a pilot as a navigator. But, of course, no one has ever attempted such a long flight alone."

"That was part of Lindbergh's strategy," Michael responded. "He chose to replace the weight of another person with extra fuel to allow for the additional three hundred miles of flight. He also added some ingenious designs like fitting spring-loaded caps to automatically grease the zerk engine fittings during the fight. He put rubber connectors on the fuel lines to reduce vibrations so no fuel would be lost if a line broke. He may have learned this trick from the Robertsons of St. Louis who hired him to deliver mail by air."

"He delivered mail with an aeroplane?"

"Oh, yes. Lindbergh has had more experience than most pilots have. He made numerous trips to and from Chicago in all kinds of weather. Sometimes he even had to land in fields and wait for local farmers to help him. When that happened, part of the mail delivery would be done by truck or car."

Mr. Brennan knew about this phase of his career. "Lindbergh was the chief pilot for the first St. Louis to Chicago airmail route."

"Yes, I remember reading about him before we left Washington," Gina added backing up her father.

"Yes, that's right, Gina. He was so well respected; it wasn't difficult for him to convince some St. Louis businessmen to back him including the Robertsons. Do you remember them, my dear? They owned the Robertson Aircraft Corporation, and persuaded the Lamberts to finance an airplane which Lindbergh was convinced could compete."

"I heard that by the time he was ready to attempt this historic trip, Lindbergh had already logged some 1,790 hours of personal flight time." For the first time, we heard from the chauffeur, a bit out of character for a hired driver, but with time on his hands, I couldn't blame him. His task today was difficult. Cars were simply crowding together with no pattern. I wondered if we would ever reach Le Bourget. It looked as if we would still be in the outskirts of Paris, taking more time to get to *Le Bourget* than it took for Mr. Lindbergh to cross the entire ocean. I didn't dare share this with the others. The conversation was too serious.

"I figured it out," said Mr. Brennan who had been calculating in his mind. "The first test flight of this plane took place after a mere sixty days."

"Incredible!" we all exclaimed.

"How did the plane get its name? Was it because of Lindbergh's association with the Robertsons?" I had broken my vow of silence.

"Absolutely." Michael treated my question as an opportunity to show off even more of his knowledge. "Lindbergh had the little monoplane christened, *Spirit of St. Louis*, in honor of the businessmen who financed the project."

At this point, we had finally eased out of the confines of the city and were on the route to *Le Bourget*. So were thousands of others from every part of the world, all lucky enough to be in Paris for this historic occasion.

Chapter Six

*We (that's my ship and I) took off rather suddenly.
We had a report somewhere around 4 o'clock in the
afternoon before that the weather would be fine, so
we thought we would try it.*

Lindbergh's Own Story in
The New York Times, 1927

The main road to the aeroport, the *Route de Flandre*, was
jammed with vehicles of every size and description.

Our chauffeur volunteered his take on the situation. "This
reminds me of the war years. The battle of the Marne. We had
an armada of taxis headed up this route. I was driving an ancient
Citroën."

"I saw a sticker on a taxi today," I remarked, the afternoon's
adventures flowing back into my mind. "It said: *I was at the
Marne.*"

"You took a taxi today? Where have you been?" Michael asked,
inadvertently displaying his controlling side.

"I … I went to a bookstore," I stuttered.

"You have all the books you could want right on the quay."
Michael's voice was stern. A miserly vein was emerging in his
character. "Why did you have to go to a proper bookstore?"

"Well, it was a special book." I explained that I had encountered
Victor at the *Quai des Grands Augustins* in front of one of the
bouquinistes where Michael knew I loved to browse. "Victor told
me that *the* James Joyce was actually living right upstairs, in the
apartment above ours." I even admitted how I felt compelled to find
a copy of his latest work. I told them I had made the acquaintance
of Sylvia Beach, the publisher. "And she told me so many stories
about Mr. Joyce." Suddenly, I realized how much I was babbling
when I saw Michael's face. He looked ready to squelch me. He had
never heard of *Ulysses* and could not understand my enthusiasm for

a book, especially with the urgency of our compatriot's imminent landing.

However, our new acquaintance seemed to share my enthusiasm. "My goodness, you have had a day," Mr. Brennan remarked. "I enjoyed reading *The Dubliners*. Tremendously Irish. Amusing. A bit esoteric. Would love to meet him in person. Understand he's a quiet kind of chap. Must be deep … yes, hum, …. My, my."

Turning into a real character yourself, I thought. I already liked this man, especially his dry sense of humor.

"Of course," he continued, "a first novel's printing is apt to be small, that is, the first published printing. The publisher, if she believes in the author, knows that she is investing in the author's future and usually takes the risk of losing money the first time around. But Sylvia Beach is a smart lady with a good head for business.

"I want my daughter to learn finances as well as art. It is the only way to enjoy success in this crazy world. Got to have a good head for money, I always say."

"Daddy, really!" Gina cut in.

"Sorry Gina dear and please, Mrs. Whitacker, don't take offense, only good fatherly advice."

I smiled and wondered what he would say if he knew that my father was a banker.

Michael had not offered any explanation about his relationship to the Brennans. Deciding that it would be inappropriate to ask, I began by saying how grateful I was for being included in the ride to the aeroport.

"Not at all," replied Mr. Brennan. "I feel as if we have known each other for a long time. Rather amazing, don't you think, our both being from Washington?"

"Yes, Mr. Brennan, it is." I tried to mask my surprise. "But how did you meet Michael?"

"Well, we had finished lunch at the little *Brasserie* around the corner from the *rue d'Anjou*, and all of a sudden, people started shouting. 'Lindbergh has made it across.' I never dreamed I would live to witness such an event. I'm so proud it was an American."

"Daddy actually met Michael on the street," Gina interjected. "It was a really friendly scene. Everyone was talking about Lindbergh and somehow Michael and Daddy began to chat and, well, here we all are."

I was amazed. I hadn't found Michael to be a very vociferous person, nor had he been one to take up with strangers. I was more likely to pick up conversations when we went out. Yet here was another side of the enigmatic man.

"Can we go any faster?" Michael asked.

I was mortified. Maybe he was not shy with these people, but where had he left his manners? We all wanted to go faster, even the chauffeur, but with bumper to bumper traffic, what did Michael expect?

"Monsieur, I cannot drive any faster. There is no room to pass. I think all of Paris is on this road." The chauffeur was certainly doing his best but the Daimler, immense with nine feet separating the windshield from the front bumper alone, could not go any faster than the little French cars less than half its size.

Looking outside, it was hard to see anything but headlights. Night was descending quickly.

"Do you think he has landed already?" I asked.

"No, I think we would have known if we saw cars coming the other way," Michael answered curtly.

At that very moment, a helmeted man riding a motocyclette passed by shouting, "He's here, he's here. He's circling the Eiffel Tower."

"After flying all the way across the ocean – alone – with no sleep, he's circling the Eiffel Tower?" Mr. Brennan was incredulous. "I say, this is a bit much, isn't it? Showing off perhaps?"

"I imagine he is lost," responded the ever-practical Michael.

"What can we do to help him?" I asked with total seriousness.

"From here, in the middle of a caravan of hundreds, driving at a snail's pace, there is nothing we can do. But somebody will help, I am sure."

All agreed.

When the sun's last ray of light had disappeared, we arrived at the high iron fence that shut off the field proper from the hordes who had gathered. Many were shaking the fence violently, acting almost crazy just to be able to get inside the airfield. Fortunately for us, Michael had a pass, which he showed the guards who allowed us through. Once inside, we could see searchlights roving the field. The light was so bright, when it came near us, it hurt my eyes and I had to look away. Every few moments, rockets soared up into the air with a great roar and as the lighted parachutes descended, the crowds cheered with delight.

"What happens to other planes who may wish to land?" I asked.

"All air traffic was ordered to remain on the ground," Michael informed me. "This is Lindbergh's night." He spoke with such pride you would have thought Michael himself had a part in this venture.

Clearly, *Le Bourget*, the largest aerodrome in the world, was prepared to give this young pioneer a hero's welcome.

By the time we were within sight of the landing field, the crowd looked like a stampede. There were maybe some fifty-thousand people, all teeming into Le Bourget as a herd. Many of these people must have climbed over the fence or at some point, succeeded in pushing the fence down.

We could hear the shouts, "Lin-dee, Lin-dee", well before we were able to see anything. We walked around for awhile, but the crowd was so thick we opted to sit in the car so as not to loose track of each other. Every few minutes, my exuberant husband jumped out of the car only to return with a sad face. "Not yet." Although hungry, we kept our minds off food by chatting. I found out more about the Brennans. Apparently, our "host" was a financier. He and his wife were staying for a year in London. Gina, his daughter, had come to Paris to study art. "She has great talent," her father told me, pride written all over his face. I suggested a hint of the Irish was in his blood given by not only his enthusiasm, but his choice of idiom from time to time. "Oh yes, he replied. "I have a bit o' the Irish in me. Now you have more than Joyce to cope with young lady!" We laughed. We were having such a great time talking that time passed quickly. It must have been a quarter past ten when we heard the roar of something other than the crowd.

"It's him," shouted Michael. This time we all jumped out of the car.

Yes, it was the roar of an aeroplane passing overhead, but I could see nothing. Then it stopped. Just when we were about to give up hope, someone nearby shouted, "I see the outline of a plane." We weren't sure. Then, only minutes later, we heard the sound again. This time the noise didn't stop; instead, it continued, growing louder by the second.

"Where do we look?" I yelled over the din to Michael. Before he could answer, suddenly, out of the pitch of darkness, the great silver moth was gliding down a path of light not far from us. We ran ahead but before we could see it clearly, the plane and its pilot were swallowed up by the crowd.

All we could identify now was the mob, as thousands upon thousands of Parisians, Americans and others cheered and waved. We worked our way into the howling mass of humanity. Someone shouted that Lindbergh had been hoisted onto the shoulders of some well wishers and was being carried around and around and away from his plane. Briefly, I caught sight of what must have been the back of his helmeted head above the crowds. He seemed to be shouting something to anyone who would listen.

"What is he saying?" I asked someone who had been pushed beside me.

"He is asking, 'Are there any mechanics here?'"

I couldn't believe that after such an astonishing flight, this brave but exhausted man would be concerned only for his valiant little aircraft.

"He couldn't be happy about this crazy crowd, but what a grin he has on his face! He's at the mercy of the mob now," reported the Frenchman standing next to us whose height allowed him a good vantage point.

I thanked the gentleman and shared the information with my companions.

"You realize," Michael added, "he has been in the air over thirty hours. He must be exhausted. But the important thing is he has arrived at his destination."

Michael and I picked up snatches of information in both French and English as we passed through the throng. The crowd had an insatiable appetite for its hero. Everyone wanted to be near the great man, pressing forward as a unit, cheering, clapping, and yelling. After Lindbergh's goggles had fallen off, we learned later, a young man had picked them up. Young, blonde-haired and looking something like Lindbergh, he donned the goggles and immediately was scooped up and paraded as the pilot. Perhaps it wasn't the true Lindbergh we had seen earlier after all. It wasn't until Harry Wheeler of New York was presented to the official welcoming committee that the truth was revealed.

"But the good news," a friend Michael had located in the crowd was saying, "is that the diversion allowed weary Lindbergh to be whisked away to a hangar. Surely he needs sleep."

Michael was disappointed not to meet Lindbergh and suggested that if he had been the pilot, his adrenaline would be flowing and sleep would be the last thing on his mind. I agreed with Michael's friend. Lindbergh must have been somewhat in shock. I don't think he ever expected such a crowd.

Mr. Brennan said that he had heard on the radio that when Lindbergh left Roosevelt Field in Long Island, there were fewer than a hundred spectators and well wishers.

"It is rumored," said Mr. Brennan somewhat haughtily I thought, "that Lindbergh has little social style."

"But he's a stickler for details," Michael yelled back over the din, annoyed by the criticism of his hero. "He is known for being analytical. Social norms aren't important to him." Michael and I had read in the paper about Lindbergh's seeking all possible information about Paris while still in San Diego during the construction of the plane. We laughed when we heard that he wanted to know how much it would cost to take a cab from Le Bourget to downtown Paris.

Naturally, our Ambassador, Mr. Herrick, took charge of the man who had brought great honor to America. The Ambassador had a big smile on his face when he saw the plane land. But when he came down to the field from his perch on the veranda-like roof of the executive building and saw the tired, dirty face of a boy who didn't know how to be afraid, his smile vanished and tears began to flow. Soon everyone was crying. The pilots from the Great War, women who had lived through the agonies of war, newspaper reporters who had seen such trauma these past ten years. They were all crying. This was not a stalwart individual, a man seasoned by experience. This was a boy, a tired and dirty, but grinning boy. It had been sixty-three hours since he had last slept. With the help of other aviators, the Ambassador was able to drag Lindbergh away from the crowds, but only after the pilot was assured of the welfare of his flying companion, the *Spirit of St. Louis.*

As a member of the American Club in Paris and the National Aeronautic Association, Paris Chapter, Michael was hoping to participate in the official reception for the heroic young aviator. He was sure that despite the mix up with the impostor, the real Lindbergh would ask the Ambassador to allow him to go to the tower before proceeding into Paris. It was the right and proper thing to do, according to Michael, as he urged our little group on, pushing through the crowds, heading for the watchtower. But as we approached the tower, Michael ran into Dennis, a flying buddy, who had just left the executive building.

"Unfortunately, Michael, the real Charles A. Lindbergh is already on his way to Paris." Dennis chuckled as he recounted the tale we had already heard. "There we were, all standing in line, exceedingly correct, ready to shake hands with the most daring and brave man in the world, and in comes this young man, his goggles still on, and we knew, we just knew, this wasn't Lindbergh! It was quite amusing actually."

"Yes," piped in another young pilot who was coming along behind Dennis. "While we were standing in the reception line, Ambassador Herrick had already taken him away in his limo to Paris. I heard that Lindbergh asked if he might be dropped off at a hotel. Of course, the Ambassador insisted that he be his honored guest at the Embassy. Actually, I think Lindbergh was really asleep on his feet and bed or no bed he was going to get the rest he deserved, no matter where he was."

"What about the plane? Is the plane being protected?" queried Michael. I thought he sounded almost as concerned as Lindbergh himself might have been.

"Yes, almost," Dennis replied. "Capt. Lindbergh doesn't yet know but some ardent souvenir hunter did succeed in cutting a good-size piece of cloth from the wing before the plane was rolled away. Actually, it was the police, French officials, and soldiers who, hand holding hand, formed a ring around the plane as it was rolled into a hanger. But, can you imagine?"

"What?" we all cried in unison, hanging on to his every word.

"As she was being rolled away, you know, the plane, Lindbergh was very upset. After so many hours together, he dreaded having to leave his companion. He kept talking about 'we'."

"Meaning himself and the *Spirit*?"

"Yes indeed. What a man. What a momentous occasion." We all agreed.

There was electricity in the air. The crowd, French, English, Americans, all were one in awe of this man and his *companion*.

"Imagine not having to take a ship to get back to the United States," I sighed.

"Not so fast, my dear. This is but the first step. We have a long way to go before you and I will be able to fly in a plane big enough for passengers, much less crossing such a distance."

Still, I was excited. Maybe not the actuality but the idea of flying back and forth to the United States had now become real.

"Hallo there?" a familiar voice shouted through the crowd. I knew before I saw his face that it was Philippe. My heart skipped a beat. Michael was delighted to see his friend as well. They greeted each other with a hug and a slap on the back.

"Your American has brought the monoplane back to its roots!"

"Did you see him? Talk to him? Michael wanted to know.

"Yes, but very briefly. Fantastic chap. Shy, quiet, not typical American." Philippe said looking at me with a twinkle in his eyes.

"Now don't be such a tease," I chided, trying to collect my self-control. My heart beat at an unaccustomed speed. "Not all Americans are as vociferous as, as, well, I guess, as we are."

"Ha, ha, you are adorable. Don't ever change, young lady," retorted Philippe. "Besides, you use words I do not understand and," he said taking my hand, "that intrigues me."

I loved his smile and melted at the feel of his hand. Fortunately, I had the presence of mind to collect myself before anyone noticed.

"The word?" he asked, " 'Vociferous', what is that?"

I explained the habit many Americans had of being noisy and long-winded. Then, continuing in French, I told him that we needed to discuss an urgent matter at some point. What I did not realize was that Mr. Brennan spoke excellent French as well and being so close, he could hear the conversation. Just then, Michael made his 'excuse me am I not part of this conversation?' cough.

I am sure that I blushed. "Oh yes dear," I responded, "do let us all introduce ourselves."

Chapter Seven

Oh! To wander Paris to exist, strolling is living.
Honoré de Balzac

Pamela had already seen from her experienced and astrological eye what my life must have been like for me living with Michael.

April, 1927

It was close to midnight by the time Pamela and Victor escorted me home. We had been at *Château Madrid* continuing the celebration of Philippe's new plane. Michael was nowhere in sight so the two kindly offered to drive me home. After asking Frederick to park the car in front of our building, Pamela went up with me to the apartment while her husband waited below.

Opening the front door, I was confronted with a startling tableau. Michael, his legs up on a table, his collar unbuttoned, was sitting before a roaring fire with a glass of brandy in his hand. His hair was tousled; his face displayed a broad grin. Another glass sat on the table, empty.

Pamela and I took in the whole scene before a word was spoken. "Who is here?" I looked around. The rest of the apartment was in darkness. "Or was here?"

Silence.

"Why didn't you come to the restaurant?" I asked angrily.

Slowly, Michael slurred, "Oh, hello there. How are you, Pamela?" Attempting to get up, he fell back again into the couch, the smirk still on his face. His free hand waved circles in the air. He was completely blotto.

Somewhere between livid and wretched, I composed myself enough to turn to my stunned friend and tried to make my voice sound calm. "Please don't worry, Pamela. Victor is waiting. I'll be in touch tomorrow. Thank you for bringing me home. I had a wonderful time." I must have sounded like a machine or a boxed voice.

Tactfully, Pamela nodded then retreated out the door but not before giving me a quizzical look. In a daze, I walked past the parlor and shut myself in the bedroom. I was shaking.

Michael slept in the salon. The fire had to put itself out.

Later the next morning, we faced each other awkwardly across the small kitchen table, sipping our coffee in silence. Michael was a man who made the newspaper the centerpiece of the table when he ate breakfast at home, which was rare since he preferred going out. Groggy from a sleepless night, I had arranged my place at the table for a coffee cup and a croissant. Michael shuffled through the paper and handed over the fashion pages. I took this as either a gesture of amends or a way to forestall becoming engaged in any sort of conversation. Still too upset to read, I held my hot cup with both hands and slowly sipped the strong French roast. Finally, Michael began to stammer. Something about being sorry. I listened, but simply couldn't motivate myself to forgive him. It was not a question of holding a grudge or even holding onto anger. Something deep inside would not allow me to accept Michael's weak attempts. Staring at my blank, impassive face, he put down his coffee and, without a word, picked up his jacket from the chair in the hallway and left.

When I ventured into the great Cathedral for the first time, the experience was nothing short of awe. I was accustomed to the small parish of Trinity Church in Georgetown where I had been baptized and where Michael and I had signed marriage documents such a short time ago. A practicing Catholic since birth, I would have to get used to my new church. So after Michael walked out, I decided to go over to the Cathedral. I needed *Notre Dame*, the old queen of our cathedrals, to give me solace. More importantly, I needed the clergy of the Cathedral. There really was no other place to turn. I had to talk to someone.

Mme. Metz had given me a little row boat when we moved into the apartment. The former resident had left it behind. I was delighted and appreciated the concierge saving the boat for the new tenant as if it went with the apartment. It was so easy to row back and forth from our home to the Cathedral. Actually, the real reason I had chosen to go on the water instead of crossing the bridge by foot may have been foolish, but I admit, I am a bit superstitious. Since crossing over the first time, I found out that the bridge leading from the *Île St. Louis* to the *Île de la Cité* and *Notre Dame* had been cursed. It happened centuries ago by a band of gypsies. The clergy, who had seen to it that the gypsies were to be incarcerated, probably for disagreeing with the tenets of the Holy Roman Catholic Church, had forced the group onto a barge to cross the river. In angry retaliation, the gypsies put a curse on both the river and the bridge they floated under. So far, there had been five bridges and each had collapsed for no explicable reason. With each collapse, there had been loss of life.

I rowed across the river, tied up the boat, and then climbed the steps up to the park behind the Cathedral. A path followed along the side and, as if the beauty of Our Lady were not enough, there were gardens of flowers and lovely shrubs all the way up the hill. The apse of the cathedral as seen from my apartment window on the other side of the river is stunning, but nothing prepared me for the impact of standing before the edifice and gazing upward. I was overwhelmed by the sheer size of this Gothic marvel, the labor that had been put into its construction (much less the funds) and the artistry exhibited everywhere.

"It took one hundred and fifty years to complete," said a man standing near me. He was holding up his hand to block the sun. "Better to study the Cathedral," he said. "Faith must have been a big commodity in the days of old."

I chuckled and agreed. "From what I have read and know of history, in what was called the 'age of faith', kings and emperors, nobles and gentry donated vast sums of money. They wanted to ensure that the teachings of the Church would be sung, taught and experienced within these towering walls." These were things I had learned in school.

"No doubt," he replied, "but I would assume the nobility and rulers also wished to ensure the support of the Church. Without the Church, they would have lost their power."

Another tourist strolled up; cane in one hand, his overcoat opened a flap and as he came closer, I noticed, at the neck, he had a priest's collar. Having overheard our conversation, he wanted to share some information about the Church's history. "In the early years, the priests used the artwork to teach the stories about good and evil. Lessons were learned from the biblical pictures of glass that make up the windows and from the frescoes painted on the walls. Statues depict saints and the Old Testament. Look over there. You can see that even the great wooden doors are carved with images from the Bible."

I told them about the beautiful picture this church projected in the evening. "At night, when I stroll along the quay on the *rive gauche*, the city has lights illuminating the façade of the Cathedral. The lovely symmetry and form show up so clearly. You can see, in the light and shadows, hundreds of statues standing above the first level of those pointed and tiered archways. It looks as if they are there to help hold up the higher structure both physically and spiritually."

We were three complete strangers held together in awe. This twelfth century masterpiece would be my refuge, a place where I could be reminded of the lessons I had learned throughout my youth, the religion taught to me by the priests and nuns in Washington. Inside these walls would be the peace needed to pause, to reflect, to pray, and to confess. Or was this wishful thinking? Could I find a priest who would help me? My marriage was a sham and I didn't understand. Was it my fault? Did I dare seek advice from priests? Oh, how much more daunting *Notre Dame* was compared to my little church in Georgetown.

Just where we were gathered, gazing up at the Cathedral, is a round marker enmeshed in the cobblestone. This marker registers the focal point from which the distance to any other place in France is measured. Then it came to me. Here we were, literally standing at the center of all of France. And just when I thought I could bear no more of the beauty and the history and the spiritual power of this place, the bells began to toll. As the chimes echoed through the air, I felt their sound and was transported to a realm only angels could know. My heart beat hard and fast and I recognized here, in this place, at this time, an omen.

Inside, after being in the bright sun, the Cathedral was especially dark to my eyes. It was also cold inside. It took some time, adjusting to the dimness and the chill, before I could locate the Confessional booths. They were on the left toward the back of the church.

"Bless me Father for I have sinned."

"What have you done, my child?"

"I had fun, I, well, I enjoyed the company of, of a … another man. I mean a man who is not my husband."

"And where, my child, was your husband?"

"He, he wasn't there, Father. I should have waited for him to arrive. I should have realized something was wrong when he did not come to the restaurant. You see, we …"

"I am terribly sorry but I do not have time to listen to your life's story, young lady."

"I am sorry, Father."

"Please be brief. Precisely, how have you sinned?"

"I have, oh dear, I have enjoyed the company of another man."

"That is what you said. Precisely how were you *enjoying* this man?"

His question seemed a bit peculiar, implying ever so much more than what I had to share, but an answer was implicit. "I danced with him, Father." Feeling foolish to confess merely dancing, I stammered, "I felt, I felt," and paused, glad the priest could not see my crimson face, "I felt good with him."

"Nothing more?"

Did he sound disappointed? I couldn't help wondering. "No, Father."

"Say three Hail Marys and do a good act of Contrition. In the name of the Father, Son, and the Holy Ghost. Amen."

I began to recite the act of contrition: "O my God."

"Oh my God!" Intoned the priest with a little more emphasis than necessary.

"I am heartily sorry for having offended Thee..." I continued.

"I am heartily sorry for having offended Thee..." said the priest.

"...and I detest my sins above every other evil..." I said with a sigh.

"...and I detest my sins..." affirmed the priest.

"...because they displease Thee, my God..." Now I was superimposing over the voice of the priest.

"...displease Thee..."

"Who art deserving of all my love..."

"...my love..."

"...and I firmly propose, by Thy holy grace..."

"...I firmly propose..."

"...never more to offend Thee..." By now, I was defiant.

"...never more..." whispered the priest. This time it was his turn to sigh. I can't say I blamed him.

"...and to amend my life." I was determined. My pupils were probably really small by now. That's what happens when I get excited, angry and determined all at the same time.

"...my life. *In patria nomines*..." The priest was making the sign of the cross on his side and I on mine. But my mind wasn't with the cross or the confession. It was analyzing. *I doubt he could ever understand women*. The confession came to me by rote. For the priest, they had a different meaning, of that I was sure. My feelings were real. The priest's understanding was nil.

I left the Confessional, knelt in a pew at the back of the Cathedral, made the sign of the cross again and proceeded to recite the Hail Marys, hoping that our lady would listen. I couldn't tell the priest what I wanted so desperately to say. I was angry and I was sad. What had Michael been doing? Why did I feel the way I did with Philippe? Was I the sinner or was Michael? My fists were clenched while I mechanically repeated pleas to the Holy Mother. *Please, Holy Mary, help me.*

I was searching for consolation as a child would demand from her mother. But consolation wasn't the function of confession. Had I been closer to my mother, perhaps I could have sought her advice. As it was, she would be the last person to whom I would confide.

I prayed the Holy Mother would listen. Above my pew were the beautiful stained glass windows. The sunlight came through but was refracted by the colored glass. But what happens at night? Without the sun, they are as dark as the Cathedral walls. Dark, this is, unless there is light within the church. Then they are splendid. People are like that too, I mused. There needs to be a light within.

Walking from the dark of the Cathedral into the sunlight, I stopped outside the great doors and waited for my eyes to readjust before descending the steps and heading down the path to the river bank. It was there where the silver waters flowed, where the air was sweet and humid, not inside the bowels of the great cathedral that I began to feel more relaxed, more at peace.

Since it was still early in the day, I decided to row over to the *Rîve Gauche*. The exercise plus the fresh air added to calm my stress. Roaming through the bookstalls, *les Bouquinistes*, on the *Quai des Grands Augustins* would help, too.

Carefully, I tied up the little boat and mounted the stone steps to street level. Visitors strolled along the river bank, browsing, peering through books, admiring prints and enjoying the aromas of the flower bouquets venders were selling in proliferation this time of year. The *quai* was busy, a microcosm of *la vie Parisienne*. Spring is beautiful everywhere in the world, but spring in Paris is particularly splendid. The air was warm and fresh and since I loved books, this pastime was one of my favorites.

"*Bonjour*, Mme. Libby."

I was startled. My attention had been focused on thumbing through a pile of old art magazines. A whole line of other fascinating bookstalls all the way down the length of the *quai* beckoned as well. Being so absorbed, I tried to ignore whoever was calling me.

"Hello, Libby?"

"Oh, Victor. I am so sorry. I didn't see you. How are you?" I hoped he didn't think I was rude.

"Very well, thank you. Thought I should take a stroll on this lovely day." Pamela's husband tipped his felt hat. He looked quite dapper with his cane, three-piece tweed suit, and spit-polished shoes.

"Yes, of course. I couldn't resist it myself. Thank you again for bringing me home last night." I did not want to say any more and was grateful when Victor began another subject. "So, among other things, are you looking for your neighbor's work?"

"And who might that be?"

"Why Mr. Joyce, James Joyce." I didn't know. We had never been told who our neighbor upstairs might be.

"Mr. James Joyce? The James Joyce? The writer?" Someone had spoken of him but I couldn't remember who or what they said about him. "My neighbor?"

"Why, yes. He lives above you on the *troisième étage*."

"On the third floor?" I was astounded. I had heard him spoken of as an iconoclastic author, but had never read anything of his. He had not been published in the United States. From what I remember, he was considered quite controversial. Not the kind of reading appropriate for a young Catholic lady, according to my mother's standards.

"Why no, I did ... didn't know," I stammered, not sure whether to admit how little I knew of this man.

Victor could see that he had put me on the spot. I think after last evening, he and Pamela must have talked about me. I had the impression that Pamela was attempting to help me loosen up and have fun, but Victor hadn't seemed like the type to want to become involved in another person's affairs. I wondered if he knew my father, although I didn't think my being my father's daughter had anything to do with Victor's kindness. So standing by the wharf, thumbing through some of the books, we chatted for awhile about this and that, nothing controversial, simply enjoying the afternoon sun. When Victor finally went his way, I had an irresistible urge to find the forbidden work. Silently, I sifted through books, too embarrassed to ask the merchant for Joyce's work in particular, even though I wasn't sure what the controversy was all about. I had a feeling that there were sexual characteristics. But not finding anything, by the fourth stall, I finally summoned up my courage, feigned assurance and in my most sophisticated French, asked if he had any of Joyce's books. The old man at this book stall coughed and smirked and shuffled his feet. I was mortified and about to run away, but the dealer tipped his hat, grunted, and made me realize that he hadn't understood a

Patricia Daly-Lipe

word I said. There are two languages in Paris. This man was from a populace who spoke only a slang called argot.

I gave up and was about to descend the ramp and fetch my boat when a younger vender approached. In a whisper, he told me about a special book shop. It wasn't too far away, he said.

The weather being lovely, I was happy for an excuse to take a stroll.

Shakespeare & Company, touted as Bookshop, Lending Library, Publisher, was located on the *rue de l'Odéon*, in the heart of the artists' district. It was owned and run by Sylvia Beach, the same Sylvia Beach who had published the first edition of *Ulysses* in 1922.

Immediately I headed there. It wasn't difficult to find and once inside, I had my first encounter with James Joyce. Not the man but a recently published book of his poems.

The shop included an impressive selection of books and was quite well organized. However, when I first entered, Miss Beach appeared to be indifferent both to me and to the cost of any of the books I had removed from the shelves. Nor could I find any placards announcing sale prices. I had never had a job in my life, but this seemed a bizarre sales tactic. It soon became clear, however, that I was totally mistaken about Miss Beach. What she preferred was to have the customer sit down and read a book before deciding to buy it. When she had established to herself that I was a serious shopper, she confided that she took pride in matching a customer with a book. Tall, slender, her hair curled *à la mode*, her face sporting a turned up chin, straight nose and deeply set eyes, Miss Beach appeared to be a serious lady.

"The Greenwich Village crowd from New York City frequently comes to Shakespeare and Company when they are in Paris. Either they visit when they arrive and became instant *regulars* or they seek us out before leaving and often tell me they regret not having found us sooner." Miss Beach added, as if in confidence, that they saved her "a great deal of postage by coming over to Paris and buying *Ulysses* in person." She loved Americans. "After all, they are my compatriots even though I left the States when I was fourteen."

"What brought you here, Miss Beach, and at such a young age?"

"My father was transferred from his Presbyterian parsonage in Princeton, New Jersey to the American Church in Paris. He served as pastor."

Since I was young, American and inexperienced, perhaps it should have been no surprise that she was considerate with me. Of course, I was also sure Miss Beach was being extra kind because she recognized my confusion about Joyce. Cradling a copy of his novel with its blue-morocco binding and printed pages of white Dutch paper in her hands, Miss Beach told me how the United States Post Office had confiscated and burned copies of a literary magazine because it contained sections of *Ulysses*. "That scared off potential English and American publishers. After I published one thousand copies in February 1922, the *Egoist Press* in London printed a second edition in October of that same year. But the Americans would have none of it. Five hundred copies were burned by New York Post Office Authorities."

I was shocked.

"But, my dear, it doesn't end there. In January 1923, four hundred and ninety-nine out of another five hundred copies were seized by Customs Authorities in Folkestone."

"How awful!" I exclaimed.

"You know," she continued, clutching her copy of *Ulysses* tightly as if protecting a small child, "Joyce gives an impression of sensitiveness exceeding any I have ever known."

I couldn't tell if she meant Joyce the man or Joyce the author, at least as he represented himself in the novel, but I was impressed with the sensitivity of this nice lady herself. These thoughts were confirmed when Miss Beach, after a sniff into her hanky, continued. "This is the first edition I published five years ago." She opened the novel she was holding so tenderly and there, on the title page, was the inscription, *Shakespeare and Company, Paris* plus a poem Joyce had written to Miss Beach as a dedication.

"We decided to publish on Mr. Joyce's birthday, February second. A good omen," she affirmed as I stared at the cherished book in her hands. "Nevertheless, despite its success, Mr. Joyce remains quite impoverished. Thanks to friends, especially Harriet Weaver, Mr. Joyce and his family have enough funds for lodging so he can complete his next great work right here in Paris."

"Who is Ms. Weaver?"

"Harriet Weaver owns the publishing company I told you about, *The Egoist*.

"I think I have heard about it, but I thought it was a feminist magazine." A girl at the New York boarding school I briefly attended had shown me a copy she had found in the library.

"Miss Weaver decided to suspend the publication of the magazine back in 1919 and concentrate instead on book publication. She used my plates to publish *Ulysses*."

Miss Beach showed me a photograph of Miss Weaver. She looked very spinsterly. When I was a student, there were so many restrictions that most anyone who did not live up to my mother's expectations was considered either *loose or low*. Now that I saw how normal Miss Weaver looked, I needed to reconsider any bias I might have had. Maybe Joyce was not that, dare I say, *indecent* after all. But beyond such considerations, now it was my turn to be animated and share information.

"Oh, Miss Beach, I must tell you. Mr. Joyce lives on the floor just above mine, on the *Île St Louis*." Any other customers in the store would have been alerted to this revelation, I shouted so loud.

Time passed quickly while we chatted. Eventually I was persuaded to take home only the book of poems. The novel was perhaps too difficult for me to understand, at least for now, Miss Beach advised.

Coming out of Shakespeare & Company, I was greeted with great commotion in the street. And not just on *rue de l'Odéon*. It seemed that the whole city vibrated with a roar of joyful shouts and chatter.

"What's going on?" I asked a passing pedestrian.

"The pilot from America is coming!"

"Who?"

"His name is Charles Lindbergh. He made it across the Atlantic and is approaching Paris." And so it was that I became acquainted with our neighbor, James Joyce's work. I also had a preview of what would come to be a major problem with Michael, even before we awaited the Lindbergh landing. I was just too insecure to put it all together and take a stand.

Chapter Eight

'History,' Stephen said, 'is a nightmare from which I am trying to awake.'

James Joyce, *Ulysses*

1928, Pamela's House

I rolled over and saw the sun peeping through the blind. My first thought was, I am back home in Washington, in my little front room upstairs overlooking Massachusetts Avenue. My childhood room has a window seat. When I was very young, the bookcase was full of toys including picture books and Mr. Ted. Later the shelves were filled with the classics and Mr. Ted. Not daring to move for a few moments, I needed to collect my thoughts and figure out how I had come back home. But as my senses awakened, my ears became adjusted to the sounds outside the window. Horns screeching, people shouting, traffic vying with nature as birds chirped over the hum of movement. This was not Washington. With the smell of freshly baked bread wafting in, I remembered. I was in Paris. Suddenly, I sat straight up. *Pamela's house, I'm in Pamela's house.* Recalling how I had come here in the middle of the night, the vision of coming home late from the writer's group; coming home to our apartment and finding Michael...my husband....naked and with another man. I just wanted to fall back under the covers and hide. But my brain kicked in and reminded me that I was an adult. I was on my own. And this was not an option. Choices had to be made and I had to be ready to make them.

Pamela had seen to everything. Shampoo was on the counter in the bathroom. Soap, towels, everything was there. All I had to do was complete my morning ritual and descend to the kitchen.

Clean and coiffed, I descended the stairs and found Pamela waiting for me in the kitchen. With a pot of hot coffee and a nice warm *brioche* just out of the oven, she escorted me to the breakfast room, which overlooked the garden in back of the house. The window was slightly open and we could hear the birds chirping and smell the blossoms of Pamela's little flowerbed.

"Your home is so lovely, Pamela. Thank you for letting me visit." I couldn't proceed further.

Not wanting to broach the obvious subject any more than I did, Pamela catered to my acting as if this was just another normal morning. We sat down to a friendly breakfast, with the newspaper in front of us and chatted about the day's events, the weather, even gossip, anything but "the issue".

In 1927, there were an estimated fifteen thousand Americans living in Paris according to the American Chamber of Commerce. In reality, the number was more like forty thousand as my fellow Americans flooded into the gay Parisian lifestyle. The Great War, seven years past, was barely a memory to these wealthy, pleasure-seeking, young adventurers. Although I was the same age and the same nationality, I could not identify with them. I sympathized with the French, vividly remembering the old man's story at the American Embassy party I had attended with my parents and the stories I heard last night at the writer's dinner. Their memories of the war could not be so easily erased.

All around were reminders of the horror they had been through. On the *quai*, dazed men walked with crutches because they had lost a leg or a foot. An armless twelve year old girl was trying to sell prints for her parents at one of the book stalls. We saw a little boy whose face was so disfigured that, even to glance at him made my stomach queasy. Hardly a street remained without crumbling reminders: a shell of a building, a vacant lot strewn with rubble, a gaping wound where someone's home had been destroyed by a bomb. Added to the visual reminders was the very real scarcity of laborers. So many men had been killed or maimed, and there was still a shortage of food and money.

Now my French friends spoke openly of the new invasion: the Americans. These were not the soldiers who volunteered to come and help the French during the war. Rather this was a new generation who, according to the French news reporters, "came in droves on their fancy cross-Atlantic ocean liners, the Ritzes of the high seas." The French weren't asking for sympathy, but they did expect some compassion; at the very least, appreciation for their pain. I had listened attentively to my French friends, but they would abruptly catch themselves. "Oh dear, Libby don't be offended. The Red Cross and the American soldiers who came later in the war were a Godsend to us, but these young *Philistines* are not of the same ilk. Please forgive us. We forget that you are not French." I took that as a great compliment.

To the French, these new *callous invaders* from across the sea had no interest in the detritus of war that was France's so recent past. They had no interest in Verdun, Ypres, the Marne or other battlefields where the blood of Gaulle had been spilled, where sons and lovers had fought so valiantly and so many had given their lives. "No," my friends said, "these Americans have no sense of history, no respect for the glory that was France."

The French papers were more sarcastically specific. They wrote about Americans coming to Paris and embarking "upon a frenzy of merrymaking. Maxim's, the *Follies-Bergère*, the *cafés* of the *Champs Elysées*, these are the places the Yankees seek - wine flows freely and many nights the French police are forced to restrain or arrest drunken Americans." Included in the papers were reports of brawls that erupted in *Montmartre*, in *Les Caves*, in *Les Boîtes*, in fact, in all the nightspots of Paris. But, the journalists also noted, "They bring American dollars and unfortunately, we French need the money." I remember seeing a drunken young American man yelling at an older French merchant while the poor old man simply wanted to sell his wares. It was no secret; this post war country was on the brink of financial collapse.

I understood the sometimes open and sometimes subtle hostility of the French. With my perfect accent, thanks to my upbringing with Mademoiselle, I often pretended to be a native and listened to bakers, butchers and other vendors discuss their woes with customers. They called Americans "*les parasites de Paris*."

In this morning's newspaper, there was an article about Prohibition in the United States. Tense from last night's trauma, the news was but a mask for my true emotions dealing with Michael. There was a mirror behind Pamela and I could see the reflection of my face. Two vertical lines were inscribed between my eyes, telltale signs of pressure and worry. Not a happy face. Looking away, I concentrated instead on my cup of hot, strong coffee.

"Pamela, I am mortified by this news," I babbled while Pamela listened quietly sipped her tea. "You know, despite all the parties, the dancing, the socializing and the drinking, mostly the drinking, there seems to be some kind of underlying melancholy hanging over the festivities. I mean, are these people finding life so boring that they have to escape by drinking and dancing all night?"

Pamela simply nodded and continued coaxing me to continue by saying nothing.

"I'm not suggesting the other night at the Chateau Madrid was like that. With the exception of you, Victor, and me, everyone there was French and it was fun." Flashes of dancing with Philippe came to mind. I had to duck into my coffee cup to hide the grin. But just as suddenly, the reality of this moment in my life, the way everything had turned around, wiped the grin from my face. I was forlorn, alone, vulnerable, and I knew it.

To escape self-pity, I continued my monologue. Pamela remained silent.

"This editorial is correct, Pamela. Passing the law on Prohibition does not solve the drinking problem in America. What right has a democracy to prevent the freedom to drink anyway?" Pamela seemed ready to say something, but, right now, it was my time to vent. "Besides all the speakeasies, the government's meddling has caused the illegal sale of liquor. Gangsters get rich and I read about murders and crimes in the States every day. Ordinary drinkers become rummies. Pamela, Europeans and you British don't get drunk. Is it because you know you can purchase liquor anytime you want? You don't have to sneak into alleys or hide behind closed doors like Americans have to do. But the Americans who come here and continue to guzzle non-stop, I just don't understand. Why are they trying so hard, pretending to be happy instead of really *feeling* it?

What is wrong? Too much drink and too many cigarettes." Looking out at Pamela's garden, I wondered how anyone could prefer the smell of tobacco to flowers. The English were famous for their gardens. Since England and France had first handedly experienced the war, this was, to my way of thinking, all the more reason for them to get blotto, not the Americans.

"Pamela, do you realize that most of us weren't even here for the Great War. In fact, very few of my generation have had any experience with death and dying. You should have been there last night ..." I had to stop. I had to keep the image from creeping back into my mind. Pamela respected my pause and quietly continued sipping her tea.

Slowly, I allowed part of last night's experience to creep into my diatribe. "Pamela, I wish you could have heard the experiences people shared at Le Rendezvous last evening. You are British, so I can say this. These Americans we read about in *The Herald*, the ones coming here just to get drunk, they are ignorant and self-centered. Have they come here searching for the *joie de vivre* of the French and think they have found it in drinking?" I had experienced this, but not with Michael. The words came toppling out and with them, an understanding I had not known or, at least, acknowledged until now began to form. "Pamela, it is as if they can't find it *within* themselves." Suddenly, there it was. An unexpected grasp of my predicament had crept into my speech. Within. The answer had come from within. I was sitting at the breakfast table, but my brain was running a hundred miles an hour. All the thoughts I had amassed through reading, museum visits, lectures, and all the experiences I heard about from the writing group came spilling out without format, without focus, without logic. Feeling tense, I clutched my napkin, the croissant untouched. Pamela remained quiet but was looking at me with some apprehension.

"Gertrude Stein was there last night. And regardless of her strange wit, this lady really has insight. I didn't see Alice, but Pamela, I know about Gertrude and Alice and it doesn't bother me." I paused, took a sip of coffee. Then, taking a deep breath, I blurted, "But Michael?" The tears came with a vengeance. Pamela found me a tissue.

Trying to collect myself, I continued. "You know, Freud would probably blame my parents. Or maybe he would blame Michael's parents. So does that make us victims of our birth?" I wiped the coffee off the table where it had spilled when I made the defeatist gesture. "The Church teaches us that God loves us and we should strive to live the righteous life according to His laws. We should confess our sins, beg His forgiveness, and go on with our lives, forever striving to be good and honorable." Hesitating, I took a deep breath. "So what happened?" The question was rhetorical. "What am I supposed to do?" I bought the napkin to my face as the tears gushed. Embarrassed at such a public display, I tried to hide behind the small cloth. This time Pamela got up and came around the table and put her arms around me.

Waiting until I was calm enough to listen, she confided, "I am not a Catholic, Libby dear, but I think we can all agree about one thing. God only gives us what He feels we can handle. He gives us these obstacles for a reason. Perhaps we are meant to become stronger for having endured the pain."

I dabbed my eyes and attempted a smile. "Yes, Pamela, I am sure you are right. It's just that," I searched for the right word, "just that, I am so confused." Looking at her kind and caring face, I said what I felt. "Thank you so much for being my friend."

"We love you and we are going to help you." This came from Victor who had just entered the room. He poured coffee into his cup, grabbed a croissant from the serving plate and sat in the chair next to mine. As he sipped his coffee, we were silent. After a few minutes, he put his hand on mine and gently asked, "Libby dear, what would you like us to do? Would you like me to call Michael?"

"I thought about that last night; no, it was this morning when I was brushing my teeth." Getting up from my chair, I walked around the table trying to elicit composure. When I finally turned and faced the two of them, my decision had been made. "Victor and Pamela, I think that although he has caused me great misery and grief, Michael and I must speak to each other, communicate, come to some understanding." Before Victor or Pamela could interrupt, I continued. "This charade can't go on!" Before either one could respond, I found myself speaking words I had not, until this moment, dared to utter. "I must find a way to dissolve this marriage. It's been a sham." With that, I brought the napkin back to my eyes and began to tremble. The tears flowed uncontrollably. Pamela rose and put her arm around me again. I blew my nose, took a deep breath and stammered, "But I don't think I can speak to him right now, not yet anyway."

I knew Victor was concerned about me, but being a typical Brit, he simply responded with, "Right." Although he went back to sipping his coffee and picked up the paper, I sensed that he was thinking, not about the news of the day, but about my predicament. Finally, putting the paper down, he looked at me and was about to say something when the telephone rang.

As he put the receiver to his ear, we could all hear the loud voice of the operator. "Monsieur Whitacker wishing to speak with Monsieur Statler." Pamela and I sat transfixed as Victor listened and nodded and said, "Yes", several times. Finally, he hung up and reported to his rapt audience, "We have arranged for a rendezvous. We will meet at twelve in my office. Michael asked after you, Libby, and thanked Pamela and me for being so kind."

Since there was nothing more to be said or done until we knew what Michael would be telling Victor, Pamela suggested a nice stroll. "Walking will be the best medicine for both of us right now." We mounted the stairs to the front hall, put on our hats, coats and gloves and left the house to stroll the streets of Paris leaving Victor to his croissant and the morning edition of *The Herald*.

Chapter Nine

Someday beneath some hard
Capricious star—
Spreading its light a little
Over far,
We'll know you for the woman
That you are.

Djuna Barnes

Pamela and I set out for a stroll by the Seine. The sun was bright but friendly, not too hot. I wore a bonnet to keep my face from the rays and a light weight coat. It was a good idea to come outside. We walked for a while in silence before she began a conversation which, I am sure, was meant to distract me. Little did she realize what I had to contribute to the subject and, of course, it worked. I was distracted.

"Did you know that James Joyce is frightfully superstitious?" Pamela began. "That's what Djuna Barnes said. According to Djuna, he always carries his book of saints with him. Whether for protection or for reference, I don't know. One story she told me went like this. Soon before *Ulysses* was published, Joyce was walking with his wife and Djuna in the *Bois de Boulogne*. A complete stranger brushed against him and spoke to him in Latin. Joyce was upset. 'Trembling' is the word Djuna used to describe him. When asked what the matter was, he replied, 'That man, whom I have never seen before, said to me - in Latin - as he passed, 'You are an abominable writer.' That is a dreadful omen the day before publication of my novel.' True story, Libby."

I had been told by Miss Beach about Joyce's superstitious nature, but allowed Pamela to tell her tale uninterrupted. After a pause, it was my turn to share news about the great man. It had occurred one afternoon when I was returning home from an errand. I was walking up the interior stairway of our building.

"Oh, *pardon*" I exclaimed as I ran smack into a small bespectacled older man with a patch over one eye. He was coming slowly down the stairs from his apartment as I was running up to mine.

"Not at all, Mademoiselle," replied the gentleman. "I have a terrible time seeing these days … Operations only make it worse it seems … very frustrating indeed."

I thought his voice was admirably expressive.

"Oh, you are English. I am so sorry. I was in such a rush I didn't even look where I was going and …"

"Irish, and please do not worry your pretty little head over such a trifling matter." Looking unabashedly into my eyes, he continued, "Ah, yes, truly this is a propitious encounter after all. ' … though a day be as dense as a decade, no mouth has the right to set a mearbound to the march of a landsmaul, in half a sylb, helf a solb, holf a salb onward the beast of boredom, common sense …' Alas, to be imbued, as I am my dear lady, with that queer thing called genius!" His eye sparkled, his mouth smiled in a mischievous way, and with one hand on his cane, he waved his other hand rhythmically to the tune of his words. At first, I thought he was crazy, but there appeared to be something ingenious lurking behind the words; that is, until he said, "I look at you and see Beauty." Certainly, nobody had ever spoken to me this way before. I simply didn't know what to do, feeling at once flattered, embarrassed, and afraid. Unconsciously, I took a step back.

"Ah yes," he added without a pause, "be not afraid, it is but the platonic yearning of an old man. Such a face … and body, if I may be so bold?" His hand extended. I almost fell over, both from tripping on the next step and being addressed with such rhetoric. I knew I was blushing, but remembering my manners, took his hand.

"Thank you, sir." I tried not to look at his face and hoped he wouldn't feel the trembling in my hand. "Please allow me to introduce myself." Mustering up confidence, I continued. "I am Elisabeth Whitacker. I, that is, we live on the second floor." I was flustered but had accomplished my task.

Bowing, he tipped his hat. "How do you do? Joyce here, James Joyce of the third floor." Replacing his hat, he made a slight bow, smiled, turned, and headed slowly down the stairs talking to himself. "Ah, star of evil! Star of pain! High-hearted youth comes not again!"

Holding onto the railing, not believing what had just transpired, I was spellbound watching the little man descend the stairs ever so slowly, so cautiously. Outwardly, he was a strange, awkward sort of man; but his mind! Yes, his mind was lucid, exciting, even a bit enticing. Again, heat began to rise to my face.

Pamela enjoyed this little tale. Our stroll was a success. We both felt relaxed.

When we returned to Pamela's house, Victor informed us that Michael had left word he would be out of the apartment for the rest of the day. We planned to go pick up some more of my belongings, but first, Pamela suggested we look at her garden. We checked the plants and literally smelled the roses. My spirits were vastly improved.

"By the way, whatever happened to the, what do you call it? The 'reading' or 'charting' you were going to do for me?" I asked.

"We will go over that tonight after dinner if you wish."

I looked forward to the diversion.

Chapter Ten

The beauty of the world has two edges, one of laughter, one of anguish, cutting the heart asunder.
Virginia Woolf

Since Michael was certain to be out of the apartment, Pamela asked Frederick to drive us over for a quick check and a chance to put together some of my belongings since I didn't know how long I would be away.

Although I was beginning to feel relaxed enough to rationalize my situation, as soon as I opened the door to the apartment, that feeling vanished. I went limp. Pamela saw the change and put her arms around me for support both emotionally and physically. Slowly, we walked down the entry hall and entered the salon. Instinctively, I looked over to the hearth. The coals were cold now.

"I can't believe he was like that. Why did he deceive me?"

Seeing his naked torso, my first impulse had been to put my arms around him. I had actually thought that at long last I could share love with this man.

"Why? Oh, why?" Pamela held me as I sobbed. *What am I to do?* I thought about my parents. *What would they think? What could I tell them? In their eyes, I would be a failure. They wouldn't believe me.* Michael had been a perfect match. My moist eyes wandered from the ashes up to the mantel where I had placed a hand-blown Venetian glass vase with dried flowers. Only last week I had found the vase at the *Marché aux Puces* when some Parisian friends asked me out. It was the older couple I had met the summer I came to Paris with my parents and we had attended the Embassy party, the couple whose son had been killed at Verdun. The French had their sorrows, losing their best men, a whole generation killed in the War. Now it was my turn to feel personal sorrow. Above the vase, I had hung an engraving of the Eternal City. Pamela's eyes had followed the same route. Suddenly, simultaneously, we both cried out, "Uncle William?" "Monsignor Hemmick?"

Color came back to my cheeks. Immediately a plan took form. Maybe my uncle could help. I could take the train to Rome.

"First you must write to your uncle requesting an interview. It should not be too specific. Wait until you see him and get a chance to know him before you plunge into such a serious request," advised Pamela.

Quickly, we went into the bedroom, gathered some clothes and toiletries and descended the stairs to the Duesenberg. Frederick was not daydreaming this time. When he opened the door, I grinned.

That night at dinner, Victor gave an account of his meeting with Michael. It had been awkward. Michael had not explained his behavior.

"Instead, he said that he was concerned about you. Clearly, he intends to make neither mention of nor apology for his proclivity. Ideally, Libby, he wants you to return to the apartment and work out an arrangement or an understanding."

I was irate. "Victor, I know that I told you I would be willing to talk to him, try to work something out, but to make any arrangement to stay with that man? No."

Victor gave me a pat and held my hand.

"How can he expect me to go on living with him knowing what I do?"

Pamela then told Victor about our plan for me to visit my Uncle in Rome. Victor thought this would be the ideal solution and agreed that the trip, plus the change of scenery, would be most beneficial.

After dinner, Pamela and I went into the library on the other side of the entry hall. She was going to share her research on my chart. Victor was more than happy to give his study over to "the ladies," he said. Besides, it would be much easier for him to spread his papers out over the dining room table.

The library was quite small. Bookcases lined all the walls, with the exception of the doorway on one wall and the window on the other. Against the wall, they had placed a small red velvet settee. The books covered every possible topic, from the classics, including the complete collection of Alexander Dumas, to *Plutarch's Lives* in both Greek and English. There were also books in Latin and a grand collection of modern novels in both French and English. On one shelf I saw a collection called *The Chronicles of America Series*. "Oh, yes," Pamela responded with laughter when I inquired about those, "we Brits are fascinated with *the colonies*." On another wall, there were books about finance, science and mathematics. The scope of subjects captivated me.

Below the window sill, next to the settee, was a small inlaid wooden table. A large blue vase filled with flowers from the garden stood next to the wedding photograph of Victor and Pamela. A square teak game table and two high backed chairs had been placed in front of the shelves. To the side of the table was a standing lamp with an overhanging Tiffany glass shade depicting leaves and flowers. Light also came from wall sconces placed to the side of the door and window. A large, red Oriental rug covered most of the wood plank floor.

We pulled out the chairs at the game table and sat down. Pamela produced a pile of papers, which she spread across the table announcing, "This is your chart, Libby."

On top of the pile was a large piece of cardboard depicting a star, names and lines. Notes were written on the various sides of the star and strange marks appeared within each point.

"Oh my. What does all this mean?"

"This chart represents the planets, the sun and the moon at the time of your birth. Since we don't know the exact time, this will be close enough to tell us much about your personality, about the way you cope with events in your life, about your parents and much more."

"Please, go on. I won't interrupt again."

"Oh, go ahead and ask questions. Now here you have Mars squaring your sun. Do you see this line? This shows anger. But don't worry. Knowing these traits can only help you. You are a strong woman, but you can be extravagant. Leo, which is your birth sign, likes to be flashy, but other signs on your chart tend to offset this somewhat. Intellectually, you veer toward a conservative point of view." Pamela traced a few lines, made some more notes, then looked at me to be sure I was reacting favorably to this information.

I must have appeared to be attentive because she continued. "Be careful with finances. You have many air signs around you. You also have great intellect. Your Aquarian moon is very powerful. You want independence. Individual rights are important to you. That is the moon in Jupiter. Jupiter is in the tenth house." Pamela showed the sign and its position on the chart.

"Pamela, I don't understand all this. Jupiter, Leo, the moon. I mean, how can I incorporate these ideas into my life? Independence, for example. How can a woman be independent? My father controls the financial side of our family. He even made arrangements with Michael. I don't know what they are. I have no money of my own. Which brings up another point. How can I ask Michael for the money I will need to go to Rome?"

True to *my* chart, I could feel anger mounting. It was really my money.

"Let me discuss this with Victor." Pamela and Victor had a singular relationship. Everything was discussed between them. Victor believed that should anything happen to him, Pamela needed to understand how to continue the lifestyle they had established. This meant that she thoroughly comprehend the banking business and the value of investments. She was wary of warning me, but she knew that Victor was uneasy about the stock market in the United States. Most of his clients were Americans and had invested deeply in the market. It was not his place as a banker to advise them but, from time to time, he did voice his concern. Pamela knew that my father was also a banker and, thank heavens, should be in a good position. However, how he would feel about my problem with Michael was something Pamela, Victor and I could only guess.

The next day at breakfast, I surprised my hosts by announcing that I would return to the apartment. I needed to be direct with Michael. Obviously, I could not stay forever with Pamela and Victor although their kindness was most appreciated. This was my problem. I was determined to solve it. While Pamela and Victor were sleeping, I had gathered my belongings and gathered up my courage as well. I needed to return to my own apartment. Both Statlers assured me it was a pleasure and absolutely no problem having me stay with them.

Patricia Daly-Lipe

Once resolved, however, I was adamant. They called Frederick to drive me home and bade me a concerned farewell.

Chapter Eleven

Experience is the name so many people give to their mistakes.

Oscar Wilde

"I didn't plan it this way, Libby. I suspected my sexual interests were, shall we say, different, but boys do these things when they are adolescents and then go on to be husbands and fathers."

I couldn't believe this was true. "Michael, you are not an adolescent now. You chose to marry me as an adult."

Pamela was having a similar conversation at her house. Victor had said something about boys experimenting. She was shocked. "Boys do that in school?"

She paused, incredulous. Finally, hoping she would receive the answer she wanted, she had to ask, 'Did you, Victor?'"

"No, my dear Pamela, I did not."

Of course, she couldn't leave it there. She had to probe and ask how he knew. He told her that he was approached. He explained that in boarding school you have little privacy. You know what is going on. He repeated that "boys do, uh, experiment when they reach puberty." He said that in many boys' schools, "they give out pills to, shall we say, keep the excitement level down."

But at the apartment on the *Île St. Louis*, our conversation had become nasty before reverting back to school days.

"Are you telling me that all boys experiment?" I had asked Michael.

"To some degree or another. It is all so external with a male, so a young man finds it rather exciting when he can … I can't believe I am having this conversation with you." He began to walk away.

"But I am so glad you are," I cried, grasping his arm. "After all, I have absolutely no experience, so it is, if nothing else, educational for me to know these things." *How I could even want to know these things was beyond me now. He was a monster, a misfit, a fiend.* But then, I was digesting the information, trying to make sense of it all. I paced the floor searching for answers and attempted to calm down. Finally, I managed to pull myself together, refocus and ask, "I still do not understand, Michael. Where does that leave us?"

Michael didn't look cross, but he didn't look embarrassed either. He simply stated his facts looking almost through me as if he had memorized the lines. "Libby, you are a beautiful woman, a bit headstrong, but gracious and charming with people. I don't know if I will ever be able to satisfy you. I need time."

I considered his suggestion. Could he change? Could I ever forget what I saw? Could I submit to his touching me knowing what he had done? The more I thought about it, the less likely our being together appeared. I walked over to the window and looked out at the river Seine. Across the flowing waters was *Notre Dame*. Would I find the answer within her gracious walls?

"What about an annulment?"

Michael's face looked grim.

I persevered, "That way, we are both free to start over."

Michael seemed to have already considered this option. "I am afraid not," he answered looking beyond me at I know not what.

"Why not? We can ask Uncle William to make the arrangements and …"

"You can expect no help from Uncle William."

"But Michel, remember that my uncle has been through the worst horrors known to man during the war. Helping us now would be nothing compared to that."

"I'm sorry, Libby." Michael turned his back and walked to the other end of the room.

At the same time that I was confronted with this enigma, Pamela's discussion with Victor was have a similar but different twist. Later, she confided, "Victor shared something personal about your family with me."

"Please," I begged, "tell me everything."

"Your Uncle Christian is swishy. Libby, I must admit that I wasn't surprised. Actually, I always suspected there was something strange or different about his so-called marriage to Alice Barney."

What Pamela did not tell me until much later was that, according to Victor, Michael was playing hardball. He did not intend to expose himself. His trump card was this information about my own family. At the time, all she said to me was, "There is no way that the Monsignor will help you, Libby."

My confrontation with Michael had left me thinking selfishly, but realistically, about what kind of life this would be for me. I remember how much control it took not to burst into tears. Just the thought of being imprisoned in a loveless marriage was demoralizing. I was also worried and scared to think of being by myself. Our conversation had suddenly stopped. We had reached a kind of stand off. I remained at one end of the room, he at the other busy filling his pipe as though the world had not fallen in.

Finally, he broke the silence. In a tone that was barely above a whisper, he pleaded, "Libby, you may not believe me, but I am sorry."

I could only stare at him, incredulous. This man whom I had married was repugnant, egocentric and inconsiderate. This was not the man I had dreamed about. This was not the life I had envisioned. Simply looking at him made me cold. I picked up my cashmere sweater and wrapped myself in its warmth. Then, just when I had given up any hope for happiness, happiness of any kind, Michael announced, "By the way, Philippe asked us both to his Mother's château this weekend. Naturally, he knows nothing of our difficulty. It seems his Mother is most anxious to talk with you. She thinks she and her late husband met your Grandfather when he was the U.S. Consul in Switzerland."

My anger with Michael evaporated at the prospect of seeing Philippe. I had to turn away and look out the window to disguise my delight. The bright blue Seine seemed to be smiling back as she tossed her waters and flashed her white foam against the stone walls encasing the *Île St. Louis. "Sous le Pont Mirabeau coule la*

Seine et nos amours …" (Under Mirabeau Bridge flows the Seine and our loves) The poem would come back to me again and again in the years to come. The next lines revealed what I was yet to learn: *'Faut-il qu'il m'en souvient / L'amour venait toujours après la peine'* (Must I remember that love only comes after suffering and sorrow)? I turned. Michael, with his arms folded across his chest, was looking at me quite smugly.

"I will accept the invitation but I'll beg off at the last minute," he said patronizingly. "You can go without me."

For the first time, my attraction to Philippe was not accompanied by guilt. If Michael had seen through me, then what I saw in his face was relief.

Chapter Twelve

He rode upon a cherub, and did fly: yea, he did fly
upon the wings of the wind.

Bible, Psalms 18:10

"I am so sorry Michael could not join us," Philippe was saying as we drove out to his château north of Paris.

"Are you really, um, sorry I mean?" The words came out of my mouth before I realized how brazen they sounded. My face turned scarlet, and heat rose to the top of my head.

Philippe nearly swerved off the road. When he regained his composure, he added, "*Maman* will be delighted to see you. She has looked forward to this."

I worried that I had truly shocked him with my audacity. I couldn't tell what he was thinking by looking at his face but I felt uncomfortable. It was a poor start for a weekend I had looked forward to so much. I was afraid the impression I left with Philippe the last time we were together was equally inept.

Months ago, Michael had given in to my wanting to know more about his work. Left alone every day to my own resources had allowed me to explore Paris, but I was curious about the business of aviation. So one morning Michael agreed to drive me to the aerodrome. This time I was clad appropriately having chosen a casual cotton skirt and blouse, my blue cashmere sweater and, most important, flat shoes. I was ready for the wind and the dirt of the *Le Bourget*.

As soon as we arrived, Michael leaped out of the motor car, started toward the hangar, then paused in mid-stride returning to give me his hand.

"Thank you, Michael." I squeezed his arm. "I will be fine. You go ahead. Just tell me where to look."

"I will let you know when I find out from the others what the plans are for today. Enjoy the sun. Stroll around. Oh, and I'll send someone out with a chair."

I laughed. He was like a small child with a new toy; he couldn't wait to climb into the cockpit. Whether I was there or not, he was going to enjoy himself. As Michael ran off to the hangar, I found a nice green grassy patch in the shade of a tree and was about to settle down when a voice softly called, "*Bonjour*, my lovely friend."

I spun around. There he was. Philippe was smiling and as he came close, he was staring directly into my eyes. He kissed me on both cheeks and then held me away with one hand on each of my shoulders. "How would you like to go flying?"

He was serious. This wasn't a joke. I could not fathom the idea. *Me? In an aeroplane?* I remembered the conversation about Lindbergh's flight among Michael's guests. *How uncomfortable, loud, dangerous ...*

"*Me?* Fly? *Me?*"

"But, of course. My little biplane plane is ready. She would be proud to have you aboard."

"But Michael is going up and ..."

"We'll surprise him. Can't wait to see his face when he catches sight of you in the air."

"Do you really think it would be all right? I mean I don't have any of the equipment, the ..."

"I have it all. Let me get everything together. It is important to dress warmly; there is no windshield, just a screen in front. Every three hundred meters above the ground, the temperature drops a little over one degree and also, there is the wind chill factor."

"That's every thousand feet," I gasped.

"We wear leather jackets, jodhpurs ..."

My face turned bright red. "You mean I am to wear pants?"

"I have some you could wear, but maybe this once we can ... no we can't. You *must* wear jodhpurs. And high boots, a scarf, a helmet and goggles."

Twenty minutes later, I was transformed. The pants were somewhat loose and long legged. I had to roll up the cuffs and to keep them from falling down, I used my scarf as a cinch at the waist. I also didn't want my garter belt to show. I kept my sweater on and put the jacket over the top of it. Philippe had thought of everything. There were boots and socks and a cap with goggles and men's gloves. When I came out of the rest room, I felt like a walking mummy. Cautiously and awkwardly, I approached his plane.

Philippe was polite. He didn't say a word about how I looked, but I would have understood if he laughed. I felt ridiculous. Taking my hand, he walked me over to the plane.

"Step up on the left wing near the side of the cockpit. That is the rear of the engine in front of you. Place both feet on the wingwalk and step, one leg at a time, onto the seat and then slide into the cockpit."

I couldn't believe I was doing this, but Philippe's voice was smooth and strong. It wasn't fear I was feeling, only a burgeoning excitement.

"You sit in front. That way I can see for takeoff and landing. Oh, and prepare for a blast of wind when the engine starts up. Adjust your goggles and attach the cinch on the belt across your lap. Tell me when you're ready."

Philippe stepped into the cockpit behind me. He could not see my trembling. Excitement was beginning to be replaced by fear as I waited for the flight to begin.

Philippe's assistant walked to the front of the plane and, putting one foot behind the other, placed his hands on the wooden propeller, turning it one complete revolution counter-clockwise, then another.

Anticipating my questions about the man turning the propellers by hand, Philippe called out, "He's filling all the cylinders with fuel before I start up."

Then to the assistant he shouted, "Ready?" The assistant nodded. "Here goes." His helper grasped the propeller with both hands and pulled it downward quickly, keeping his balance so as not to fall into the deadly mechanism as the propellers spun around on their own, so fast they became a blur. At the same time, the noise was earsplitting. I could barely hear Philippe as he shouted, "Fuel, okay. Tach, oil pressure, good. We're all set." He turned the plane out to the field and facing the wind, revved the engine. The wind blew back on us with tremendous force. I clutched the railing bar in front of me so tightly my fingers throbbed. The plane began to shake. I grit my teeth and prepared to face my biggest adventure yet. I, Libby Whitacker, was going to fly.

"I have to check the rpm," he shouted.

I had no idea what he was talking about.

"1250; ready to go." Philippe advanced the throttle and the plane began to run like a race car across the grass, then before I knew it, we were up. The wind blasting against my face, my eyes stung even behind the goggles; the helmet clung to my head like a glove, but it kept me warm.

"Sorry about the oil," yelled Philippe as some of the caster oil from the engine was being whipped by the wind and splashed against the screen in front. It was much smaller than a window and offered little protection, but being so tense, I barely noticed the oil. Clutching the panel in front of me, hardly able to breathe, I said a silent prayer as the plane jerked left then right. Suddenly, the plane dropped. Thankfully, it came right back up, but as it did, my entire life flew past my mind's eye as I prepared to die. My lungs were ready to burst until I realized that I had been holding my breath. Each time the plane seemed to be falling, my heart pounded hard against my chest. And each time, just when I had given up hope - probably less than thirty seconds at a time - the plane rose again. Gradually, as the wind blew forcefully against my face, it gave me reassurance and I heard myself shouting for joy even though my eyes were still closed. Instinctively, I trusted the noisy engine and was convinced, or at least was willing to convince myself, as long as I could hear the racket, we would stay aloft. After counting to ten, I opened my eyes and dared to look down. The earth was at least one hundred feet below.

When the plane leveled, I kept my eyes open. What I saw held me spellbound. Through the wires crisscrossing between the wings, the countryside, the hedgerows, a stream, the barn that served as a hangar and the tops of the trees just behind and below all looked like a painting. Mingling lines, the roads, fences, stream beds, crop boundaries, all coming and going. I was seeing the earth as never before. It seemed both real and not real. Looking straight ahead, to the side of the twirling propellers, I could make out the mountains, soft blue-grey in the distance and once I thought I saw a hint of the Paris skyline. The view went to the rim of the world. Being in the air, looking down, presented me with a new perspective, so different from what you could see riding in an automobile or on a train or a wagon or just walking.

Although my head vibrated from the deafening roar of the engine, I could also discern a whistling sound. It came from the wind crossing over the wings, two sets of wings above and below where I sat. They nodded and dipped as if playing with the breeze and seemed to take on an intelligence of their own. At the same time I enjoyed the movement in space and the vista below, yet a part of me remained a bit apprehensive. Trying to talk myself out of fear, I reasoned that if I could concentrate on the wind sounds, the whoosh and whistle, it would make me feel secure. But, in the end, knowing that Philippe was piloting this plane was what gave me confidence. Wanting to thank him, I tried to turn around, but the restraining straps did not permit much movement. As we continued over the land and below the wisps of clouds, I began to relax. Soon, I forgot fear and simply enjoyed the feel of flight. Philippe always warned me when he was going to turn or dip. "Do not be afraid, we are very secure," he would shout; at least I thought that was what he was saying.

As if playing a game, we waved at people in open coupes, bicyclists, farmers in the fields and children playing in their gardens who stopped their play to look up when they heard the drone of the motor. I marveled at the geometric patterns stretching out to the foothills and the lovely colors of the fields and the mosaics made by the streams meandering across mud flats. I was mesmerized and had become even immune to the noise. I was also oblivious of time, but Philippe must have known that he should not venture too far nor stay up too long. All too soon, he began his descent.

The landing brought me back to reality. Again, I closed my eyes when the plane lurched and dipped. This time my prayer was for a safe landing, but my eyes only stayed closed a moment. I watched as the plane approached the grass. Then, looking over the side, it suddenly seemed as if we were going to crash. Terrified, I think I screamed. But when the wheels bounced, confidence returned. Once the plane was traveling down the runway, Philippe pulled back the throttle to slow down. We had landed safely! I wanted to whoop for joy and tell everyone I knew. As Philippe taxied the biplane back to the point of departure, I searched for onlookers who might be outside the barns or in their motor cars, but saw no one.

By the time we pulled up to the flying school building, it was mid afternoon. As Philippe helped me climb out of the cockpit, I was finally relieved that I had agreed to wear jodhpurs. Then, before we saw him, we heard Michael shouting. When we did locate him, it was clear he was not pleased. A big scowl crossed his face. Perhaps he was jealous; upset knowing someone else had taken his wife up before he had. Or maybe it was neither jealousy nor resentment. He was simply shocked and amazed that I would actually consent to be taken up in the air at all. He mumbled as much to Philippe as he opened the car door for me to get in, not even noting my strange attire.

It took me awhile to change out of the cumbersome outfit and back into my skirt. I hoped no one else had come in to use the toilet since my clothes were hung on a nail behind the door. The facility was primitive and for me, a glance at the ways of men. There was no mirror, no brush or comb, an old piece of broken soap by the basin and a rag for a towel. Nevertheless, I was grateful for the opportunity to fly and was not beyond coping with a little mess as long as I looked decent when I came out. When I did emerge from the lavatory at the back of the hangar, the two men were waiting for me in front, standing side by side but not speaking. Philippe took the borrowed clothing, acknowledged my thanks and, looking grim, somewhat stiffly walked away.

During the drive back to Paris, I was bubbly like a child, chatting about the views and the wind and the sounds of the whistling wires, intoxicated with the excitement of flight. Michael didn't say a word.

Chapter Thirteen

O seasons, O châteaux,
What soul is without flaws?

Arthur Rimbaud

My mind shifted to the present. Philippe and I were in his little car, not the biplane. We were going to meet his mother at the family château and because Michael had reneged at the last minute, we were alone without the fright of flight or supervision to intervene. I should have been more discreet and not made such a gauche remark about being sorry that Michael was not coming. That was a poor beginning to what I was hoping would be a delightful weekend jaunt. There was a long silence. Finally I mustered up the gumption to initiate a new conversation.

"Paris is beautiful and exciting and I am delighted to be living there, but I am so happy to be able to come to the country. Look at those poplar trees. The way they line all the roads is spectacular. They're positively regal. We don't have such grand avenues in my country."

Philippe appeared to relax at this, a more innocent opening. "Yes, the poplars are lovely in the daytime but one must be very careful driving at night. A bit too much wine and one might steer right into a majestic trunk and the trunk would win." The tension dissipated. We laughed. The rest of the drive was spent on neutral topics like the weather, the landscape, and French history. All too soon we arrived at the de Beau's estate. The large iron gates stood open, framing the entrance to a long, narrow cypress tree-lined dirt drive. On the right, a small lake reflected the parkland beyond. A rowboat was pulled up on the far shore. "I used to row every day when I was a boy," Philippe said pointing to the boat. Through a grove of trees, I could see a small patch of grazing land and a flower garden; then we arrived at the green lawns of *Fontaine-les-Nonnes*.

The château was a surprise. Once a convent in the 12th century, its architecture was beautiful, warm and inviting, more like a home than a château. Philippe watched me as I absorbed the beauty of the estate. "It was originally built in the 12th century, but most of the building was destroyed in the 100 Years War. Then at the end of the 15th century it was rebuilt so most of what you see emanates from that era." The façade reflected the glow of the afternoon sun, giving the structure stateliness without foreboding formality. A spacious lawn ran down the front of the building. To one side stood a small round structure, its walls completely covered with ivy. "That's the *pigeonnier*," Philippe pointed out, "where pigeons and doves roost."

I loved the elfin building. There was sweetness and warmth and gentleness about it.

"It is lovely, isn't it? Remarkable that some caring individual many years ago took the time to draw up architectural plans and build a home for the birds. And behind," continued Philippe, "is the *"jardin potager* – how would you call it in English? – soup garden. We try to grow all our own vegetables."

I was enchanted. There was also something about the buildings and the land that reminded me of my grandparents' summer home in Canada where I was born. Called *Idalia*, it too had been a stately building, three stories high, each floor a bit smaller and capped by a cupola. Surrounded by a porch, the house appeared round from a distance. Behind the house were steep cliffs leading down to the edge of Lake Ontario. I remember so much activity as servants bustled around serving tea, making up beds, sweeping, polishing the cars, looking after children, tending to incessant guests. Since the family was originally very large, there were over a dozen bedrooms.

But unlike *Idalia*, the château did not appear quite as large nor was there any obvious activity. Everything about this place was tranquil.

The *Comtesse* came down the front steps as the elegant Bugatti pulled up the gravel drive. As soon as we descended from the car, Philippe gave his mother a kiss on both cheeks and hurriedly explained that my husband had been detained in Paris. His mother gave her son a searching glance before taking my hand and greeting me warmly.

"Please have our guest's bags put in the little blue room, Philippe dear." Before he could comply, an elderly woman wearing an apron, a long blue cotton dress and flat shoes with ties appeared and took the bags. I noticed her give a slight bow as she walked past the Countess.

"Antoinette will show you to your room. You no doubt wish to freshen up after the drive. We shall have tea in the sunroom when you are rested."

I was not in the least tired. I didn't wish to be rude but I was eager to see the property before the sun went down. The lake and the gardens and the *pigeonnier* intrigued me. "The air is so fresh and we have been sitting for so long," I began, hoping my accent was clear and precise. The *Comtesse* smiled. She could see I had pluck. I just hoped she didn't think I was without manners. On the other hand, hopefully she should be pleased that her home held such appeal.

"I am glad that you like *Fontaine-les-Nonnes*. When you come down, I will walk with you to the lake, but then I must make arrangements for tea."

The Comtesse de Beau was petite and fragile. As was the custom, she had dressed only in black since the death of her husband. The ankle length dress had long sleeves and a lace collar that seemed to be tight around her throat. The black accentuated her delicate appearance.

Philippe caught up with us as we stood by the side of the sparkling water.

"We used to have picnics here, in the shade of the trees. My husband loved the water and this small man-made lake was as much as we could hope for in this part of the world. He used to take the children out in a boat like the one over there. It always made me anxious. I cannot swim, you see. But the children were delighted to tour the lake with their father."

She must miss him very much, I thought, knowing better than to voice such a comment.

Patricia Daly-Lipe

Philippe came over and gave his mother a hug, then turned to me. "Come, let me show you around." Without waiting for a reply, he took me by the hand. "We will see you back at the house, *maman*?" But he didn't need an answer. His mother had already begun the short walk back.

We followed narrow paths through verdant woods and green, lush mini-parks, past the tool house and the fenced-in 'soup' garden. Philippe ushered me into the small chapel. Inside were the tombs of nuns whose inscriptions dated back to 1105.

"During the war, the Germans occupied this place, but the chapel was completely protected. My parents had put up signs saying 'Danger Explosives' on all sides."

Behind the chapel, chickens rushed about the haystacks and in the distance, enormous work horses plowed the fields.

We strolled through the flower garden where big red and yellow dahlias bloomed

"Please wait one moment," he requested, as he climbed over the fence into the garden. When he returned, he took my hand and led me to another fence. On the other side was a large pasture. He whistled and from the far end of the field, two forms materialized. They were two black horses. As they galloped toward us, their manes flying, their tails flowing behind, their hooves pointing, I started to move back. "Don't worry, they will stop at the fence," laughed Philippe. The handsome pair did just that, halting right in front of us, nostrils flaring as they exhaled mists of air with loud snorts. Their ears tipped forward, focused on Philippe. The one with a white blaze running down his nose raised his head and whinnied.

"Is he unfriendly?" I asked.

"Unfriendly? Certainly not. He's impatient. He is the youngster. They always expect a treat when I whistle. Here, give him one of these." From his back pocket, he produced two carrots he must have retrieved over the fence of the vegetable garden. I was captivated.

All the way back to the house, as Philippe chatted, I couldn't help laughing and smiling.

"And so, are you ready for tea now, young lady?" Philippe asked as we entered the house. I nodded. "I think *maman* is in the sunroom waiting for us."

124

We sat in the sunroom, which was lit artificially at this hour. The sun had set, but in my heart, I felt its warmth. I had glanced at the mirror in the guest bathroom. My cheeks were rosy and, although my hair needed combing, I found myself looking at a happier version of myself than I had seen in a long time.

Comtesse de Beau served tea, holding the china pot amazingly steady with her long, thin fingers. She wore no nail polish, makeup or rouge and her remarkably unblemished skin had few lines. *Had I misjudged her age?* The black clothes were deceiving. She sat upright, not touching the back of the elegant Louis XVI chair just as I had been taught by Mademoiselle to sit. *"A young lady must never slouch."* To be perfectly poised all the time was tiring, but the *Comtesse* appeared quite comfortable. I could not imagine her sitting any other way. Though petite, the *Comtesse's* demeanor and discourse evoked immense energy. She was well versed in many subjects. Her late husband had been a historian and I deduced that he had shared much of his research with her.

I tried to imagine what it was like for a lady of her, or of my mother's age to be living in such a turbulent time compared to the world they knew before the war. Here in the country, history and time stood still with few outward changes. On the contrary, in Paris, although the buildings remained the same, with the exception of the Eiffel Tower - once the tallest building in the world - people were changing and their habits were changing. Only recently, ladies had given up wearing corsets. It was Paul Poiret, the French fashion designer and decorator who, as part of his innovative fashions, replaced the corset with the girdle. He had also revived the high-waisted Empire style, but all that was before the Great War, the era when these ladies enjoyed their youth, when girls dared not show their ankles and words were spoken with care and accuracy. In those days, nobody knew what the *heebie-jeebies* meant. It was a time when music was soft, unlike the jazz that has become so popular in Paris these days. I pictured the turn of the century to be a time when romance came easily in the soft glow of candles or gas flames, not in bright electric lights and on big screens in the cinemas.

It was quiet here in the country, but in Paris, the noise from motor cars was almost as loud as the calls of the vendors. But when the *Comtesse* was young, it would have been the clip clop of horses' hooves on the cobbles and the rolling of the steel wheels as carriages passed by that she heard through the windows of her home in the city. Then automobiles came to the streets of Paris. At first, they were slow and quiet. The maximum speed had been ten miles an hour at the turn of the century when my mother was a young bride. My thoughts were cut short when the *Comtesse*, after quietly sipping her tea, picked up the thread of conversation.

"I am afraid what my husband said is true, history repeats itself. I worry that the Great War will not be the last of its kind. I pray every night my son, and someday his children, will be spared the horror to which his father was subjected."

Philippe informed me that *Fontaines-les-Nonnes* was headquarters of Colonel Bon during the Battle of the Marne. "It was fought from the ninth until the thirteenth of September, 1914. My parents and I were right in the middle of it. I was only nine." With a look of disapproval from his mother, he abruptly stopped speaking, picked up his cup and quietly sipped his tea. I learned later that his father had died only months after the battle.

We sat sipping tea observing a respectful silence. When everyone seemed more relaxed, I decided to broach a new subject. "*Madame Comtesse*, I believe you said that you knew my Grandfather."

"Oh, yes indeed. Such a distinguished and multi-talented man." The more she spoke, the more I wished I had known him. At the same time, I began to feel accepted as a genuine friend of the de Beau family. This was proven later when Philippe had gone out to do some errands. His mother confided that she preferred romantic novels to nonfiction and scientific journals, not a fact she wished her son to know. Thoroughly French, the *Comtesse* delighted in philosophy and the arts. I told her about my visits to the Louvre. She was intrigued by my description of the *Surréalistes* exhibit.

Chapter Fourteen

To express the emotions of life is to live.
To express the life of emotions is to make art.

Jane Heap

A few days after our venture to *Le Bourget* to welcome Lindbergh, Mr. Brennan had called to ask if I might enjoy accompanying him and his daughter to an art reception. Michael was going out that evening with a group of aeronautical experts, so I felt that it would be quite appropriate for me to join the Brennans.

"It's an exhibit of some of the *Surréalistes'* work including Eileen Agar. She's British. Dad met her in England. She has quite a following here in Paris." Gina was bubbling with excitement when they came to pick me up. This was her world and I was eager to be introduced to it.

"Will your work be on exhibit?" I asked innocently.

Only two days younger than I, Gina was a serious student of art and envisioned a career as a painter. She had such self-assurance. Here was I, the same age, supposedly secure and stable as a married woman, but without the slightest idea what I was supposed to be doing with my life.

"My work on exhibit?" Gina cut into my thoughts. "Not yet; I mean, I am not quite ready to show my paintings and drawings. I am only a student now. I have yet to find my niche."

"I love your work, dear. You mustn't be so modest," rejoined her proud father.

"Thank you, Daddy, but I really would prefer waiting a little. Here we are." The car stopped in front of a gallery.

"Bonsoir, Mesdames, Monsieur, soyez les bienvenues." The doorman opened the passenger side first and saluted us. Mr. Brennan gave the man a tip and escorted us into a lively gathering. Besides the paintings, there was an eclectic array of people. Here, it was

as it used to be. People's attire identified their social class. I saw a woman, probably in her mid forties, dressed in a long yellow gown leaning against a pillar smoking a cigar. In the opposite corner stood a young man with a shaven head talking to a dwarf with a green cape wrapped around his entire little body. In the center of the room, a fat man wearing a pink suit was saddled up to an elegant lady smoking a cigarette that extended from a long narrow puffer. It was their enthusiasm for the avant-garde offerings lining the walls that brought such seemingly dissimilar individuals together. A fascinating mix.

"Bohemian, but most entertaining, don't you think?" asked Mr. Brennan as if reading my mind. I blushed. My face must have reflected my thoughts.

"Have you been to *La Cigale?*" This came from a lady wearing an elegant sequined black sweater, obviously a Chanel. "It's on the *Boulevard Rochechouart*. Derain and Braque have created sets for the ballets of Milhaud and Poulenc. Chanel did some of the costumes. I see you have been to her salon."

"No, yes, I mean ..." Flustered, I didn't recognize half of those names.

"Oh yes," continued the lady, oblivious of my ignorance. "In fact, I understand Jean Cocteau is doing an adaptation of *Romeo and Juliet* there."

"Really. How terribly exciting." I tried to sound familiar with the subject.

"Are you talking about the *Cigale?*" piped up another guest. "Only a third rate music hall but everyone who is anyone goes there. And then, of course, it is off to *Graff's* for supper."

"I hear there was a fight there the other night...at *La Cigale* I mean," offered the lady with the sequined sweater.

"A fight. Good heavens, why?"

"Well," the lady began in a voice so soft that everyone around her had to lean in to hear what she was saying. "... some of our artistic friends ... you know, the *Surréalistes* ... well, they were angry with Satie for allowing Picabia to make the sets."

A chorus of *Ohhhs* echoed around her.

"Picabia is, as you must know, a great enemy of Picasso."
Ahhh.

"It was the *Surréalistes* who started the fight."

I listened to all the chatter and sighs and realized how much I had to learn about Paris, the artists, the places, the people. *Goodness knows, my life has been incredibly sheltered.*

"I am so glad you asked me to come, Mr. Brennan. I wish I could go out every night. There seems to be so much happening that I don't even know about."

"We are pleased you are enjoying yourself. You must let Gina explain this exhibit to you. I am afraid it is quite beyond me."

Gina, overhearing her father's comment, took me by the hand and led me to a wall of paintings on the far side of the room away from the boisterous crowd.

"The manifesto of the *Surréalistes* is: explore the 'more real than real world behind the real'." Gina laughed at my quizzical expression. "No I am not crazy. It does make sense. You see, it has to do with psychic experience. André Breton defined Surrealism three years ago, in 1924. He said their aim was to resolve two contradictory phenomena, dreams and reality, and create a new reality, a *surréalité*, which will, as he said, 'reestablish man as psychology instead of anatomy.'"

"Intuitive reality, that's what it is all about. 'Intueti' is Greek for 'to see inside'," chimed in a young man in baggy pants and a full blowsy red shirt. "Not to say that it is one without the other: the inner domain versus the outer. Nor is it one and the other at once. Hardly. Instead, it is one after the other; a kind of attraction, an *interpenetration*, if you know what I mean." His eyes focused, as the French so naturally do, directly into mine. I couldn't escape his gaze. Only able to muster a nod, I quickly turned my attention away from him and toward the paintings.

"Don't worry, Libby, he's hardly a threat. I have seen him before attending lectures at the Sorbonne. He is quite attractive though, isn't he?" Gina took me by the arm and led me to another wall of paintings. "You need to understand that some of these paintings were the result of the artist being able to disengage herself from all external stimuli and from all the logic of rules, the shoulds and coulds, and allow her creative powers to flow. Have you read any of Freud's work?"

"No, not really. I have heard discussions of his great findings about the unconscious mind. I wish I knew more." Here it was again. Great artists, authors, and aviators. Incredible movements of thought, discoveries inside the mind of the human psyche and outside, the mechanics of flight. It made me dizzy, all the many fields of knowledge I was being introduced to and at such a fast pace. The world was changing and I was changing with it. I could sympathize with the *Surréalistes*; reality was obviously more than getting up in the morning.

"You see this one?" Gina pointed to an illustration I recognized simply as a contorted and confusing canvas. Images unrelated to each other were vying for attention, or so it appeared to me, attracting and repelling like the young man had stated.

"So the idea is to bring the subconscious to the surface?" I asked meekly.

"Absolutely. I see you are acquainted with psychoanalysis. Fascinating science, don't you think? Carl Jung, a *protégé* of Freud, has written that painting is one way to interpret dreams. Freud asked, 'How does the painting help you interpret the dream?' Jung replied, 'Because, like a dream, I don't attempt to control either the content or the form of the painting. I let it flow spontaneously from my unconscious.' Studying his painting, Jung was sure he could learn the content of his dream."

I must have looked skeptical.

"You see," explained Gina with the authority of a good student, "fantasies come from the unconscious. There is no suitable language, but painting that can capture its essence." Pointing to another canvas, "You see, this is more than so-called abstract art. Abstract means to take from something observed, as from nature and convert it to some type of pattern or design. In a non-representational painting, some fragments of nature can be identified, but the *Surréalistes* go a step further. The surrealist artist is concerned with the subject, so there should be a recognizable theme the spectator can identify."

I was trying hard to understand, but my eyes weren't seeing all this intellectual information.

"What have we here?" I had gone back to the painting with the unrelated objects dancing around. "It is like some kind of crazy dream."

"Precisely. You see what Jung was talking about. And why shouldn't the dream be as real as our waking moments?"

I couldn't help smiling.

"*Surréalistes* are not only artists; they can be authors and poets as well. Perhaps you would like to read some of Paul Valery's work?" ventured Gina. "He feels all things are part of a single whole; nothing is casual, nothing is alone. Truth must come through more than the syntax."

A voice interjected, "'The independence of objects is ... only an appearance. Their apartness, their noncontact, is appearance. And my illusion of liberty ...'"

"Oh daddy, you are too, too clever. Have you seen everything?"

"Enough. Let's go out for *souper*. Maybe we can find one other person to join us and play *Cadavre Exquis?*"

"Cadavre Exquis?"

"A popular *Surréaliste* game. You'll see."

"Yes," added Gina, as we reached the entrance and were preparing to find our coats and leave. "It is a kind of unconscious experience like automatic writing. Did you know that way back in the fifteenth century Leonardo da Vinci suggested the possibilities of self-revelation through automatic drawing?"

"Ah yes, but have you seen the work of Salvador Dali? He once said that he was actually terrified by the images which appeared on his canvases!" This came from a lady I did not know but who appeared quite well acquainted with the Brennans. Tall and slender with dark brown hair, grayed at the temples, she was a striking individual. Her patrician face was accentuated by a well-defined chin, a straight and prominent nose, and penetrating, somewhat arrogant eyes that stared at me from below wide, arched, dark brown eyebrows. She was probably close to fifty years old, I thought, given the strands of telltale grey and slightly wrinkled facial skin. She wore a simple white silk blouse with wide padded shoulders and long puffy sleeves and a wide belt around her small waist which showed off her slim figure. What a surprise when Gina greeted her with open arms and said, "Natalie. How nice to see you." Then, turning to me, "Let me introduce you to our new friend. Libby Whitacker, may I present Natalie Barney."

Could this really be Uncle Christian's stepdaughter? It was hard to contain my shock. I wasn't sure what Ms. Barney had heard about me.

Natalie did recognize my name. I think she also identified my uneasiness combined with curiosity.

Somehow, I found my voice and muttered an appropriate response when she inquired how I "fancied" the exhibit.

The Brennans invited Natalie to join us for supper, but she declined, saying she had a prior engagement. I was relieved to hear this. Although curious to know more about my uncle's stepdaughter, I wasn't quite ready. I wanted to spend time alone with Gina and her father. Clearly, they had much to teach me, which would be enough for one night.

We were driven up to Montmartre, across the *Place du Tertre*. This was once the center of artistic creativity before so many artists resettled in *Montparnasse*. Montmartre is the highest elevation in Paris. The view is breathtaking with all the sparkling lights of the city below.

"Picasso used to call this area *'Bateau Lavoir'*. At least that is what his friend Max Jacob dubbed it," chuckled Mr. Brennan.

"Laundry Boat?" I translated wondering what the connection was between laundry and art.

"Well, Max was a poet, and I assume, preferred to see things that were appealing or, at least, proper. When Picasso set up his studio here, it was miserable, noisy, unhygienic - a real firetrap. But, despite its appearance, this was the center of Bohemian life some twenty years ago."

I wondered if maybe Gina had inherited some of her artistic temperament from her father since he appeared to be so well informed and enthusiastic about art. Their interest was contagious and I myself was beginning to enjoy the so-called Bohemian life.

The ivy covered *Lapin Agile* at *22, rue Saules*, last of the tree-shaded Montmartre taverns, once patronized by my favorite poet,

Guillaume Apollinaire, was our destination. Gina told me that I might even see Picasso there, since he still came back to the neighborhood from time to time. It was here, she told me, that Picasso said, "When you paint a landscape it should look like a plate."

Greeted by *Lapin Agile's* owner, "Old Frédéric", bearded and wearing a velvet beret, we were escorted inside. Immediately, I could smell the fragrant odor of Brandy Alexanders along with the pungent smell of Gaulois cigarettes.

"Did you know that Absinthe was outlawed?" Mr. Brennan asked me after we had located a small marble table off to one side but still surrounded with people and smoke. I had to ask Mr. Brennan to repeat the question because it was so noisy. When I understood he was talking about the green drink, I admitted my ignorance of alcoholic beverages.

"Called *the Green Fairy*, it was popular among writers and authors because it is believed to stimulate creativity."

"Does it?"

"I am not sure that it does more than stimulate hallucinations; that is, if it is taken in strong doses."

"That would be true of any alcoholic drink, wouldn't it?"

"Perhaps, but Absinthe has wormwood as one of its ingredients. Van Gogh became an addict when he was living here with his brother Theo. He had to leave Paris and go south to live in Provence. It was the war that put a stop to Absinthe. Pilots would lose control of their aircraft. It was found that many of them had consumed Absinthe before flying. There is an ingredient in wormwood that causes cortical blindness."

"Cortical blindness?"

"Temporary brain blindness, as opposed to eye blindness. It was also feared that any traits acquired from drinking Absinthe could be passed on to the progeny of the drinker."

"Dad, you can only drink a moderate amount of Absinthe before you get blotto."

"Oh? And young lady, how do you know this?"

"Daddy, everyone knows these things. Please don't worry about me. I tasted it once. It is so bitter that we had to add sugar and water and then it turned from green to white. I would rather watch it than drink it."

"Where did you get it?" Mr. Brennan sounded concerned.

"It was called Pastis, but it is the same as Absinthe."

Relieved by the clarification, Mr. Brennan explained that it was not the same at all and he warned both of us to be careful all the same. Then, to our amusement, he went to great trouble to explain the health benefits of circulation and the digestive process and proceeded to order a carafe of red wine.

We never did play the *Surréaliste* game. Instead, as our glasses were replenished and delicious *hors d'oeuvres* were served, the conversation evolved into Mr. Brennan's relationship with his wife and, surprisingly, his interpretation of Catholic dogma.

"No, I don't want my wife by my side all the time," Mr. Brennan said. "I need to have my own space, my own interests, and, occasionally, special time alone with my daughter, *our* daughter. I did think about leaving Anne once. Of course, divorce is out of the question. We are Catholic." Mr. Brennan paused, and sipped his wine looking more inward than at his surroundings. "I needed more in a relationship than *casual acquaintance* would allow," he said almost to no one in particular.

"Daddy!" exclaimed Gina. I am sure she had never heard her father talk like this before.

Looking up and noticing his daughter's stunned expression, Mr. Brennan attempted to explain. "I love your mother, Gina, but sometimes I wonder if she loves me. There is, excuse my being blunt, maybe it's the wine, but there is no passion. She knows me; oh does she know me. But she … Oh dear, I have gone too far. I am sorry." He took Gina's hands into his own. "Only take my advice. Keep the spark alive. All this drinking and partying you young people do is not what it is really all about. Life is about intense feeling, feeling that the world consists of none other than you and your own true love. I have to respect my wife's choice. In the final analysis, 'the Father is the separator. The Mother brings together.'"

Fortunately, the rest of Mr. Brennan's revelations were drowned out as the show began.

Chapter Fifteen

Perhaps the only one in the world
Whose heart could answer mine,
And who, entering my deepest night
Could enlighten it with a single look.

Gerard de Nerval

I wasn't about to tell the *Comtesse* all about my eye-opening
adventures, but I did share the basic philosophy behind the
Surréaliste exhibit we had seen.

"You must acquaint yourself with the art treasures we have in
this part of France as well," she advised. "Only a short drive from
here, you could visit *Meaux* where the archives with the *Illuminated
Manuscripts* are kept. I should be happy to make arrangements if
you wish to visit the Cathedral."

Philippe and I spent much of the weekend touring the countryside,
visiting *châteaux*, churches and museums, and chatting. We saw the
Illuminated Manuscripts in *Meaux* as well as the gardens designed
by Le Nôtre next to the old Gothic Cathedral. Each night, happy and
tired, I returned to the petite blue room. Octagonal in shape, it felt
cozy and warm like a nest. Philippe had found a robin's egg when
he was a small boy. The color had so delighted him that his mother
had this room painted robin's egg blue. The bed was covered with
a well-stuffed eiderdown and when I lay down, my head sank deep
into big, fluffy pillows as I drifted off to sleep and dreamland.

My dreams were vivid. The first night, I dreamt that a priest was
asking me to find a proper place to bury an object. The decision had
to be made and it had to be mine. I held back from participating. I
did not want to make this decision but the priest kept demanding.
When I awoke, I was damp with perspiration. Eventually, I drifted
back to sleep. The next dream was different. I was walking on a
grassy hillside carrying a large bag. I wore a wide brimmed hat,

a sweater over a simple frock, black tights and flat shoes. In the distance, train tracks could be seen crisscrossing through the valley from a tunnel in the mountains. A young boy approached and asked where I was going. I told him that I was going to get on a train and travel to town. But the tracks eluded me as I kept walking and walking and walking.

Hadn't Gina told me that future events are sometimes revealed in dreams? Outside, a white mist veiled the green front lawn and flowerbeds. In daylight, the flowers had been full of color, now they were a combination of somber, muted tints. It must be dawn, I thought, but the mist hung along the top of the trees blocking the early sunlight. One of the Latin words my father taught me was *revelare*. It is the base word for 'reveal'. The etymology is 're' meaning again, once over, or back, and *'velare'*, to 'veil'. So to 'reveal' something was to 'remove' or 'pull back' the veil. This was precisely what was happening outside as the mist partially hid the lush garden. What were my dreams unveiling?

Sunday at midday, we took time off from history and art. In the early morning, we had attended mass in the modest chapel near the château along with Philippe's mother, the servants and *Monsieur l'Abbé*, a local retired priest who loved to dine with the *Comtesse* after the service. Philippe asked that we be excused; explaining that the two of us would have lunch in the country. There were still so many sights to show his guest, he added.

By early afternoon, we had seen enough of churches and historical sights. It was too nice a day to spoil by being indoors. The mist had disappeared and the sun displayed her wily powers, sending brilliant light down to dazzle those venturing outside. In the village, Philippe bought a bottle of *Côtes du Rhone Gigondas* wine, a loaf of bread and the Brie cheese so famous in this region. "It is called *'Le Roi des Fromages'*", Philippe said with such pride one would have thought the cheese had come from his own kitchen. We drove to a peaceful spot and parked the car. Philippe came around to open the door for me. Then he went to the trunk and brought out a blanket to spread on the grass. A quiet stream sauntered nearby. Birds chattered in the trees, probably preparing their young for the flight south, a trip they would be taking all too soon. Flowers winked at us between the tall grasses that swayed in the light breeze. Clouds, soft and small, crossed the sun overhead in the otherwise clear blue sky. The summer was ending too quickly. This was a day to cherish before the cool autumn winds robbed the leaves of their verdancy and whisked them away.

I sat on the blanket, my long legs bent to the side, one hand balancing myself, the other holding a glass of wine. Philippe perched on his knees and spread out the small repast.

Our eyes met and locked. The moment could no longer be avoided. I stopped breathing; my heart pounded. With an inevitable force, our lips met. I dropped my glass, closed my eyes and surrendered. My arms went around his neck. Our bodies melded together. I was conscious of his smell, strong and masculine. I felt limp and would have fallen, but his arms supported me. Gently, he lay me down on the blanket and continued the kiss.

"This is the kiss I have longed for from the moment I laid eyes on you," he said.

This was the kiss I had imagined in my dreams, I thought in silent reply.

A few days after Lindbergh's famous flight, Michael had invited his flying comrades to our apartment. When I came home from buying fresh bread at the local *patisserie*, they were all congregated in our salon. Seeing me pass by the doors of the salon on my way to the kitchen, Michael invited me to come back and join the group. I think he meant for me to listen to what they had to say, not to participate in the discussion and frankly, when I settled into the *fauteuil* at the back of the room, I was a bit lost, unable to follow the scientific aspects. However, when they spoke of Ireland, I perked up for that was the day I had met our distinguished neighbor, James Joyce, on the stairway.

"I say it was only luck that got him to the coast of Ireland, the luck of the Irish anyway," Michael was saying. I couldn't wait to tell of my meeting the great author, so picking up from Michael's reference to Ireland. I began softly, "Speaking of the Irish ..." However, the enthusiasm in the salon was so intense that my quiet, ladylike manner was simply not heard or was ignored as the men continued discussing the great flight. Since no one noticed, I decided to slip out of the room. I wanted to read Mr. Joyce's book, especially now that I had met the man. Tiptoeing down the hall, I passed the kitchen and went through the door to the bedroom. It was getting dark. I found the lamp and turned it on before drawing the curtains. Kicking off my shoes, with a brief glance in the mirror to check my hair and lipstick, I settled down on my bed, propped myself up with two big, soft pillows and began to read the great Joyce.

Pomes Penyeach consisted of a mere dozen poems. The price of this volume was inconsequential when measured against the feast for mind and soul contained within its covers.

Sylvia Beach had compared Joyce's poems to Blake's *Songs of Innocence and Experience*. As I perused Joyce's verses, I came across 'Ah star of evil', which Mr. Joyce had muttered on the stairs. The next stanza read, *'Nor old heart's wisdom yet to know / The signs that mock me as I go.'* Yes, I had heard this plea before. The French had a saying, *'Si la jeunneuse savait, si la veilliese pouvait!'* (If youth only knew, if the old only could!) Here I was, very young, yet fortunate enough to be surrounded by a world so invested with knowledge that I could scarcely keep up. I was grateful and I was intrigued. There must be some special reason I should be in Paris with all the activity in the arts and in aviation. Returning to the poem, I read, *'Why then, remembering those sky / Sweet lures, repine when the dear love she yielded with a sigh / Was all but thine?'* I was enthralled. More lines followed. I read them over and sighed. For a moment, I closed my eyes and allowed the feeling of heretofore forbidden warmth fill my body. After a few minutes, I opened my eyes and continued, coming across a poem called Again.

> *Come, give, yield all your strength to me!*
> *From far a low word breathes on the breaking brain*
> *Its cruel calm, submission's misery,*
> *Gentling her awe as to a soul predestined,*
> *Cease, silent love! My doom!*

Blind me with your dark nearness, O have mercy,
beloved enemy of my will!
I dare not withstand the cold touch that I dread.
Draw from me still
My slow life! Bend deeper on me, threatening head,
Proud be my downfall, remembering, pitying
Him who is, him who was.

Again!
Together, folded by the night, they lay on earth,
I hear from far her low word breathe on my breaking brain.
Come! I yield. Bend deeper upon me! I am here.
Subduer, do not leave me! Only joy, only anguish,
Take me, save me, soothe me, o spare me!

Interpretations are the result of selective understanding. For me, the mood was right for romance. The words conjured up soft, amorous images. Again I closed my eyes; my head settled back on the pillow and succumbed to a fuzzy daydream.

A man's body bent over mine casting a long shadow across my face and shoulders. His breath was sweet, his gaze soft and steady; his dark eyes penetrated mine. Although I could not see his features, I knew he was smiling. His hands caressed my neck, then moved slowly down my shoulders. My flesh burned under his touch; my breath came in short gasps. He leaned forward. His lips pressed against my eyelid, as gentle as the flutter of a butterfly wing. He kissed the other eye, then the tip of my nose. Our flesh parted for the span of an eternal second and then I felt his breath on my lips. His lips pressed against mine and I could taste him. He lowered himself onto me. His body pushed me deep into the mattress. My nipples hardened painfully as his hand moved slowly inside my blouse and ...

"Napping are you, darling?" Michael stood at the foot of my bed.

I opened my eyes, struggling out of my dream, blushing furiously as if he could guess my thoughts.

"It's all right. Stay where you are."

Patricia Daly-Lipe

I sat up, looking for the sheet to pull around myself and realized that I was fully dressed. Seeing Michael did not tempt me in the least. He wasn't the man in my dream.

"The fellows and I are going to run down to a little bistro in um, *Chez Clément*, I think it is called, the one with all the spoons bent and twisted. Anyway, it is only for a nibble. Don't mind staying home, do you dear?"

Without waiting for an answer, Michael left.

I struggled to find my way back to my imaginary lover. I tried picturing him, remembering what his touch on my skin was like but I couldn't bring him back. Then I was wide awake and the romantic feelings were gone, gone so completely that I swung the other way. In fact, I was furious. I wanted to scream or hit something and I wasn't even sure why.

That was then. Now it was really happening to me. The kiss. My arms responded without command as I held him tightly. After some minutes, he gently disengaged himself and lay at my side, his head resting on my breasts. For a long time, we were silent. Finally, Philippe sat up and, looking down at my flushed face, whispered: "I should not have done that, Libby." I felt the tears start. "But I am not sorry," he continued. I smiled. "You see, I …"

"Please, Philippe" I pleaded, my arms reaching for him, "please don't say anything. Please."

It was so clear; it was so simple. It was so natural. It was also, we both realized, so impossible.

I clung to him for a moment longer, unable to turn my feelings into words. The tears welled up from my soul. Haltingly, I told him everything that had happened. The shock of finding Michael naked with a man. My flight to Pamela and Victor Statler's home. Between sobs, I told him all that had happened since I had opened the door on Michael's secret.

What could I do? If only I had met Philippe in Washington. The tears could not stop. Philippe held me tight.

We made an attempt to begin the picnic but ended up leaving the bread and cheese to the squirrels and birds. Holding hands, we strolled along the side of the stream. About a mile down the path, under the trees lining the bank, we kissed again, this time lightly, without urgency, as though our relationship had been in place a long, long time.

Eventually, we turned back toward the car. Before opening the door on my side, Philippe took me by the shoulders to face him and said,. "I want to be with you, Libby." I slid my arms around his neck once more, unable to speak.

"I want you, Libby. I want you for the rest of my life." Then, looking straight into my eyes, he said, "We will find a way." Melting into his arms, I yearned to believe him.

Chapter Sixteen

*A man is better than a girl. Consider him from the
viewpoint of the evil which is almost always pleasure's
real attraction. The crime committed with a creature
completely like yourself seems greater than that with
one who is not, and thus the pleasure is double.*

Marquis de Sade

I found a small book with its page open to the above quotation
on the table next to Michael's bed when I returned to an
empty apartment late Sunday night. After such a glorious
weekend, with Philippe's last kiss was still warm on my lips, it
was a slap of cold reality.

While unpacking the small bag and hanging my clothes in the
armoire, my mind raced as I tried to reconcile two diametrically
opposed emotions: the newly found passion with Philippe and this
awful passage from the Marquis de Sade. Even with all that had
happened I could not believe Michael had this sinister side to his
personality. No, someone else must have left this book.

From what I had read at the *Bibliotheque Nationale* and
observed on the streets and at various functions, on a Bohemian level,
homosexuality appeared to be free and innocent, even charming and
gay, at least in Paris. However, according to the laws and most social
circles, there was little or no tolerance for it. For some, homosexuality
was a personal torment. Many of these men and women struggled
to have relationships with members of the opposite sex, sincere in
wanting normal lives, but ended up becoming frustrated, often to
the point of becoming emotionally disturbed and unable to cope or
function in society at all. Others, however, simply accepted their
affinity and enjoyed same sex relationships without reluctance or
stress. Alone amongst themselves, they were confident; but out in
the open, or faced with others, their courage evaporated. Deep down,

they were only too aware of the censure that was being heaped upon them.

Homosexuality has existed since the beginning of civilization. It was documented in ancient Greece that a Greek General who did not have a young boy at his side was considered suspect. It happened in Rome during the Italian Renaissance and on throughout the history of mankind. I researched, trying to understand this custom, this concept, this life-style, but was still having trouble accepting its reality when it came to Michael.

I paced the floor, looking out the window from time to time to see the flowing steel-blue water of the Seine, the sun's rays dancing on its restless wavelets. It wasn't the movement, but the energy that talked to me. What was I doing with my life? The river never stopped. No matter the weather, it rushed on, sometimes rough; sometimes smooth, but it continued its course. Imagine the river stopping all of a sudden for no reason. It would not happen. Life is like that, a continual conflict of extremes, like the consistent but unpredictable nature of the River Seine.

Memories of rough seas came back. The voyage across the Atlantic had been a nightmare. At times, the sea turned violent. The vessel had rocked back and forth causing hideous nausea. The cold, damp, salty air that made my lungs ache. Desperately seeking relief, I wished somehow I could have stopped the ship. I remember whimpering, "Please stop, please. I want to get off. Please stop!" The memory brought back the taste of bile. Was that sea voyage an omen? A poem by Apollinaire came to mind. *How slow life seems to be, / How violent the hope of love can be.*

I continued pacing the floor trying to piece together what had suddenly become of my life. I was a married woman. Like every girl at the debutante parties, my goal was to marry. But did I want it or was it simply the wishes of my parents? Was it so important that the man or the relationship was beyond consideration except in terms of status? On the other hand, once married, what woman really knows her husband in just the first few weeks or months? My pacing speeded up. The books on the shelves, the walls with their history, the paintings, all around me were stories to stimulate deeper insight, but nothing was giving me the answers I sought. With a deep breath, I uttered the truth. I was ready for the full passion of love. The precious moments with Philippe were proof. I was talking to the window then back at the bookcases, walking back and forth but seeing nothing. If only I had believed in my misgivings before the wedding. Did I really think I could marry a man and those feelings would somehow miraculously happen? How stupid, how ridiculously stupid. Yes, I had entered marriage with my eyes closed and my ears closed and my mind closed.

It was the way everything in my life had always been: planned, organized and cerebral. That was how I had been brought up. It was my parents' motto to always be in control. I had feelings, but brushed them aside. I had instincts, but ignored them; that is, until I met Philippe.

Pamela called. She had been invited to one of Natalie Barney's soirées and had asked if I might accompany her. Natalie had said she would be delighted to include me. This was going to be a new lesson to learn as I was to be exposed to yet another lifestyle.

Chapter Seventeen

As an artist, a man has no home in Europe save in Paris.

Friedrich Nietzsche, 1888

"Pamela, I am so sorry not to be ready on time," I muttered, as I pulled a soft grey-green wool sweater over my shoulders. I sneaked a peek in the mirror. The shade was flattering, bringing out the color of my eyes. As I combed through my closet for a proper pair of shoes to match my dress, I began to feel giddy about going out.

"You know the funny thing is, with all the excitement, I wasn't even embarrassed to be wearing pants," I concluded after telling Pamela all about the famous flight with Philippe. We both laughed. I hadn't told her about my visit with the *Comtesse* and certainly not about the picnic, but she must have noticed how completely alive and radiant I was and guessed the source. She was chuckling to herself, and it didn't bother me a bit.

Paris was a Mecca for artists in the twenties. With the Industrial Revolution, which had its beginning in 19th century England, America was becoming the super power of industry and consequently, wealth. There were men like Carnegie, Rockefeller, Andrew Mellon and John Pierpont Morgan, Jr. With such affluence, a new class, the *nouveaux riches* developed. This newly rich public was being flaunted and taunted by novelists like Fitzgerald, Hemingway and Faulkner. The idealism of Walt Whitman had given way to the realities of e e cummings.

pity this busy monster, manunkind
not. Progress is a comfortable disease:
your victim death and life safely beyond
plays with the bigness of his littleness

I was told that Cummings had volunteered as an ambulance driver in France during the war, but he endured more than the experience of seeing the suffering of war. He suffered personally when he was placed in military detention. It was three months before someone verified that Cummings had been falsely accused of treason. Now that the war was over, e e chose to spend most of each year in Paris. When asked why he decided to use the lower case for his name as well as his choice to abandon the pronoun 'I', e e said, "It is a way of reminding the reader of my poems that the self is not always important as it seems to some – or most." I thought about this statement when I read other writers' works. The more I read, the more I came to respect e e cummings, now with all little letters, reading his poems over and over, each time digging deeper into the meaning – and into myself.

The French economy was in desperate straits and American dollars were welcome. The exchange was so favorable that even poor American artists and writers could come across the ocean and afford to live here for as little as a dollar a day. The artists and writers usually stayed. The others created a stir and left.

In our school, Emerson's essays about the symbols of nature and man's attachment to nature were studied and enjoyed. However, since the war ended, society seemed to be looking in a different direction. Many of the *intelligentiari* were turning inward. In Vienna, Sigmund Freud was tearing the veils from the subconscious and the unconscious. Others who were looking outward involved themselves with technology to change the environment. Television was beginning to play an important role. Experimentation was in vogue. If pictures could be sent across the ocean, only lack of imagination would hinder further discoveries.

As I prepared for the drive to Natalie's, Pamela and I chatted about all of this.

"And then look at the arts," I was saying. "First it was Dadaism and then Surrealism, the two mostly at odds, but both *experiments* in art. Even the English language has become an experiment, letting the words take over. I mean, we, you and I, Pamela, come out of a particular linguistic convention, a socially correct manner of speech. So when I write, I can't help using the words and phraseology that I have learned. Perhaps I am hindered in what I wish to say because of the manner in which I was taught the language. But Mr. cummings' poetry goes beyond conventionality. His words grasp the heart of the subject. And Coleridge. Give him one vivid word and he will mix it with two of his own and out comes sheer creative brilliance, a star!" I was ready to continue, but Pamela interrupted.

"I am impressed, Libby dear. You have not been wasting your time."

I had done my homework. Despite being young, this American lady, I decided, was going to be part of the gathering, if not as a participant, at least conversant and knowledgeable enough to follow the discourse.

"Changes and more changes and, Pamela, it seems as if everything is happening right here."

"Why not?" Pamela chuckled.

The *City of Light*, as Paris had been christened, spun in a whirlwind of activity. Everyone drank with abandon, everyone smoked, and everyone had an opinion.

Deciding to tease Pamela, I put on a straight and serious face and recited something Mr. Brennan had said. "Of course, you know that the national psyche of France professes that art is as important as love or food. In fact, for Parisians, art, food and love are synonymous."

Pamela laughed. She and her husband had lived in Paris much longer than I, but she said my enthusiasm and free spirit was infectious. I certainly felt lighter. If I could fly in an aeroplane, I could do most anything.

Picking up where we had left off in the conversation, Pamela suggested, "But it is only natural that artists from around the world would be drawn to France, isn't it Libby?" I murmured "Yes," as I searched for a shawl to match my dress.

"And what city more beautiful than Paris? Remember the poem, 'Oh, Paris is a woman's town with flowers in her hair?'" *Yes, the poet was right*, I said to myself surveying my jewelry.

My final attire consisted of a soft green frock brocaded in silver. Its lines were straight, flattering and simple. At the bottom, there were white ostrich feathers along the hem. Around my neck, I wore the pearls my mother had given me as a wedding present. If only she could see me now. I chuckled with a big grin, a grin that said, "I am on my own and going my *own* way." With the grey-green sweater tossed over my shoulders, I was ready. Pamela and I descended the staircase, arm in arm, to the Deusenberg where Frederick stood waiting.

Natalie Barney had attracted a marvelous gathering, packed with people laughing, chatting, some waving their arms and some in serious discourse. The room was festooned with garlands of red and yellow roses. Pretty young girls dressed in Greek tunics with yellow roses in their hair glided around serving dainty sweet-smelling pastries warm from the oven while at a table in the back of the room some of Natalie's friends took turns serving Dragon Smoke tea from southwestern China in dainty china cups and saucers. The mood was uplifting, euphoric; everyone was smiling and having a good time.

Daphnis and Chloë, I thought as the sound of a violin interpretation carried me above the laughter and the chatter. Registering the animation of the scene before me, I was astonished that tea was the only beverage being served. In *cafés* and bistros, such vivaciousness would be the result of the consumption of alcoholic beverages.

Meeting new people was not my strong suit but I was getting better at it. Besides, here no one seemed to care whether I participated in the conversation or not. Each artist appeared eager to share some great insight or revelation using his or her own words and listeners were always welcome.

This night was special. Natalie had organized the evening to pay tribute to the great avant-garde American writer, Gertrude Stein. Many of the guests were American writers and artists. Ernest Hemingway, a particular favorite of Miss Stein's, was there.

"The artist destroys his talent himself, by not using it, by drinking so much he blunts the edge of his perceptions, by laziness, by sloth, by snobbery, by hook and by crook, selling vitality, trading it for security, for comfort." Mr. Hemingway lectured as a group of admirers stood about him transfixed. I wondered how much of what he was saying came from his own experience. He looked more like a football player than a writer with his broad shoulders, muscular body and strong masculine face. His large lipped mouth was hardly constrained by the drill-sergeant's mustache. And when he walked, it was with a tough guy swagger like the big men I had seen down by the barges, the ones lifting the crates out and stacking them on the *quai*.

"He could well be part of the bar scene," I chuckled to Pamela as I accepted a cup of tea.

"My young friend, this man has a great reputation and it isn't exactly pristine."

Mina Loy was there to pay tribute as well. Although she was middle aged, she was an imposing figure. Her grey-blue eyes were both soft and piercing. She had patrician features and wore her perm-waved black hair parted in the middle. She was taller than I but not by much. I was five feet seven inches and taller than most of my girl friends. A slender lady, she flaunted her figure by wearing a tight hobble-skirt that almost hid her enlarged ankles and a large brilliant lemon colored blouse with magenta flowers that was eye catching. I stared at the poetess as she spoke, mesmerized by her long dangling earrings that swung wildly as she nodded and gestured with each expressed idea.

"We have lost mysticism so it is to abstract art that we have turned."

Miss Loy appeared to me as a cross between a Victorian lady and a modern woman. Her stature was patrician, but her shoulder length earrings betrayed something more contemporary, almost bohemian.

A poet as well as a painter, Mina Loy agreed to read some of her recent poems. I was fascinated. Never before had I heard this kind of verse. Futurist poetry had certainly not been part of the curriculum at Holton-Arms School for Girls in Washington.

> *Ostracized as we are with God*
> *The watchers of the civilized wastes*
> *Reverse their signals on our track*

Pamela was ready to move on to another circle of guests, but I wanted to stay and hear more.

We are the sacerdotal clowns
Who feed upon the wind and stars
And pulverous pastures of poverty

Our wills are formed
By curious disciplines
Beyond your laws

Later, Virgil Thomson played and sang Miss Stein's portraits of *Susie Asado and Preciosilla.* Gina had told me that he had come to Paris only two years before but straight away ingratiated himself with Gertrude Stein. Kindred spirits, I supposed, because they had already collaborated on many innovative stage productions. I recognized hymns as well as popular tunes and even a waltz in the piano piece he was playing.

"Playful music," remarked Pamela. "Spontaneous and uplifting, don't you agree?"

"Oh, Pamela, I love that music. So familiar but so different all at once."

The highlight of the evening came when Natalie read passages from Gertrude Stein's *The Making of Americans*, a thousand page novel she had first published as a series, which, Pamela told me, Hemingway had arranged. "This was published in Ford Maddox Ford's *The Transatlantic Review*. Have you read the *Review*?" whispered Pamela so as to not interrupt Natalie. "No," I admitted, but was determined to buy a copy. The passages being read were captivating.

"Disillusionment in living is the finding out nobody agrees with you not those that are fighting for you. Complete disillusionment is when you realize that no one can for they can't change. The amount they agree is important to you until the amount they do not agree with you is completely realized by you. Then you say you will write for yourself and strangers, you will be for yourself and strangers and this then makes an old man or an old woman of you."

"You realize, Libby dear, Miss Stein's books as well as many contemporary works, even Mr. Joyce's *Ulysses* are not truly stories per se."

"I'm sorry Pamela, I don't understand. If the books are not stories, then are they just an exercise of words?"

Some of the guests had been talking about Joyce and his use of language. They had mentioned a word I had never heard before. The word was *claritas*. From the conversation, it sounded as if *claritas* meant radiance, but what did it have to do with writing? Perhaps Pamela would know.

"Joyce had used that word in his book, *Portrait of An Artist As A Young Man*, Libby. It means wholeness, harmony and passion."

"Sounds like the Catholic Church's vision of God?"

"Perhaps. Yes, you could say that these writers are pursuing the same path as the Church, trying to understand what our lives are all about. Happiness and pain, ugliness and beauty. Joyce and this great lady, Gertrude Stein, are not writing books for a story line. They write so that we can have an experience, like an adventure with words. Miss Stein's writing consists of structurally spontaneous compositions with words coming across like music with harmony and rhythm."

Just then Miss Stein passed by and, having overheard part of our repartee, offered her view. "I like the feeling of words doing as they want to do," she said. I was contemplating that thought when she continued. "… and as they have to do when they live where they have to live. It is thought thinking itself." Pointing at my head, she concluded, "That is where they come to live, which of course, they do." Before I could reply, and frankly, I am not sure I could have replied anyway, Miss Stein had turned and continued her stroll through the crowded room.

Pamela was pensive. As we sauntered about, she pointed out that the origin of the word text is *textus*, Latin for *weaving*. "Therefore, a work of art that is written is analogous to a fabric embroidered, like your shawl."

"Oh, I see. So in a literary work, the weaving is done with phrases."

"Yes, you might say that the petit point comes with dashes, all carefully woven to be worn with only the right words."

I burst out laughing. "Oh, Pamela, you are an amazing lady." We walked on, pausing here and there to eavesdrop on conversations, most of which were about some type of art form.

As we wandered, questions flowed through my mind. Why does Miss Stein write so much about America when she has chosen to live in Paris? And Natalie, why was she so much happier to live here than in her own country? Perhaps, I was only seeking justification for my own feeling of finally *coming home*. Maybe for them too, it was simply the romance of the language.

As I was in the midst of these thoughts, we ran into the guest of honor again. This time, as she was deep in conversation with another person, I had time to look at her before she noticed us. Stout, only five feet three inches tall, she was an impressive little woman. When she turned and saw us and before Pamela could say anything or perhaps even leave, I boldly walked over to Miss Stein and asked, as one American speaking with another American, why she chose to remain in Paris. Was it the French language she wished to acquire? Miss Stein scoffed at that idea.

"No, no. For me, living among the French is important precisely because that way I can keep my own language to myself." We laughed. She wasn't as intimidating as I had thought she would be. "The twentieth century, my dear, is difficult enough without confusing languages and customs." Before I could agree or disagree, she was onto a new subject.

"Everything cracks; everything is destroyed; everything isolates itself in this new century," she said, using words as only she could.

I thought about the idea of television. "One day," I told Miss Stein, "that invention will pull the world together on a screen." Although she didn't seem terribly appreciative, I proceeded to tell her about an article I had read recently in *The Herald*. The headline read: "Television Sends Hoover's Voice, Image Through Space." Television? It had been my first encounter with the concept.

In Washington, we had a radio, a mysterious, small polished wooden box through which you could listen to people making speeches or reciting plays. Only a few months before, some prominent men in London were not only listening to, but actually speaking to men all the way across the ocean in New York.

We had limited telephone service in Washington, but certainly not to anyone living across the ocean. This new communication equipment was called a radiophone. My father had stock in A.T. & T. and surely made quite a bit of money from this new wireless device. It was like a voice voyage. Father explained that Dr. Alexander Graham Bell made the human voice able to travel a million times further when he invented the telephone. Now the art of telephony had progressed. It seemed fact had outrun fancy. Someone's imagination had become actuality with this new invention called television. The newspaper article claimed we would be able to listen to and see Secretary Hoover, who was running for President, address the nation hundreds and, some day, thousands of miles away.

Exciting news, but for me, living in the early years of the twentieth century, a time when the phenomena of the sciences are considered more splendid than the customary cycles of nature, it was a difficult concept for me to accept. There is something desensitizing about the science of industrial arts. For me, the daily routine of nature is more comfortable. I prefer feeling a chill in the air when the trees exhibit their palette of colorful leaves in the fall and in the spring. I love to close my eyes and smell the new flower buds.

I told Miss Stein and Pamela about the television article and they agreed. It was interesting but somewhat insensitive.

Then I tried describing my aeroplane ride to Miss Stein. "Imagine, passing above the earth, being in the sky, free as a bird, flying wherever you want to go. Perhaps one day we might be able to fly even beyond our own planet up to the stars."

But Miss Stein thought I had missed the point, or maybe she hadn't heard what I said. While I was going into the future realm envisioned by Jules Verne, Miss Stein had her feet planted firmly in the present.

"To me, the twentieth century is a more splendid thing," she said, her eyes concentrating on some inner vision, "more splendid than a period when everything follows itself." I merely nodded. Miss Stein paused, reflected, and decided to complete her thought. "So, you see, my dear, I feel that this century is a splendid period, not a reasonable one in the scientific sense, but splendid."

Patricia Daly-Lipe

Formidable was the adjective that came to mind in describing Gertrude Stein. It was a polite word and although correctly applied to her wit, it did not apply to her form. Physically, Miss Stein was massive, in width not in height. She was also massive relating to volume as her boldly spoken words wound around me and clung with her energy and enthusiasm. When she had finished speaking, I had the impression of her huge stature towering over me even though I actually looked down at her. *Those big dark eyes*, I thought, *they look into the most secret recesses of my soul. Perhaps that is what writers do.* But having it done to me was exceedingly uncomfortable. It was a relief when someone else caught her attention, although with unfeigned curiosity I continued to watch as she walked around the crowded room as if cultivating personae for her next book.

"Pamela," I said afterwards when we were being driven back to my apartment, "my mind is soaring. So much creativity, so much talent, so much clout and all in one room."

Pamela was delighted with my excitement and for awhile listened attentively. Then, eager to add to my enthusiasm, she asked if I was aware that Guillaume Apollinaire, whose poetry she knew I treasured, had been a friend of Picasso's. After I recited a verse from *Under Mirabeau Bridge*, I asked Pamela to tell me more.

"Picasso befriended Apollinaire precisely because he was a poet."

"Pamela, I am having difficulty following you."

"According to our Miss Stein, the egotism of the painter is not the same as the egotism of the writer." I must have looked at her with question marks in my eyes. Pamela explained, "A painter sees himself as a reflection of the pictures he has painted. A writer, on the other hand, sees himself or herself first as existing inside him or herself whether or not she or he is secure with the outside world."

"You mean, the writer has to be secure about himself, who he is and what he is all about, before he can write? I thought most writers were insecure about themselves and their work."

"Perhaps that is true of some. But think about your neighbor Mr. Joyce. A good writer should not see his ego reflected in his work like the painter. Remember what you told me about e e cummings?"

"Take out the 'I', you mean?"

154

"Precisely. Since Picasso clearly knew how to paint, he didn't need to go to other artists to learn. Of course, he studied the old masters, but I am talking about his contemporaries. No, he went to writers because what he needed were ideas and thoughts. According to Miss Stein, that is why Picasso, a man who expresses himself only in painting, has only writers as friends."

"Dearest Pamela, you're beginning to sound like Miss Stein yourself," I chided.

"I shall take that as a compliment."

By this time, we had arrived at my apartment building. I was sorry we had to part. It had been such an enjoyable evening.

After waving good-by to my dear friend, I unlocked the big blue *porte cochère* with the large key that had barely fit into my handbag. Not wanting to disturb our concierge, I was careful to tiptoe on the black and white tile floor in the dimly lit passageway. Although I was quiet going past Madame Metz's dark apartment, the dear lady was probably peeping through her tiny viewing window above the doorknocker. At the end of the passage, I slowly and methodically continued to tiptoe up the cement stairs, careful to hold on to the iron railings for balance and security. On the way up, I paused for a second on the first landing. I could picture Mr. Joyce. The memory of that encounter was still so vivid. I was sorry that he had missed such a glorious evening. Someone at the soirée told me that the Joyces were in the Netherlands for a holiday, but for me his essence was here, on this landing, cane in hand, his tiny glasses tilted askew on his somewhat prominent nose, a twinkle in his mischievous Irish eye, the one without a patch.

I arrived at my landing, and with a sigh, turned the smaller key into the door of our apartment. The fire in the hearth was reduced to a few smoldering embers. Like our love, if what we felt for each other even deserved that cognomen. There was no sign of Michael.

Chapter Eighteen

Never less alone than when alone.

Samuel Rogers

Being alone was good when I was busy reading, studying, exploring the city, visiting museums. But often, when the realization that I was in fact alone, really alone, came to mind, especially at night, I became restless and tense. When nothing was planned and I was at home during the day, I found myself staring through the window as if the world out there could help answer my questions.

Our apartment was on the second floor of a converted old mansion on the *Quai d'Anjou*, the road that encircles the *Île St Louis*. It was small but had been more than adequate for our needs when Michael and I first moved in. More important, the view was breathtaking. The river passed below and beyond, the silhouette of the city sprawled out in all directions. Stone buildings pointed to the sky and tree limbs flowed back and forth to the tune of the breeze. In the mornings, I took my coffee and read the morning news in the largest room, a combination study, salon and dining room. A long hallway, the floor fashioned with a parquet geometrical design, led to the front door and passed a small kitchen area on the right. The bedroom was behind the kitchen through a tall double door. The bedroom, a sad place, a room with two beds inhabited by two people who never touched.

All the ceilings were eleven feet high except in the kitchen, which was probably a closet before the renovation. The bathroom was down the hall, across from the study making it accessible to guests, but it was awkward for me since I had to go through the kitchen and down the hall to get to it from my bedroom. The building was very old and the remodeling and upgrading must have been quite a challenge. There had been no electric or gas appliances before. Some apartments still didn't have bathroom fixtures or kitchen stoves, so we were quite lucky. A few tenants still had to walk down the stairs to the halfway landing for their bathroom facility. But despite some inconveniences, we were all grateful to be able to live on the *Île St. Louis*.

This island was a jewel at the heart of the city. Buttressed by tall stone walls, fortified against the sometimes strong currents of the Seine, the island was first called *L'Île des Vaches*, meaning 'Island of the Cows'. The ramp going down to the river across the street from our building was the access for cows to get water for drinking and bathing. By the 17th century, however, the island was in too ideal a location to remain pastureland.

In less than a hundred years, it had been converted to an architectural masterpiece that put the rest of Paris to shame. "An entire city, built with pomp, seemed to have miraculously sprung out of an old ditch," suggested a book I was given by our *concierge*. Pierre Corneille wrote those words. The year was 1643.

Our island was covered with classically beautiful *hôtels* constructed from stone with graceful wrought iron decorations. The façades are narrow because of lack of space, but the buildings are deep once you enter their *portes cochères*. The *quais* around the island were named after the three great houses of France, the last vestiges of monarchy: Orléans, Anjou and Bourbon. We inquired around and were glad to learn that the Commission of Ancient Monuments was protecting the old historic buildings on the island along the river. Louis Mercier, years and years ago, wrote that "the island is a *quartier* hemmed in by the river and separated from the *Cité*. It seems to have escaped the great corruption of the town, which has not yet penetrated here."

But it is not just this island that I love. It is all of Paris. e e cummings wrote:

Paris, thou art not
merely these streets trees silence
twilight, nor even this single star jotting
nothing busily upon the green edges of evening;
nor the faces which sit and drink on the boulevards, laughing
which converse, smoke smile, thou art
not only a million little ladies fluttering merely upon darkness –

these things thou art and thou art all which is alert perishable
alive; thou art the sublimation of our
lives eyes voices
thou art the gesture by which we express to one another all
which we hold more dear and fragile than death,
thou art the dark dear fragile
gesture which we use

In essence, Paris is the center of France, the elite hub. But it also had a provincial personality. This character trait did not come from the *haute monde*, the upper-class Parisians of Le Tout Paris. It came from the people who worked daily. These people were the real reason Paris was a world center. After working in and around the city streets all day, at night they return home to their own *quartier* and live as those in the provinces live. They maintain the same routines, the same traditions, but are still within the confines of Paris.

By now I had walked all over the city and knew at least some of its secrets. I knew that the *quartiers* of Paris were connected to the center of Paris by trams and the underground Metro. Paris was not one big city but a collection of villages that coexisted. There was a separate history of Paris not found in books, a history hidden behind the façades of old houses and store fronts and within the intimacy of manicured gardens. And there was romance, on the riding lanes in the *Bois de Boulogne* and along the *quais* and pathways that lined the Seine.

Beside the history in the majesty of the grand architecture of the *Place des Vosges*, there existed the reality of the daily routines which in themselves were history. Here was the saga of the food stores and eating places, the *boulangeries*, the *patisseries* and the *bistros*. In the shadow of the great halls of the *Louvre*, the goat herder still brought his goats to the door if you chose, and milked them for you. And although the urban goat herd still survived, it was only within the past couple of years that the urban cow-keeper had disappeared.

Every morning, my routine was to go down to the open market. Every neighborhood had one and ours was a short distance away at the other end of the *Île St. Louis* near the park. I loved discussing weather, politics, and thoughts of the day with the venders. I even learned the local dialect.

My time in Paris was not being wasted. I had made many new friends and was eager to read the books they recommended. I visited the Louvre not once, but almost daily. For me, Paris itself had become a book. However, there were also many times when I would look up from reading or gaze around a museum or park and realize, "I am alone." That is when memories attacked like a swarm of bees, stinging my brain to the point of tears.

Thoughts like, "No one had hugged me except my governess and she was paid to be there for me." Then there was the warm and now insecure memory of my time with Philippe. Had I reacted with such abandonment because I needed to be loved so much? Had I gone too far? Was I a wicked person? What would Philippe think of me once he had time to reflect?

Philippe did reflect, and he did surprise me. Now I needed to talk with someone, not necessarily to share my news, but to toss some of my ideas around, to exchange some of my newly acquired *insights*, but most of all to gain perspective. Sitting at my desk next to the window, I looked out. The city beckoned. Yes, I needed to go outside. Being alone was not a solution.

"Yes, operator, please connect me to ..." The phone was picked up at the other end. "Pamela? Libby here. I'm calling to see if you're up for a stroll. It is so beautiful outside and ..."

"Wonderful. I'll be ready in a jiff and meet you in front of your building. All right? Excuse me?"

"Yes, Pamela, I am still here ..."

"To Victor's office? That's a lovely idea ... meet him for lunch? Brilliant."

Once I had found that Paris the city was also a village, I felt less overwhelmed. Already the summer had passed and cooler days were becoming the norm. This day, the unwearied sun gave just enough warmth to lift the spirits.

One of my insights as I walked around the ancient streets and alleyways was that in Paris, the past, the present, and the future were all combined. It was a combination as complex as the human condition itself. I was young but the streets and places I was walking through had stories going back generations.

Although history was everywhere in the city, so was nature, a constant without the need for history. This was where I found peace. In nature, those who took the time to notice would find, if not inspiration, at least solace. Of course, Paris had huge manicured gardens as well as little formal floral spaces, but it was along the quays that the city felt restful as only a village can. While the Seine flowed through the heart of the city, along her sides, stretching the length of most of the quays, the *peupliers* and the *plantanes* soared, casting shadows over the streets and mesmerizing all who were fortunate enough to stroll beneath their great limbs.

Soon after moving to our apartment on the *Île St. Louis*, I asked our concierge, "What are those trees called?" pointing to the ones that lined the boulevard and the quays outside our windows. "They are the *Peupliers-trembles*," she replied with the pride of ownership as all of Paris appears to be to those who called it home. "These trembling poplars like humidity and grow more rapidly near rivers." She went on to explain that their botanical name, *populus tremuls*, was given because the leaves shiver in the wind. In the spring, the leaves form tiny cotton balls. The breeze chase wisps everywhere. Our apartment was full of these fluffs of cotton when we moved in.

"Thank you, Libby, for getting me outside to enjoy this absolutely perfect morning." Pamela smiled and waved her hand in the direction of the tree-lined quay straddling both sides of the Seine. We were walking along the *Quai aux Fleurs* after gingerly crossing the cursed *Pont St. Louis*. So far, there had been no loss of life on this structure; nevertheless, Pamela and I wasted no time going over to the other side.

The French love being outside and they love to talk. We passed men and women of all ages, laughing and chatting in small groups on the sidewalks. Slowly, we walked alongside the *terrasse* outside a neighborhood *café* and observed people sitting at tiny iron tables. The terrasse was separated from the sidewalk by moveable privet hedges in yellow painted boxes. I had seen enough to know that these locals might sit for hours sipping only one drink. At no charge, the *café* supplied pens and writing paper if customers wanted to write letters, newspapers if they wanted to read, or draughts if they wanted to play draughts (or checkers as we Americans call the game).

Further on, we passed a *boutique*, a milliner's shop, a *boulangerie*, and a *pâtisserie*. Each neighborhood had its own cluster of food stores for morning shoppers and women's apparel, gift items and other fun, non-essentials to satisfy afternoon shoppers. Climbing slowly up the cobblestone street was an elderly man, hunched over with a harness strapped to his shoulders. He pulled a cart full of bandboxes, but smiled as he single-handedly hauled his load down the narrow cobbled road. Across the street, a small group of children stood in front of a charcoal stove outside the door of a wine shop. They appeared to be hoping to coax a few free roasted chestnuts from this old man's grill.

There was much coming and going up and down the narrow streets. People busied themselves with their lives.

As Pamela and I walked, observed, and from time to time commented about the difference between the French and our compatriots, the Brits and the Americans, I kept wondering to myself how I could have married someone like Michael. He would never have enjoyed a casual stroll. He would never have behaved like these people, laughing simply because they enjoyed each other's company, delighting in roasted chestnuts or sitting at a *café* watching the world go by. But I loved every moment and was grateful that Pamela seemed to be enjoying it too.

Now we were working our way around the *Île de la Cité*, heading for the *Pont Neuf*, which we needed to cross to get to the *Grand Musée de Louvre*. Just ahead, on the *Pont des Arts*, with its metal substructure of half moons stretching across the Seine, we saw a row of men crowded together shoulder to shoulder, leaning over the railing. "Do let's take a look," I suggested to Pamela. With their backs turned to the city, the men faced the out-flowing river. Perhaps there was an overturned boat in the water below or some other type of catastrophe. She finally agreed. We hurried to the end of the island, peered over the wall and looked down at the river. Nothing unusual. Across the small expanse of water, we stared at the silent line of men and tried to discern what they were focused on below. Then we saw it. They were staring at a rowboat, a flat-bottomed rowboat with three fishermen leaning over the hull fishing. And that was it. The row of silent serious faces was merely watching the fishermen fish.

"Well, it may not be exciting, but isn't that a perfect example of life in Paris?" Pamela gave me a quizzical look. "No, I'm not crazy. These people are taking the time to look while we are always rushing." She wasn't following my thoughts. "Pamela, don't you think perhaps we could learn from them? I mean, learn to slow down and enjoy the moment?"

Pamela simply hunched her shoulders as we resumed our walking tour. But the sun beamed enough warmth that even my curt British friend could not resist showing enthusiasm for the moment. With a flourish of words, she exclaimed, "What an absolutely splendid day this is, Libby."

I smiled at her sudden enthusiasm.

We walked on in silence. Although the air was warm and moist and the view of the Seine soothing, my mind was on a separate track. I was remembering Natalie's party. Something she had said was nagging me. "The other night, Pamela, do you remember Natalie asserting that you can judge nothing while you are in it? That happiness is an 'aftermath'."

Pamela did not respond.

"Oh well," I said, wanting to break the silence. "You are right, Pamela, it is a beautiful morning."

"Perhaps, Libby dear, you are reading too much."

"You mean reading too much into what people are saying or reading too many books?"

"Both. And do be careful of Natalie. You two are not of the same ilk." Before I could understand what Pamela meant by that remark, a horn sounded. Pamela jumped. I laughed.

"You still aren't used to those, are you?"

"Now I may be older than you, young lady, but I am not that old." Pamela was almost forty. "But I must confess, I do miss the serenity of the peaceful horse and buggy era, though I guess the country set were late bloomers for this noisy, smelly contraption.

We used to go everywhere with our horses, either astride or in the pony cart or with our parents in the carriage."

"Let's sit down, have a little rest before we proceed any further." I could see Pamela was getting tired and I wanted to hear more about her life.

By now we had crossed the *Pont Neuf*, the oldest bridge in Paris and a beautiful structure. We were on the right bank and walking along the *Quai de la Megisserie*. Along the wall, we found a nice shaded place, sat down and surveyed the scenery dominated by the flowing Seine. Down by the water's edge, two lovers were locked in an embrace. I looked at them wistfully, then caught Pamela studying my face. To distract her, I turned and pointed out the cyclists whizzing by. Some were ridden by errand boys delivering baskets full of bread and vegetables. The smell of the fresh baked bread lingered long after the bicycles passed from view. Other bicyclists were out like us, simply enjoying the fresh air.

Birds serenaded us in the trees while squirrels hopped in and out of makeshift shelters, collecting rations for winter. Further down the river, a man washed his dog. Down the slope, another man lay sprawled across the grass, his beret hanging over his face keeping the sun out. Even from where we sat, we could hear him snoring contentedly. No hassles, no cares, everyone just enjoying the day.

By mutual agreement after ten minutes, we rose to continue our stroll. A little further on, an old man and a young boy were sitting beside the *Quai du Louvre*, the points of their fishing poles bouncing in the wavelets. Just beyond them was a painter. Dressed in brown baggy pants and a tan rumpled jacket with a black beret on his head, he had his arm extended in front of his face and was staring at the bridge with the paint brush held perpendicular to his eyes. The way the easel was set up, we could see his painting.

"He is measuring the perspective of the bridge with his eye, isn't he?"

We paused to admire his work. So as not to disturb him, Pamela whispered, "Yes, I think so. And look how he has captured the intricate architecture of the lovely old *Pont Neuf* on canvas. Even the stains are beautiful."

"Oh yes, can you see the strokes he made depicting the swirl of the river's currents? I love the colors, the reflections of light, the greens and blues and browns in the water gushing under the bridge. It would be wonderful to be able to paint like that."

We continued our stroll and soon reached the venerable Louvre Museum. This time it was the gems of nature we were after, not the gems inside the Museum, so we decided to walk along one of the paths in the *Jardin des Tuileries* and find a bench.

Children played with their hoops and balls and some young boys sailed their toy boats in the bubbling waters of the fountain. The sun continued being kind, considering the time of year. The leaves had already turned, many scattered along the pebbled path, but the birds, fooled by the warmth, had delayed their southern migration and contentedly crooned their summer serenades in the trees.

"I guess the trees are more in tune with the season than the birds. I hope the weather does not suddenly change and catch some of them in a freeze," Pamela said after she settled on the bench and had time to catch her breath.

Pigeons wheeled around the great Palace courtyards distancing themselves from their more sophisticated cousins in the tree branches. Pamela loved the sound and sights of nature even though she had become basically a city person. The architects of the Romantic era thought of Nature as being more than a word in the dictionary; but for the city planners, the dictionary was modern life and the buildings and streets of the city were its center. Paris with her many parks offered just enough nature to satisfy both schools of thought.

"In England we still have so many relatives with country homes that we can spend almost every weekend in the country, hiking and picking flowers. Victor enjoys the stables. He is quite a handy polo player, you know."

I smiled, thinking of my father who rode, not in polo matches, but as a member of the hunt in Washington. He and his friends had formed a club over the state line in Chevy Chase, Maryland. I also remembered my mother insisting that I go with her to the banquets with their bonfires and rituals for the returning huntsmen. I considered these primitive and unpleasant. If the huntsmen were successful, I had to go inside the club house and get away. The game was red fox. To me, killing such a pretty and innocent creature was awful. Perhaps polo was a better sport. Thinking about equestrian activities led my mind in another direction. I could almost see Philippe's grin as he held the secret treat in his back pocket, and his whistle to summon those big, beautiful, black horses.

Pamela must have noticed the smile crossing my face, but she did not ask the cause. Some thoughts were better left untold.

A small boy with a push toy that looked like a pony with wheels instead of hooves made his way close to Pamela's ankle. She pulled her foot back just in time. The child stopped, gave a slight bow and gravely said, *"Excusez-moi, Madame,"* before continuing down the path followed by his nanny.

"What a polite child." Pamela was rarely impressed with the manners of the French, the British standards being so high.

"Have you ever thought about having children?" I asked.

"Oh yes. Unfortunately, we have not been blessed with any. Perhaps this is as it should be. We love each other very much and Victor has never complained or made me feel uncomfortable about it."

"Oh God, I wonder what my future will be," I sighed. "I think it would be nice to have a child. However, I would have to be happily married to a normal man. Sorry." I grimaced. Pamela decided to remain silent.

We watched the children and the birds and the comings and going. Couples taking a stroll, occasional schoolchildren and older Parisians enjoying the afternoon sun, one old gentleman tossing breadcrumbs for the birds. Then, out of the blue, I found myself chatting about some of the things I had been learning these past few months "You said, Pamela that maybe I was reading too much, but I'd like to share some of the things I have learned."

"Certainly, Libby. Please don't be offended. I am anxious to hear about your studies."

"Thank you, Pamela. I have been reading the research that Dr. Freud has been conducting. In a sense, it is similar to what you were telling me about astrology. Remember, 'the universe is contained in the mind of man'? Freud doesn't express it quite that way, but he is giving us techniques to delve into our subconscious, exploring dreams, using what he calls psychoanalysis and free association. His protégé is Carl Jung who talks about archetypes and what he calls 'the collective unconscious'."

Pamela looked at me quizzically. I guess she wondered where my mind was with this new scientific mumbo jumbo. But with dreams and hopes and feelings coming to me all at once, I just needed to vent and was most appreciative to have an audience.

"Then in the art world, there are the Impressionists," I said. "They show us what is outside: the atmosphere of the place." I avoided Pamela's dubious glance.

"This is a new school of art. Being able to depict the air, the weather and the mood changes of the sky, all this leads to a dramatically new vision of the world."

Pamela did avow that she too loved the Impressionists. "Sometimes, I feel my very being is absorbed in gazing at the Impressionists' paintings," she said with surprising zeal. "I wonder, Libby, if you might say that my absorption reflects something greater than just enjoying what the painting depicts."

Was she going to return to astrology talk? She noticed my wrinkled brow and decided to explain herself.

"What I mean is, perhaps I am touching on what my friends in the Theosophical movement called the etheric body…"

"The etheric body?"

"Yes, it is another level, beyond the astral level."

I decided not to question any of this.

"… which would make the experience I am having with my eyes, my sense of vision more of a spiritual encounter. Perhaps hidden behind the artistic image I am viewing, there lies an *eternal, hidden element*."

I wasn't ready to talk about things supernatural, although something about my dreams had given me a hint. At night I could travel anywhere, be anyone, experience a veritable release from the confines of my body. However, although I prayed to God and Mary and Jesus, the eternal, hidden element was not yet a personal experience.

I was also aware of my immaturity. At this point in my life, my emotions and feelings veered toward something more basic and concrete. So to bring the conversation back to earth, I asked, "Since you were talking about the Impressionists, do you remember Gina? She has been experimenting with the palette knife using contrasting primary colors." Pamela clearly wasn't aware of painting techniques so I veered off into yet another direction still wanting to make my point or perhaps just find a point to make.

"All right, forget painting. Think about the aeroplane, Pamela. When Philippe…" just mentioning his name made me blush, "took me up in his plane, I will never forget what it was like looking down on the world from above and what how strange it felt getting lost, at least visually, when we flew inside a cloud." Pamela smiled at my enthusiasm.

"So you see what I mean?" I continued, not at all sure she was following me in this, but getting a better idea for myself where my thoughts were headed. "With all the scientific inventions and research, with the feats of aviation and with the experimentation in the arts, shouldn't we have a greater understanding of ourselves?" By now, Pamela must have thought I was crazy, but before she could offer advice, I returned to the original subject. Did I want to have children? I had not forgotten. That was what had spurred me on; something so personal that it hit my every nerve and forced me to reach out with my mind trying to come up with a formula for myself.

"If we could understand ourselves before having a child, wouldn't it be better for the child?" I took a deep breath. This was a sensitive subject for me. My childhood had been so lonely and my relationship to my parents was strained at best. "I don't think I am ready to take that responsibility yet, even if I were secure in my marriage."

"Perhaps one day?"

"Perhaps," I said with a smile. I had my secrets. But Pamela persisted and eventually, I was able to share something special.

"By the way, Pamela," I began tentatively, "Philippe has asked me to go flying again. He wants to take me to Provence. What do you think?"

"Oh, Libby, how divine … But … I don't know. You are still married to Michael. But…Oh my….maybe?"

Patricia Daly-Lipe

Pamela did not give me outright approval. Of course, I didn't need her permission, but it would be nice to have had her support. I wasn't so naïve as not to realize that I was venturing into something far more significant than sightseeing, but I wasn't ready to admit it openly. Fear kept the truth in hiding.

Pamela studied my face. I was hurt. She knew what an awful muddle life had become for me. She and Victor had spent endless hours trying to think of a way for me to have my freedom and my respectability too. Philippe was not only a fine, honorable man; he was a part of an old, established family. Since his father's death, he had inherited the title, Count, and had assumed all the responsibilities that went with it, handling them very well. If our relationship were to become permanent, something would have to be done about my marriage.

"Oh, 'what the heck', as you Americans like to say," Pamela replied, after what she knew to be too long a pause. I held my breath. "You should bloody well go."

I threw my arms around my astonished friend.

"But," she added, "Let's not tell Victor."

I was bubbling. "Provence. The land of light. Home of Cézanne, Matisse, van Gogh. I love their paintings. Don't you? It really would be a treat to see the places they painted." The smile could not be wiped from my face. I babbled on and on, but what I was really thinking was not something I was ready to talk about. Pamela fell in with the game as we continued the superficial conversation.

"Oh, Libby." Pamela was smiling herself. "There you go again. You are learning so much. I am studying finance and business, but you are way ahead of me in your art and philosophy. You really should think about writing a book." We vacated the cement bench and strolled arm in arm the few blocks to the *Place Vendôme*, the banking center of Paris, home of the plush Ritz Hotel, Cartier and everything expensive in Paris.

As we passed the *Place de la Concord*, Pamela asked, "Do you remember Ambassador Herrick's speech the day after Lindbergh's flight? No? Well, let me tell you some things your ambassador said. Introducing your pilot, Ambassador Herrick told the story about King Louis XVI's execution. After the guillotine fell, the priest

168

cried out to the assembled mob, '*The spirit of St. Louis* ascends to the skies.' Here we are, Herrick said, in 1927, and the spirit of St. Louis has returned."

"Pamela, thanks for telling me. I wasn't there. Michael was, but he didn't tell me that story. It is compelling, isn't it? Sometimes things happen simply because they are supposed to." Where did that insight come from? I paused to reflect. Then looking to Pamela for confirmation, I asked, "Don't you agree?" She smiled and took my hand as we strolled down the lane.

Our walk was over. We had arrived at Victor's bank. He was pleased to see his wife and me looking so enlivened. The long walk had done us both good. From the bank, it was only a short distance to the Hotel Maurice with its lovely old-world charm and elegance. The lunch was pleasant, which is to say, in a country where meals are a high cultural experience, this was more of an English venue and not terribly filling, but the conversation was agreeable. When we had finished, Victor suggested we take our coffee and *petits fours* outside on the terrace. Finally, with coffee in hand, he could delay his news no longer. "I must go to New York," he began. "And unfortunately, I must go alone."

Pamela turned ashen. "You *have* to go? When? How long?" She hated to be left behind; as much as she claimed loving her independence, her life was still very connected to and contingent upon her husband.

"There is an important conference in two weeks. I wish I could fly, but Lindbergh has only given us a glimpse. It will take years before they will build the planes to fly people commercially across the ocean, so I am afraid I will be away several weeks. Allowing for the ship's passage, the round of meetings scheduled in New York ..."

"Will you be seeing my father, Victor?" I interrupted. Being keen about Victor's trip, I had failed to notice Pamela's pained expression. Considering the circumstances, my eagerness was out of place. Still Victor responded in the same tone hoping more than likely his wife could use the time to adjust to the news and compose herself.

"I will be seeing your father. That brings us to the important point. What do you want me to say?"

Pamela remained quiet while her husband and I talked. I had written my father. He had responded but in such ambiguous terms, I couldn't be sure what he really thought. He did confirm, however, that he would send me an allowance once a month. I didn't know if this meant that Michael would no longer receive funds from him. If that were the case, Michael would have to rely solely on his own inheritance. I wasn't sure what that would mean for him and I didn't care.

"Why don't you plan on staying at our house when I am gone?" Victor invited. "Pamela hates to be alone and I am sure she would be delighted with your company."

Chapter Nineteen

If you are lucky enough to have lived in Paris as a young man, then wherever you go for the rest of your life, it stays with you, for Paris is a moveable feast.
Ernest Hemingway
(borrowed in part from Gertrude Stein)

Philippe and I dined together often and took many lovely strolls around the winding streets of Paris. From the *Faubourg St. Germain*, home of many literary salons, to the *Boulevard Montparnasse* where, at *Place Vivan*, Leon Trotsky and fellow exile, Lenin, had sat playing chess while awaiting the collapse of czarist Russia. Hand in hand, we wandered into the ghettos of artists like Lipschitz, Zadkine, Soutine and Chagall where Philippe, his dignified status masked by an old weather-beaten overcoat, chatted freely about art and politics, philosophy and history. I fell more and more in love every day with this brilliant man who showed so much compassion and sensitivity.

One evening after attending a performance at the Opéra, we decided to linger and enjoy the warm evening air. We chose a small *café* on the edge of the *Place de la Bastille* and ordered two Anisettes. There is nothing more Parisian than sitting at an outdoor *café*, the ultimate people percolator where solitude and companionship, meal or snack, coffee or wine all mix perfectly. And near every great Parisian *café*, there is also art. Philippe told me about the *bals musettes* that used to be danced around the Bastille. I contributed nothing to the conversation; just basked in his words, mesmerized by his eyes, oblivious to the lively chatter around us as other young people talked about nothing and everything. It was practically morning by the time we arrived at my apartment. Biting my lip, I realized how close we had come to spending what little was left of the entire night together. Etiquette and rules passed down from strict upbringing prevailed. Then again, *Madame la Concierge* would have known and that would have been difficult to live with.

Meanwhile, Philippe's main concern was my position in regard to the Church. He had spoken to his prelate, but was not encouraged. I had written another letter to both my parents, although I still did not dare put into words Michael's perversion. I wrote that we were living separate lives and that I wished I could have my freedom. Perhaps they could intercede to the Church on my behalf. I also telegraphed of Victor's imminent arrival. Although they were looking forward to meeting Victor, their response to my needs was cold. They affected not to understand anything about me or my life style. Perhaps they never had. Obviously, to them, their daughter's behavior was embarrassing and irresponsible. I suppose they thought I was simply acting out some kind of youthful rebellion or perhaps, in their eyes, I was succumbing to the wild life that was Paris as depicted in Fitzgerald's and Hemingway's books.

But it was not a wild life. I was participating in one of the most interesting and exciting periods in all of history. Change, experimentation, challenges were happening everywhere in and around Paris.

One of the changes and challenges was the sport of racing. Aerial races were at their zenith after the Great War. One-man design teams, backyard mechanics and veteran pilots were eager competitors in the sport of air racing in the United States. In France, enthusiasts had the support of the French government. I knew that Michael was eager to compete. He had been among the first group of aviators to receive a private pilot's license. However, being an American, he had to affiliate himself with a French citizen to qualify. Someone reported to Philippe that he had. Despite his betrayal and all the grief it caused me, I was curious, if not concerned, to know if Michael had found his place in the sport of aviation. Trying not to be vindictive, I consoled myself with the thought that what was meant to happen, would. Philippe had said as much; he was sure we would be able to arrange the legalities so we could share a lifetime together.

It was a joy to drive to the aeroport with Philippe and watch him work on his monoplane. Philippe fancied flying, but unlike Michael, he was not at all interested in racing. He preferred the mechanical aspect of flight. With the assistance of a friend, Philippe was constantly modifying his new plane, the one he had christened so many lifetimes ago. His monoplane, called a Puss Moth, was not dissimilar from the one Lindbergh had flown; at least it appeared that way to my nonprofessional eye. I still enjoyed flying in the biplane and hoped he would never get rid of it. The new plane was enclosed so you couldn't feel the fresh wind blowing in your face or hear the sound of the straps singing in the breeze. I loved to smell the damp air and to peer over the side and spy on the goings on the ground below.

I hadn't seen much of Michael. After our confrontation, he had politely offered to move out of the apartment – it was the only polite aspect of his behavior in my opinion – and he didn't appear to mind my being seen publicly with Philippe. Besides, it was, after all, his doing. I did wonder, however, how he explained our relationship to his friends. Only once when I came home early from an evening at the Theatre with Philippe did I find Michael in the apartment.

Philippe had ended the evening with a passionate kiss at the door and as always I responded with *a soft, liquid joy* as Mr. Joyce had described it. It was hard to maintain the proper decorum. I hoped nobody, especially Mr. Joyce, would see us. It was getting difficult to say good night and enter the apartment alone. I could not halt the misery my body and emotions endured for not allowing myself to give into passion. This particular evening, when I had closed the door and was facing the library, I saw Michael's coat and umbrella thrown over the Louis XV chair facing the fireplace. He must have come in to get some of his clothes. I had no idea where he lived, but I knew that from time to time he had come in to collect clothing and other personal items.

Putting my purse and keys on the hall table, I looked up and concentrated on my reflection. My flushed face peered back at me from the gold framed mirror. It would not be a good idea for Michael to see me in such a disheveled state. He might guess what I had been doing. Arranging my hair, I was distracted by a groan from the back of the apartment.

It had to be Michael. Was he all right? Should I go look? Just as I was finished pulling my hair back with the comb, I heard it again. I paused, listening attentively. Again, a long and what sounded like a painful guttural groan. Dropping my comb, I ran down the hallway to where I thought the sound came from, the bath.

Michael was there. In the bathroom. The door was slightly ajar. Fortunately, I stopped before bursting in. What I saw was not an injured man. It was Michael enjoying the pleasure of a solitary man, slowly and methodically urging his need to its fulfillment. I was momentarily paralyzed by the image in the mirror. It reflected a man plainly possessed. I had never seen a man in this state before. I could feel the heat rising to my cheeks; my whole body began to tremble.

Slowly, I drew away from the door. Clearly, Michael was not remotely aware of a witness. He was oblivious to everything except the intensity of his own pleasure. I allowed myself another look. I had never seen a man's organ before and certainly had never seen it erect. The heat seared through my body. I felt vulnerable and, how could I describe it? I felt liquid. In a trance-like state, I watched his fingers slide up and down, his face contorted. I couldn't watch any longer. Turning away, I tiptoed down the hall. On my trek back, I heard the loudest moan of all. *"Ahhh"*.

My knees practically buckled beneath me. Feelings, foreign until now, made me light-headed. At the same time, confusing thoughts played havoc with my mind. What had triggered this physical response? Mine and his? What caused him to feel this way here in the place we once shared? The apartment is filled with my perfume, my flowers, my lace and linens. Could it have been me he is reacting to after all? Is it I who am truly the one he loves? If he does, could I take him back?

The image of his huge organ returned and I had to squeeze my eyes shut as if to ward it off. Seeing him in this most intimate encounter with himself, could it be that Michael did not have a male lover after all? This was my husband. I *was/am* still married to this man. A picture of the two of us in front of family and friends, committing to a life together was depicted in a photograph on the mantel. I remember kneeling before the priest, before God, and the priest laying his anointed hands on the ring Michael had placed on my finger saying: "God all-powerful, send your Holy Spirit, the Spirit of union, to sanctify this ring. Through Christ our Lord. Amen." I still wore the ring. What else had the priest said? *"Et ne nos inducas in tentationem. / Sed libera nos a malo."* And lead us not into temptation, but deliver us from evil. Was it seeing his manhood that made me feel this way? Was I evil to be tempted to yield to his affections?

Meanwhile, part of my mind was still functioning logically. I reached the front door and, trembling, managed to open it silently. Then with fervent force, I slammed the solid wood door shut making a huge racket. Michael would think I had just then come in. I heard him pull the chain over the toilet. Taking a deep breath, I affected innocence and called out, "Michael, is that you?"

After a few minutes, he emerged from the bathroom, looking embarrassed. His fingers were clenched in his palms and his head made an involuntary jerk as he struggled to find the right words. All the way down the hall, he mumbled something about missing papers. His face was flushed. Did he notice that mine was red as well? I thought he might change his mind. He might take me into his arms. Did I want him to? Did he love me after all?

There was a moment when I believed he would say or do something. I held my breath as time stretched. We stood facing each other. Neither of us spoke but neither looked away … looking, but not touching. Finally, Michael glanced down, fumbled in his pocket, withdrew a key and announced quite formally that the motor car he had driven over had to be returned. I nodded and watched him go. Michael never returned to the apartment unannounced.

Evidently Michael paid the rent on time. It was an awkward arrangement. The concierge knew what was happening and had no doubt spread the news all over the neighborhood. I decided my father should be told the truth as well.

Meanwhile, I had no success with the priests of *Notre Dame*. Since Michael refused to cooperate, they said there was nothing the Church could do for me. I wondered whether they even believed me. It was a man's world. Our strange lifestyle did not affect Michael's life in the least, but it was ruining mine.

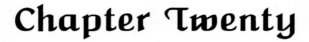
Chapter Twenty

Joyce's trick was seeing symbols everywhere.

Beyond the world of opposites
is an unseen, but experienced,
unity and identity in us all.

Joseph Campbell

Finally, the day arrived for Victor's departure. He was sailing on the country's most luxurious liner, the *S.S. France*. Pamela and I escorted him to the *Gare Saint Lazare* and waved as the train steamed out, heading for the port of Le Havre. To cheer Pamela up, Philippe and I planned dinner parties, reserved seats at concerts and obtained tickets to the Opera.

At the end of Victor's second week away, I was asked to bring Pamela to the *Comtesse de Beau's* house for dinner. An American student had arrived in Paris and the *Comtesse* was eager for him to meet English-speaking people who lived in Paris and could show him around.

Her Parisian *pied à terre* was located near *L'Hôtel des Invalides*. I had been there before with Philippe for an occasional Sunday dinner or lunch during the week and I believed the *Comtesse* enjoyed my company. But I also noted Philippe no longer tried to hide his love for me. Such openness was at once unfamiliar and refreshing.

At this house, more than at *Fointaine-les-Nonnes*, I could feel the presence of Philippe's late father. Very masculine, the house was paneled with dark wood. Heavy brocade hung on the windows, and dark Oriental rugs ran the length of the hallways and down the stairs off the library. The library itself was an enormous room with books tiered on floor to ceiling shelves. A large Louis XV desk stood adjacent to the only window at one end. Despite its severity, this was my favorite room. The *Comtesse* liked punctuality and expected us in her *petit salon* upstairs on time. Although the residence fascinated

Pamela, we had to hurry. Nevertheless, along the way there was little she did not notice. For one thing, she remarked, probably more than one generation of the family had lived in this house. There were so many prints, lithographs, paintings, *objets d'art* everywhere and yet the house appeared cozy and comfortable.

Philippe intercepted us half way up the stairs. He kissed me right on the lips in front of Pamela. As he slipped his arm around me, I blushed, but didn't try to discourage him as we walked as a threesome up the rest of the stairs. At the landing, we turned left passing many family portraits hanging along the hallway before entering the *petit salon*. The *Comtesse* and a young man were deeply engrossed in conversation. Pamela and I were apparently the only other guests this evening.

Only a year older than I, Joseph Campbell was bright and zealous about his studies. He had come to Paris to study medieval philology and Old French and *Provençal*. With his boyish enthusiasm, he appeared much younger. Perhaps it was my domestic incertitude that made me feel older. His ears were set high indicating, according to Pamela, a love of music, and his mouth was almost sensuous. With bushy eyebrows set low over pale blue eyes, it was hard to avoid his gaze. So when he made a point and fixed his eyes on you, his look was so intense, you were glued to his every thought. He wore his wavy, thick hair combed straight back with a part to the left exposing a broad, clear, intelligent forehead.

The *Comtesse* encouraged me to enter into the conversation. Joseph did most of the talking, about America, France, history and literature. However, when it came to Shakespeare and Company, suddenly we had something very much in common.

"Yes," he said. "I went to Shakespeare and Company. When I arrived in Paris here's this *Ulysses, Ulysses, Ulysses*. So I bought the book and took it home, and when I got to chapter three, it started out with illegible verbage. It read, 'Ineluctable modality of the visible; at least that if no more, thought through my eyes. Signatures of all things I am here to read…' It had been published by Sylvia Beach, at Shakespeare and Co. at…"

"Yes, I know," I cried. "Number 12 *rue de l'Odéan*."

"Right. So," he continued despite my outburst, "I went around there, you know, in high academic indignation: 'What do you think of this!' I demanded of the little lady at the book shop."

"Surely you weren't going to return it?" Until now, Pamela had sat quietly throughout this entire conversation amused by Joseph's boyish American ardor.

"Well no, not really. But I did feel, you know, offended." We could picture his schoolboy posture.

"And Sylvia Beach – I didn't know who she was – just took me on and sold me the books that would convince me of Joyce's brilliance. I took them back to my room and that was almost the end of my interest in medieval philology."

So Sylvia Beach had assisted Joseph just as she had me. I was impressed with the impact this book was having on Joseph's life.

"*Ulysses* is a phenomenon here in Paris, but it was banned in America, you know."

At first, I didn't want to infringe upon Mr. Campbell's enthusiasm and his pride in knowing the great Irish author's work, so I said little except to mention Miss Beach's recommendation of Joyce's recent book of poems.

"That was a very wise recommendation since Joyce's writing on the whole is almost impenetrable." That word again. My face was turning crimson at Joseph's choice of adjective just as it had at the *Surréaliste* exhibit.

"Miss Beach gave me clues to deciphering the words and phrases. I thought if she could lead me through the first section, I might understand his style and continue. Instead, I have this huge collection of references she sold me: mythology, the classics, history - oh yes, she also recommended a book about music. She said that music was something Mr. Joyce lived for and that there were musical references throughout his works."

"That must have been very expensive!" Pamela exclaimed, going straight for the practical aspect. "I mean, having to buy all those reference books."

"Yes, but they were worth the money. She also sold me a journal that was just published in November called *transition*. It is written by Eugène Jolas. In that issue, Mr. Jolas sketches the early chapters of a book Mr. Joyce is calling *'Work in Progress'*. Mr. Jolas and his wife told Miss Beach that they are publishing this journal because they like to 'daydream about new forms in art and language'. But you know, that is precisely what is happening in Joyce. I remember one line of his that the journal referred to. Let's see. It goes something like this: 'Do you tell me that now? I do in troth. And didn't you hear it a deluge of times? You deed, you deed! I need, I need!'"

Then suddenly embarrassed by his tirade of sorts, Joseph concluded. "So that's what I am learning. I am now fascinated with Mr. Joyce and I am beginning to understand his words." Before we could respond, he looked at each one of us, smiled and said, "And there you have it."

Miss Beach really wanted Joseph to understand Joyce thoroughly and he was beginning to. We both were truly privileged by her attention. In fact, in his case, I thought, her attention may have changed Joseph's future, as well as his career.

"And did you work it out?" asked my back-to-basics British friend who did not know Sylvia Beach at all.

"Yes. *Ulysses* is actually based on Dante's *The Divine Comedy*, the second stage in particular, the *Inferno*. Now that I see the parallels, I can follow Joyce's thoughts. Hell is simply the experience of your limitations. No one can show you the divine dimension of life that transcends your experiences. That is the state of the characters in *Ulysses*: they are bound, locked in the hard ring of their ego systems, devaluing the mystical dimensions. I am not finished with the book though. Besides, it should take at least two or three or even four readings before I should be able to appreciate fully Joyce's nuances and innuendoes. Strange and magical, even mystical things happen when you least expect." His face was radiant. The *Comtesse* watched the young man intently, clearly eager to learn from him. Enthusiasm must be the key to staying young in spirit.

His explanation of *Ulysses* fascinated me also. I wanted so much to be able to read that book. Listening to Joseph made me think some of my own questions about life might be intrinsically tied to Joyce's ideas. For the moment, however, I was happy with Joyce's poems.

"Fortunately his poems are not that difficult. I have found them to be lovely: quite soft and sensitive," I piped in before I realized the implications of what I had said as my face turned pink.

"That's wonderful. I am sure you will agree that we need more poetry that reveals what the heart is ready to recognize."

I could not believe Joseph had just voiced what I had believed ever since I could remember.

Philippe sat through this whole repartee, a silent observer. I am sure he noticed the blush. I had told him that I wanted to read the poems to him, but not until we were alone. He loved me so much. I could see it in his eyes. We had talked about how difficult it was for him to behave like a gentleman when we were together. We needed to get away from Paris. And so he had planned to take me to the south of France before it became too cold. It was a trip he had been living in his mind for weeks. I know he hoped I could then relax. Without admitting as much in words, we both looked for honesty, compassion and romance.

Chapter Twenty-One

The meeting of two personalities is like the contact of two chemical substances: if there is any reaction, both are transformed.

Carl Jung

We embraced. The ruins of the château of the Marquis de Sade loomed above.

After flying down from Paris with me in the front cockpit, Philippe landed his little biplane on a field near the hill town of Lacoste. We gathered our belongings and walked the short distance to the town where we were greeted like heroes. Everyone wanted a ride in the plane, but Philippe was patient. Slowly and with the ultimate in manners, he was able to get beyond the crowd and find proper and private lodging for a few nights. I stood behind Philippe as the arrangements were finalized not wanting the caretaker to see my excitement or my unease.

When we had settled in our room, Philippe, sensing my hesitation and mood, hastened to suggest we just leave the bags, unpack later and instead, take a hike to the top of the town, to the famed château of the Marquis de Sade. I trembled remembering the note that had been left in my apartment. I had never shared this with Philippe and didn't want to admit knowing anything about the Marquis to him now. He had placed so much time, energy and care into planning this trip for me. To him, it was the beauty of Lacoste, not the ugly ghost of the Marquis he wanted to share.

While I nervously removed my toiletries to freshen up, Philippe talked about the history of this place. "The château was begun in the eleventh century."

Not letting him complete his thought, I grabbed his hand. "Do let's go up and explore."

Patricia Daly-Lipe

Romance was going to have to wait. He had to be patient. I was tense. Philippe wanted to see me in a happy mood, so he followed me out the door.

Hand in hand, we hiked up the narrow stone roads and the walled-in steep stone paths that ascended from the ancient village up to the ruins. But by the time we reached the summit, clouds had formed and within seconds, the rain beat down on us. We ran for shelter as thunder cracked and lightning flashed. The only refuge was what was left of the *château*. The structure was spooky, sinister, cold and, – how else to describe it? – it reeked of transgressions. I knew too much. With me squeezing his hand tightly, he led the way into the dark shell of the castle.

There was no light except from the flashes of lightning. Treading carefully, Philippe groped the wall until he found a spot we could lean against and be at least partially protected. He held me close and attempted to take my mind off the fearsome storm as well as the foreboding structure.

"Please don't worry, Libby. This castle has remained empty and unfinished for years. It's hard to believe, but I understand there is a distant relative of the Marquis who plans to restore it."

I looked around each time the lightening lit up the walls. There was no evidence that anyone had ever actually lived here, but maybe it was what I couldn't see that would be worth saving. I trembled at the thought.

Climbing up the hillside path, what we had seen before the rain began was a nearly roofless castle that had not weathered the elements gracefully. The ghosts of this sadistic adventurer were probably hovering in the rooms below. This thought made me shiver, but Philippe, thinking I was chilled, gallantly put his coat over my shoulders.

"I am sorry this happened. Look at you, my poor dear. You are so frightened." He held me tenderly.

This time when the lightning flashed, it was immediately followed by a loud crack of thunder. It must have been close because the walls themselves seem to tremble. We ducked out from under the overhang and ran down stone steps to a corridor. Carefully following the passageway, we found ourselves going deeper into the bowels of the castle. On this floor the rooms were empty and it was pitch black. At least we were out of the worst part of the rain.

"Please, let's not go any further." I was terrified. "I don't mind getting a little wet." It was completely dark until suddenly there was a crash and we saw lightning flare from an opening in the stone. What looked like dragons and monsters formed shadowy silhouettes on the wall directly across from where we stood.

Philippe held me tightly. I snuggled against his body, but still shook uncontrollably. He ran his hand through my hair and kissed my wet curls.

"I have waited so long, dear Libby. Waited to be with you, alone and away from the eyes and ears of Paris." Just then the thunder broke again. He held me even more tightly until I relaxed a little. Since the storm was not about to end, still holding me in his embrace, he asked, "Maybe to help take away your fear, I could tell you something about the Marquis?" As long as he continued to hold me, it didn't matter what he spoke about. I nodded.

"He was born in 1740, this so-called Marquis. His real name was Donatien Alphonse François, but he became the Count de Sade when his father died in the mid 1700s. He fought in the Seven Years War then was imprisoned by his own commanders."

"Imprisoned by his own commanders?"

"His commanders had good reasons, Libby. The Count's behavior was scandalous."

Now I hoped Philippe wasn't going to describe what behavior was scandalous. He had me distracted from the storm, but I was not comfortable with the subject. Nevertheless, he continued.

"At one point he actually married, but he couldn't have had much time with his wife because for twenty-seven years he was incarcerated, including several years in the Bastille." He paused and gently smoothed my damp hair back from my face with his hand. "Libby, remember the lighting of the *Colonne de Juillet?*"

The memory made me smile. It was another special time for us both. I remembered listening to him talk about history as we sipped our drinks in the wee hours of the night at the *café*. We were sitting outside and as the other young couples around us were talking, all I heard was Philippe's soft voice and I remembered thinking to myself how much I loved this man. And now, here I was being held by my love, alone with him at last.

"How times have changed," I whispered thinking more about our own relationship than the fate of the Marquis.

Philippe's hands were moving around my shoulders and caressing my back drawing me closer. I looked up to his face but it was dark and I couldn't see his features, only the outline of his head. He could have done anything to me at that moment. "Libby, I love you so much but this is the wrong place so…" He took my hands in his and returned to his tale. "The whole time de Sade was in prison, he wrote. He called his work romances, but part of his writing included six-volumes, the *Philosophy of Vice*. Frankly, I am not at all sure you can call his writing noteworthy." *I know. Please don't tell me more*, I thought to myself.

Philippe glanced down at me, probably realizing this was not an appropriate subject to be discussing. As I didn't say anything, he must have assumed I was nevertheless interested in his little history lesson so he continued. He most likely wanted to clarify his position on this sordid subject as well.

"I must tell you, my dear Libby, that once I understood what he believed, I was not in the least tempted to complete any of his books." He paused and looked out into the night. The rain was still pounding and the clouds were thick, dark and ominous. "If you really want to know what the Count was all about, I can tell you this much …"

He let go of my hands and brought me closer with his arms. I could feel his need, his and my desire to kiss, to hold each other, to feel every part of each other's bodies. Not yet, not here, not in this place. I think it was the only thing he could think of doing to avoid making a move too soon, using words as a diversion.

"If I continue telling you about this man, it may sound coarse." I was trembling, but not from fear of the storm anymore but from fear of my feelings. Now it was I who wanted the talk to continue. "Shall I?" he asked but in a tone that sounded more like, 'please don't make me'.

But I mumbled yes while sinking deeper into the folds of his arms. Feeling his strong, muscular body against mine, my heart throbbed. A desire, a new sensation, was taking over. Instinctively, with my head nestled under his chin, I sighed as my body seemed to be loosing control. I hoped he didn't hear me sigh, but he was so close. He began lacing his fingers through my hair with one hand, holding me tightly with the other. Then suddenly, he stopped. Again the fear: not here, not now. Taking a deep breath, he looked away. With the storm raging in the background, almost by rote, as if he had memorized the lines for a school assignment, he began reciting the Count's tale.

"de Sade believed that since sexual deviation and brutality occur in nature, they must be considered natural." Turning back to face me, he whispered, "Libby, this man was a monster. All his volumes of writing dealt with some form of deviant sexual behavior: women tied up in chains, self-flagellation and even necrophilism." I shivered, sorry to have encouraged him to tell me these things.

As we stood huddled next to the opening in the wall, lightening flashed again and I briefly imagined seeing an eerie surrealistic, ghostly male figure reveal itself on the stone bulwark across the yard. I could almost hear the wails of women emanating from the rocky floors beneath my feet and cries echoing down the maze of hallways descending to the dungeon I knew must be below. Once more, I shuddered and involuntarily snuggled even tighter into his embrace.

The lightning flashed again, this time followed by a roar so loud that it was as if the very foundation moved. I jumped; but with his arms holding me tightly, I was less afraid than when the storm began. I began to distance myself from the scene. The storm was now more like a performance with Philippe and me as the privileged audience.

But just as it had begun so quickly, so it ended. The show was over. Cautiously we climbed back up the passageway and stepped out onto the wet, sandy soil. The air was heavy. More rain was likely to come, so, hand in hand, we hurried down the hill. The lull did not last. Raindrops grew into hail bullets, and the wind became serious as its volume increased.

Back in our room at the lodging, Philippe helped me remove my wet outer garments. Outside, the rain tapped rhythmically against the glass window panes, a soothing almost sensuous sound now that we were inside and getting dry. My hair was dripping wet, but I needed to take off all my clothing first before I caught a chill. As I sat on the side of the bed, Philippe got down on his knees and attempted to pull off my sticky, damp stockings.

"No, please, I can do that."

He looked hurt.

"No, I mean, oh Philippe, please." I held out my arms. Impulses and desires replaced thoughts. Any indignity I might have felt in any other circumstance vanished as my eyes focused on his. "Please, please come up here with me." Philippe stood, removed his shirt and raised me off the bed and into his arms. As my trembling hands undid his belt and helped him pull his trousers down, I felt his manhood. At the same time, cautiously and tenderly, he removed what remained of my undergarments. Our bare bodies came together. Pulling back the duvet, he gently laid me down arranging the pillow beneath my head. My eyes spoke what my mouth could not. His eyes responded saying yes.

"It was you I saw; it was really you," I whispered vividly remembering the half-dream I'd had with Joyce's book of poetry lying by my side. Philippe didn't understand and probably, he didn't hear me either Yes, now, his body was saying. Yes, I replied my arms around him, drawing him down. Yes. Our lips met. With his body settled over mine, he could feel my breasts, my pounding heart, my desire. Outside the window, the clouds had moved away, the rain had stopped and a full moon was released from hiding. A soft light shone on the bed.

Yes now. I responded to his love completely. He tried to be slow but he was too ready. Gently but firmly he penetrated. There was a moment of pain, but what followed was a sensation I had never experienced before. Involuntarily, I moaned, *"Ohhh"*, as my whole body shuddered. My legs tightened around his back, my arms clasped him firmly as I felt him throb. When he let go, his stream surged throughout my body, sending a pulsating but pleasant tremor that left me breathless. Yes! At last, at last. Yes, finally. At last we were one. Yes. I sighed as tears trickled down my cheeks, tears of joy.

We slept like that, our bodies enmeshed. Philippe looked pleased as he dozed, eyes closed, his mouth a little open but clearly turned up at the edges. He slept with me held tightly in his arms. In the morning we made love again. I had never felt so relaxed, so happy.

When I finally got up, I realized we had stained the sheets. "Don't worry, I will take care of that," he said. "You must wash. Did you bring a douche?"

"What is that?"

Suddenly he realized how innocent I really was. He found a soft washcloth and told me to cleanse myself meticulously.

However, when I went to wash, I was not concerned with repercussions. I was in a magical place. The reflection in the mirror showed a glowing, radiant face. My eyes sparkled bluer than ever. No longer a virgin, I was a woman at last and it felt wonderful. For the first time in my life, I wasn't embarrassed to be naked. *So this was what it was all about?* I felt like running back and starting all over but when I peeked in the bedroom, I could see that Philippe had already removed the sheets. We had several more days to spend together. I would have to be patient. We should go outside, enjoy the fresh warm air and this quaint little village. Besides, I was famished.

Chapter Twenty-Two

. . . the full potential of the acorn is be the mighty oak.

Unknown

Philippe and I spent the day walking through the narrow stone streets of Lacoste. I saw the town as a veritable tapestry of stone. Texture, tone, contrast, stones of every size and every variation of brown and grey converging here, spreading apart there and coming back together.

Lacoste is in the shadow of the Luberon Mountains. The main industry had been stone mining. With the invention of cement, the mining had practically stopped. Now, although money was made from lavender and sunflowers, the legacy was evident everywhere. Stone walls, stone steps, stone streets, stone buildings, stone everywhere, stone cold or hot depending on the angle of the sun of Provence.

The warmth of the southern sun replaced the odious emotions I had felt in the cold stone castle of the Marquis de Sade. Here below in the town, the sun shimmers off the stones on the streets and on the walls. It feels good. Of course, I was also responding to the warmth and tenderness I felt with Philippe. As we walked together, he talked about some of the trials this town had been subjected to in the course of French history.

"They say conflict tends to connect. In battles the families of soldiers unite for the cause. Generations have passed up and down these steep streets of Lacoste. Some generations stumbled and fell; others recovered but did not learn. It's as though this town was too old to accommodate modern conflict. Lacoste had enough scars already. Through all the battles and conflicts, this tapestry of stone had somehow withstood and stoically stayed still defying time."

There were many *pigeonniers* similar to the one at Philippe's château. In the rest of France, pigeons were considered a delicacy and reserved for the nobility to eat. In Provence, everyone raised pigeons, and for more reasons than simply a food source. Many used the birds for sport. In Lacoste, the crest of the *pigeonniers* always faced north because of the Mistral, the warm strong wind famous in this part of the world. To keep the birds off homes and shops, they are built with glazed tile roofs. This discourages nesting. Lacoste itself was like a large *pigeonnier*. Its buildings slant; in fact, the whole village is slanted at the same forty-five degree angle on the side of the hill.

"Lacoste, maybe because of its position on the hill or maybe because of its geographical location, has always been a favorite stopping off spot," Philippe explained. "Many of the ancient voyagers traveled through here on their way to and from Rome. You remember Gilbert? We met him at the Bistro."

I shook my head. We had met so many people, particularly because of Philippe's plane which had been left in the field below.

"No, well it doesn't matter. The story he told was quite amusing as well as being a great anecdote for the period."

I loved Philippe's stories and his way of telling history as a tale of someone's escapades.

"According to Gilbert, there once was a man who lived in Lacoste many, many years ago. The way Gilbert told the story, the man was out on his terrace enjoying his wine, the warm afternoon sun and the view. All of a sudden, in the distance, on the top of the mountain range, the man saw something very strange. He called to his wife and said, 'Come out! Come out quickly! There are elephants on the mountain.' His wife came out, gave him that knowing look only a wife of many years can give, tapped his hand and said, ever so gently, 'Enough.' Putting the cork in the wine, she turned back into the house taking the bottle with her. What he saw must have been Hannibal." Philippe and I laughed and laughed. The French. They have a wonderful view of life, and how lucky I was to be loved by this particular Frenchman.

The petite hill town stands adjacent to two mountain ranges, *Le Petit Luberon* and Le Grand Luberon. Hannibal's troops were said to have marched past this town two thousand years ago although there is some debate about the legitimacy of this. But I cherished the story nonetheless.

Our stroll brought us to a *café* at the edge of the village. To get there, we had to walk up a narrow cobbled street that rose steeply. Stone steps led further up to a terrace where there was an open bar. The view was spectacular, a palette of color, a panorama of purple and yellow and blue. The valley and the mountains were off to the west and the quaint brown hilltop town of Bonnieux could be seen in the distance across the lavender fields to the south.

"Did Hannibal succeed?" I asked Philippe once we settled at a table near the railing.

"No, he was eventually captured by the Romans." He handed me a glass of water to add to my *pastis*. *Pastis*, I learned from my well-informed beau, probably came from the old *provençal*, the original language of this area. It meant *confused* or *mixed*. Most appropriate I thought, as my drink, diluted from the water, had turned white. With our glasses in hand, Philippe began again to tell me about Hannibal. By this time, other guests on the terrace had begun to gather around to listen to the tale. The local people are so friendly and they love to share stories.

Encouraged and, I think, energized by the locals' interest, Philippe continued his saga. "To avoid being executed, Hannibal took poison." The group gasped in unison. Then, with a twinkle in his eye, he looked around and added, "So you see, he ended up dying by his own hand. That is control. That is power!"

Just as I was about to raise my glass in a toast to Hannibal, Philippe continued. "And what do you think was in Hannibal's mind when he drove his elephants over the mountains?"

I didn't know. No one else seemed to know. But we were all intrigued.

"Looking good," he declared.

"Looking good?" I didn't follow this line of thinking. The others giggled.

"*Oui*. Looking good. Because, my dear, on Hannibal's head there was a wig." He paused, waiting for the effect. "Hannibal wore a wig into battle to cover his lack of locks. Julius Caesar used his chaplet for the same purpose. He too wanted to look good."

By this time, everyone inside the *café* had come out to the terrace to listen. Philippe's tale was followed by roars of laughter. The atmosphere was electric.

Later, when we had been served cheese and bread, Philippe asked for a bottle of local red wine. Another round was served to the other patrons of the *café* and the history lesson continued, this time by one of the local gents.

"Centuries after Hannibal's famous ride, Lacoste became Protestant. Twice, the village was razed and its inhabitants slaughtered. Catholics considered the *Vaudois*, as the inhabitants were called, heretics."

"The town was last razed in 1585. The new town was designed for defense as a fortress and a haven," explained one of the other local inhabitants who had joined us from the bar inside.

I asked about the Great War and was told that Lacoste had been spared, although many of her inhabitants who had served the cause had not been so fortunate.

As the group chatted with Philippe, I stood up and went over to the railing to look out at the view. Taking a deep breath of the clean, dry, warm air, I savored being right where I was. Now that I had a better understanding of the area's history, I could almost visualize the battles that must have ensued in the valley below and the elephant silhouettes marching across the mountain ridges which defined the western side. In front of me was a play, a light recital as the sun passed down to the west. Long shadows crisscrossed the fields and hills. Lavender and green turned into purple and blue. This setting, this place with its magnificent views and its grand history was as majestic as it was congenial. In the midst of my reverie, Philippe came up from behind and put his arms around my waist. I was in Heaven.

That night we proved to each other how much we really cared. I think we slept only a little. We had much to explore and I was an avid learner. By the time we did get up, it was almost noon.

After a light lunch, which was also our breakfast, we decided to spend what was left of the day sightseeing. We walked down and

Patricia Daly-Lipe

around the old stone fortress town for hours, then decided to look for a quiet place to sit and relax. A shopkeeper told us about a spot often sought by artists. Outside the walls of the town, down a short trail, was a grove of worn-out, old oak trees. He said artists loved to paint and draw the gnarled limbs.

On this side of town, the land was carved into terraces painstakingly planted with gardens of vegetables and fruit. The streets ended and became rocky paths meandering between ancient stone walls. Further down, pastures, lavender and sunflower fields, grapevines, olive and citrus trees formed a mosaic on the valley floor. Just before the rocky slope plunged into the valley, we spotted the oak grove. Jagged rocks and boulders broke through the earth as if a restless giant hiding underneath the surface had decided to toss them out in a fit of anger. There were stones everywhere, but the tough, old oaks had settled their family in this spot. It took little imagination to see arms outstretched, legs leaping and torsos twisted. At the same time, it was a peaceful place and we welcomed the cool shade.

"There is a shadow the length of my hand. It looks wicked, don't you think?" I was pointing down to the dark lines cast on the ground by shadows of the oak tree we sat under.

"It is not of shadows and dark matters you are thinking about now is it? We are so lucky to be in such an enchanted place. Don't you agree?" Philippe looked at me with concern. My voice was tired from all the walking up and down. But he was right. I was not so much tired as depressed. We had been so happy, so much in love, but I guess it hadn't occurred to Philippe that what we were really doing was running away from reality.

Trying to reassure me, he pointed out, "The world is changing and we are constantly changing too." He stroked my back softly, massaging my tense muscles. "Our job in life is to accept change, to learn from it, and to grow." I know he wanted to remove my frown forever, to make me happy. "Remember, Libby dear, the full potential of the acorn is to be the mighty oak. Look at these sturdy, majestic trees. Their leaves are falling now, but they will endure the seasons." He paused and then, fixing his eyes on mine, he added, "We can learn so much from nature."

Looking up at the gnarly twisted branches spreading out above my head, I couldn't help being inspired. Leaning against my lover, I was at peace. Then that troublesome inner voice once again broke into the silence.

Pointing to the rays pouring through the huge, grand oaks, I said, "You see those beams of light coming through the leaves?" Philippe nodded. "That is the way the renaissance artists depicted God or the presence of God." He nodded, but said nothing. "But," I continued, "look down now, down at the ground. I see patterns and inky images like lizards and reptiles crawling on the dark, damp earth." Tears came to my eyes. "This is how life is, isn't it?" I rested my head against his chest and sighed. "Spiritual light and black reality."

Philippe held me tightly.

"I love being with you, dear Philippe." I put my arms around his neck and kissed him on the lips. "You are like the sunlight, warm and safe and sure. I wish the world were like that, warm and safe. I dread going back and having to cope with the Church and their reluctance to set us free." Tears threatened to flow.

"My dear Libby, you complicate life. Please believe me. If we are meant to be together, and I believe we are, then God will allow it. We must be patient. Life is not that complex. People like to make it complicated but it does not have to be that way." He kissed my moist eyes. "Life is really simple, *ma chérie*. You can say, 'I love you', and those few words can mean everything." Philippe drew me even closer and we kissed. Time stopped and the moment extended forever as we lay beneath the oak trees in each other's embrace.

Later that evening, when we returned to the *pension*, Philippe asked Brigitte when mass was offered. Brigitte was what Philippe called a *'bonne à tout faire'*. She did everything from washing the sheets which embarrassed me, to preparing breakfast and taking money while the owner sat in her tiny cubicle of an office smoking, drinking endless cups of coffee and getting fat.

"You are in luck, *Monsieur le Comte*" she said

"In luck? What do you mean?"

"*Oui, Monsieur le Comte*. Let me explain. Lacoste was always a Protestant town."

"Yes, so we were told."

Brigitte ignored the interruption. "In feudal days, Bonnieux, the town on the hillside across the valley, was the Catholic village. The land between was the scene of bloody battles between the two faiths. Only recently have the Fathers restored the Catholic Mass to our Church. The priest comes here once a month and tomorrow will be his day with us. So, *Monsieur le Comte*, you are in luck."

Chapter Twenty-Three

...ET UNUM SANCTUM CATHOLICUM

Catholic Mass

The stone Romanesque church stood apart from the village separated by a stone square with stone walls sectioning off small plots of grass. The entrance was a small door to the side. Bells announced the beginning of the service but few people who were gathered on the square appeared concerned or interested. Philippe and I ventured inside. The church had low ceilings and rounded Gothic arches, primitive compared to the high pointed arches of *Notre Dame*. Candles with their incessant flickering shadows provided the only light against the cold stone walls. We chose a narrow wooden bench midway up the aisle. In front of the bench was a *prie-dieu*, a hand-woven woolen pillow for kneeling. The bells stopped tolling to be instantly replaced by the most magnificent music reverberating throughout the sparsely attended church.

"What a fine organ they have here, and what a superb organist," remarked Philippe. He looked relaxed and happy, holding my hand.

"Introibo ad altare Dei."

The priest appeared accompanied by two young acolytes carrying the Great Book. They walked down the center aisle to the altar. The hymns and prayers were familiar: the same Latin psalms and prayers I had repeated all my life. The sermon was short. No offering plate was passed. Then the priest began the liturgy. The congregation chanted in French:

"Jesus your light is shining within us;
Let not my doubts and my darkness speak to me.
Jesus your light is shining within us.
Let my heart always welcome your love.
Jesus your light ..."

Patricia Daly-Lipe

I tried to feel part of the chant, but I couldn't stop fidgeting.

Raising his hands, the priest proclaimed *"In nomine Patris et Filii et Spiritus Sancti,"* making the sign of the cross. The parishioners began to file up to the altar to receive the body and blood of Christ. When our turn came, Philippe stood up, went to the aisle and waited for me to walk in front of him. I remained kneeling. I could not go. Philippe looked at me and realized I was right. Neither of us could go to the altar. If he had taken Communion, he would no longer have been in a state of grace and would have been ex-communicated. Then we could never be married in the Church. We sat holding hands, our prayers said silently. Being together was a blessing in itself but we sought the blessings of the Church as well.

"... et unam sanctam catholicam et apostolicam exclesiam," we repeated with the priest and the others. The service was over. I genuflected toward the altar, made the sign of the cross and left the pew. Faith was in my heart, but my mind was confused. Placing my hand in his, I walked with Philippe down the aisle to the entrance.

The sun blinded me at first as we left the dark tomblike interior of the church. Bells tolled; mass had ended. For this town, it would be three weeks before the next Catholic service. As our eyes adjusted to the light, we decided it was too nice a day not to continue our exploring. I wanted to see every building, every stone. I wanted to totally absorb the place. I was going to carry the memory of this visit, especially my time with Philippe, for a long, long time.

We had barely begun our tour when I stopped and turned to Philippe. "Did you know that the son of the Emperor Franz Josef committed suicide because the Church would not grant him an annulment?"

Philippe was caught completely off guard, but he was getting accustomed to my spontaneous pronouncements. He shook his head knowing I would see this thought through no matter what he did or did not say.

"His father forced him to marry the Belgian princess, Stephanie, whom he did not love. He had pleaded with the Pope to grant him the freedom to marry someone else. Can you imagine? Even royalty is refused. They say it was a double suicide. The Crown Prince and seventeen year old Baroness Marie Vetsera shot themselves, or each other, in the royal bed at Mayerling."

"Where did you hear that, my dear? I heard quite a different version of the story."

Such gloomy thoughts were piercing my heart. Torn between the requirements of a religion I had been raised in and the love I was now experiencing, I couldn't resolve the conflict. There was a battle being waged between my soul and my body. Philippe declared that he wanted to spend the rest of his life with me and, unlike Michael's declaration before the priest, Philippe's avowal included love. *Why should I be deprived of a proper and meaningful marriage?*

Philippe did not see loving me as a sin. On the contrary, for him I was a miracle. He turned me around to face him and softly placed his lips on mine. "Don't worry darling, there will be a time for us," he whispered.

"I'm sorry," I murmured through tears.

We strolled down the hill toward the vineyards and the lavender fields. I should know better than to vent my frustration on this wonderful man. I loved him more than I had loved anyone in my life. Somehow, everything would work out. We held hands and walked in the sunlight, the same light made famous by Impressionists' paintings.

To change the subject and draw me back into the moment, Philippe tried to explain how Impressionist painters viewed nature.

"Since the colors of the sky and the tones and variations of color change on the land from instant to instant, the goal of Impressionists was to seize one of these fugitive appearances and capture the moment in a single session. They painted outdoors, on location. It is called *en plein* air painting." My sweet and well-informed man explained to me how the artists saw that tree trunks were not necessarily brown, nor was grass really green, nor the sky necessarily blue. Instead, the motif of nature was multicolored with hues and tones that changed perceptively as the sun moved across the sky. "This was the first time an artist could take his paints and easel outside, because now pre-mixed paints were being fabricated in collapsible zinc tubes that could be transported easily. These artists painted hurriedly and vigorously, not stopping to refine their strokes. Their paintings reflected the energy and the spontaneity, both of the artists and of the world they were observing. And, Libby, this energy I am describing expands beyond the frame."

"What do you mean by *beyond the frame?*"

"When you look at these paintings, you do not find one focal point. You find instead, webs of connections, and finding these webs you follow up and down and around. You become involved."

I was amazed and couldn't wait to pass this on to Gina although she probably already knew these aspects. How did Philippe acquire all this diverse knowledge? Was it the French system of education, or was his mother the source? Perhaps it was simply a gift he was born with, this brilliant, inquisitive mind he had. I was falling deeper and deeper in love. He seemed to be able to explain everything in the world and always from a positive, righteous and good point of view. I had never known anyone like him before, not even my father who was so erudite.

"Nearby, in Aix-en-Provence, the first truly modern painter, Paul Cézanne, had his studio," continued my art authority.

"What do you mean by *modern?*"

"He was modern because he was the first artist to truly challenge the old definition of what is perceived as real."

I was lost. Sensing this, Philippe explained.

"Cézanne joined the Impressionist School of artists in Paris for a time, but in his heart, he was convinced that loneliness was the basic condition of modern man."

I frowned. It was still hard for me to feel happy when I was alone. Maybe I was too immature to understand.

"He spent almost all of his adult life in a studio he had designed himself. Alone."

We were passing the oak grove and following the path all the way down to the fields.

"Life is in constant flux," he reminded me. "Cézanne attempted to interpret this movement that is life. In his paintings, he focused on what the eye of the spectator sees as his mind processes the images before and around him. He painted *Mont Ste-Victoire* many times, because he saw the lights and tones ever changing. His palette changed as he asked himself, 'Is this what I see?' The best that an artist could do, he maintained, would be to give a sense of the infinite potential in unending mutations, the potentialities of life."

"This sounds as if Cézanne was a religious man."

"I am sure he was, Libby, but in a different way from you or me. For Cézanne, art was religion."

I thought about the mass we had just attended. *Wasn't the same spiritual feeling to be found out here in nature, in the beauty of all that was around us as we walked down to the aromatic fields of lavender?*

As if reading my mind, Philippe responded. "Cézanne wrote that the aim of art and the artist should be the elevation of the spirit."

"Is he still alive?"

"I am afraid not. He died a year after you were born. Picasso says that Cézanne was the father of us all. I imagine Gina has shown you some of Picasso's work so you probably know better than I about the generation that inherited from this master."

"I think Gina told me once that it was someone before Picasso, so it was probably Cézanne who sought to change the surface of a painting from merely depicting reality to making the canvas a reality unto itself."

"It may well have been, although I am not aware of that statement."

We walked in silence, smelling the perfume of the flowers and feeling the soft warm breeze from the south. In the distance, the church bells echoed across the valley. Later, back at the *pension*, I read from the book we had bought in the village, a book that included letters written by Cézanne. Reading these and listening to Philippe, it dawned on me that I was learning not only about art, but about the ultimate beauty of God's work. How wonderful it would be to be able to paint the wealth of color, sights and scents of Provence. Nature had much to teach and, for the first time in my life, like those artists before, I was learning to understand its lessons.

"Culture is usually defined by historic events, isn't it?" I pondered out loud while we were waiting for the second course to be served at dinner that night. "I mean, it is supposedly man who governs, dictates, controls. But when we were sitting in the oak grove looking over the stone wall at the fields and the mountains, the sky a brilliant blue overhead, I realized what affects people most. It is not other people. It is nature."

Philippe smiled. He was way ahead of me, but I wanted him to know that I was learning. So I continued. "We saw the same sky, the same lavender fields, the same sun-drenched landscape the Impressionists saw and probably generations of artists and poets before them have seen. Philippe, don't you agree that it is the *spirit* of this place that is so overwhelming."

Philippe only stared at me. In his face I saw love and tenderness. There was no need to agree. We feasted in each other's eyes and barely touched the second course of the meal. Skipping dessert, we couldn't wait to go back to the room and consummate the passion that was so palpable between us.

I know I blossomed in this landscape. I felt more alive than I ever had. My sensitivities were at their height: the smells of nature, the soft and pleasant sounds, the colors and contrasts, the feel of the warm sun on my shoulders and back, and at night under a starry sky, my excitement at the exhibition of grandeur that is our universe. The sky during the day in Provence was bluer than I had ever seen and the celestial exhibit at night was brighter and clearer.

Besides the walks each day, at noon, when the soil sizzled in the hot midday blast from the sun, Philippe and I enjoyed each other in our room, experimenting and experiencing with such fervor that I was often left out of breath and soaked with perspiration from both our bodies. Afterward, we would stand at the window looking out over the terraces of fruit trees and flowers, and at the fields of sunflowers and vineyards below. Here and there were long rectangles of reddish ground gone fallow for a season. Standing with Philippe's arm around my waist, I was comfortable being quiet and content with the sound of silence. Nature was meant to be shared. Philippe helped me become part of nature and it felt wonderful. I was not alone any more, not in any sense.

Chapter Twenty-Four

The historian relates the events which have happened, the poet those which might happen.

Aristotle

Paris was grey. The rain-spattered streets were grey. The buildings were grey. The naked branches of the trees were grey. Overhead, the sky was missing. Clouds hung low and continued to spill rain over the city. Activities involving sustenance, maintenance and cleansing went on as usual despite the weather. Horses hung their heads low as their hooves sloshed through puddles; drivers hung their heads low with large black capes cloaking them against the torrents. The Seine snarled as it pitched and peaked down its harnessed channel. Clearly, the mood was gloomy. It matched my own as I stepped off the running board and watched my lover withdraw my valise from the trundle of his little sports car.

Back in my apartment and alone, I put down the bag and went to the window. Looking out at the raw gloomy scene, I was reminded of a poem by Paul Verlaine. I had heard it sung, soft and low, like a chant. It didn't match my mood then, but it certainly did now. I hummed:

Il pleure dans mon Coeur   *It is raining in my heart*
Comme il pleut dans la ville. *Just as it is raining in town.*
Quelle est cette langueur   *What is this listlessness*
Qui pénètre mon coeur?   *That penetrates my heart?*

Better not sit here and be melancholy, I thought. Rising from the window seat and looking at the furnishings and the small collectibles we had begun to assemble, I recalled the hope I had of something wonderful. A home and love. But it was not to be. Tearfully I turned back to the window and allowed myself to be mesmerized by the scene outside. The Seine was dark, lashing out with rage at its stone confines in the wind swept torrents of rain. I closed my eyes remembering when, so many months and lifetimes ago, as a new bride, full of expectations and promise, I had first entered this apartment. The first place I headed was the window. It was Spring, a bright sunny day. I had opened both windows to allow the fresh breeze and tiny cotton balls to enter the apartment. We laughed, Michael and I, at the cotton balls. Expectations and hope, those were my thoughts and feelings that first day. Then I remember the next day sitting by the window. Apollinaire's poem had come to mind. Suddenly, a realization came to me. The poem; that poem...the words, the poem's words...now so prophetic...*Sous le pont Mirabeau coule la Seine et nos amours... Must I remember that happiness comes after pain or sorrow...La joie venait toujours après la peine...*

Sous le pont Mirabeau coule la Seine	*Under Mirabeau Bridge flows the Seine*
Et nos amours	*And our loves*
Faut-il qu'il m'en souvienne	*Must I recall that*
La joie venait toujours après la peine	*Happiness always comes after sorrow*
Vienne la nuit sonne l'heure	*Let the night come, sound the hour*
Les jours s'en vont je demeure	*The days pass, I remain*
Les mains dans les mains restons face à face	*Hands in hands, let us stay face to face*
Tandis que sous	*While underneath*
Le pont de nos bras passe	*The bridge of our arms shall go*
Des éternels regards l'onde si lasse	*Weary of endless looks, the river's flow*
Vienne la nuit sonne l'heure	*Let the night come, sound the hour*
Les jours s'en vont je demeure	*The days go by, I remain*
L'amour s'en va comme cette eau courante	*Love goes by like this flowing water*
L'amour s'en va	*Love goes by*
Comme la vie est lente	*How slow life seems*
Et comme l'Espérance est violente	*And how violent is the Hope*
Vienne la nuit sonne l'heure	*Night comes, sound the hour*
Les jours s'en vont je demeure	*The days go by, I remain*
Passent les jours et passent les semaines	*Days pass and weeks pass*
Ni temps passé	*Neither the past time*
Ni les amours reviennent	*Nor the loves come back again*
Sous le pont Mirabeau coule la Seine	*Under Mirabeau Bridge flows the Seine*
Vienne la nuit sonne l'heure	*Let the night come, sound the hou*
Les jours s'en vont je demeure	*The days go by, I remain*

The days go by, still I stay...How violent the hope of love can be. My sweet pleasures with Philippe were juxtaposed with the pain thinking about Michael. Closing my mind to the present, I was back with Philippe. A smile spread across my face and I hugged myself as a warm glow filled my soul. My life was whirling, just like the river outside the window. But the smile soon fell and my shoulders drooped as I stared at the flowing water. *Neither the past time nor the love can come back again.* Please don't let this be.

Watching the wild movement of the river brought back more memories. The rough trip we had endured sailing across the Atlantic. We never had a chance to feel like newlyweds. Any naïve anticipation of romance disappeared when the ship started to roll into the high surf and the nausea set in. Please stop the motion. *Please, please, I pleaded to the wall of my cabin, to the railing on the deck, to the rolling waves.* Please stop. No longer a whisper, one night by the railing I lost all self-control and yelled to the universe, *'Stop, stop, I want to get off!'* But the seas ignored me, the ship rolled on and my stomach was left behind.

So many memories, so many thoughts. My head spun out of focus bouncing from Philippe to Michael and back to Philippe. I loved Philippe. *Please, dear Lord, don't let Philippe leave me.* I prayed but my prayers were more like begging. *Didn't I deserve this man who had unselfishly given me the gift of love?* But according to the Church, this love was called a mortal sin.

The vow Michael and I had made at our Washington wedding was "until death do us part". But I never felt this way with Michael. *Please, God, show me the way. Show me that this is right.* Philippe said we were meant to be together. *I pray the Church will come to understand and grant us the right to be a couple in the sanctified state of matrimony.*

With my elbows on the window sill, my face in my hands, I stared into the gloom outside. Captivated by the gushing waters of the Seine, I tried to overcome the depression that was seizing my soul, but the tears began to flow like the water below.

Patricia Daly-Lipe

When Victor returned from New York, Pamela invited me for a *petit souper*. It would be informal, just the three of us. Victor had met my father.

Chapter Twenty-Five

Leave off the agony, leave off the style,
Unless you've got money by you all the while.

Julia A. Moore

"I explained the entire situation to your father," Victor pronounced after we had begun our meal which Pamela called *paysan*. She was radiant and well she should be. Her love had come home safely. While we ate cheese, country bread, a large mixed-green salad and drank a good full-bodied red wine, Victor recounted his visit in the States and his meeting with my father. After dinner, we went into the library for coffee.

"I must say, he is a very impressive man," continued Victor balancing his *demitasse* in one hand and his customary glass of Cognac in the other.

I smiled both at Victor's posture and at the memory of my father. The meeting schedule in New York City had lasted three days and it was most likely in the evening after the scheduled conferences and seminars that the two met.

"I was nervous about confronting him with your news, but once we met, we got along quite well."

I sat on the soft, red couch with embroidered pillows and held a *demitasse* in my lap, but my mind was far away.

"He was very concerned. He loves you very much. That is clear. However, he does not want your mother to know any of this."

"I wish he would stop protecting mother. He does everything for her, worships her, but never lets her do anything practical." I was annoyed and couldn't help speaking my mind.

"He has decided to set up an account for you with my bank. I am to teach you how to use it: make out checks, balance your checkbook, all that." I was amazed, happily so, and very touched by

Patricia Daly-Lipe

father's confidence in me. The way he treated mother, I didn't think he believed women were capable of anything related to money.

"Money will come from the same fund he established when you first married Michael. This is the currency he sends every month for your needs."

"That means Michael won't get any money from my family."

"Quite," replied Victor tersely, his face revealing what he thought about Michael. He wasn't smiling.

Chapter Twenty-Six

...tell me all ... I want to hear all ... Tell me all. Tell me now.

James Joyce

I spent the winter months alternating between immersing myself in the daily routines of the neighborhood, visiting the morning produce markets and talking about the weather, the season, the recipes *du jour* with the merchants and learning, everything from history to art. I also wrote in my journal, walked for miles at a time and spent hours relishing in the magnificence of the museums.

One article in the newspaper caught my eye. It extolled the arts as a product of peace. Paris was at peace and its art community was flourishing. Gina called from time to time and we attended openings and *soirées* together. Philippe took me to the Opera and to the *Ballet Russe*. Occasionally we stayed up until all hours listening to American Jazz. The French violinist Stephane Grappelli and the Belgian Gypsy guitarist Django Reinhardt formed the nucleus of the Hot Club Quintet, which popularized American-style jazz. Grappelli translated Louis Armstrong and Joe Venuti on the violin and was quite the rage in Paris. I was keen on the sweet music of swing, but was learning to appreciate jazz, a more complicated form of music. These late jazz evenings were followed by breakfast in the early dawn at *Pre Catalan* in the *Bois* or at *Les Halles*.

Despite the hour, Philippe would dutifully escort me back to my apartment, not his. We did not make love. Not only did we feel strange in an apartment the world at large still considered mine and Michael's, we were frightened about where this fervor might take us if we were not careful. When we were alone together, it was only by the strongest of wills that we were able to keep the passion in check.

Neither one of us was giving up trying to get the Church to annul my marriage. While Philippe was calling everyone he knew connected to the Church, I was talking to the priests of *Notre Dame*, trying to understand why the Church could not and would not understand my position. Why was Michael excused from their vindication when he was actively involved in sinful behavior? After our explosive passion in Lacoste, Philippe and I were trying hard to behave in what the Church would consider an appropriate manner. It wasn't easy.

"Why can't you understand?" I wept as the priest shrugged his shoulders and walked away. I should have said, "Why don't you admit that you *do* understand and simply refuse to help me? You are a man. Of course you sympathize with Michael!" Instead of retreating out of the church right away, I pounded the cement pillars with my fists until my fingers bled. It didn't matter if anyone saw me. In fact, it was too bad no one did, then maybe there would be a sympathetic ear.

Philippe heard rumors that Michael had found a place of his own. Although he saw Michael from time to time at *Le Bourget* in the damp, cold, winter months when there was little activity, he didn't speak to him. Besides, Philippe was totally occupied with his Puss Moth.

One day, Madame Metz informed me that James Joyce and his family were moving out of the building. I was disappointed, having wanted so much to get to know this man. Then, just before they left, a note arrived under my door inviting me to come up for a chat. The note was signed by Mr. Joyce himself. Both honored and terrified by the invitation, I tried to comport myself in a casual manner as I climbed the stairs to the floor above, taking a deep breath at every second step.

Mr. Joyce was alone in the small apartment on the *troisième étage*. Pamela had told me that she had heard from Natalie that Mrs. Joyce and their daughter were in Switzerland. They were there to meet with Doctor Carl Jung.

Joyce's note indicated that he had been made aware of my problems. Although he didn't say as much, he had most probably been informed by Madame Metz.

"Please come in," called the author in his melodious, tenor voice.

I entered the dimly lit apartment. Books were everywhere. On the floor, on the shelves, piled high on tables, and scattered across a small sofa. In the corner sat a large writing table with one lamp. This is where I found Mr. Joyce, hunched over his desk, straining to see through thick lenses, his left eye patched behind the glass.

"Come in please, Mrs. Whitaker. I apologize for the dark, but my eye is most sensitive to light."

"Please, Mr. Joyce, please call me Libby," I said, tentatively moving closer.

"Don't be timid, Libby. Come see my new gift," he said, beckoning me to look over his shoulder.

With seemingly great pride, he showed me his typewriter. At first it appeared the same as any other typewriter, but then I saw the difference. The characters were well over the normal size.

"This machine was procured for me by Harriet Weaver. Do you know her? She's the editor of the *Egoist*. Both she and this machine help me with my work."

"What are you writing about?" I asked taking a step back.

"The history of the world," he chuckled. Despite the chuckle, I think he was serious. He swung around in his chair and gave me a big grin. Even with glasses and one eye patched, I was struck by the boldness of his gaze. After a moment of silence, he staring at me and me feeling both awkward and embarrassed, I lamely ventured, remembering the words of Joseph Campbell, "Everyone is talking about *Ulysses*. They are saying that it took you a very long time to write it."

"Fifteen years or to be exact, a lifetime," he replied tersely. Then without looking up and without preamble, he declared, "The Hemingways have decided to divorce."

I had heard.

I remember sharing the information with Pamela. I had been in an ugly mood, kicking tree stumps, frowning even when walking along the Seine and snapping at Mme Metz. Pamela knew something terrible had happened.

"It isn't fair!" I grumbled.

"What seems unfair, my dear?" she asked.

"Ernest Hemingway and Pauline have married."

"Well, that is very nice …"

"Yes, yes, I know all that, but they have married in the Church!"

"How can that be? Hemingway is married to Hadley. And what about their son? Bumby, I think his name is." Pamela was shocked.

"According to the MacLeishes, Ernest convinced the Church that he had been baptized by a priest who had walked between the aisles of wounded men nine years ago. He was one of the wounded. He'd been an ambulance driver in Italy."

"But Hadley? What about Hadley?"

"Ernest says Hadley is a non-believer and, can you believe, 'has never been his wife'."

This was more than either of us could accept. "Hadley and Ernest were married in a Protestant Church in New England, but the Catholic Church is willing to consent to its being invalid. Since the Church, the Catholic Church, does not recognize marriages that are not performed by a priest and since Hemingway did not ask for permission to marry outside the Church, the Church acknowledges that it was not valid which leaves Hemingway free to marry as if for the first time." I took a deep breath after venting my indignation. "Ernest claims he attended mass fairly regularly most of 1926 and 1927 and," I was shouting despite myself at this point, "he says, and I think he is being theatrically defiant, he says that he has *set his house in order* this year."

Pamela listened sympathetically to my raving.

"In his own words, he is a very dumb Catholic. Dumb isn't the word I would use. Pamela, can you believe he justifies any mistakes he may have made by supposedly admitting that he always had more faith than intelligence?

Pamela shook her head in disbelief.

"Apparently he has taken his talent for fiction and put it to use in his own life," I added tersely.

"Libby, where did you hear all this?"

"I just heard it from a friend who attends church in Montparnasse. She said that this was the excuse he gave a Dominican priest who was sent to make an inquiry. What lies! What fabrication! No wonder he is such a good writer." I paused taking a deep breath. My nerves were frayed. "Do you know what else he told the good Father?" The question was rhetorical. "He said he had so much faith that he hated to examine it in depth, but he was trying to lead a good life. A good life. Leaving his wife and his son for a new lover!" By now, I was shaking with rage. Of course, there was absolutely nothing Pamela could say or do, still I wanted her to know. Maybe just to purge myself of this horrible reality. At the very least, she could sympathize. Ernest Hemingway now was a married man for the second time and he did so with the blessing of the Catholic Church.

"Hadley must be a saint or have some agenda of her own to allow such a thing," reflected Pamela. "I am afraid that I will never understand, nor wish to understand, the politics of the Catholic Church. This is a severe blow, isn't it, my dear friend?" Now that was an understatement!

Here I was in the presence of this amazing and distinguished writer and he had to bring up the Hemingways. But thankfully, before I could interject with a comment of my own, he continued, "Of course you know I may have to go through the formality myself. I don't mean divorce. I mean of marrying Nora."

Now I was shocked. "But, Mr. Joyce, you have two children and ..." I didn't know what to say.

Joyce chuckled. Switching the course of conversation, he pointed to a platter I had not noticed before. It was squished unobtrusively between two piles of books on one of the tables.

"Please, young lady, help yourself to some of Nora's scones. My Irish Princess made them just before leaving. And do try her famous greengage jam."

I wasn't sure about the green plum jam, but I took a scone. Just holding it might help calm me down a bit. Being in the same room with the great Joyce was enough to have me on edge, but bringing up Hemingway and then his comment about Nora...well, my nerves were jumping. *Could he tell?*

"Please sit, my dear lady," he said pushing a chair out for me.

Obediently I sat. With the scone in my lap, I noticed sheets of papers scattered around his desk and on the floor but my focus was really Mr. Joyce himself.

Suddenly, picking up where he left off, "You will not find a man more devoted nor loyal than I to my dear Nora and to my children." Yes, I had seen their relationship as they walked in and out of our building together. "But I will not serve that which I no longer believe … No, young lady, the paper, the ceremony, that is not what it is all about."

I was stunned. "Mr. Joyce, you are a Catholic, and …" Had I missed something by not reading his books?

He must have read my mind for he said jokingly, "You know I have gone to great lengths to see that my books are written with so many conundrum and riddles that they will keep professors of literature, historians and critics busy for centuries to come. This assures me a kind of immortality, don't you agree?" We both laughed. "I can see them now, all hunched over, analyzing every word, every phrase, looking for references, and references of references."

Ezra Pound, not his favorite person by any means, had derided his work. He quoted by heart what he called Mr. Pound's epitaph: "Nothing short of a divine vision or a new cure for the clapp can possibly be worth all the circumambient peripherization." Joyce was mumbling but I was picking up most of it.

He paused as if collecting his thoughts, his gaze back on me. "I am so sorry, my dear lady, only some coffined thoughts milling around my brain, in mummy-cases, embalmed in spice of words."

"That is what Stephen said in *A Portrait of The Artist!*" I exclaimed in delight. Joyce was visibly pleased. "That is you; I mean, the protagonist is you, isn't he?" I asked naively.

"My dear young lady, to quote from my own work: 'The artist, like the God of creation, remains within or behind or beyond or above his handiwork, invisible, refined out of existence, indifferent, paring his fingernails'."

We both laughed.

"May I ask you something perhaps quite personal, maybe even sacrilegious?"

"But of course." He almost looked pleased at my use of the word 'sacrilegious'. I was sure he had absolutely no idea where this was leading but how kind of him to listen. I was even surprising myself with such cheek.

"Mr. Joyce, have you ever considered leaving the Catholic Church?"

He was silent for a minute, then without looking at me, he said, "I shall quote Stephen, then you can judge for yourself. 'I said that I had lost the faith but not that I had lost my self-respect. What kind of liberation would that be to forsake an absurdity which is logical and coherent and to embrace one that is illogical and incoherent?' So, young lady, there you have it."

He laughed and laughed. Still bewildered, nevertheless, I couldn't help joining in his mirth. How could anyone not be relaxed and happy with this delightful man? Such a paradox. To look at him, you had to feel some pity for the patch over his eye and his dependence on a cane for balance, but to hear him, quite the opposite.

"Mr. Joyce, as you climb the stairs past my apartment, I have heard you speak Italian with your family. Why is that?"

"To preserve my native tongue for my writing. Also it is as close to Latin as we can get in everyday speech. Or maybe I just like waving my arms when I speak! However," he said, suddenly changing from jovial to stern, "I asked you up here for a purpose."

I shuddered.

"You are a beautiful woman." He was looking steadfast at me. "Go and find someone to love. Go and learn what the heart is and what it feels. Do not let the Church or anyone's rules stop you from happiness. I love my Nora. I do not need rules to tell me that. Look at the world today. I can tell you," he said, pounding his fist on the table, "I have been more virtuous than most of this lot." He looked angry, but then slowly his expression changed to sadness. "Young lady, I hope I am wrong, but the world appears to be tumbling. Look at the historical trend: from theocracy to aristocracy; from aristocracy to democracy. But democracy, my child, is neither the end nor the solution. No, the end, the last phase is chaos. And chaos, I am afraid, characterizes our own age. Materialism, individualism, explosion of pride, but on such a vulgar scale. Yes, this is what defines our present day world. Sterility of spirit is on the rise." Again, he pounded the table. I watched, but dared not retrieve the papers that fell off the side. "Where is certitude?" I was glad he was not looking to me for an answer.

"Yes," he said, his face taking on its own look of doom and distress, "we are on our way down."

With this, any sign of his prior cheerfulness was completely gone. Elbows on the table, his hands holding his head, eyes closed, he looked emotionally drained and I knew it would be best to leave.

Grateful and somewhat flattered that he had given me a portion of his valuable time, I rose and headed quietly toward the door. He must have been extremely uncomfortable with the eye operations he had undergone plus the migraines which Mme Metz had told me he suffered. Imagine this great, though desperately ill, genius taking the time to consider my predicament. Now I had to consider if I followed his advice, it would mean defying tradition and convention. For years to come, I would remember his words.

Just as I opened his door to leave, he called out, "Go and experience the reality of existence!" Then with great emphasis, his voice resonant, he proclaimed his famous "Yes!"

Chapter Twenty-Seven

Ah, dangerous salients of youth, loving in a crucial month.

Lawrence Durrell

Joyce's words came back repeatedly: "Go find someone to love." *I had once. Why should being back in Paris change that? What had happened should happen again.* As if we had agreed upon a plan, without discussion Philippe and I rekindled the fire that was started in Provence.

Putting memories of the ugly revelation in the salon behind me, I placed fresh cut flowers in every room and potpourri in the bath. The apartment became imbued with my presence. Newly acquired art, including a small Picasso, hung on the walls. Light and bright, the apartment became the home I had wanted. I called Philippe and suggested we not go out. I was going to make a modest dinner at home.

"I can't cook, but I will try."

He was delighted. He would bring wine, a bottle he had brought from Provence. The mere mention of that enchanted place warmed me.

When Philippe came to the door, I greeted him, perfumed and cheery. As I hugged him, I knew. I felt his desire. No words were wasted. Placing the wine on the hall table, he scooped me up and carried me to the bedroom and gently undressed me. His touch was tender as he slowly caressed and gently sucked my nipples, kissed my shoulders and snuggled fitting his long limbs over mine.

I kissed his chest and let my tongue play, my arms wrapped around his body as my hands caressed the taut muscles of his back. I wanted to experience every inch of this man. Never before had I taken the body so seriously. Now I knew and craved the profound pleasure the bones, the skin, the muscles aroused. As I explored him, Philippe responded with more passion. Thoughts vanished. Instinct took over. I was throbbing and wet and, when I could no longer wait, I surprised both of us as I boldly grabbed his stiffened, swollen organ and drew him in. Immediately our rhythms blended: rising and falling, rising and rising higher, rising and exploding. No one told me how I would feel making love. Even after my bliss, I found words of little avail. I rose; I flew; I was transported; my nerves tingled to my fingertips and toes; I was beyond my body and his, floating, somewhere.

Later, we opened the wine, had a few bites of bread and cheese, but dinner was left untouched.

It was daylight when Philippe rolled out of bed, dressed and after a lingering kiss, left the apartment. I passed the day in a daze.

Chapter Twenty-Eight

I murmured to Picasso that I liked his portrait of Gertrude Stein." "Yes", he said, "everybody says that she does not look like it but ... she will."
'The Autobiography of Alice B. Toklas'

"You know," Gina said one day after viewing a new exhibition of Picasso's latest technique, "he seems to have little by little lost his own vision. His colors are no longer his own. They are the fairly ordinary colors that other painters use. Like Matisse. I wonder what is going on in his head?"

I remembered how Pamela had related Gertrude Stein's observation that Picasso sought inspiration not from other painters, but from writers and poets like Apollinaire. But it wasn't for me to question Gina. After all, this was her field of interest. Besides, I appreciated her teaching me about art.

"It amazes me how much you can see in a painting, Gina. How can you know by looking at the colors and the texture and the style, exactly what the artist is thinking?"

"Painters use art as an outlet for their emotions. Writers do the same with words. For both, it is an urge, which, no matter what else is happening in your life, has such force that it pulls you on. It forces the oils to slide and stick on the canvas or the words to come tumbling out on the blank page. The artist cannot hide behind his art; he is his art. He is almost a victim, a victim of his own creative urge." Gina spoke with such vehemence that if I were not looking at her I would have thought she had grown six feet tall.

Her enthusiasm had helped to spur me on in a quest for more knowledge. Proof was my library. It was getting rather sizable. Hard to resist when the books were so reasonably priced at the stalls of the *bouquinistes* on the West Bank.

"Gina, I want your opinion."

"Sure," she replied.

"I read that Freud thinks the origins of art are found in what he calls the – wait, let me find the page – yes, here it is, 'irremediable psychological conflicts which lie at the root of culture.' That's a demeaning, negative view, don't you think? I mean, aren't most artists today leaning toward a more spiritual uplift? 'Creative ecstasy' I think you called it? Isn't that the creative urge you talk about?"

"Actually, I believe art does come from the subconscious. You know, all I suggested months ago was that you be aware of Freud's influence on art. I didn't realize what a true scholar you turned out to be. Your research is impressive. Perhaps I could convince you to come with me to some of our lectures at the Sorbonne?"

"You can really drive this thing?" I asked as Gina ushered me into a 1926 Model T Ford. Gina's father had the car delivered to her as a gift before his return to the United States.

"She's nicknamed *Tin Lizzie*. Now you watch me." Gina sounded bold, but it was probably more to bolster her own confidence than to convince me. She revved the engine in front and then leaped into the driver's seat. With her left hand, she moved the floor gear stick that was next to the door forward into gear, at the same time releasing the left pedal with her foot.

"You have three pedals and two feet. How are you supposed to drive?"

"Don't be silly. The right one is the reverse and the center one is the brake. This one on the left has to come out after the handle on the floor goes forward. At least I think that is right." Gina was flustered. With some sputtering and a great deal of screeching and clamoring, we were moving forward.

"Noisy, isn't it?" I yelled; I had to yell the racket was so bad. Since there were no windows, I hung onto my hat with one hand and the seat with my other, realizing that should anyone get in the way, we would have to stop abruptly. *Could Gina handle a crisis like that?*

"Can you stop this, this Lizzie?"

"What? Oh, right. Yes, I can, but I need plenty of room and time. I do have this Klaxon horn. The center pedal is the brake, but Daddy told me that in an emergency to push the reverse pedal."

We moved along slowly, the valves singing, one tone for each of the four cylinders, harmonizing with the bombastic exhaust escaping out the rear. This was Mr. Ford's attempt to dress up the Model T before he went to the Model A this year. Gina's father must have more confidence in his daughter than I did was my thought as we bounced our way to the conference.

"Let us be ashamed of our superficial life; it is full of lies. There are only two possibilities: one is that we are not able to see the truth, the other is that when we have once seen it glimmering before us and the path that is leading to it, we are devoured by the eternal thirst it follows to the end. He who is filled with love for truth goes out into life like a hero without weapons, but under the spread-out wings of an archangel." These were the words being used by the instructor, Antoine Bourdelle, a distinguished sculptor whose lectures were regarded with utmost respect by other artists and students of art.

Gina and I had arrived just in time for the talk. Joseph Campbell was there and when he saw us, waved for us to come and join him and his friends in the upper rows of the lecture hall.

One of Joseph's friends, a student from Yale University in the States, nudged me and whispered, "Did you know that the Professor had all but given up on the youth of America until he met Joseph and Charles?"

"Our Joseph and Charles Lindbergh?"

"Yes. Professor Bourdelle had been in Paris four years before he met the two Americans. Both Charles and Joe impressed him tremendously and it was here in Paris, not in the States, that he met them." His enthusiasm was contagious. I could understand Joseph's popularity and as his friends, Gina and I were well received too.

After the lecture, we went to a new restaurant, *The Cupola*, in Montparnasse and enjoyed a fine dinner and a chance to chat. From the start, Joseph admitted he didn't know a thing about art, but he was determined to learn. Apparently, the abstract, non-representational art really puzzled him.

"Yesterday I was strolling in the *Bois de Boulogne* and I came across the new exhibition hall. Have you seen it? It houses work by a group of artists who call themselves the Intransigents. I don't know what these paintings are about, but I am going to find out. If what *Le Maître* Bourdelle says is true; namely, that art requires that the artist devote all his or her life to it or give it up, then these works must have some significance. As *Le Maître* says, 'If you are not willing to devote your life to it, you might as well stay at the beach'."

We laughed, but I knew Joe was serious.

"But since I am not an artist," he continued once the laughter subsided, "I want to learn what the inner meaning of art is."

Before I could tell Joseph what I had learned about non-representational art, the waiter came by asking about drinks. Joe, a non-drinker, ordered coffee. The rest of us shared a bottle of red wine. When the order had been placed, Joseph pulled out his notes.

"Bourdelle said, 'Beauty is everywhere. Nature is always beautiful. When nature seems ugly to us, it is because we do not understand it.' " Glancing up, Joseph looked directly at Gina and finished the quote. "He said: 'You can make a masterpiece of each human face.' "

I caught Gina reddening, but she quickly composed herself. I don't think anyone else noticed. Glancing down at her copious notes, she chose her own quotation. "Art vividly shows us the grand lines of nature. We should not lead superficial lives. Nature is everywhere and it is always beautiful. If we don't see the beauty, Joseph, isn't it simply because we don't understand?"

He nodded and smiled.

"Such a great responsibility for the artist, isn't it?" This came from one of the other students. The table was small and round, and everyone was encouraged to participate in the discussion. The students began vying for a chance to share their thoughts, mostly about the role of the artist. I was wondering if anything would come of Joseph and Gina's friendship, then scolded myself for not paying better attention to the discussion at hand.

"I think you mean the responsibility of enticing the viewer to look at nature and see her beauty. The artist himself is not important.

He is like a glass through which the rest of the world can view nature. Am I not right?"

"Yes, that's it! Remember what the master said? 'Only the artist can see the essence of life'" This came from a student sitting across from me, a young man probably only eighteen or nineteen years old. If this were so, I was not privy to the *essence of life*. I wondered if I had any hope of seeing with the eyes of an artist.

"The artist suffers the irresistible urge to translate this ultimate reality through painting or writing, or even music or sculpture," offered another serious student. And so the conversation continued. For these students, art was a religion or, at the very least, a way of life. I listened, but I was also very aware of the differences between them and me.

To my relief, all agreed that there is a part of every man and every woman, not only artists, that is aware of the aesthetic. Now was my turn to contribute. Remembering some of the Greek my father had taught me, I decided to offer my own insight.

"The Greek word for aesthete is *aesthetes*. It means *one who perceives*."

Gina clapped her hands. The students were thrilled. A big grin covered my face. I had been accepted as one of the group.

"Yes, precisely," said Joseph toasting me with his coffee. "Bourdelle said ... now let me find the exact phrase ... Here it is: '*C'est la personnalité qui conte!*' It is the sense of self or the individuality that is the source of creativity. Let's see if we can take that a step further." We are looked mystified. "Perhaps I can give you an example."

We sat, watched, and listened to the words that gave a glimpse into the mind that would perhaps one day make Joseph world famous.

"As Libby said, you 'perceive' which is to say, you are thinking about something that you see. But do you ever have a glimpse beyond your thinking, your perceiving, of that which transcends anything you can think about yourself?"

We fell silent, trying to comprehend, each in his or her own way. I wondered if this was the spiritual world I should examine, so different from the teachings of my catechism classes.

Gina brought us back to earth reminding the group about the influence of Freud and Jung; the tug of the unconscious and the world of dreams. "Only look at the direction Picasso is taking, siding with the *Cubists*. Art will never be the same. The thing in itself is no longer the object of interest. Artists and writers are drawing from dreams and automatic reflexes and the realms of the unexpected and the accidental. At least," she added meekly, "I think that is what is happening." Once again, it was Gina's turn to blush.

"Precisely," commented another student. "André Breton defined *surréalisme* as pre-psychic automation. It is supposed to be outside reason and logic. Maybe that is what you meant, Joseph?"

"Right. And not dictated by traditional aesthetic or moral judgment."

"Have you seen the work of Jean Miro?" someone else asked. "He is also a *Surréaliste*. His colors are bold and he is not reticent about using black. I love his powerful shapes. I feel like I am walking into any landscape I want. I mean, I really get lost in his paintings. They allow me to look back to my past, which is somewhere still hidden inside my head. I feel as if his paintings open doors for me. Do you all understand?"

Some shrugged their shoulders; others nodded. The idea was still new for many of them. I couldn't help smiling. Philippe had already taught me so much about this artistic conflict. In fact, those were almost his exact words, "You can walk into the painting." My memories floated back to Provence; to Philippe and me sitting under the old oak trees. *I wish he were here. He would have so much to share.*

Later that evening, after most of the students had left, Joseph, Gina and I wandered off to a tiny hole-in-the-wall off the *Place Pigalle* to share a *café noir*. Joseph confided that although he was a Catholic, he was beginning to find some of its canons difficult to accept.

"I won't ever give up religion," he said, "but I may give up Catholicism."

I gasped.

"You know, Joyce's problem, at least the way I perceive it in his writing, is the same as mine."

I almost blurted out what Mr. Joyce had told me in confidence, but stopped just in time. Instead, to engage Joseph in further discussion, I put the question back to him. "What do you mean, Joseph?"

"The problem is when you're deeply built into the system of the church and you're losing your faith, it's no fun. I mean, it started when I was studying biology. There's absolutely no relationship between the biological evolution of the human species, the animal and plant world and what you get in the Book of Genesis."

I could relate quite easily. The nuns and priests had taught strict adherence to the biblical text. But I had always felt the biblical stories were more symbolic than real. As if reading my mind, Joseph spoke about the problem being how to understand the Bible stories without losing the symbols.

"That's it Joseph!" I cried out.

"Yes and no. This is where Joyce has helped me. We are not talking about anecdotal historical symbolism of the sense of these great universal symbols that come to us through our Christian heritage."

"We're not?"

"No. It is on the wings of art, an opening out of a mythological reading of these symbols."

"Joseph, I don't understand."

"Libby, Joyce disengaged himself and left the labyrinth, you might say, of Irish politics and the church, to come to Paris. He became part of the movement that we were talking about earlier."

My eyes were opened to something that I instinctively knew would change my life. Hearing someone as bright as Joseph voice these concepts gave me confidence. I was in Paris for a purpose. The timing was right. The discovery of modern art, the ideas being tossed around, this was the place I needed to be. A new world was opening up and I was part of it. Now I was being given the gift of strength to consider that the church might be wrong. Why should I be condemned to eternal sin and purgatory for loving Philippe? The *mea culpa* had to stop. The spiritual was out there. It was in nature.

Patricia Daly-Lipe

And my determination was to enjoy and learn from all of it. This outing, the whole evening, had been a great success.

Chapter Twenty-Nine

"Wall St. Lays an Egg"
                    Headline, *Variety*, Oct. 30, 1929

"PHONE, RADIO, CABLE, BEAT ALL RECORDS,
Market Break Strains Every Form of Communication
Between World's Cities"
                    The New York Times, Oct. 30, 1929

Black Thursday. October 24, 1929, a day to remember all over the world. The New York stock market took a terrific tumble. Although this original crash was followed by a small rise, by Tuesday the twenty-ninth, the market went back down and down and down. *The New York Herald* published a display of photos. Hundreds of men filled the streets of New York, tearing up worthless receipts. There were reports that some could not deal with the loss and the shame to their families so they jumped out of high-rise windows. Perhaps an exaggeration; but it was true some families did lose everything. Entire fortunes dissolved overnight. Banks closed. Businesses closed. Consumer buying decreased causing the need for cutbacks in the work force. Bread lines began to form. A shanty town sprang up in Central Park, New York City. America, the great land of opportunity, wealth, and eternal youth was losing its splendor and graying at the temples; all this, the newspapers headlined.

In 1929, Hoover, the man whose image had been transmitted via television two years before, won the election, but his Republican idealism left the country gasping for breath. In October, 1928, Hoover had stated that after the Great War it was no longer necessary to have the government control and operate many instrumentalities of productions and distributions. "We were challenged," he said, "with a peacetime choice between the American system of rugged individualism and a European philosophy of diametrically opposed doctrines, doctrines of paternalism and state socialism." To accept the European ideals would have meant, according to Hoover, the destruction of self-government.

But by 1930, the party for individualism and hands-off policy was over. *Blue Skies* was the song of the moment. In 1932, with no end in sight from the Great Depression, Americans voted in a Democrat, Franklin Delano Roosevelt. The Republicans had failed. In his acceptance of nomination, Roosevelt attempted to give desperate people a ray of hope. "Give me your help," he asked, "not to win votes alone, but to win in this crusade to restore America to its own people." Roosevelt, or FDR as he was called, emanated a charisma and charm the American voters sought. "The country needs and, unless I mistake its temper, the country demands bold, persistent experimentation." His voice was heard and on November 4, 1932, Roosevelt won by a landslide. However, not every American was thrilled.

"There is a man named FDR
Who travels in a private car.
Sometimes he goes out to fish,
In a batteau? Not this tish.
Nor in his yacht like you or me,
HE uses Uncle Sam's Navy.
For his fun we pay the freight,
Laugh fool, laugh, or get the gate.
There may be some who think he's fine,
Like dupes of Black Father Devine.
While you and I who clearly see,
Know he's a mountebank, only."

This was a poem my father sent soon after the election. Somehow he anticipated the crash and our family funds were in good order. My parents' lifestyle in Washington continued with some inconveniences but no disasters. The hungry and poor of Washington must have marveled at the big black limousine as it deposited the banker at his bank, the banker's wife at Elizabeth Arden's and the banker's servants on their various household errands.

I worried about some of our American friends here in Paris. Had they lost everything? What would they do? To my great relief, although not something I wanted to share with others in light of most people's dilemmas, my allowance would continue unchanged. Diligently, I was trying to keep my checkbook balanced, and so far had only been humiliated by two overdrafts. Victor had covered both incidences. However, at his wife's bidding, he called me into his office after the second offense and sternly admonished me against any further debits.

Philippe was also coping with the effects of the Depression which had moved across the ocean to Europe. He was organizing the reestablishment of farmlands, both agricultural and livestock, with funds allocated by the Treaty of Versailles. Elsewhere, factories were being rebuilt making France the most modern industrialized nation in Europe, or in the world. Although the government was a mess, democracy still prevailed in France. Philippe and his mother hoped and prayed that the same could be said of Germany. It could not.

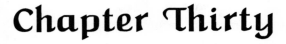

Chapter Thirty

It was the best of times; it was the worst of times...it
was the spring of hope, it was the winter of despair,
we had everything before us, we had nothing before
us ...

Charles Dickens

Philippe and I continued to spend a great deal of time together. I was secure with my kind-hearted French gentleman. With him, I was treasured, loved, wanted and spoiled.

When I was not with Philippe, I allocated time to read or study. Sometimes I attended lectures with Gina, sometimes we went to art openings, galleries, or simply toured the museums. With Philippe, I learned more about other things as well. His lovemaking brought out a warm, compassionate nature I never knew I possessed. That alone would have held me in Philippe's presence, but it was more than his loving. Often we flew to different places in the provinces for lovely weekend excursions. In his presence, I had no fear. Touring the countryside, visiting churches and museums, he always had some insight on the place or the history. I called him my *quiet genius*. There was not much he did not know, but rarely did he exhibit his knowledge unless it was pried from him. I loved to pry.

A note arrived from Uncle William. He had been informed of my request for an annulment. After years of failure, I decided to write to him despite Michael's warning. It was clear, however, either he did not understand the nature of my problem or he was ignoring it. I had told him that we were not in love, that we had not consummated our marriage and that I wished to be released from the bond of marriage. I didn't tell him what I had seen that fatal night when I found Michael with a man. Now it was clear, despite my qualms about admitting Michael's proclivity, this might be the better option, no matter how it made me look and no matter how hard it was for me to say it. From the little information he did have, Uncle William said he would under no circumstances approve my request or assist me in any way.

The marriage had to be dissolved. This deception could not continue. I loved Philippe and despite my using the diaphragm given to me by the pharmacist in Lacoste, I was pregnant. I had not told Philippe. I didn't need a doctor to know. My breasts were swelling and tender, and I had not had my cycle for two months.

Djuna Barnes knew about a doctor who took care of these things. I loathed that option. In England, cautious conception was approved by the Anglican Church, but it was banned by the papal encyclical of Pius XI. Catholics had no choice. I had been so careful, but we had continued our relationship, sometimes with such passion and complete abandon that something was bound to happen. I did something that I shall regret the rest of my life. Something I never told Philippe.

On the pretense of visiting some English friends of Gina's, I traveled by train and boat to the British Isles. Djuna had made all the arrangements. When the procedure was over, I stayed at an Inn in a nearby village and though I bled more than I would have during my monthly cycle, I felt no pain. I rested, taking only short, slow walks along the picturesque paths in the lush green countryside. In the village, I found a small Catholic church and confessed my sin. The priest must have heard this confession before. He was quiet and compassionate, so different from the French priests.. I told him everything and almost thought he would release me from bondage, especially when he said, "Homosexuality is defined by the Church as a sin of vanity." In the end, however, there was nothing he could do. I had gone too far this time. I had committed a mortal sin. I could never again take communion, at least, not in the Catholic Church.

Several months later, back in Paris trying to put my trauma behind me, I decided to call Michael. He was attending to the sale of his mother's Paris 'headquarters'. Just prior to Black Thursday, Michael's mother had fallen down the stairs of her house in West Virginia and hit her head on the tile floor at the base of the stairway.

The doctors said it was a blessing that she died a few days later since she would have been a complete invalid had she survived. His mother had been demanding enough without being incapacitated. Not a kind thought, but she was a very difficult person. Most probably she was tipsy when she fell, and for Michael and probably his father as well, Mrs. Emma Whitacker's death was a relief, but for far different reasons. Michael had recently returned to Paris after the funeral, which was held in West Virginia. Apparently, no one there had asked why I had not come and therefore Michael had no need to give an excuse.

Surprised by my call, nevertheless Michael accepted my invitation to come to the apartment for dinner and conversation.

My life was still so much a part of Philippe's that being alone with Michael in the apartment presented very little noticeable tension. I had prepared a simple meal. He brought a nice bottle of wine. Feeling like old friends, we chatted about this and that, including his mother's funeral.

After dinner, Michael began, "I did want you to know something I never dared admit to you before."

I held my breath. Michael was about to shed a very deep and powerful light on our relationship and I was anxious to hear it through. He began by admitting that his mother had played an important part in his marrying me. I fit all the norms imposed by this matriarch. Michael said he wasn't sure of his proclivities at the time. I thought he probably was, but didn't want to interrupt. He assured me that he had thought, and still did think, I was charming, beautiful, bright, polished and in every sense, a lady. He, however, would not, could not satisfy my needs. I blushed. Suddenly, Michael became very tense. His eyebrows came together causing lines to form across his forehead, a portent of the aging process caused by stress.

"Libby, I need to be honest with you." His face looked almost menacing. What was he about to admit? Looking at me intensely, he whispered, "You deserve that much at the very least."

But it wasn't about himself that Michael wanted to discuss. It was about me and my liaison with Philippe. That pleased him. What an ironic twist. I always assumed it was a relief for Michael to know another man was around to take my attention. What Michael did not know was the ultimate sacrifice this relationship had caused me, something I hadn't even shared with my lover. Now I had so many secrets that perhaps the Church was right. I didn't deserve an annulment.

"Michael, although our situation did not work out as planned, I am grateful to be living in Paris and I do love Philippe. I think you know we would like to be married." *If only this had happened a few months ago. The timing was wrong.* No matter what happened, I was condemned. But this was not something I was about to share with Michael. I still clung to my hope that happiness was possible. Before I could continue, Michael blurted, "I am prepared to help you."

Tears streamed down my cheeks. Michael handed me his crisp kerchief. Facing each other, we sat for many minutes before either of us could speak.

Chapter Thirty-One

The surest way to get a thing in this life is to be prepared for doing without it, to the exclusion even of hope.

Jane Welsh Carlyle, 1849

Michael confessed his homosexuality. It was a courageous admission. I hoped he had a lover to be with him after it was over. But why should I? After all, I had been through Hell. My marriage, a sham, had cost me dearly. Lost was my self-respect, my religion, and, for all intents and purposes, my immortal soul. I sincerely hoped and prayed and I still pray believing God will understand and forgive and that time would heal.

However, despite his admission and despite his acquiescence to an annulment, the Church stood firm. Too many years had passed, they told me. *Too many years? Too many years!* Did any of these priests have the foggiest idea what I had been through during those many years? How could they? By loving God so much, they had lost track of what it was to be a human and especially a human in love. It was a sham. For a solid week, I stormed from one theologian's office to the next. No one could console me nor did any of my friends blame me for being furious. In the end, I simply gave up. I didn't even have the support of my own family, although my father was willing to send me monthly checks, which was some measure of support.

This is where The Church steps in, I deduced. Not to assist, sympathize, and have compassion. There seemed no other reason to believe in God than for security and an unwavering answer to the whys of life as proclaimed by the Holy Catholic Church. I couldn't even attend mass with Philippe any more. It would make me a hypocrite.

Time was passing. Something had to be done. I asked Philippe if he would check on or stay at my apartment until my return. Knowing I was headstrong and recognizing there was no rational argument against my proposal, he resigned himself to a long separation. I would depart by ship for the United States. The laws of my country would free me from the bond of marriage, even if the Holy Roman Catholic Church would not.

Chapter Thirty-Two

Le chancelier Hitler expose les grandes lignes de son programme interieur et exterieur (Paris-soir, 24 mars 1933) Il demande au Reichstag réuni cet après-midi à l" Opéra Kroll les pleins pouvoirs.

Chancellor Hitler exposes the broad outline of his interior and exterior program. (Paris-soir, March 24, 1933) He asks that the Reichstag assemble full powers this afternoon at the Opéra Kroll.

January 30, 1933, Hitler is appointed Reich Chancellor (Prime Minister). On March 4, 1933, Franklin Delano Roosevelt takes the oath of office as President of the United States of America. On July 14, 1933, East European Jewish immigrants are stripped of German citizenship.

The Atlantic Ocean, 1933

After Hitler took over Germany, rumors of war began to rumble. However, in the United States, President Roosevelt was serving Martinis to the Press Corps in Washington to announce the end of Prohibition. At the same time, I was sitting at the table of the Captain on the *Aquitania* crossing the Atlantic Ocean.

The party was jovial. It was an honor to be at the Captain's table. This new environment should prove the beginning of a distancing, both emotional and physical, from a past I both cherished and regretted. It was with a heavy heart that I left Philippe, but it was with an equal and opposite emotion that I left the priests of Paris.

The chatter at the Captain's table brought me back from my somber thoughts.

"Do you know what W. C. Fields said the other day?" asked a matronly woman not waiting for a reply. "He ordered a martini and the waiter asked, 'Would you like a twist of lemon, sir?' W. C. replied, 'If I wanted a soda pop, I would have ordered it.' Isn't that marvelous?" The lady laughed somewhat hysterically. Most of those sitting around the table simply grimaced.

"I did know the late Sir James," replied the Captain in response to a gentleman sitting across from me. "He was, shall we say ... with all due deference ... an imposing figure." Everyone laughed, except me. I didn't understand the joke. Seeing my quizzical look, the Captain explained.

"We are speaking of Sir James Charles, a man of rank in many senses. His pennant flew from the masthead of the *Mauritania* and was the ultimate cachet of nautical rank and dignity. The famous/infamous Sir James had voluptuary table practices, a preview of *Maxim's* and the *Café de Paris*." My mind leaped back to the memory of that lovely lunch with Pamela now six years in the past.

Continuing, the Captain explained, "Sir James knew no limit. Stewards would roll in whole roasted oxen one night, grilled antelope surrounded with peacock fans the next. Chefs in two-foot high hats built turrets of Black Angus beef that towered above the arched eyebrows of the diners. Sir James imbibed in all of this and became so portly, so 'full of honors' that his mess jacket had to be constantly reinforced in its internal integrity to support all his ribbons and medals." The Captain glanced around to be sure everyone was listening. Noting that all other conversation had stopped and all eyes were indeed upon him, he continued in a low, almost raspy voice.

"One evening, as he was leading a full-blooded assault on turtle stew au Madeira moated in citadels of pastry, he died." I gasped, covering my grimace with my serviette, but the Captain laughed.

"I watched in disbelief. Yes, he was dipping his stew and sipping mountains of gin followed by rivers of cognac and Mumm's as he and his guests did every night. It was Sir James' way of slushing down the people fleeing prohibition. Oh yes, I watched; it was nothing new. However, this time the staunch paradigm of nobility and nautical prowess had reached his limit. He simply tumbled over and died ... died in the line of duty. I loved him. We all loved him. What a life!" The Captain held his glass up high, "Hear, hear!" Everyone joined the toast with a fervent, "Hear! Hear!" Glasses clicked. People shouted and laughed heartily.

"They had to open both wings of the *Mauritania's* halfports to take him out. It was a noble exit!" More laughter followed.

I began to relax. It was hard not to in this company.

"You all have read Somerset Maugham, haven't you?" shouted one of the guests, his glass lifted precariously close to my head. "Such a sharp writer. Maugham said, 'Excess on occasion is exhilarating. It prevents moderation from acquiring the deadening effect of a habit.' " Extending the glass, then raising it in a salute, half its contents slopped across the table before reaching the puckered lips of the man who had rendered the great quotation.

I was mesmerized by the jovial nature of this group and grateful to have survived the rollicking wine glass.

Harold Genin, whom I later discovered was head of ITT, the company that had allowed my father to come through the Depression without loss, sat at the foot of the Captain's table. I perked up when he began to describe the changes he had observed in Germany.

"Yes, it is the end of the Old Order," he was saying. "Germany has amazing strength both militarily and technically. We must be wary lest she use her power to our demise."

The conversation at the writers' dinner I had attended so long ago came back. It was foreboding when the older poet had said, "I know the Treaty of Versailles forbade them from manufacturing military aircraft or tanks. But we would be naïve to think that there will be no more battles, no more wars." His prophecy that the German Republic would fall and, God forbid, something tyrannical would take its place, might come true after all.

Mr. Genin was saying the same thing; in effect, that the Great War might not have been the *war to end all wars* after all. Then he made a comment that startled me. The changes he had observed, the so-called *old order*, included the Catholic Church. *Could this mean there is a chance my petition might be heard? Would there be someone in the Church who could understand and forgive?*

Countless courses of food were served. The evening seemed to have no end. Finally at midnight, the group began to disperse. Some of the men descended to the gambling halls. Some of the women went out to the lounge to smoke. I returned to my cabin and went to bed.

In the morning, I awoke fully refreshed. Perhaps I had dreamed my way out of the present crisis in my life. Dreams were supposed to be able to do that. At least, that is what Pamela had told me. She had also said that somehow the subconscious absorbs all the information of our daily lives and sorts it out. Our dreams become the resolution. Pamela may not always be correct, but something had occurred during the night to help me relax. I went through my morning ritual and dressed, eager to go on deck. I couldn't wait to look at the sea and smell the salty air, the same air and sea that had made me so sick on the voyage with Michael. Memories began to crowd into my mind once more, but they were disregarded as my inward barrier took its stance.

The wind almost blew my hat off. With one hand, I held onto its brim, with my other hand, I hung onto the railing. The tweed coat was more than adequate to keep me warm. Through an open porthole came the words and music of a Charles Trenet record.

La mer	*The sea*
Qu'on voit danser	*That one sees dancing*
Le long des golfes clairs	*Along the bright bays*
A des reflets d'argent.	*To the silvery reflections*
La mer	*The sea*
Des reflets changeants	*With changing reflections*
Sous la pluie	*Under the rain*
La mer	*The sea*
Au ciel d'été ...	*To the summer sky ...*

The song brought recollections that passed beyond the sea. Happy times. But my pleasant memories came to a crashing halt when someone inside played Trenet's other song, *"Que reste-il de nos amours?" What is left of our loves?* and I had to grit my teeth. It was difficult to stay focused. Concentrate on being happy, I told myself. *Please God, let me have this small piece of happiness,*

Patricia Daly-Lipe

please. The sea began to melt into the sky above, the horizon missing somewhere behind a distant haze. To anyone looking down from above, there was but one lone passenger by the rail, watching but not seeing, lost in a horizon all her own.

Chapter Thirty-Three

What has gone? How it ends? Begin to forget it. I will remember itself from every side, with all gesture, with every word. Today's truth, tomorrow's trend. Forget, remember!

Finnegan's Wake, James Joyce

Divorce was legal in the United States, but it carried a terrible social stigma. Nice people did not do it. I had agonized over this decision for six long years. My father and mother would not approve, but there was nothing else I could do.

The reunion with my parents was as strained as it was brief. They were of another generation. They would not, could not understand, adhering instead to the school that believed in the three virtues of True Womanhood: piety, submissiveness and domesticity. I could see their regal respect for the first two, but as to the latter, I doubted mother even knew the word. Perhaps making our menus with the cook or planning automobile tours with the chauffeur or even formulating a schedule for the governess was considered domesticity. It was cruel for me to chastise my mother that way, but here was an instance when I needed comfort and care and I, her only child, was being rebuffed.

One evening, my father asked to see me alone behind the closed doors of his library. It was then that I told him the truth, that Michael was a homosexual. He didn't seem ruffled by the news and probably had assumed as much already. He said he had written to Uncle William as well, but didn't realize I had received a reply. He was also surprised by my uncle's response. Then I told him that Michael had confessed.

"So that settles it, right?" No, I told him, the Church was unwilling after all these years to acquiesce. Father said he would continue writing letters to the Church on my behalf, but he was unwilling to discuss this with mother. I have never understood why she needed to be protected, but I couldn't disobey his wishes.

My nanny was gone, but Mr. Ted remained. He was the one toy they hadn't given away. I was glad to hold him once again just as I had as a child. This time, he was going back with me.

The few Washington friends I had were not terribly kind. Social norms clearly cast me out. I was wearing the Scarlet Letter. When departure day finally came, it was a relief. I left from Union Station on the first of several trains for my voyage west.

If only I could have flown. After flying in Philippe's little plane so often, I had become very comfortable in the air. Since returning to the United States after his famous trans Atlantic voyage, Lindbergh had set another record flying across the continent in just under fifteen hours and soon after, Frank Hawks had beaten that record by flying the same route in twelve hours and twenty-five minutes. Here I was, taking days to cover almost the same distance.

My discomfort, however, wasn't just because of the length of the trip. On the fist day riding the Pennsylvania Railroad heading out of Washington to New York City, all the windows were wide open because of the afternoon heat. The outdoor grit covered everything and everyone. Only in the diner was there any comfort. In that car, the railroad had installed air conditioning. When I asked about the fresh cool air, the steward told me that the apparatus for treating air had been invented by Willis Carrier back in 1902, although even further back in 1895, George Vanderbilt had developed a method for air conditioning the Biltmore, his estate in North Carolina. I had only experienced this fresh, cool air circulation in movie houses. Sometimes the air was so cold that I had to bundle up to prevent my teeth from chattering. Father had told me that there was air conditioning in the chambers of the U.S. Capital as well. I wondered if the congressmen wore long underwear. On the other hand, in this sticky heat, just thinking about the cold air made me wish I could stay in the diner for the duration of the trip. However, passengers were encouraged to eat quickly so everyone could be served.

The train I transferred to in New York was the famous *Broadway Limited*, also part of Pennsylvania Railroad. Most of the old wooden cars had by now been replaced with streamlined passenger cars. Father had purchased these tickets for me. This posh train, which would take me as far as Chicago, also supposedly included status and prestige for its passengers. "There simply is no better way to go." The ride was fairly smooth but I felt gritty all the time. Any long trips I had taken before were always nautical, traveling across the Atlantic. Despite periodic episodes of nausea, when I was out on deck, I could inhale the clean sea air.

This train was very similar to the ones I had taken in France from Le Havre to Paris. In both, the window could be left open to enjoy the breeze despite the billows of steam and cinders that blew past and sometimes made their way inside. When the grit became too dense, I headed to the observation platform at the rear of the train, where the roar of the high speed over the rails, although nearly deafening, was nevertheless invigorating. Back there, you could watch as the tracks came out from underneath and receded backward. Smoke passed over the train and formed a funnel behind. The smell was pungent but the crisp air made my cheeks glow and gave me energy.

In Chicago, I changed trains again, this time to board the Overland Limited run by Chicago & North Western Railroad. We traveled as far as Omaha before my car was transferred to a train belonging to the Union Pacific Railroad. This went to Ogden, Utah. In Ogden, my car was again transferred, this time to the Southern Pacific Railroad. This train stopped in Reno on its way to Oakland, California.

These passenger cars were large and comfortable offering steam heat, electric lights and plush appointments. The sleeping cars were all steel. Called heavyweights, each car weighed almost one ton per foot of length. On all legs of the trip, I was fortunate to have a roomette all to myself and chose to sleep in the upper bunk. The porter going west, an elderly Negro, was very kind but punctilious, religiously adhering to a tight schedule. When he came down the aisle ringing his little bell, I knew he had attached the bed ladder which I was expected to climb down immediately and get freshened up for my scheduled breakfast time. On all the trains, I signed up for early seating. When I returned from my toiletries, my bed would already be made and reinserted into the ceiling. Even if I wanted to,

I could not return to lie down until the proper hour. With the bed out of sight, the area became a nice cozy sitting room. Here I would read until dozing off with my head against the window and the vibrations of the train lulling me away from the literature. It was nice to be alone, but from time to time it was also fun to roam through the carriages and chat with other passengers.

On the last leg of the trip, I found a perfect spot to view the passing scenery. This train had a Pullman car beautifully decorated with southwest Indian designs painted on the clerestory ceiling. Windows opened at the upper level to allow fresh air to flow through the car.

As the trains rolled on, crossing a countryside I had never seen before, I relaxed more and more. The scenery changed from the harsh, bright greens and reds of the East into the soft gray-greens and pinks of the West. Lush gave way to lean and sparse as plant growth was more of a challenge in the dry sandy soil. Sitting at the window looking out, there was something also very soothing about the sound of the train: metal on metal as the heavy car wheels lumbered along the tracks, soft and low and melodious. The train's music enhanced daydreaming, carefree and comforting. At night I slept soundly and had pleasant dreams. Truly, this journey represented more than an adventure. It represented a passage in my life, perhaps finality, possibly a resolution. It also represented a beginning.

As the days passed, distancing me further and further, both physically and emotionally from my problems, I began to recognize something new about myself, an awareness of personal strength and confidence.

With plenty of time to read, it was helpful that I had brought along so many books, some purchased in Paris and some picked from the family library in Washington. I even brazenly brought the copy of *Ulysses* I had bought at Shakespeare & Co. Joseph had let me know when he thought I was ready to understand or at least appreciate the famous book.

Leaning back in the puffy upholstered seat, the window to my right, good lighting, and the scenery whizzing by, I thought this might be the perfect time in my life to attempt the great Joyce. With a six-month domicile in Nevada being required, I would need something more than light reading to occupy my mind. Little did I realize then, in the tranquility of the train ride, that once we arrived at the Reno train depot, a new challenge would be presented.

Chapter Thirty-Four

Lying awake, calculating the future,
Trying to unweave, unwind, unravel
And piece together the past and the future.
Between midnight and dawn,
 when the past is all deception,
The future futureless, before the morning watch
When time stops and time is never ending . . .

T. S. Eliot

My time alone on the train had been productive. It had been time outside of time, where nothing had to be done, where responsibilities could wait. It was a period when I could enjoy the timelessness of the night while the wheels rolled over the rails below. In all, the trip lasted only five days, but it seemed longer because the disparity was so dramatic.

Then, just as I began to relax, everything changed.

We arrived at my destination: Reno, Nevada. Stepping out into the bright Nevada sun, I rubbed my eyes trying to adjust to the glare. Young men in caps holding notebooks and pens rushed about, accosting passengers as they alighted from the train. Besides the notebooks and pens, the young men carried thick books under their arms or in satchels.

"What are they doing?" I asked the redcap who was helping me retrieve one of my larger trunks.

"Those are reporters, Ma'am," he replied with a smirk. "You see, they run around looking for name tags. Then they check out the names in the Social Register. See there's one under his arm," he said pointing to one of the reporters who was heading my way.

From what I could see, these men were rude and brazen. Imagine checking the names on the luggage to find someone to write about. "Who do they write for," I asked.

"Oh, papers like the *Daily News*."

"Tabloids!" When the young man I had seen approaching came closer, I realized he was looking for me. Immediately, with no preamble, he began soliciting questions. He already knew my name. I urged the porter to stay with me, but after my last bag was located, the young redcap went to assist another passenger. Left alone, I wasn't sure what to do next.

"Here, let me give you a hand." A nice gentleman took my valise and, giving me his arm for support, helped me descend the metal steps from the train.

Holding my broad-brimmed hat in place with one hand to keep it from blowing off in the strong, dry wind that was gusting across the flat, sandy soil, I was most grateful to receive any kind of assistance, particularly male assistance to protect me from the prying reporter.

"Thank you so much. It is very kind of you."

Putting the bag down, the gentleman removed his hat, and with a slight bow introduced himself. "Samuel Locke." He repositioned the hat and put out his hand to formally shake mine. "I am here to accompany my mother. That is to say, it is she who is here for the business of divorce, not I. Forgive my bluntness, but I assume that is what has brought you here as well?" He introduced me to a petite but refined lady, impeccably attired. Somehow I had missed meeting these two on the train.

I nodded to his question while shaking his mother's hand surprised that such an attractive person as his mother should find herself in my same position. However, I was fatigued and, though this young man was pleasant and polite, I wasn't in the mood to prolong the discussion. What I really needed was a nice warm bath.

As it turned out, the Lockes, mother and son, were staying at the same inn as the one booked for me. This simplified my introduction to Reno considerably.

Samuel's mother was a perky little lady. When Samuel introduced me to her, I was conscious of her blue Irish-looking eyes. Her son had the look of the Irish too.

"Yes," she responded to my compliment about her eyes. "I was born in Ireland, in County Galway. Have you been to Ireland?"

I had not, but told her it would be lovely to visit someday.

After a brief chat, it was clear that she had the tenacity and strength of character the Irish are known for. This was not a lady who could be fooled by anyone nor was she going to be a shrinking violet in any man's presence. I wondered what sort of person her soon-to-be-ex-husband might be.

Meanwhile, I yearned to unpack, undress and soak in a hot bathtub. Fortunately, my room had a bath. Not all the rooms did. When I remarked about this, Miss Spencer, the Inn keeper and owner, shared a startling fact. There were no bathtubs at all anywhere in the United States until sometime after 1840.

"When they were first introduced," she said, "most people undertook to prevent their too frequent use." This was hard to believe. At home during Washington's hot, humid summers, we would often take baths three times a day. Perhaps this no bathing concept was western logic. "Oh, no," she assured me. "It was the physicians who opposed the practice of bathing in tubs as being dangerous to public health. Laws were passed in most states and cities prohibiting and discouraging the use of bathtubs in private homes or hotels. Oh, yes indeed. The Commonwealth of Virginia even passed a law taxing the owners of bathtubs the sum of thirty dollars per year. In some places, it was against the law to take a bath without the advice of a physician." I could see that even out here in the middle of nowhere, I was going to learn many things. There is no telling where Miss Spencer obtained her information, but I was sure she was correct with her facts. She appeared to be well-educated and running an Inn is no easy task for a single woman.

Finally, when my bags and trunk were delivered and the registration was signed, I was provided with a key and taken to my room.

Time to relax. I unpacked while the tub filled, grateful that the travel office my father chose had found such an exceptionally fine Inn. With lavender powder, I made bubbles in the bath water, crawled in and soaked. The smell brought back memories of Provence. I remembered learning about the difference between lavender and lavandin and Philippe insisting on the real flower, the lavender found only on the higher elevations. Philippe. Just saying his name brought tears that fell into the sudsy water. As I closed my eyes, I could see the past float across my mind. Then a bell clanged.

Snapping back into the present, I wondered if this meant we were to gather downstairs. There would be plenty of time in the days ahead to arrange my wardrobe, so I picked the top garment, dressed quickly and prepared to descend.

The Inn had a large porch with chairs and small tables on two sides of the building. Since it was warm, I chose a wicker chair facing the west where I could watch the mauve, purple and blue shadows as they enveloped the scene before me. A young woman in a white apron came out and asked if I wanted wine or tea. Totally relaxed and clean for the first time in days, it was nice to have the sunset to myself. I requested a glass of red wine.

At dinner, Samuel and his mother asked if I would sit with them. It was a small world after all. As it turned out, Samuel's sister was married to a Frenchman and lived in Paris. I had not met them, but was acquainted with their address. Both mother and son had been to Europe frequently. Mrs. Locke enjoyed music and Samuel's sister had considered making piano recitals her career before she met her husband, Raymond deGiterre. Samuel preferred riding polo ponies on the beach near Bordeaux. He enjoyed the ponies but he didn't play polo. I couldn't help comparing these two with my beloved Philippe and his mother. While both ladies were extremely bright, well-read and well educated, Philippe's mother was more reserved, dignified in a quiet way. Mrs. Locke, on the other hand, was vivacious and vocal. Both ladies, however, loved to talk. And talk she did, about travel, about literature and even about politics and historical events. No one could compare to Philippe, but Samuel appeared to have a similar sense of adventure. While Philippe loved his aeroplane, Samuel loved his boat, a sport fisherman he kept in Coral Gables, Florida.

Samuel told me about his father and how he came to live in Miami. "Anticipating the boom of southern Florida, father moved his family from St. Louis to Miami in 1909. He helped pioneer and develop the city, dredging what are now Palm Island and Hibiscus Island as well as developing other areas. He would take people out in a little boat, point down into the water and say, 'This is where we will build your new home.' "

After his mother had gone upstairs to retire for the night, Samuel told me that his father was a man of excess in every sense, including an accumulation of mistresses. Samuel had sided with his mother and consequently was disowned by his father. As a youth, against his father's wish that he learn about business and remain in Miami, young Samuel had been sent north by his mother. He attended a private boarding school for five years in New England followed by a couple of years at Yale University. Although an excellent student of mathematics and physics, Samuel also had a penchant for art. He left Yale to live the bohemian life in New York City.

"I have published several poems in the *Village Gazette* and am trying to sell my paintings in various Village galleries." I listened, but after what Michael had put me through, I was unwilling to accept any story told to me by any man as the gospel truth. At least, not yet. I was also tired from my travels and having some difficulty adjusting to the heat. The evening ended amicably, but I was happy to return to my room to be alone and quiet. It wasn't long before I fell into a deep sleep. No dreams this night.

As the days passed, with more leisure time, I enjoyed listening to the wonderful stories Samuel told about the New York Stock Exchange where he worked part-time and his many tales about the poor and struggling artists and writers and poets, actors and dancers of Greenwich Village. Samuel said it was a place where "nobody questions your morals, and nobody asks for the rent." I had visited Greenwich Village once with some girlfriends and remembered that we had felt like tourists in a foreign country with its small buildings and narrow, winding streets. It was very different from the rest of Manhattan. I loved the park, Washington Square, where artists gathered to smoke, chat and play chess. An almost European atmosphere permeated the area. Some of the creative people who called Greenwich Village home included Theodore Dreiser, Eugene O'Neill, Mabel Dodge and Isadora Duncan, whom I had seen perform in Paris. She was a friend of Natalie's. Greenwich Village in the twenties and thirties distinguished the arts in America, just as Paris was the Mecca in Europe.

Samuel agreed to a point. "The Village has a European flavor. But the parties are unique," he said. "I was attending one party last winter that was truly noteworthy. The host, an old friend, asked if I might be of some assistance. 'But, of course,' I replied. The Fitzgeralds were at it again. 'We need to get them out of here. Can you hail a cab and have them driven home?' I was only too happy to be of assistance. The unfortunate couple had developed a habit of becoming unpleasantly blotto at soirées. I hailed a cab and, opening the door to the rear compartment, shoved the tipsy pair inside. Slamming the door, I told the cabby up front to drive on. As I turned back to the party, there, just in front of me, across the road, were Scott and Zelda lying in a snow bank. Laughing and screaming with delight, Scott held a bottle high in his right hand and waved."

"How on earth did they end up in the snow?"

"They had simply gone straight through and out the other side of the cab." I laughed with Samuel picturing this absurd image of the two. Their reputation was well established in Paris.

"It is a shame really. Such a good writer, but an irresponsible, high-flying boozer. Scotty and his crazy wife Zelda used to carouse through the Riviera you know, and their fights are legend. Not that I was pure, you understand," Samuel added with a wink, "but I didn't like the fighting aspect and I regret his wasting time when he is such a talented writer."

After this and other stories and late evenings, I was always happy to retire. Perhaps the hot, dry air made me sleepy, but it was nice to be alone. Once in bed, I would gingerly pick up the copy of *Ulysses*. In the beginning, reading Joyce's work, I tried to do what Joseph had advised, "Read for the sound not the content." The sounds produced a harmony. I was beguiled. It wasn't as if Joyce were teaching me a lesson. Rather his words created a kind of spiritual balance like music. Joseph had put a note in my book. It was a quote from Victor Hugo. "To put everything in balance, that is good, but to put everything in harmony, that's better." That was precisely what I desperately needed, harmony that would make the issues in my life sing or chant, not chastise. Mentally and physically exhausted, I drifted off into the realm of dreams, the book lying against my stomach. Reading Joyce's book was going to take a long, long time.

In the morning, I liked to dress quickly and go outside before anyone else awakened. It was me and the universe, alone and together. In one passage of Joyce's other book I had brought along, one that was easier to understand and that I had read once before and wanted to reread, *Portrait of An Artist As A Young Man,* the character Stephen jerked his thumb toward a window and pointed to the goings-on outside and said, "That is God ... Hooray! Aye! Whrrwhee! ... What? Mr. Deasy asked ... A shout in the street, Stephen answered, shrugging his shoulders."

This I could understand. I remembered the day Pamela and I saw the men staring into the waters of the Seine, happy to simply watch a fishing boat. And here, the morning sunrise over the beautiful vistas of Nevada was worth a good, long stare. Purple mountains in the distance circled open plains of pale tan desert and soft golden knolls dotted with grey green creosote bushes. After a rain, yellow flowers sprinkled the land with happiness as the sun glittered on the watery mirage in the distance. It was a surrealistic scene, but a scene reflecting the presence of God too. Like Stephen, I had seen God in the screech of an owl at night, in the sound of rain on a tin roof, in the cries of bliss from revelers in the night.

With shock one morning, I was told my name had appeared in a Washington, D.C. newspaper. The Innkeeper was able to procure a copy for me. There it was. The headlines in *The News,* our daily paper in Washington, read *Wealthy Banker's Daughter Seeks Divorce For Non-support.* I was being ridiculed, derided and mocked by these insensitive so-called newsmen. *That frightful little German paper hanger named Hitler is preparing to invade Europe and all they can worry about is my divorce?* Never again would I relax in a public place. For a country boasting equality, democracy and a classless society, America was, as far as I could see, more snobbish than anything I had experienced in Europe. I, Elisabeth Perry Whitacker, might just as well have been the Princess of Wales. I dreaded speaking to my parents and was glad to have this time in the desert, three thousand miles away.

The days wore on, weeks turned into months. The fairness of my complexion made it dangerous to expose myself to the full strength of the desert sun. When accompanying Samuel on afternoon strolls, I often donned long sleeve blouses and broad brimmed hats. When he invited me to travel with him to nearby Lake Tahoe, I accepted. One side of the lake was Nevada but on the other side was the state of California. Although leaving the state was against the rules for those awaiting a divorce, everybody did it. But we abided by the rules. Besides, Samuel enjoyed the Nevada gaming tables. I simply delighted in the ambience of the place. On this first trip, we left the casino early so we could tour the region. Samuel was a gentleman and behaved himself, only taking my hand for support. But life was casual in the West. By the time we had completed our little countryside tour, darkness descended and before we knew it, night had fallen and it was too late to motor all the way back to the Inn. There was no moon and the road had been tricky even in the daylight. When Samuel suggested we stay the night at the lodge next to the Casino, I didn't insist we get separate rooms and he didn't ask. I had to admit, it was wonderful to be held again by a man.

At first I penned a letter to Philippe every day and it was a joy to receive his, although written weeks ahead, in the afternoon. As the days passed and my time became more preoccupied with Samuel, a day or two would slip by without a letter to Philippe. Naturally, I wrote nothing about my weekend jaunts, but when we were away for several days at a time, more than a weekend, I sent no letters. This must have upset Philippe. I rationalized that he would understand that I was safe and secure and probably with friends I had met. A nice American couple is what I had written. But he should have been concerned. While I continued my correspondence, I was permitting those old passions to rekindle and the fire was getting stronger as the days and months went by. A little wine, soft music and a warm body to snuggle against. Dancing to a slow rhythm coming from the night music in the shadows on the sand. Allowing a casual kiss to turn into more under a starry sky was hard to resist.

Too quickly the six months were over and the court appearance took place. As the law required, I vowed that I would live in Nevada. I stated that I had been subjected to unreasonable circumstances in my marriage and wished to return to the status of a single lady. My petition was granted, money was exchanged and I was free to leave. The first statement was for their books only.

After Mrs. Locke was granted her divorce, she asked her son to take her on a tour of the West Coast. Samuel reluctantly acquiesced.

"Libby, I promised mother that I would accompany her and I must. It would be dangerous and difficult for her to travel alone. But it is not easy for me to leave you."

"Samuel, do you really have to go?"

"Can't we see each other in a month?" he asked taking my hands.

"In a month? Where would we meet?" I could feel his intensity and his devotion in my hands.

"In New York."

"I don't know."

"Please think about it. You have my telephone number and my address. I will leave mother in Florida and then take a train up to New York. Please say yes. I want to see you. I want to be with you." He pulled me to him and kissed me ardently. I responded, my emotions losing control. This time there were no shadows or night music, no starry sky or wine. We were in my room. With no self-consciousness, we undressed each other and made passionate love in the bright light of day.

Now I was torn. Philippe had never left my mind, but Samuel had been here for me, and I could not ignore the fact that I had enjoyed his company.

When Samuel escorted me to the train depot, it was difficult to say good-bye. And when my train left, I was leaning out the window as far as I could despite the grit, waving until he was but a speck on the horizon. There was much to think about on this return trip east.

With the passing landscape going from arid to lush, I began to feel myself coming back to a more formalized existence. My nails needed a professional manicure. My hair needed to be cut in a proper style. My skin was in desperate need of creams and oils. And despite many attempts to allow the words to flow freely, I had made little headway with Mr. Joyce's novel. On the other hand, I had consumed several volumes of so-called *light* reading and could now relate to the heroines feeling as only a woman who has been caressed and loved could feel. It must have shown because men I didn't even know smiled at me and I smiled back. Their interest was not in the least offensive, but for protection, my wedding ring was back on my finger.

Chapter Thirty-Five

He was an outcast from life's feast.
James Joyce, Dubliners

My return to Washington was brief. This time, my mother and I had completely drifted apart. How could it be otherwise after what Mother, showing me the newspaper article, called "this brash venture"? Like Joyce, I was an outcast. Washington was no longer home.

Father was also annoyed by the newspaper headlines; nevertheless, he assured me he loved me and would see to my financial security. On the other hand, he would never allow for more than a fixed income. Clearly, he did not trust women with money. Equally annoying to him was the President whom he felt would squander the entire national economy for his New Deal. Before I left, father handed me another poem he had written.

My father, poor misguided gent,
Wasted a life, a life misspent
By working hard and working late
To gather pieces of the eight!
Poor Dad!
He'd fuss and fret and toil,
And burn the blooming midnight oil
For nothing but a little cash
To buy the daily beans and hash.

Poor Dad, he was so mild and meek,
He'd work six days in every week,
And fourteen hours in every day
To try to keep the wolf away.
Now father, meaning well, but dumb,

Amassed a rather tidy sum
With which he planned to buy some beers
To brighten his declining years.
Then came the New Deal; simple Dad
Awoke one morn to find that he
Was now a Public Enemy,
A louse, a Scrooge, a National Cyst,
An economic Royalist!
So Dad, industrious but dumb,
Is now the source from which will come

The Coin to buy the Gasoline
For some poor under-dog's machine,
To bring the More Abundant Life
To every loafer and his wife.
From Dad will be extracted sums
For filling the bellies of the bums,
For Radios to case the halls
Of all the chronic ne'er-do-wells,
For booze, so Labor's Little Nell
Can tell the Boss to go to Hell.
Poor Dad, a faithful, trustful Goon,
Was born thirty years too soon!

A moral lurks along the hall
In all this fancy fol-de-rol,
And it is this - that any cheat
Who sez you ought to work to eat,
Is simply nuts - cut off his hand:
Sit on your tail, or stay in bed,
The Government will see, by Gad,
That you get yours from chumps like Dad!

Perhaps I was being paranoid, but the last stanza, although politically pointed, might also have been directed at me. "Who sez ... you get yours from chumps like Dad!" *He would never respect me. I could never please my father. I couldn't go to work. I couldn't run for office. I couldn't do anything that might smear the family name. All I could do was marry well. I did and look what happened. What now? What about Samuel? Should I give up on Philippe and go to New York? Would my parents approve? Probably not.*

It was evident that I could not stay in Washington. Although my father and I could discuss politics to our mutual enjoyment, I was, nonetheless, an embarrassment to my parents. Having been away in another land, another culture, another mindset, I had nothing in common with my contemporaries in Washington. Moreover, as far as society was concerned, as a divorcée, no matter what the reason, I was a failure. To the young men, the eligible bachelors of the city, I was a high risk. And to my now married girlfriends, I was also a high risk. My thoughts returned to Philippe. I loved my house on Massachusetts Avenue, but it was the memories of childhood that I relived, not the harsh realities of the present.

As the days passed, my longing increased. I could hear the bells of Saint-Gervais, then the chimes of *Notre Dame* followed by a symphony of sound echoing throughout Paris. In my mind, I opened the window wide and listened, enticed to the chorus of church bells. The city was calling me back. Closing my eyes, I could see the lovely sun-drenched glittering waters of the Seine below my window in the apartment on the *Île St. Louis*. History told of floods, the water level rising until it was even with the bridge. But I couldn't imagine such a thing, not the gentle river I had known and loved. Just up the road from my island, a new bridge to be called *Le Pont de la Tournelle* was being constructed. It would be open soon. On the other side of the river, I could see a *péniche*, a houseboat, tied to a big iron ring on the stone wall of the *Quai de la Tournelle*. Paris, not Washington, was now my home. It was time to return.

A single woman, but only according to the American legal system, to the Church, I was an outcast, an ex-communicant. As a divorcée, I was ineligible for remarriage. Still, there was hope. Hadn't Philippe told me years ago in Lacoste, "If we are meant to be together, and I believe we are, then God will allow it. We must be patient." I wanted to believe it was true.

The authorities in the Roman Catholic Church ruled otherwise. Philippe wanted to marry me anyway, but I knew that to defy the Church would mean the loss of everything that was his. He would lose his title, his inheritance and his acceptance in French society. I could not allow him to turn his back on all that was his by right. It was on a remote wing of a prayer that the Church would change.

The trip west, even the dalliance with Samuel, had given me a stronger sense of myself. Finally, I was happy to be alone. I could talk to strangers. I had enjoyed myself on the ship coming across the Atlantic. I could converse with people I met on the train. And in the town of Reno, I could listen to nature while sitting on the Inn's porch alone and be at peace. I loved Philippe but I could be realistic too.

Nevertheless, I would return one more time to fight for the right to be Philippe's wife. I would confess all if that was what I needed to do. Was happiness possible only accompanied by sorrow as Apollinaire's poem said? *"La joie venait toujours après la peine."*

On the slow trans-Atlantic voyage, I resumed my journey across the pages of *Ulysses*. Little by little, Joyce's words became less ambiguous. He had little use for the Church. God was calling to us in nature. Outside my cabin, I stared at the sea, the surf and the sky. *"That's God,"* I cried.

Chapter Thirty-Seven

I have a feeling that there is just about one more good flight left in my system and I hope this trip is it. Anyway when I have finished this job, I mean to give up long-distance 'stunt' flying.

Amelia Earhart, 1937

There is something about flying, something that goes beyond the mere excitement of the flight itself. The French were not only leaders in the world in aviation, but they were color-blind. Race was not an issue in France as it had been in the United States. In Washington, our servants were all black. It was expected. I would never have considered a Negro child as a personal friend. They certainly did not attend Holton Arms School. On the other hand, I could not fathom why they couldn't learn as easily as we. My father wouldn't tolerate such talk when I brought it up on more than one occasion. But the French proved that they could learn and it was an American Negro who led the way not only for those of her race, but for women as well. Bessie Coleman, whose father was a laborer and her family poor, overcame all the obstacles. She had an inner drive that I am convinced we all have, but so many ignore.

Bessie left the United States and came to France thanks to her mentor, the publisher of a Black Newspaper in Chicago. In France, she learned to fly a twenty-seven foot biplane called a Nieuport. When she was twenty-nine, she was awarded a license from the *Federation Aeronautique Internationale*, the first black woman accorded such an honor. At the time, this was the only organization whose recognition guaranteed permission to fly anywhere in the world. By the time she returned to the United States, she was a celebrity. She had literally soared above her roots.

Sadly, Bessie lost her life soon after coming home. It happened in a flimsy World War I Army surplus plane, the only plane she could afford. It cost her her life. The year was 1926. But Bessie Coleman had begun something special and she exemplified a lesson that my country is still trying to learn. More importantly, she had taught me something.

I had always been on the fringes of aviation, always watching the men fly, a passenger, but never a pilot. Yet, here was a black woman who had the courage to overcome her sex and her race. I was never allowed to do something on my own such as work or attempt a career. Reading about Bessie Coleman and other women who were beginning to appear in the news for various exploits and endeavors, I realized how timid, how feeble I was to allow others, even my father, to control what I did with my life. I was more than a toy for a man. More than a future wife and mother. *What was I meant to do using my own wits, my own talents?* I had to search in my heart.

Another pilot, Antoine de Saint-Exupery, wrote, "And now here is my secret, a very simple secret; it is only with the heart that one can see rightly; what is essential is invisible to the eye." And then my friend Joseph Campbell counseled that "The entire heavenly realm is within us, but to find it we have to relate to what's outside." Inside, outside, the bottom line was to believe in myself and seek my own way.

For the rest of the world, meaning the white male population, flying a plane in the late twenties and thirties was considered simply romantic. In 1937, eleven years after the death of Bessie Coleman, I read about another woman, Amelia Earhart, who took romance one more step. Highly publicized, her flight was a commentary on two levels. Aviation had advanced so rapidly: from Lindbergh's courageous solo flight across the Atlantic in 1927, and whose triumph I had witnessed on that crowded field of *Le Bourget*, to this flight only ten years later. Amelia Earhart, a thirty-nine year old aviator, was proving it possible that not only could a woman fly; she could take a plane around the entire globe.

So I was not unique in wanting independence. The thirties were an era when women were just beginning to come into their own. Amelia was a woman who enjoyed adventure. As she wrote, "I only wanted to have fun." Her husband, book publisher George Palmer Putnam, promised her complete freedom if she married him. That was different from anything I had ever known. He was willing to encourage her desire to circumnavigate the earth by air. But then I understood his rationale. In his mind, it would make a sensational story for publication.

In June, 1937, Amelia began the round the world flight. I was in Paris. Just as they had for Lindbergh, the French were again rooting for this American pilot. My French friends and I listened to the radio for the latest news and scanned the papers for each and every detail.

Beginning in Miami, Amelia flew to Puerto Rico, then to Brazil, across the Atlantic to Africa. Crossing the African continent, she traveled over the Red Sea, across India and down as far as New Guinea. During her flight from Lae, New Guinea, to Howland Island she was monitored by a ship. Within hours before the beginning of her flight, she had a long discussion with her husband about putting a light on Howland Island. No light was placed on the island. Her last recorded message stated her location. She was a good one hundred miles off course with low fuel. No trace was found of her, her navigator or the plane.

Since I had followed Amelia Earhart's career with fascination over the years, I couldn't help weeping when I read of her disappearance. This had been a woman who had pioneered beyond the flight, a woman who had hoped for the day when women would know no restrictions because of sex, but would be individuals free to live their lives as men were free. I practically idolized this lady and agreed with her philosophy. I saw no reason why, given the proper temperament and skill, a woman could not succeed where even men had feared to tread.

Putting myself in Miss Earhart's shoes, however, was something else. On my own now, living an independent lifestyle at the age of thirty-two, I tried to emulate the strength and courage of conviction that Amelia and Bessie possessed. But my courage was waning as I waited for the Church to come my way. As for aviation, although I enjoyed my flights with Philippe, when it came to piloting, I was happy merely to be a passenger. There must be something else I was meant to do.

In 1937, another important chain of events were happening that would change the world as we knew it. In 1937, Pablo Picasso created a masterpiece depicting the horrors of wars in Guernica. And that same year, British Prime Minister Neville Chamberlain made this statement: "We should seek by all means in our power to avoid war, by analyzing possible causes, by trying to remove them, by discussion in a spirit of collaboration and good will. "

Instead of taking a stand and drawing a line in the sands of time, Chamberlain entered into a policy of appeasement with Germany. The end result was that Adolf Hitler took advantage of the additional time to strengthen his hold on power and perpetrate a holocaust not just on the Jews of Germany, but on much of Europe.

When I was in my early twenties, I wrote this in my journal: *I used to think order was contrary to creativity. I was a rebel, although I did not think so at the time. The Surréalistes here in Paris are teaching about the illogical inner self. Between them and the insight of Freud and Jung, I am learning about a part of me never explored before, my subconscious. I am trying to document my dreams. Then I attempt to translate the images, symbol and stories and learn from them. What I have discovered is the importance of discipline and control. It is as if I have traveled a full circle. From this perspective, I understand that order tames disorder and it is out of this new order that creativity is born.*

Perhaps my new insight came naturally, a part of the process of simply getting older. Or was it possible that I had changed my outlook because the times were changing?

A geometric enclosure of the sun's reflection,
A glistening, glimmering flash of light
    as transient as the life of man
Contained within a rectangular frame
Limited by the curvature of time.
The sun's rays glaring back at me,
No image, no lines, only brilliancy

*Then a shattering, a crash, an unexpected thunderous
Tinkling.
Sounds, movement, magnified dread
Resounding long after the streaks appear:
Parabolic immobility:
Reality.*

*The breeze blows.
The simplicity of silence reigns once more.*

I called this poem, *The Reflection of Man's Image*, being the latest in a myriad assortment of musings and observations entered in journals I had carried with me over the years. This poem was written three days before Hitler's storm troops invaded Poland.

"Look at the image concealed within the emotion," I read in a book by Carl Jung. The human being is an enigma and my life has been a puzzle, the pieces often falling off their proper positions.

I had been reading a little, perhaps too much of Jean Paul Sartre's book, *Nausea*. Recently published, it was quite the rage. "Everything has been figured out, except how to live," he wrote.

While I philosophized, the sun yawned and stretched its rays obliquely over the earth.

Chapter Thirty-Eight

Pity this busy monster manunkind
Not

e e cummings

Europe was arustle with scurrying diplomats. According to the newspapers, the French Foreign Minister had paid calls on France's allies and found them oddly heedless. *Life Magazine* ran an article, *Europe's Little Nations Flirt With Germany and Italy*, which said, "As soon as his back was turned, the Yugoslav Premier and the Polish Foreign Minister rushed to Berlin and the Rumanians went Fascist and anti-Semitic." A stampede had started with powers moving away from democracies and away from the League of Nations. They were running toward the great Fascist powers of Central Europe.

Although the Pact of Paris had been signed with many nations promising to renounce war as an instrument of national policy, it did not look as if the world would escape the perils of war. Hitler invaded Poland and Britain was about to declare war; but for me, the fight was over. In the end, the Church had its way. I could never marry Philippe; at least, not in the Church. To have it any other way was out of the question. Although he said he was willing, even wanting to do it, I could not allow Philippe to give up everything for me. I loved him enough to give him up.

I will always remember that night. We met; we held each other; we kissed; we made love. But in the morning, I had to tell him.

"Philippe, *chéri*, I love you too much."

"What are you talking about? Shall I say that I love you even more?" He laughed, not understanding me. He was still lying blissfully by my side.

"Philippe," I began and then could say no more.

"What is it, Libby, my sweetheart. What is wrong?"

"We … We have no choice," I stuttered, the tears flowing out of control. "The Church will never give in. We will never be able to marry. We cannot continue like this."

The words came slowly and in spurts. Philippe was stunned. "You must get married. You must have a family. It is expected." I could say no more. The guilt of not telling Philippe all that I had experienced weighed me down, crushing me. My trip to England, my unfaithfulness with Samuel. I had been an evil person. Philippe deserved better. Completely defeated and with an exhausted heart, I told the man whom I loved more than life itself that it was best for me to return to my homeland. Philippe just stared at me, his eyes glazed, his lips trembling. He stared and held my hands so tightly it hurt.

To match my mood, Paris was closing down. From the beginning, the approaching and inevitable war was unlike any other. It was a long, numb waiting period. Endless days of apathetic delay while more and more soldiers were mobilized, and visit after visit exchanged between Ambassadors and Ministers. Could war be declared cold-bloodedly after so much deliberation and discussion? The days crawled by. The moon became bigger and brighter as Paris was stripped of her lights and museums emptied of their treasures. More and more numbers of mobilized reservist classes were placarded on the walls. Then one glorious morning, the final sheet, *"Mobilisation Générale"* was added to the others and we knew the war had come. Delirious shouts, shrieks and tragic, moving speeches came over the radio while, still unbelieving, we drank champagne with shivers running up the spine.

That was the beginning. Walking around in a daze with a sick feeling in the pit of the stomach. That was when all Parisians began to take the news seriously. They and we knew the things we needed to do, many for the last time. Just do what is to be done in a dream, an awful dream of war. Paint the windows blue. Stuff black paper in the cracks of the shutters, pack what you can, and wander through the apartment or the house and garden for the last time.

In the country, at *Fontaine-les-Nonnes* and other estates, all the menservants had gone and women served the meals and worked the garden. After being embraced by the children and decorated with flowers, the horses were requisitioned. I cried, remembering Philippe's beautiful horses racing up to us to get their treats. The Mayor of the village came to see what houses on the place could be used by refugee families from Paris. Philippe and I pored over the atlas and listened to English broadcasts in French, German broadcasts in English and the French in Arabic. Great white spaces in the newspapers indicated an absence of news or news not permitted to print.

In the daytime, marketing was done on bicycles since gas was scarce and needed to work the electricity and water. Strolling in the sun or shopping we could forget. But at night there was the black-out accompanied by soldiers walking around the houses and commons looking for a ray of light from a careless window. The moonlight, once romantic, was now terrifying. Glorious nights filled with future terrors. Long hours in the middle of the night imagining the whir of aeroplanes coming with a macabre purpose. The heart beats fast. The air is filled with the vibration of planes. A tree of ice stretches its branches through the veins.

Philippe and I knew our time together was coming to an end. Hand in hand we walked through familiar haunts. But now, all the Parisian *gouaillerie* had gone. People solemnly walked through the streets with those ugly gun-metal tubes containing gas masks. We strolled past Schiaparelli. A great iron shutter had been pulled down where shocking perfumes were once exhibited. The familiar doorman was replaced by a young boy and inside a lonely girl stared blankly out of the door as she mechanically folded sweaters on the counter. "No, there is no collection just now. We expect to stay open, but we don't know how things will work out."

We crossed the *Place Vendome* to see the gay old crowd at Morgan's, but no one was laughing. The glass corridor along the private offices of the bank wore the new blue paint. A group of worried directors from the American Hospital grimly discussed war policies.

After wandering all day like ghosts through a deserted, hole-cemented, sand-bagged Paris, we headed for home, my home on the *Île St. Louis*. A police car clanged by playing mi-sol, mi-sol. Later it passed us again going the other way this time playing mi-sol-do-mi, mi-sol-do-mi.

Despite war clouds, I was fortunate. Pan American Airways System had been able to inaugurate its first regular nonstop transatlantic passenger service. Unlike Lindbergh's little monoplane, this was a gigantic Clipper. It had not one, but four powerful engines controlling its four propellers. But this was more than a plane; it was a ship with wings. The inaugural flight from Europe was to take place in the waters off Lisbon. I booked passage. The booking was expensive, three hundred and seventy-five dollars, but this might be my final fling and if we crashed, I would have had the experience of a lifetime to end my days on earth.

Although disagreeing with my decision, Philippe was willing to fly me this one last time in his little monoplane. Most likely he thought our being together would convince me not to leave.

Driving to *Le Bourget*, we passed young soldiers, *la fleur au fusil*, dahlias crammed into the guns with the bayonettes. Even the great canons wore bouquets in their nozzles. All the time, the feeling that this could not be happening, that it was just a bad dream, engulfed us. *Don't think about all these men, these writers and composers and bankers that we have seen for the last time. Just drive down the roads of France. Just keep driving.*

The first night we stopped in Bordeaux. It was crowded with Americans. They camped all day in front of the United States Lines offices waiting for the latest sailing bulletins. They sat on the *café* sidewalks, played Bridge at the *Hotel Splendide* and stumbled down the dark streets at night in a real provincial black-out. If there is moonlight, the buildings of a blacked-out city rise high in the sky, proud of their naked white beauty. But under the stars, Bordeaux sank deep into the darkness of the earth. We looked for a place to eat.

One of the best restaurants in the world, or so they say, the *Chapon Fin* at Bordeaux had never been a gay place. It is a dark ghetto where cryptogram rocks bite on dull tarnished mirrors and where no one has ever been known to laugh. It is damp and chilly. Scorned is the soft indirect lighting or crystal glitter of fashionable restaurants. One eats perfect food and drinks the finest wines under a grey light falling through dirty glass or from bare electric bulbs. But never has such good eating reached the depth of despair as now. People gathered like those condemned to eat their last favorite meals. Ours was *Charentais* melon with old Sauterne, *Chateaubriand Bordelaise* and *crêpes* with *Chateau Latour* '16, *soufflé* and *Fine Champagne* of the special reserve.

The next morning, we flew across the water to Spain where we landed and spent a passionate night before proceeding to Lisbon. At this point I think, we both put the reality of my leaving, going back to America alone, into a box and closed the lid; that is, until the last night.

In those final hours with Philippe, as the sun began to rise and spread heavenly pink clouds to announce her approach, I held dear Philippe so tightly that there were marks left on his sides. And, with reality emerging from obscurity with the light of the sun, I almost relented. It was crazy both to leave my wonderful Frenchman and to climb aboard the *Dixie Clipper*. But somehow, despite my body crying "no", the mind prevailed, and on June 28, 1939, I was one of thirty passengers taking off from the ocean to the sky.

Chapter Thirty-Nine

The present in New York is so powerful that the past is lost.

John Jay Chapman

These flying boats did not need the expensive concrete runways that were all too few and far between in the '30s. Our Boeing 314 was a stately flying boat and its sumptuousness rivaled the ocean liners I had taken to and from America. Sleeping berths, lounges, luxurious lavatories, hot meals on real china and silver goblets served by white-coated stewards were all part of what Pan Am Airways offered us. There were two levels on the plane. The passenger deck was laid out as a series of lounges with couches. As you moved to the back of the plane, there were steps up into the next compartment caused by the curvature of the bottom of the plane. At night, the couches were made into beds. The main lounge was transformed into the dining room at mealtimes. Despite the kind attention to our every need by the stewards and the luxuries proved by Pan Am, it was frightening to think that we were in a winged ship weighing some 82,000 pounds and flying over 12,000 feet above the ocean.

My destination was New York City. In that large metropolis, I thought I could escape the pressures of society. I would get lost in the crowds. It had been years since the newspaper article disgracing me and my family had appeared. To the rest of the world, it would be a forgotten moment in time.

I could still feel Philippe's last embrace. *"Les vrais paradis sont les paradis qu'on a perdu."* ("True paradises are lost paradises." Marcel Proust) Looking out the round porthole-like window, I let my mind soar with the clouds. Far below, the sea was thrashing around but this voyage in the air was smooth. Not like the crossing so many years ago with Michael. *What would become of me now? Leaving my only true love behind, what was there to look forward to?* I was so absorbed in thought that when the steward tapped me on the shoulder, I jumped.

"So sorry to disturb you, Miss. Just wanted to know if you would care for some champagne?"

Grateful, I thanked him and was able to come back to the present. It was time to share the excitement of this first trans-Atlantic passenger flight with my fellow passengers.

Just before we made the final descent, I again looked down on the ocean where the waves rolled against the shoreline of Long Island. Outside my window, the wind was blowing eastward. "The wrong way! The wrong way!" whispered the wind. Too late, I chided. The plane circled the city before turning into the wind for its landing.

I had survived. The flight was a success. We landed safely amid much fanfare in Port Washington, Long Island, New York. It was easy to locate my friends in the throng of welcomers. They were in front of the crowd behind the gate next to the terminal. These were some of my former classmates who now lived in New York City. They had made a banner and waved it in the air.

I was stiff after the long flight, but couldn't complain. The trip had been uneventful and smooth. My girlfriends were ecstatic about coming to meet me after this inaugural flight. As they smiled and shouted and waved, I descended the floating ramp with great trepidation. I had survived the trip. But I had come alone. Trying to be composed, forcing myself to put on a good face, I wobbled down the plank. Flash guns popped in my face, but these reporters weren't there to cause trouble. It was all part of the celebration.

"Just call me Lindbergh the Second," I laughed. The recirculation in my legs took its time, but I didn't fall. The girls were hugging me and grabbing my belongings and practically carrying me to the car. Despite my *scarlet letter*, these old friends from Holton Arms School were loyal. When I wrote that I was coming and planned to stay, they had searched and found a small apartment on the Lower East Side for me to see. Partially furnished, it was available as a sublet. Without much thought, I took it.

Noise. That was New York City. Unadulterated noise. No romance, little history, at least compared to Paris. A busy place with busy people. No outdoor *cafés*; no time for chats. Skyscrapers cutting out the blue, the sun having to sneak around the spires and towers to spread its rays. The Flatiron Building, the Times Building, the City Investing Company Building, the Singer Building and the giant Woolworth Building, all great towers of wealth, stood cold and grey. A Central Park limited by and surrounded with buildings. To me, New York City resembled an immense dark dragon with streets for veins and automobiles for the blood pulsating as its life source. *"pity this busy monster, manunkind / not. Progress is a comfortable disease ..."* Even out on the river, the image was distorted as tugs fouled the air with heavy black smoke puffing from their stacks. I was suffocating and had only just arrived!

My Uncle Christian came frequently to the city for his own social gatherings. Soon after moving in, he checked to be sure the accommodations were appropriate. I liked my uncle despite what I now knew about him. He was probably the only member of my family who was sympathetic to my plight. I should have been furious with him knowing what I did. He too had cheated on his wife, but, he explained, "Alice wanted to marry me knowing I had relationships with men. Libby, I loved her sincerely and I satisfied her in all ways. Do you understand?" If my mother could have heard this conversation she would have died! But I learned something. Some men can swing both ways. What a woman of the world I was becoming!

Now I was alone in the big city. In Paris, although alone much of the time too, my aloneness was productive; at least that's how it seemed. In New York, my creative energy was stifled.

Negativity filled the newspapers, the radio, the streets, even my friends. In New York, everyone spoke in gloomy tones and it wasn't just because my ears were out of tune with Americanisms. Despite what one would have thought, this wasn't caused by the war. On September 1st, German troops invaded Poland. Britain and France declared war on Germany. Two days later, what my Parisian friends had dreaded came about: World War II. I was sick worrying about Philippe. I was also worried for all my friends who had remained in Paris. To New Yorkers and the rest of this country, the war was overseas and far away. According to *The Herald*, Americans were told to leave France, but no commercial ships were making the voyage. Mr. Joyce had left Paris. He knew the threat from the Nazis was not confined to Poland and Czechoslovakia.

As I stood in the small bedroom of my compact apartment, the tears began to flow. I grabbed a hanky, blew my nose and walked back over to the paper left on the couch. According to the news, it was only a question of time before the United States would get involved. But here in the big city, the pessimism in the air that had nothing to do with the war. Years earlier, Gertrude Stein had declared, "You are a lost generation." Now the phrase was popular in New York. Hemmingway used the quote as an epitaph for his novel, *The Sun Also Rises*, which he had published the year before I arrived in Paris. Was I part of that lost generation? Perhaps, considering the way my life had played out so far. It felt as if my candle had been blown out. I had given away my zest; my enthusiasm, my passion.

This apartment was on the sixth floor. Outside my windows, what I saw was not my beloved River Seine or the buttresses of *Notre Dame*. I didn't smell the fresh air or hear the birds in the trees lining the *quais*. Instead, I saw buildings, cement monolithic sculptures and skyscrapers with windows that looked nowhere. Instead of the perfume of flowers, I smelled exhaust, fumes and dirt. Even the rays of the dim sun seemed to have trouble finding my window.

I stared out seeing nothing, my thoughts drifting back to another place, another time, another me. *Was it really true that I had lost the only love I had ever known? Oh, Philippe. Was all that time in Paris then a lost time? Coming to New York, was it a good idea after all? Can I really get lost in this metropolis?* The tears were back. Turning away from the window, I walked back into the gloom of the living room. Pictures I had acquired from the *bouquinistes* along the *quai* hung on the walls.

"Oh how could I do this?" I cried out to no one. "How will I ever survive away from him?" Over in the corner, above the Louis XV chair, the one that I had been so proud to find at the *Marché*

Patricia Daly-Lipe

Aux Puces, was the large framed etching of St. Peter's. I took it off the wall. It was heavy. Carefully I opened the back, removed the glazier's points, took out the picture and walked to the window. The wind was blowing. I watched as St. Peter's swung down through the buildings and disappeared from sight.

"So take my life as an example," I said to the universe. "Take it as a perfect example of what people are talking about. Use my life to show what the lost generation is really all about."

I spent hours alone, hugging Mr. Ted, the one reminder of a happier time.

Chapter Forty

Spring is like a perhaps hand
(which comes carefully
out of Nowhere) arranging
a window, into which people look (while
people stare
arranging and changing placing
carefully there a strange
thing and a known thing here) and
carefully changing everything carefully ...

e e cummings

New York, 1940

In 1939, Libby's father died suddenly and unexpectedly of a heart attack. She returned to Washington for the funeral, but her relationship with her mother remained strained. Returning to New York, she decided to call on the man she had met in Reno. Samuel had a flat in Greenwich Village. He was working on Wall Street but still enjoyed the bohemian life writing poetry and painting. Libby was happy to be with him; at least, she convinced herself that she was happy. She did enjoy his zest for life and his creativity and he enjoyed being with her. So in 1940, with the blessing of his mother, who adored Libby, they were wed by a Justice of the Peace. Only days after the quiet little ceremony, Libby called her uncle in Washington.

"I have made a mistake," she cried. What she couldn't tell Uncle Christian or anyone else was that no man, not even Samuel, could ever erase the love she still felt and would always feel for Philippe. Her uncle, though somewhat sympathetic, was stern. Mistake or not, she must simply make do, stay with Samuel and learn to be a good wife. She had already made enough mistakes in her life. He should know, he said, having made mistakes of his own.

Patricia Daly-Lipe

Later that year, the couple moved to California where Samuel, because of his talent for drawing, was hired to be a supervisor in the developmental aircraft design department at Consolidated Aircraft in San Diego. Only two hangars down from where Samuel worked was a building bearing a significant plaque. This was the very location the *Spirit of St. Louis* had been constructed in 1927. Times had changed. The *spirit* had changed. The plane Samuel was designing, the B-17, was not destined for history and myth, romance and courage. It was designed as a strategic weapon, a bomber for the Second World War.

January 13, 1941, eight months after the German occupation of Paris, James Joyce died at the age of fifty-eight. He had taken his family to Zurich to spend the war years, but soon after their arrival, he succumbed to an unsuccessful abdominal operation and was never able to complete the trilogy that had begun with *Ulysses*. The second book, *Finnegan's Wake*, had been completed after seventeen years of hard work while living in Paris. This was the book Mr. Joyce was laboring on when Libby had visited him in his apartment on the *Île St. Louis*.

One year after Pearl Harbor, Catherine was born. She would be Libby's only child.

Spring, New York City, 1961

In 1958, Catherine's mother, Elisabeth Perry Whitacker Locke, had been admitted to Scripps Hospital in La Jolla, California. Catherine was a sophomore in high school at the time. The day of her mother's surgery, she and an older girl who was looking after her took a hike behind her house. They walked up the barren hillside with its dry brush, such a contrast to the sparkling blue water of the Pacific and the bright white beach of La Jolla Shores. From the top of the hill, the view went out to the horizon where the sky and the sea blended. It was a beautiful sight. Catherine's sadness, her fears and concern for her mother lessened as she sat looking out to the edge of the world. That night the emotional pain returned. Her sitter drove the child of fourteen to the hospital where, before she could see her mother, Catherine was shown into the surgeon's office.

274

"Do you have any relatives who are close to you?" he asked.

"No," answered Catherine. Her parents had been divorced since she was ten. She had not seen her father since.

"You have no aunts, uncles, grandparents?"

"No," Catherine replied not comprehending the significance of his query.

"Then," he said looking serious and unhappy, "I must tell you everything." She squirmed, folding and unfolding her hands. "Your mother had a malignant tumor removed from her lower intestine. We have removed as much as we can but I am afraid the disease has spread. Your mother has cancer." He paused, letting that horrid word sink into the mind of the child. "You must not tell her. It would be better for her emotional health if she did not know she had cancer. But I have to tell you," he paused again wishing he did not have to say this, especially to someone so young. "There is nothing more we can do. She may have to come back for another operation so we can cut back some of the growth and make her life more comfortable. However, you must understand, there is no cure." He looked at Catherine, carefully scrutinizing her reaction. It would have been difficult in any situation, but her youth compounded the problem. "Catherine, you must keep this information to yourself. It will be hard, but she must not be told. She needs to live her life to the fullest. Knowing would bring her unnecessary grief." Catherine could not even cry; she was stunned.

Now unable to face her mother, she left the surgeon's office and walked out of the building. Behind Scripps Hospital was the rocky shoreline. She walked down and found a place to sit. Looking out at the expanse of the sea and listening to the pounding surf as the waves crashed into the cliffs below, Catherine tried to absorb the information. That night, after a brief visit with her mother, she wrote in her diary:

"A deep, dark mantle holding the secrets and torments of many a soul is the sea. Covered by jagged geometric peaks, the depths remain silent. Many are the anxieties and sorrows that are washed ashore or sunk below to relieve a tortured soul. Far greater is the power of a tide than the strength of war. As the waves rise up continuously, so does time. But the sea is heedless of hours and minutes, unmindful of a lost generation of mankind. To go down to its floor, to the depths of its clutches, would be to reach the black of the infinite, to bear the weight of its load or to die a joyless soul.

"A wave rises up like a fierce white bird, clawing the rocks with dying strength, and then weakening, sinks back down to the sea."

Catherine never described her own feelings in her diary. Since her childhood in La Jolla, California, the ocean had always been the place she turned to contemplate, find relief tossing her emotions into the tide. Perhaps she had never faced reality at all. Perhaps, rejecting that reality, she had put on a stubborn face and continued as if her life were normal. But it was far from normal. Certainly not the normal life of a teenager.

Two years passed. Catherine graduated from high school and enrolled in college. Now in New York City, no longer a child, but not quite an adult, she was still bewildered and confused. This week she had come down on the train from Vassar College because once again, her mother had to be hospitalized. Of course her mother knew. How could she not? But all this time she had continued to keep the secret, speaking to her mother as if the things that happening were simply routine. Catherine was staying at the Vassar Club waiting for her appointment.

The telephone rang: "Room 505, fifth floor, turn left down the corridor … Dr. Daniel at 12:30."

Catherine's feet carried her robotically down the sidewalks, block after block. To anyone who took the time to notice, the young lady appeared to be merely another body coming from or going to, but then everyone is in a rush in New York City. She walked, looking, but not seeing. Suddenly someone laden with bags from a department store jostled her as they passed each other and Catherine found herself standing at an intersection, uncertain which way to turn. There were crowds all around. The light was soon to change.

Snapping out of her self-imposed trance, she suddenly became aware of the car horns honking, the pedestrian footsteps clacking across the sidewalk, the hammering coming from up high and the deep rumbling from the subway deep down in the bowels of the city.

Reality returned with a vengeance. Where was she? Had she passed the cross street? No. The hospital was straight ahead. Reality. Her mother was in that hospital. This had been her third surgery. She was so ill and so alone in her pain. Passing a storefront window, Catherine caught her own reflection.

Something in me refuses to believe, she told herself. *Hold onto yourself*, an inner voice instructed. She remembered her mother's expression at home when, assisted by a nurse, she too had glanced at her reflection in the mirror. It was a shock to see what had become of her body: a pale, shriveled, stooping shadow of its former self. Catherine's eyes glistened with tears, but she took a deep breath, preparing for the performance. Her true feelings could not surface.

This life's play demanded the image of a cheerful young woman, a proper daughter for a mother she had barely had a chance to know. Being a college freshman, she was supposed to be a happy. Books and intellectual inquiry were to be her sole occupation. Instead, she was experiencing an emotional trauma some never experience in a lifetime.

The appointment with Dr. Daniel revealed nothing new. The operation was only a patch, a postponement of the inevitable.

> *"Already I have shed the leaves of youth,*
> *Stripped of the wind of time down to the truth*
> *Of winter branches. Linear and alone*
> *I stand, a lens for lives beyond my own,*
> *A frame through which another's fire may glow,*
> *A harp on which another's passion blow ...*
> *Blow through me, Life, pared down at last to bone,*
> *So fragile and so fearless have I grown!"*

Catherine found this quote in a book by Anne Morrow Lindbergh. Libby had given this book to her daughter with a brief explanation of her participation in Charles' landing at *Le Bourget*. But the words haunted Catherine as she looked down at her mother's frail body in the hospital room. Her mother attempted a weak smile. Catherine held back the tears.

Chapter Forty-One

A man lives not only his personal life, as an individual, but also, consciously or unconsciously, the life of his epoch and his contemporaries.

Thomas Mann

Memoirs have power. They do more than recount the mere facts of the day. Daily notations reflect history from the only true vantage point: the personal perspective. For Catherine, a time in history, Paris between the wars, came to life in 1961. That year Catherine's mother, the refined and reserved Libby Perry Locke, lost her long battle to cancer.

Only eighteen at the time, Catherine knew very little about her mother's past; little, that is, until she unlocked a hidden trunk. Inside were bundles of letters, each tied with a thin blue ribbon, each letter inscribed with sweeping lines of beautiful calligraphy, and each posted with a collection of French stamps. Opening one, glancing through, and then opening another, she found that the letters, written in French, were all from someone named Philippe. The most recent letter was dated 1954.

At the bottom of the trunk, tattered and torn, Catherine found a journal. Written in her mother's familiar blue script, the journal began in the spring of 1927. As she opened the journal, a piece of paper fell out.

For years, Catherine had obeyed the doctor. She had not told her mother about the cancer. But her mother must have known and conversely didn't want to tell her daughter. This was confirmed by the note.

I leave this story to my daughter or to whoever wishes to learn from it. I am finished. It is time to return to the light. One last thought. Don't be fooled, dear Catherine, into believing that the only reality

is what you see and hear and smell, a reality of sharp distinctions. There is so much more.

To prove her point, Libby had added a quote from the poet Rainer Maria Rilke:

"Angels (they say) don't know whether it is the living they are moving among or the dead. The eternal torrent whirls all ages along in it, through both realms, forever, and their voices are drowned in its thunderous roar."

Catherine knew her mother was watching.

Chapter Forty-Two

*Time cools, time clarifies, no mood can be maintained
quite unaltered through the course of hours.*

Thomas Mann

1961 and 1939

G reat Uncle Christian told Catherine the story. Philippe
had followed his love across the ocean, taking the last
ship out of the port of Le Havre before the war. All
commercial flights had been halted. Libby had asked Uncle
Christian to accompany her to the docks. If he had not been there,
would Libby have had the strength to see her task through? Her
uncle watched from an appropriate distance as Philippe began his
descent down the gangplank. Libby clenched her handkerchief
in her left hand. Her face betrayed her anxiety. This was the
most difficult thing she had ever done. Uncle Christian watched
as Libby slowly walked up the gangway to meet Philippe. They
met halfway. Philippe started to put his arms around Libby but
she stopped him. Tears rolled down her cheeks. They stood like
that, facing each other for a long time, before either one could
speak. Libby spoke first. Even from a distance, Uncle Christian
could see Philippe's face. The handsome young Frenchman was
staring into Libby's eyes, staring as if in a trance. Not only his
face, his whole body displayed the strain and hurt he must have
been feeling.

"I couldn't see him speaking," related great-Uncle Christian.
"Your mother was crying softly." Catherine could picture the scene.
This was the man her mother had loved more than life itself and
she was telling him to go back home. Maybe if he had grabbed her,
shouted at her, resisted her, but he did not. Christian didn't know
what words Libby had used, but it seemed such a long, long time

they stood, not touching, but looking into each other's faces before they parted.

Finally, when Philippe turned and slowly walked away, it was "agonizingly slow", Uncle Christian said describing Philippe's return up the gang plank. "Never pausing or looking back, he re-boarded the ship." Libby was left alone on the gangway. "I could see her body was on the brink of convulsions. She seemed to be trying to take several deep breaths. Finally, she gained enough composure to proceed down again and rejoin me." Christian said he took her hand, but they did not speak. He settled her gently in the front seat of his car, walked around to the driver's side and headed back. There was nothing he could say or do to comfort her.

When they arrived at her apartment building, Libby barely uttered a complete sentence. "I knew she was holding back the tears that would consume her for many hours as soon as I left."

Philippe never set foot in the United States. He returned to France only to face another conflict. War came to Europe with vicissitude and vengeance. In 1940, Paris fell.

Although she followed the progress of the war in Europe, Libby resolutely turned her back too. The past was past. The same year that Paris fell, Libby married Samuel.

POSTSCRIPT

"Pass in, pass in," the angels say,
"In the upper doors,
Nor count compartments of the floors,
But mount to paradise
By the stairway of surprise."

Ralph Waldo Emerson

1999

A few months before the end of the millennium, Catherine and her husband traveled to Canada. Their destination was Port Hope, Ontario, where Libby was born in 1905. The house in Port Hope called *Idalia* had belonged to Catherine's mother's family for three generations over a period of sixty some years. This home, built high on a bluff overlooking Lake Ontario, was used by the family mainly in the summertime. Since Libby was born in August, her birth took place in the Canadian home.

Idalia was sold after Libby's father died. Catherine was eager to see it for the first time. She had brought along photographs from her grandmother's album. Perhaps the new owner would allow her inside.

They drove all over the small town and could not find the house. It was only after they inquired of a distinguished looking older couple who had lived in Port Hope for many years that Catherine and her husband were directed to the home, now on a much smaller property than appeared in the old photographs. Today it is surrounded by a hedge wall and a large iron gate. Unfortunately, because they had arrived with their two dogs in a camper, the owner, who had turned the home into a Bed and Breakfast, would not allow them inside. It was unreasonable and cruel, but try as she might, Catherine could not change the owner's mind. She and her husband were only allowed to take photographs of the exterior. Having driven this far, Catherine decided to visit Our Lady of Mercy, the church where her mother's birth and baptism would have been recorded.

The ladies at the Church business office were delighted to meet Catherine. Hers had been a distinguished family in this town. Fortunately, one of the ladies knew where to find the very old papers which were stored separately from more recent documents.

The marriage certificate of Libby's parents in 1903 was the first paper they looked at. In the 1905 listings were the names of infants baptized. Third from the bottom was Libby's name. Her baptismal name, her parents, her home location, objections, of which there were none, the date, the priest and the witnesses were listed in columns to the right. Her Uncle William had been a witness. He must have been a student at the time because he was not listed as being a priest.

As they looked at the old document with a magnifying glass, they noticed an arrow leading down to the left of Libby's name. It took a couple of times putting the paper through a copy machine to enlarge the type before they could distinguish the handwriting at the bottom of the page. This is what was written: (The dashes represent blurred images.)

"In the course of the years she married one Michael -------1927 Washington, DC. On Nov. 20th I received notice from the Matrimonial Curia of the Archdia---- Baltimore SA ... that this marriage was annulled by it on July 14th, 1937; Appellate Court St. Louis ----- SA. Aug 12th 1937 ... " This was followed by a signature which could not be distinguished. It was the *spirit of St. Louis* coming once again into her mother's life.

How was it possible that Libby had never received this document? Was notification lost crossing the Atlantic in those pre-war years? Or, had Libby changed her mind about Philippe?

Catherine would never know.

ABOUT THE AUTHOR

Patricia Daly-Lipe grew up on both coasts of the country. She was born in California and spent most of her younger years in La Jolla. Her mother, however, was a Washingtonian. After her parents' divorce, when Patricia was ten, she and her mother spent an equal mount of time in Washington, DC. In 1960, after graduating from The Bishop's School in La Jolla, Patricia made her debut during the Christmas Season in Washington, DC (as her mother and grandmother had before her), while she was a freshman at Vassar College. Seven months later, her mother died.

Left alone, she remained in Washington for the fall semester taking courses at the Institute of Languages and Linguistics and at Georgetown University before returning to Vassar to complete her sophomore year. The following September, she went to Belgium and studied Philosophy, in French, at Catholic University of Louvain *(Université Catholique de Louvain, Institut de St. Thomas d'Aquin)*. Most of the following year was spent living in Paris and Rome. Her great-uncle was the only American Canon of St. Peter's. Because of him, Patricia was invited to many receptions within the Vatican and was introduced to diplomats, celebrities and royalty. She returned to Washington and worked for the *Evening Star Newspaper*.

After her marriage dissolved, Patricia raised her three children alone. Later she had the opportunity to return to Vassar and complete studies for a B.A. degree in Philosophy. When her children were themselves in, or preparing for college, she completed a Master's degree and a Doctor of Philosophy in Humanities, specializing in Creative Arts and Communication. During this period, Patricia also taught at various schools and colleges and wrote for an online magazine, a monthly periodical and a newspaper.

Returning to Virginia to be near her children and grandchildren. Patricia is happily married to her very first boyfriend from La Jolla, Steele Lipe. She serves as President of the DC Branch National League Pen Women, Historian for the Daughters of American Colonists and works on events for the Historical Society of Washington, DC. Please visit her web site: www.literarylady.com

This novel is the result of over fifteen years of research and writing. Based on her mother's life with factual historical references, the story line is nevertheless fiction. A Best Books Award Finalist, *Forbidden Loves* also received the coveted JADA Trophy.

Printed in the United States
120886LV00002B/1-99/P

9 780980 062939